MONA
in
THREE
ACTS

MONA
in
THREE
ACTS

Griet Op de Beeck

TRANSLATED BY MICHELE HUTCHISON

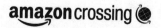

Previously published as *Kom hier dat ik u kus* by Uitgeverij Prometheus in the Netherlands in 2014. Translated from Dutch by Michele Hutchison. First published in English by AmazonCrossing in 2019.

Published by AmazonCrossing, Seattle

www.apub.com

ISBN-13: 9781542005449
ISBN-10: 1542005442

Cover design by Kimberly Glyder

Printed in the United States of America

for you
forever
("and where you are is where you are not," T. S. Eliot said)

Perhaps all the dragons in our lives are princesses who are only waiting to see us act, just once, with beauty and courage. Perhaps everything that frightens us is, in its deepest essence, something helpless that wants our love.

—Rainer Maria Rilke

we forget that we consist of just enough water
to form a tidal wave

—Dennis Gaens

PART ONE

1976–1978

1

They say your eyes get used to the dark, but here, in this tiny room in the corner of the basement, it's pitch black. Last time, I counted out loud and I got into the hundreds and I still wasn't allowed out, so I'm not trying that again.

"I'm not scared." My voice echoes in the silence. "I'm not scared, because I'm nine years old and that's big and big girls don't get scared." I won't be here for much longer. Mommy will come downstairs in a minute and let me out. I'll say sorry and promise never to do it again.

I'm not a good kid. Alexander is. Mommy says that a lot. She calls Alexander "my darlingest." That's not a real word, she made it up just for my brother. Sometimes he's really annoying and mean, to be honest. Like the time he ruined my painting by drawing three big brown stripes right across it. When I went to tell on him, Mommy said that nobody likes tattletales and he's still too small to realize that what he did was wrong, but you should have seen his face when he was making the last stripe. Anyway, he's six and that's not a baby anymore. Alexander has already called me some nasty names and whacked me on the head, which didn't hurt of course, but still. I know he never does things like that when Mommy's watching, so she doesn't know about it.

Mommy calls me "Mona-love" when I'm good. I'm good when I help with the dirty dishes or the cleaning or when I set the table. I'm good when I tidy up, when I wash my hands before eating. I'm good when I'm quiet when Daddy wants it to be quiet, or when I do well on a test at school, and other stuff like that. But sometimes I forget I'm supposed to be good. It just happens by accident. I might be drawing and I scribble on the tablecloth by mistake. Or I'm playing with Alexander in the garden, and he falls over because the game is too rough for him. Or I say something I shouldn't say. Or I come home from school with a torn skirt, and I don't know how it happened but Mommy has to buy a new one. Like money grows on trees. I've also taken candy from the cupboard when it wasn't allowed. Which is actually stealing. When I got caught, I said I didn't know it wasn't allowed, which was lying. And last week I was very mean to Sophie from my class. But, well, she was making up rules that didn't go with the game and that was why my team lost and then I called her a nasty pig. Of course I know that's not nice, but it just slipped out. I have to learn to think before I speak, Mommy says, and she's right. I'm not always good at that. Sophie cried and told the teacher I called her a pig, and then the teacher was really mad at me. I was scared she'd tell Mommy, but she didn't. That was lucky.

I hold my hand in front of my eyes to find out whether I can see it. Maybe a little bit? Or is it just because I know it's there? I'm sitting on the floor because I can't find the stool that's here somewhere. The floor's hard and cold, my bottom is already beginning to hurt a bit. Anyhow, I'm going to stay close to the floor because there are spiderwebs hanging from the ceiling, and I don't want to get them in my hair. If I had a tissue, I'd blow my nose, but I don't have one so I suck the snot back up. I can do that by breathing in hard through my nose. Mommy thinks it's filthy when I do that, but well, she can't hear it now. "A girl without manners doesn't get anywhere in life." She says that a lot.

I try not to listen to the sounds down here, a strange kind of tapping and a quiet buzzing. I don't know where they're coming from, and I start to think there might be a monster in here or something. I know they don't exist, but sometimes, here in this little room, I forget

4

that. Well, not really forget, but it's like my brain is switched off. I'm a scaredy-cat, Mommy says, I have to be tougher. She's right, of course, but I don't know how.

I could be stronger—for a nine-year-old, I mean. Only not in the dark—I hate the dark, and spiders, I'm scared of them, and mice, and big dogs. But only if they're really big. I like little dogs. Little dogs always seem friendly. Like they don't know what sadness is, unless their owner shows them. I saw that once, my best friend Ellen's dog lay down with her when she was sick, really quietly. Usually he's jumping around and wagging his tail and barking because he's happy to see Ellen. When he was lying next to her on the rug beside the sofa, I decided that dogs might be the nicest animals in the world, along with white rabbits, those little ones, and baby goats, like the ones on the farm we went to with school. If I had a goat, I'd call it Alexander just to mess with my brother. Geese seem nice too, only Daddy once told us to be careful around them, they can bite. I thought that was weird because geese don't have teeth. Then Daddy said they do it with their beaks, but that's stupid because you bite with teeth, otherwise it's not called biting, is it?

I don't know how long I've been in here already, an hour, or maybe four hours, I'm not sure. Maybe I'll die of just sitting here getting bored. I try to crack my knuckles one by one—Daddy doesn't let me do that, it gives you rheumatism later, he says, but I like the sound. I'm not allowed to put my hand in the bins of nuts in the supermarket either, but sometimes I do it because it feels so nice, and afterward my hand is all salty and I can lick it off, but Mommy thinks that's gross.

I can hear someone coming down the stairs. Phew, it's her, I can tell from the sound of her high heels. I can't help smiling a bit because I'm so happy my punishment is over. I have to stop smiling before Mommy sees me, otherwise she'll think I'm not sorry. I hear her clearing her throat like she always does when she's angry. The door opens.

"Well?"

My eyes shut on their own because Mommy has turned on the light in the part of the basement where she's standing.

"I'll never do it again."

"What else?"

"Sorry, Mommy, I'll never do it again." I wrap my arms around her waist.

She taps my left shoulder twice with her hand. "Yes, yes, that's enough. Go upstairs now."

I'm so happy that Mommy always forgives me each time. Only mothers can do that, I think, always forgive you whatever you've done. When I'm upstairs in the bright light, it takes a while for my eyes to get used to it.

Daddy is just coming into the kitchen. "Hello, kids," he calls out to me and Alexander. "How did you get those cobwebs in your hair?"

I don't answer. I don't dare.

"People who don't want to listen have to pay the price."

Daddy doesn't respond. He looks at me. "Everything OK?"

"'Course," I say and walk into the dining room. I'll read, I think, because I have a really nice book and it cheers me up. Daddy walks past me. It looks like he's going back to his dental office.

"Do you have more patients?" I ask.

"No, I have to do some other work."

"Can I come with you? I'll read my book."

"Oh, Mona," Daddy says.

Before he has the chance to say anything else, I say, "I'll be really quiet, I promise. I won't tell you anything about my book, because it's so exciting I just want to keep reading."

"Go on, then," he says, holding the door open.

I'm not allowed in here much, but I love Daddy's office. It smells like the funny things he uses to repair people's teeth. There's a diagram of what a full set of teeth looks like, which is kind of boring, but I don't say that. There's a special kind of electric armchair that Daddy can move up and down with a switch. I like to lie down on it. There's a massive lamp above it that's really bright, perfect for reading if I position it right. I don't want to disturb Daddy, so I hop up right away, without his help. The back of the chair is in exactly the right position. Daddy sits down at his desk and gets some files full of papers from his bag, then he begins to leaf through them, jotting stuff down from time to time.

I like sitting here like this without talking, him working and me reading. Daddy really loves working, he hates salsify, which is a vegetable, and the new postman who sometimes leaves the newspaper sticking out of the mailbox so if it rains you can't read it anymore, and if Daddy's watching television, he sometimes talks to no one in particular. My dad is very clever because when he does crossword puzzles he does the five-star ones, and you can't get any more stars than that.

"You reap what you sow." Mommy says that a lot too. There are lots of sayings that Mommy says all the time. You're supposed to remember them and learn something from them—she explained that to me once.

I wish we could stay here like this forever and that I never had to go to school and do stupid math problems, and that I never had to lie in bed without being able to sleep, and that I never had nightmares, and that I never had to go to the room in the basement, and that I never made anyone angry, and that I won a prize for being the nicest girl in the world. The clock in the hall strikes nine, loudly, like someone is banging a gong. I don't like that sound and neither does Daddy, he says, but the clock used to belong to Daddy's parents, so it has to stay here, he says.

"Past your bedtime, off you go," Daddy says.

"Yes," I reply. I try not to sound sad about it.

2

I know it's not actually allowed because I'm not ten yet, and I have to cross the big road, but who's going to know? Since it happened, our house has been full of people all the time. Drinking beer.

I stand at the back door, look around, no one can see me. I close the door, run to the garage, get my bike out, and set off.

I'm guessing it will take me about fifteen minutes to get there. It's a lovely day: blue sky, the odd friendly cloud, an amazing amount of birds. From down on the ground, all the birds look black, from close by they're not, though, most of them aren't. Crows are, and blackbirds, well, the males are. Daddy taught me the French word: *merle*.

I like biking, especially when the sun is shining and the warm air comes blowing at you. That's what I think about inside my head. It's good to think about nice things.

I bike past the baker's, the lady at the counter sometimes gives me candy, completely for free. When I say "Thank you, ma'am" politely—because politeness gets you further in life, Mommy says—the lady smiles, and when she smiles, you can see her golden tooth. It's a bit scary, but because I know I don't want to look at it, I look even more, of course. That's like trying not to think about potato chips when you know you're not allowed to have any, which makes you want some even more.

I bike past Sophie's house as well, she's nice but a bit smelly. She smells a little like trash in the summer, and sometimes like attics where nobody's been for a while. When the teacher made us sit together in class last year, I was kind of unhappy about it. But Uncle Artie said that if you smell a bad smell for a hundred and eighty seconds, you get used to it, that's what scientists say. I don't know if he really got that from scientists or if he just said that to make me feel better, but it did actually help. Each day when school started, I sat extra close to Sophie, and then I counted to a hundred and eighty, not too fast, while I breathed in hard through my nose. And then it was easier to put up with it that day. School starts again soon. I wonder who I'll sit next to this year. I hope next to Ellen. Ellen's my best friend and I'm hers. She hates mosquitoes, bees, flies, and card games, she loves yellow and ice cream, even in the winter, and if she has to sneeze, which she does all the time, really all the time, she sneezes at least three times, and sometimes lots more.

I reach the crossroads, the traffic light is red. There aren't that many cars on the road today, because it's Sunday. Most of them are blue, I notice. Ours is green. The same green as ponds when the sun's shining on them. When my dad brought the car home for the first time, about four years ago, I didn't like the color. I was disappointed he hadn't picked red or, if he had to, yellow. But it was a Citroën DS, my dad said proudly, an old car, much prettier than today's cars. I had to agree with him. The headlights on the cars looked like eyes, like it wasn't a machine but a person. I thought that was funny. He bought it from a patient, he said, so he couldn't choose the color. I got that.

In general, I don't like not being able to choose. Like at school, where the teacher always says what we're going to do next. Sometimes I wish I didn't have to go to school. But then I think about always being on vacation, and then I'm not sure that would be much better.

I'm almost there. I know where the scrapyard is because we always drive past it when we go to visit Granny. Which is lucky. The sun is in my eyes, but I can handle it. Being able to handle a lot of things is helpful in life, my mom says. Just a bit farther and I'll be there. I get down, lean my bike on its stand, and walk around the building. It's an ugly gray rectangle with a door, some windows, a big gate, and a flat roof. Everything's closed, of course, which is the point and the reason I waited until Sunday. I didn't want anyone looking over my shoulder. And I knew I'd be able to get into the yard, there are only some short posts at the side so people can't steal the cars.

The wrecks are at the back, on the plot next to the poplar trees. It hasn't rained for so long that the hard, sandy soil is dusty, and back here it's full of gravel, the small, sharp sort. One little stone already got into my sandal, but I can't be a wimp. If I stop to get it out, a new one will just get in right away. I walk on and take a good look around. What a mess: wrecked cars and parts all over the place, there's a funny stack of cars in the corner. They're piled on top of each other like Duplo blocks.

Suddenly I see it, it's at the front left: our pond-green Citroën DS. At first I keep my distance, trying to take in what I can see. I count to sixty, which is long enough. How smashed it looks. The two left wheels are off, the front bumper has disappeared, and its whole nose is dented. It hasn't got a windshield anymore, of course, and part of the roof is missing, mainly on the passenger side. I take a few steps closer, and then a few more. I want to look into the car. There's not much to see on Daddy's side, except that everything's broken, and dirty, only the steering wheel is still there. Then I go and look on Mommy's side, where it's different. There's dried blood on that funny rod above the dashboard and on the seat. A lot. The blood isn't red, more brownish. I get even closer, my head almost inside the car. It smells of gasoline and burning meat and paint. I look more carefully and see bits of skin. And hair. Strands of Mommy's blond hair. I stay there for a long time, just looking. Sometimes you have to take a good look.

When Granny came to wake us up, me and Alexander, the day before yesterday, in the middle of the night, I knew right away that something was wrong. We're children, you don't just wake children up at twelve minutes to five. Granny didn't look at us, she just said we had to come downstairs, that Daddy would come soon, and then she went downstairs herself. Alexander and I followed her. Alexander said he was thirsty. My grandma went to get him a drink, and we had to sit on the sofa, Daddy would be here right away—those exact words, which I thought was strange. Alexander got Coke, and I immediately regretted not asking for anything myself. Coke's only for special occasions. Now it was too late, I couldn't send Granny back to the kitchen, it wouldn't be polite.

It seemed to take an eternity, Granny's so-called right away. I looked at the photo on top of the television, the one of me and Alexander together in a kiddie pool in the garden. He was still a baby then and I was a little girl. I'm smiling awkwardly, posing for the photo. I look a little strange in it, I heard Mommy say once to Uncle Artie, and I think she's right, "but Alexander looks scrumptious." That's what she said: "scrumptious." It made me think of a big monster that eats children, and I quickly tried to think about something else.

Suddenly Daddy was there. He'd come from the garden, I think. He was wearing his nice suit because they'd gone out for dinner that night. Now it was all dirty. Mommy wouldn't be happy about that. There was a kind of massive Band-Aid on his forehead. I saw Daddy looking down at his shirt like he knew what I was thinking.

"I'll be with you right away," he said before disappearing upstairs.

Yes, yes, right away, whatever you say, I thought, then felt bad for being so mean. Daddy doesn't just get us out of bed in the middle of the night for fun, so he must have a good reason for going upstairs first.

Meanwhile Alexander had started driving his red toy car up and down the legs of the coffee table like they were roads. *Doesn't he realize something's wrong?* I thought. *Maybe it's good if he doesn't, because he's only six.* I wasn't such a baby when I was six, I don't think, but Mommy says it's because he's the youngest. She says the youngest is allowed to stay small for longer.

We're never allowed to go with them to restaurants because restaurants are for grown-ups, Mommy says. When they go, they always put on their nicest clothes, and Mommy wears the earrings Granny gave her—white pearls shaped like big tears. And then she puts on makeup, and she sprays hairspray onto her hair, making the whole kitchen smell sour and soapy.

When Daddy came back, he was wearing different clothes. These ones weren't dirty. Daddy's forehead was sweaty, which often happens in the summer, only now it was nighttime and not that hot. He sat down in between me and Alexander and said, "You have to listen carefully because Daddy has something to tell you." And then he was silent. For a long time. Even Alexander had stopped playing and was watching Daddy carefully, like me. Neither of us dared to say anything or ask about the Band-Aid on his head. Daddy was just staring into space like he'd forgotten what to say. He balled one of his hands into a fist.

Granny got a chair and joined us. "Go on," she said. I looked at Granny. All of a sudden, her face looked gray. I think she'd been crying, because there were red blotches on her neck and face. Mommy gets them too if she cries, which she hardly ever does. Mommy is a woman who can cope with a lot—she says that to Daddy sometimes. "Oh, do what you have to, Vincent, I can cope with a lot." It's not easy for Mommy, with us and all that.

I heard Daddy taking a deep breath. "Kids"—he always says that, "kids," even though I'm big now—"I've got some bad news: there was an accident, earlier tonight, and it's not good." Then he stopped talking again. Granny began to sob loudly, with tears and snot. She walked out of the room, probably to get a tissue, because it's not a pretty sight, snot running from your nose. Then Alexander started crying too, probably because he wasn't used to Granny crying. I laid my hand on Daddy's arm in case it would help him finish his story. He didn't seem to notice. There was just silence and silence.

Then Granny came back from the kitchen. She had stopped crying and she looked neat and tidy again, and finally she said, "Your Mommy didn't make it." Since no one reacted, she said, "She died."

Alexander sobbed and gasped for breath. "Is she dead? Is Mommy dead?"

"Yes," said Daddy. Just "yes," nothing more. He went on staring at the wall next to the door like there was something to see there.

I didn't start to cry, which bothered me. I tried to send tears to my eyes, but they wouldn't listen, so I looked down, like at my belly button, my chin almost on my chest, like sad people do. Granny didn't move. Daddy stood up, walked into his office, and closed the door behind him.

There we sat, Granny, Alexander, and me. Nothing moved outside, or inside either. It was quiet. I heard the sound of the fridge, a quiet buzzing. And the ticking of the clock. And Alexander's sobs. I thought about Mommy and what she had said before she left. "Behave, won't you, for Granny. If I hear you haven't been good, you know what will happen." She sounded a bit angry already, even though we were always good for Granny. Afterward I thought about the black outfit she'd been wearing: a black skirt with a red belt and a black blouse. It looked really nice. I'd told her that when she came down the stairs, and she'd smiled. Mommy liked getting compliments on her clothes, I knew that. When she'd smiled, it had made me happy. Was she still wearing that outfit now? Did it get dirty too? It probably did, just like Daddy's suit. Would they wash it for the funeral, or would she get something else to wear in the coffin? I was certain she'd want to be dressed in black. *Maybe I should tell Daddy that,* I thought. Daddy didn't know anything about clothes. Mommy always said so. I wondered what Alexander was thinking about. He was sitting on the rug with his knees pulled up, his tear-stained face turned away. I really wanted to say something to him but I didn't know what. So I just stayed where I was. It seemed best.

As I stand there, next to what was once our Citroën DS, I realize I never told Daddy about Mommy's clothes. I have to go home. Soon it'll be too late for the clothes.

I can't tell anybody what I've seen. Alexander is much too young and all the grown-ups will just get angry because I did something that wasn't allowed.

When I get home, everyone's sitting more or less in the same place. No one noticed I was gone. Granny serves cups of coffee and beer, people are sitting around talking and drinking. If you didn't know any better, you might think it was a birthday party.

Uncle Olivier sees me and smiles. I go up to him.

"Will you tell Daddy that Mommy would want her black outfit on, the one she was wearing on the night of the crash? They were her favorite clothes. If they're dirty, we can wash them."

"All right," Uncle Olivier says. He looks around the room. I wonder whether he heard me. "Why don't you go and find Alexander? He's playing outside with his cousins, I think." They want to get rid of me.

"Maybe I should tell Daddy myself."

"Leave him be for a while." Uncle Olivier lays his hand on my back, gently at first, then he kind of pushes me toward the door. I go look for Daddy. He's sitting on the sofa under the window, surrounded by two aunts and the neighbor, and he's talking away. After being silent in the night, he's turned into the opposite in the day. He's talking the whole time, like a machine that doesn't stop turning, but I'm not allowed to know what he's saying. Whenever I get near him, there's always someone who sends me away.

Last night before I went to sleep, Daddy came into my bedroom. He hardly ever does that. He stood there, next to my bed. "Sleep well," he said.

I waited for more, stared at him with the sweetest expression possible. I wanted to ask something but I didn't know what.

He gave me a kiss on my left cheek. "Sleep well," a bit quieter now.

"Yes," I replied. When he'd closed the door and everything was dark, I wondered if I'd be able to sleep. *Or to cry,* I thought, that would also be good.

3

First day of school. Yesterday Granny said it was good for us to go back to school, back to life as it used to be. I repeated the words inside my head: *Life as it used to be.*

It's not that I'd rather stay home, but I don't feel like school. And certainly not the fourth grade, because I think it's going to be boring. In fifth grade at least you get French, something new.

It's almost seven thirty. I'm lying in bed and the sheet is annoying me, it's not spread out right beneath the blanket anymore, and the blanket is so prickly. Can I think of an excuse? I can't pretend to be sick because Daddy would see through that right away.

Suddenly my bedroom door opens—it's Alexander. "We have to get up or we'll be la-ate."

"That's true," I say. "I'm coming. Will you go get dressed?" It can't be right for a boy as young as Alexander to have to keep an eye on the clock. So I start the day with a guilty conscience. I often have one. Uncle Artie explained the expression to me; I'd come across it in a book for older children. I like to read books for kids over ten and sometimes over twelve because I can understand them, even though the people who write them and the lady in the library with the big nose seem not to think so. Uncle Artie said it has to do with feeling sorry about doing something and thinking you should feel sorry. Then I thought, *I know all about that.*

Daddy has more work than he used to. He's often already in his office in the mornings when we go downstairs, and then it's best if I don't disturb him. It's not Daddy's fault that there are suddenly so many people with toothaches. He can't just send home difficult patients with rotten molars. So I toast some slices of bread for Alexander and myself and give him a glass of milk. Actually, he can do it himself but he likes it better when someone does it for him—he's a bit lazy.

Sometimes my little brother is awfully dumb, like for example when he wants to join one of my games for big kids, or when he dropped the vase I made, or the time when Mommy said he was being too wild and that calamity would come of it; Mommy used that word a lot: *calamity.* But sometimes, once in a while, I think he's sweet. Sweeter in any case than Berend, Sophie's big brother. He smells just like his sister, plus he hits people when he gets angry, and he burps so loud you can hear it a long way away. It's too bad for Sophie.

When I've made our lunch and gotten two apples from the fridge for a snack, I call Alexander. "Coat on." He thinks it's much too warm, he doesn't want to wear a coat, he makes a face. "It just seems too warm," I say. "It's cold in the mornings and I don't want you getting sick." Just like Mommy always said, I realize. He sits down on the ground in a grump, like he's three years old. "Alexander, do I have to get angry?" He shrugs, gets up, and goes outside, without his coat. I don't know what to do now. If it takes any longer, we'll be late for the first day of school. He used to listen to Mommy. I carry his coat under my arm, pick up my satchel, and go outside. I throw the coat at his head—that way, he has to take it. He ties it around his waist and holds out his hand to me. He never used to do that.

As we walk to school, neither of us speaks for three whole blocks. Maybe Alexander is wondering what on earth he's going to tell his school friends. Ellen in my class knows about Mommy but the others don't, as far as I know. Granny said that Daddy will inform the new teachers.

"Look, a cat," Alexander says. He's wanted a cat for ages, but Mommy didn't like them.

"It's a pretty one," I say. "It's got lovely white paws."

Alexander walks over to stroke the animal, but it darts off into the bushes. If I could choose, I'd get a dog. A little white one like Ellen's, and then I'd call him Blackie because that's a joke. But actually, I shouldn't think about it, because I'm never going to get one.

Once we arrive at the boys' school, Alexander clings to my side. It's his first day at big school, but before the long vacation he said he was looking forward to learning to write and count and read.

"You know that your teacher's heard about Mommy? She'll look out for you, all right?" I just hope she really will.

"All right," my brother says, though he doesn't sound very convinced.

"Go find your friends. Look, there's Jeremy. I have to go now or I'll be late." I push him into the playground. I can't always be taking care of him.

This year we've got Miss Van Gelderen. She's not that nice or funny or whatever, but she's also not a real witch like Mrs. Volderman, who teaches third grade, so I'm happy. Ellen comes and sits down next to me right away in the classroom because we were allowed to choose our places ourselves. "If there's too much talking, I'll move you around next week. But first you're getting the chance to prove that you're big girls." *Ooh, that's going to be difficult,* I think, Ellen and I love talking. And we always get so bored at school that it's almost impossible not to.

"But first an announcement before we start. Mona, sweetie, could you come forward?"

Ellen squeezes my leg under the desk. *Go to the front—me, now?*
The teacher keeps on talking as she gestures to me, waving her hand like
a policewoman directing traffic.

"Mona had a sad experience a couple of weeks ago. I don't think
all of you know about it yet. Come here, sweetie, come along." Usually
I like to stand up in front of the class, but right now I'd rather float up
into the sky, far away from here. When I reach the teacher's side, she
rests her hand on my shoulder. "Go on, tell them."

Tell them? What should I tell them? That my mother's dead, that
she was killed in an accident I know nothing about? That I didn't cry?
Only briefly during the funeral, but actually that was because I'd never
seen my dad cry before. Should I say that only people cry, and not animals, that I read that in a book? That I'm wondering how long it will
be before the creepy crawlies get through the coffin and into Mommy's
body? That every evening I really try not to think about those creepy
crawlies, but when I close my eyes, I see white things that look like
worms? Should I say that my dad hasn't said anything since the funeral,
except for silly things? That my granny comes around a lot but she just
starts dusting or cleaning the patio or ironing clothes, which we've
already got Marcella for, and that she only wants to play cards with us
because she doesn't know any other games? That sometimes, like when
I'm reading a book, I'm happy because it's a funny story, but then I feel
really bad afterward because that can't be right, can it?

"Or should I tell them?" the teacher asks.

"Yes." I look at the wall at the back of the classroom. There's a bul-
letin board with a poster of a sunset in colors so ugly they can't be real.

"Mona's mom and dad had a car accident. A truck drove into them.
Mona's dad is fine, but her mom was taken to the hospital and the doctors tried everything but it was to no avail. Her mom died there, didn't
she, Mona?"

I nod, though all I can think of is—*A truck? They took her to the
hospital?* That explains why the roof was off on Mommy's side. Why

did Daddy tell my teacher this and not me? Without asking permission, I go back to my desk. It was "to no avail." That's a strange way of saying something. Ellen gives me a sad look. She shouldn't do that. If people are kind, it makes me weak. And it's not good to be weak in life, Mommy always said. She said Uncle Artie was weak, his flesh was weak, that's what she said, and that was why he kept getting into trouble.

"So, now you've been informed, children. Let's take out our math book."

I don't want to think about math. I don't want to think about trucks and hospitals. I can tell Daddy what my teacher said—who knows, maybe he'll tell me even more things I don't know. Or maybe I'd better not, there's a chance Daddy might get upset, and he's already finding things difficult. I try to concentrate on nice things. Like the extra-thick layer of chocolate I spread on my bread this morning because nobody was looking. Or the friendship bracelet Ellen gave me at the end of vacation when I was allowed to play at her house for the afternoon. Or that time that Daddy almost tripped over the rolled-up carpet at Uncle Artie's.

Ellen nudges me. "You have to do these problems, this row here." Luckily, Ellen's there. She always knows what to do.

4

School's out. We'd have to work hard today, the teacher said in the morning, but to me what we did was just as boring as the days before it. I'm waiting for Alexander at the gates to the boys' school. He shuffles along, bent over slightly, a little boy with an oversized backpack.

"How did it go?"

"All right," he says.

"And did you learn something new?"

"Yes."

"What?"

"I forgot." Then he asks if I'll play Sorry! with him at home. "Please, please, please." I understand why Mommy found it difficult to say no to him. She was stricter with me. But that was all right because I needed it, otherwise nothing good would ever become of me.

When we get home, there are two extra cars parked in front of the door, Granny's and Auntie Rose's. I wonder whether Daddy likes Granny coming by so much, because I'm not sure Daddy would be friends with her if she wasn't a relative. On Sundays, when Mommy used to say we were going to visit her, Daddy would usually reply, "Can't you say I had to deal with an emergency case?" And then of course Mommy would sigh. I understood. It's not nice to have to do everything on your own with two children. And it's not nice for Granny either;

she'd usually bake a tart if we were coming, or a cake, and then she'd be stuck with it. While children are starving in Africa.

I open the door and hear that the visitors are upstairs. They seem to be disagreeing about something. When I go into the bedroom, I see that they are putting Mommy's clothes into gray garbage bags. A few of her skirts and blouses are lying on the bed.

"Those are Mommy's clothes." I try to make it sound like a problem.

"The wardrobe needs to be emptied so other stuff can go in there." Granny sounds like the look on the teacher's face when she doesn't want us to talk back.

"We're going to give them to Goodwill," Auntie Rose says, as though this will make it better, "except for the things that would suit me or Auntie Emma, perhaps. That's what we were talking about."

"But they're Mommy's clothes," I try again.

"Yes, child," Granny replies. "Could you take your young legs downstairs to fetch us something to drink? All this dust is making me thirsty." She stuffs a couple of sweaters in a bag and turns away from me.

I gallop down the stairs and go into Daddy's office. There are people in the waiting room, but for once I really don't care. I knock on the door and storm in. "They're getting rid of Mommy's clothes, all of them." My voice breaks. Daddy looks at me, as does the old lady lying in the chair with her mouth open and a cloth under her chin. A tube sucks up her saliva and it's making a spluttering sound.

"Calm down, Mona. You know you're not allowed to come in when I'm at work. What's Georgette here going to think?"

The old lady smiles, tube and all. She doesn't seem to mind much.

"Her clothes." I continue to stare at him. I don't know what I expected exactly, but something, in any case.

"We'll talk about it later. Granny thought it would be a good idea to tidy everything up. Now I really have to get back to work, Mona, the waiting room's full." He looks at his patient again. "My apologies for the interruption, Georgette. Now I'm going to—"

I turn around and close the door behind me. When I'm back in the living room, Alexander tugs at my sleeve.

"You promised you'd play Sorry!."

"In a minute, Alexander."

I take a good look around the two large rooms. The photo of Mommy and Daddy when they got married that was above the cabinet that used to belong to Daddy's parents is gone. The shoes that were under the radiator in the corner: gone. I go to the cupboard with her wool and her knitting: empty. I rush back upstairs and check the jewelry box in the bathroom: empty. The book that she was reading is back in the bookcase. Granny is tidying everything up, everything. I go back into the bedroom and glare at her. She doesn't look back.

"Did you bring water for us?"

I don't reply. When I'm angry, I forget my manners.

Auntie Rose asks as she folds up a blouse, "How was school, Mona?" Just like asking someone "Is the soup good?" while they're bleeding like a pig from a gash on their knee.

"All right," I say, just as Alexander did. I bite my lip.

"It's better if you're not constantly reminded of what happened," Auntie Rose says then.

"Back to life as it used to be," Granny adds.

Then I go downstairs.

"Get Sorry! out of the cupboard," I say to Alexander. He runs to the playroom and then puts the game on the table. "We're allowed to have Coke," I lie. "Do you want some?"

"Yes, yippee!" he squeals.

I go into the kitchen, get the biggest glasses I can find, and fill them almost to the rim. "Chips too?" I shout. I climb up onto the counter and find two bags of sweet pepper potato chips on the top shelf.

"Yes," Alexander shouts.

That evening Granny cooks us dinner. Meatballs in tomato sauce with mashed potatoes. I actually do like that, but I don't feel hungry. Maybe it's because of the chips.

"You need to eat properly," she says.

"Yes," I say, putting down my knife and fork.

"The other meatballs are nicer," Alexander says. He means the ones Mommy makes.

Granny looks at him. "Eat, sonny," is all she says.

"Where's Daddy?"

"He'll be along in a moment when he's done."

"When will he be done?"

"I don't know."

I have to go to bed at eight thirty. I didn't get to see Daddy. Once I'm under the covers, I think: *I'll stay awake until midnight if necessary, and when I hear Daddy on the stairs, I'll go to him.* He won't mind. He did say we'd discuss it later.

I don't think I made it until midnight. In the morning I woke up, and the only thing I could think was that he must be angry with me. I know I'm not allowed to just go barging in, it's against the rules. Or maybe I made him sad. Even more sad. Maybe he didn't like Mommy's things being tidied away but he didn't dare tell Granny that. After all, he should be grateful for everything she's doing for us, so yes. I'll be extra nice to him today. Hopefully he'll forgive me then.

As I brush my teeth, I think: *Maybe they're right. Maybe it is better not to be reminded anymore.* The same way I try not to think about monsters, and about wriggly worms in coffins and Sophie's smell. Luckily she sits far away from me in class now.

5

It's Christmas Eve tonight. Daddy and Alexander and I are going to celebrate it with just the three of us. We don't have guests coming until tomorrow. Mommy always said that Christmastime meant stress-time, and when I see the way Granny's carrying on, already spending all afternoon cooking for us, I think she must feel the same.

They say children look like their parents, but I don't think Mommy looked like Granny. Except perhaps her nose and also that they're both strict for my own good, but Granny a little less. I think I mainly look like Daddy.

Most children love Christmas because of the presents. Ours have been lying there shining under the tree for a couple of days now. It's hard only to be allowed to look at them, but Daddy wouldn't let us open them until Christmas Eve. And now we've had to wait for him for ages because there was another urgent case. An old man who was roaring in pain, Daddy told us. I felt sorry for him, even though I didn't hear any roaring. I also felt sorry for us because we'd waited so long already.

Alexander opens his first, a big box of Playmobil, something to do with firefighters. He looks happy. Mine is a big box too. The paper's blue and blue's a pretty color, so it's already looking good. I take it off carefully so that I can make something with it later. And then I see it: it's a doll. Really, a doll. As big as a baby. Her eyes open when you sit her upright and shut when you lay her down. Her mouth's a little bit open and she's wearing a yellow romper with white stripes. I hate dolls, I don't get what to do with them. This one smells like plastic and bedrooms before the windows have been opened. I really wanted a punching bag and boxing gloves, like Sophie's brother, Berend, or maybe roller skates, or some of that special watercolor paint like Ellen's got. Her mom says it's called aquarelle and you can make much prettier pictures with it.

I had actually made a card with a drawing on it and I'd written what I wanted inside. It was supposed to be for Santa, that card. I knew he didn't exist, but last year Mommy had me make a card because Alexander still believed in him. But in November, just after the first toy catalog had come in the mail, Daddy suddenly said that grown-ups had invented Santa. We were eating tomato soup with those bits in it. I think Alexander was upset. "Yeah, I know, Daddy. That guy in the big store, he's not real. He's just an assistant Santa," he said. But Daddy explained that parents bought presents for their children and said Alexander was a big boy now, and it was better he knew the truth. My brother pouted. I immediately thought about the card, of course. I'd put a lot of work into it. In the end, I just adapted my drawing a bit. There are also regular people who have beards, and I turned the cloak into a coat, like for regular people, and I added a little Christmas tree in the corner, so then it became a card with my Christmas list on it. I put it on Daddy's desk more than three weeks ago so that he'd have enough time to go shopping. He didn't mention it, but I just thought he didn't want to ruin the surprise. And now this doll? Granny probably bought it and didn't even see my card.

"There's a bottle too, so you can feed the baby milk," Daddy says. He's taking everything out of the packaging for me. He's being so nice I don't dare say how ridiculous the doll is. Anyway, that wouldn't be polite. I pick up the bottle, put the doll on my lap, and feed her the so-called milk. In the meantime, I look from the doll to Daddy and back again. He smiles at me. I like it when Daddy smiles.

Personally I don't think Daddy's very handsome. Of course everyone has to make up their own mind about those things. Mommy must have thought differently. He's got a beard that prickles when he gives you a kiss, and I always think beards smell a bit like dirty dishes. When I was smaller, only eight, he didn't have one and that was better. He's got small brown eyes, a reasonably big nose and big ears, and his ears flap a bit. My daddy's also got bushy eyebrows and hair that stands up on top of his head. He's also got hair on his chest and arms and legs and back and on his hands and ears too. When I look at him, I'm glad I'm a girl. I hope for Alexander that he hasn't inherited all that hair.

After about two minutes, I set the doll upright. "Now she has to be burped, right, Daddy?" He nods, gets up, and asks whether we want any candy.

We watch TV together. We're allowed to choose what to watch and we've each got a whole dish of candy. I've stuck the doll on the other sofa so that she can watch along with us comfortably. And to get rid of her. Maybe the card got lost. Or maybe one of Daddy's patients took it and it's somewhere on a lonely person's shelf. That would be all right, actually, because at Christmas you have to be nice to lonely people, my teacher says. People who don't have anyone else are lonely, according to the teacher. Luckily we're not like that.

6

Uncle Artie has the radio on. Uncle Artie loves music and nice clothes and he runs races against us. He hates soccer and other sports on TV. And he never talks to me like I'm a kid. The speakers are singing "Save Your Kisses for Me."

"I know what that means," I say proudly, and I giggle.

Granny puts a plate on the drying rack. There's been a crack in it for a long time, but she still doesn't throw it away. It's because she lived through the war, Daddy says. Granny never throws anything away. Except for some things, I've realized.

"It won the Eurovision Song Contest, that song," Uncle Artie says.

"I know. There were four people in white suits who were singing and doing a kind of dance, waving their arms." Mommy hadn't liked their suits, she said at the time, when Eurovision was on. I was allowed to stay up for it because I was big enough.

Uncle Artie sings along. He tosses away the dishcloth he was using, lays his arm on my shoulder, takes my hand, sticks it out, and dances around the kitchen with me. He smells of flowers and cigarettes. He's wearing a lavender-colored shirt and a kind of scarf, very different from Daddy's clothes. I always love Uncle Artie's clothes.

"Me too," Alexander, who has just come in, cries.

"No way," I say. "I was first."

But Uncle Artie spins me around, my arms above my head, lets go, picks up Alexander, and dances around with him until the song finishes. There wasn't much of it left but I'm still annoyed.

Granny gives him his cloth back without a word. Granny thinks people should always be working, it seems to me. Uncle Artie makes a face behind her back, crossing his eyes and sticking his lower lip out over the top one. I think it's funny, but maybe he shouldn't, because if Granny saw she wouldn't like it.

Granny wanted to have the big Christmas party at our house, she thought that would be the easiest because there's enough space in our house. Auntie Rose, Auntie Emma, and Uncle Olivier will be coming later too with their children. They've got five kids altogether. Five and a half in fact, because Uncle Olivier and his wife are going to have another baby in March.

There are going to be two of Mommy's sisters and two of Daddy's brothers. I think it's good that it's even. Even though it doesn't work out if you count Granny too, since she's on Mommy's side. But Granny only half counts because she'll be in the kitchen almost the whole time, I can tell you that already.

Yesterday she got started on the food: Vol-au-vents with croquettes, both homemade, even the croquettes. As an appetizer, soup made of something I've forgotten, with homemade meatballs. Chocolate mousse for dessert. It really is an awful lot of work to make that all yourself. I offered to help, but then it would only take longer, Granny said. That's probably true. Mommy always said I had two left hands. When I was little, six maybe, or four, I thought she meant I was born wrong, now I know it's just an expression. Granny slaves away for us, just like Mommy used to do, and she's actually really old—fifty-nine. There isn't a cake big enough for that many candles.

It's almost three and the first guests are arriving. Auntie Rose, who always comes too early. Not long after her, the others arrive, one by one. Uncle Olivier is almost thirty minutes late—little Walter just wouldn't wake up from his nap, apparently. Uncle Olivier always talks really loud. I don't know why. It amazes me that Walter can sleep through it.

Everyone sits down and I'm allowed to take a tray of snacks around. There are pieces of melba toast with cream cheese and an almond in the middle, or with crab and a leaf of parsley, or with steak tartare, mayonnaise, and a pickled onion. They look beautiful. Everyone chooses one except for Auntie Emma, who is watching her figure, like Mommy always did. Uncle Artie takes two and winks. "There are plenty," I say and wink back. Daddy pours everyone a glass of fizzy wine, which is the right thing to drink at a party. My cousin Emilie is sitting next to Auntie Rose, so after I've finished making my rounds, I put the tray down on the coffee table and nestle up to Daddy.

The boys immediately rushed off to the playroom, and Walter is sitting among the toys Auntie Elke put on the floor for him. He stares intently at the tower of colored rings, arranged from big to small. Walter gets them off and puts them in his mouth, which isn't how you're supposed to play with them, but I'm not going to get involved.

Uncle Artie is the first to raise his glass. "Let's drink to a wonderful Christmas, a better New Year, and to Agnes, wherever she is now. Cheers!"

Agnes—I haven't heard that name for so long. I wonder whether Daddy still talks about Mommy to other people, in the evening maybe, when we're in bed and can hear guests downstairs. Like a ridiculous amount of mosquitoes, a whole living room full, all buzzing at the same time—that's what it sounds like. He hasn't said the word *Mommy* to us since that time, nine days after the funeral, when I asked him why we had to get rid of her clothes. And now Uncle Artie has dared to say her name? I can feel how uneasy the silence is. Granny gets up and goes into the kitchen under the pretense of fetching something. Auntie Rose and

Auntie Emma sip from their glasses in silence. Uncle Olivier smiles at his brother like he's saying, *Everyone makes mistakes, it's not that bad.* I like Uncle Artie but I don't understand how he doesn't realize he upsets people. I always do my very best not to upset people. Daddy stares at his shoes. I don't move.

Then suddenly the door to the hall opens and Alexander comes in crying. "They're cheating."

Everyone replies at the same time.

"Go on, Mona, go upstairs and play a different game with your brother. He's the youngest and probably can't compete with his cousins."

"And Mona," says Auntie Emma, "tell the boys to be nice to Alexander, otherwise I'll be forced to come up."

I don't want to go is what I think. It might not be very well behaved of me, but I really don't want to go upstairs. I want to stay here, like Emilie, even if Auntie Rose has started talking about the handbag my uncle gave her yesterday, which isn't that interesting. I want to hear what they all say. They might even mention Mommy again.

But Daddy says, "Come on, sweetie, hurry up."

I'm angry at Alexander. Why can't he ever stay calm like the rest of us? I shout up the stairs in irritation, "Why do you always have to play with the big boys? They're stronger and smarter than you, that's just how it is." At which point he cries even louder. That's all I need. "Little brothers can be a real pain." I just say it, and I don't even feel guilty, because I'm not sorry.

In the evening, we're all called to come eat. They stuck all the children together at a separate table. I hate kids' tables. Like I hate green gummy bears, which taste horrible, and gymnastics benches and having to stop reading in bed.

It just seems like much more fun at the grown-ups' table. Uncle Artie is always laughing, and Daddy talks a lot. Now he's telling people about the patients of a friend of his who is a doctor. There was a patient with a shampoo bottle stuck up his ass—that's what my daddy says, "up his ass." Everyone laughs, which is understandable. My father says his explanation was that he'd slipped in the bath and that's how the bottle got into his butt. This makes everyone laugh even more. I don't think they'd laugh if it happened to them. Granny doesn't find it very funny either, I can see that from her face. Granny has a deep wrinkle between her eyebrows, as if someone has used the back of a kitchen knife to cut a groove in clay, and when she frowns, the groove gets even deeper. Mommy had that too, but less.

We've already finished the main course, our plates are clean, or almost. The whole room smells of frying. A lot of people have complimented Granny. Auntie Rose said how much better homemade croquettes taste, and almost everyone agreed. I told Granny that they were the tastiest croquettes in the world and asked whether I could have one, not because I was hungry, but because they tasted so good. I didn't actually really need a croquette but I thought it might make Granny happy after all that work. She said I shouldn't overexaggerate about the croquettes and that they'd make me fat.

Daddy didn't give her any compliments, which is a bit of a shame.

Granny and Auntie Rose go off toward the kitchen, each carrying a pile of plates. Daddy shouts after them, "Can you bring back a bottle of red?"

"And the corkscrew," Uncle Artie adds.

When Granny returns, she's empty-handed and begins to tidy away the glasses. Auntie Rose puts a bottle of Coke and another of water on the table. "Who wants soda, and who wants coffee?"

"And who wants wine?" my father roars gaily. He keeps his hand on his glass to make sure no one can take it.

"I think enough wine has been served," Granny says, pulling her mouth into a thin strip.

"I'll get it," Uncle Artie says.

But before he has the chance to stand up, Granny insists, "I think enough wine has been served."

Uncle Artie bursts out laughing, he never really cares, but Daddy doesn't find it funny. I can see that from the way he does something with his mouth, twisting it to the right.

"This is and will remain my house. Artie, feel free to get another bottle. You know where to find them." He doesn't raise his voice, his face has gone red, he stares at Granny, in rather a mean way, I think.

"I've gone to all this trouble," Granny says, "on a day that's difficult for me, the first time without her, and I won't sit back and watch things deteriorate."

"Deteriorate? You just can't handle a bit of fun. Having a difficult time is no reason not to be able to enjoy ourselves on a day like this."

"A bit of respect for your wife who only recently left us would be nice."

"What do you know about what I do or don't respect? It's Christmas. And my family's here, and we're thirsty. And I think we need to celebrate properly so we can bear it all on a daily basis. By 'it all,' I mean your meddling, your cleaning frenzies, your judgmental silence."

I'm panicking now. What is Daddy saying? Granny doesn't deserve this. Mommy wouldn't think so either.

Auntie Emma says, "Come on, Mom, let's go to the kitchen. I can help with the dishes."

Auntie Rose interrupts her. "No, we're not going to do the dishes. Is this the thanks we get for standing by you all this time, and our mother even more than us?"

"I never asked for it," Daddy cries. "Marcella's here to help with all the practical stuff, and her breath doesn't stink."

Daddy does have a point. Sometimes when Granny talks, it smells like the fish heads and bones Mommy used to make sauce from.

"How low can you go, Vincent? Insulting your own mother-in-law. Someone who has done everything for you and your children."

"I never asked for it."

He already said that, I think.

"She's not doing it for you, she's doing it for the children. Our mom would never work her knuckles to the bone for you—never. Not after everything we heard. You think Agnes never told us what went on here?"

Much quieter than the others, Auntie Emma says, "Let's calm down. Come on now, it's Christmas."

But Auntie Rose is on a roll now. "Oh, you want to let him get away with it again? You know what Agnes thought of things. How she complained about his absences, his stinginess, his lack of interest in the children, his lack of interest in her? How his brothers and friends and neighbors always took priority—always. How she had to cook for the whole mob of them and fetch drinks too. And that she was sick and tired of it. And I won't talk about the other thing with everyone sitting here."

Then Uncle Artie gets involved. "And why do you think my brother was always inviting people over? Because Agnes was such a warm, cheerful, loving, supportive wife who gave him and her children everything they needed?"

At this, Granny goes to the kitchen with Auntie Emma following. None of us at the kids' table move.

"Artie," Uncle Olivier says, "let it go."

"All right, but he should be allowed to say something in his own defense. We all know that there's another side to the story."

"The children," Auntie Elke says, moving her head in the direction of where we're sitting. She says it quietly but we still hear.

"The children should know that there's more to life than Christmas trees and presents. What's more, these children have known that for a long time. Besides, they don't understand what we're talking about anyway." Uncle Artie throws his napkin down on the table, knocking over a glass with a little bit of red wine still in it. Red wine stains.

Daddy is standing up. He shouts to make sure that Granny can hear it in the kitchen, I think. "Nobody has to take care of me or my children. We can manage ourselves. You all have no idea what—"

Auntie Rose doesn't let him finish. "That's true. It's not like we lost our sister! Surely we don't have a clue what mourning and grief can do to a person. Not a clue." At which point, she disappears to the kitchen. Emilie darts after her and closes the door behind them.

I don't understand all of it, which is annoying. Maybe Auntie Rose is just saying those things to hurt Daddy. That's what people do when they're angry. Once, when I'd won at Dead or Alive four times in a row, Sophie told me that I might not have died in the game but that my mommy had in real life. I nearly cried. But later the teacher explained that Sophie only said it because she was angry and then Sophie said sorry.

All the other kids stay in their seats. I wonder if I should go to Granny. I'm worried she'll stop coming. Who would cook for us then? What she makes isn't always that good but sometimes it is. Daddy can only warm things up, and fry eggs on weekends, and Marcella's never cooked for us, so I don't know whether she can or not.

"Calm down now, bro," Uncle Olivier says to Daddy. "Why don't you have some coffee? Or go get a breath of fresh air?"

I think *a breath of fresh air* is a funny expression. I always imagine little men with oxygen tanks taking puffs like divers.

"Like coffee and fresh air can fix this," Daddy says, calmer now.

He sits back down. Auntie Elke pours him a glass of Coke and puts it in front of his nose. There's silence. Auntie Elke rubs Daddy's back. He doesn't react, just like he never does when I do things like that. It makes me feel better—I mean, at least in terms of that.

7

I have to do a drawing of spring for school because spring officially starts tomorrow. I'm not that happy about it, but it might also be because I'm not very good at drawing, for a ten-year-old. Mommy said I didn't have much of an artistic bent. I thought *bent* was a strange word to use, but she was right. It's been more than six months now since she left us, and I still keep hearing all the things she used to say to me. Granny says I should just practice drawing more.

Daddy is nervous today and that makes me nervous too, which doesn't help with the drawing: weird tree, grass too high, a bird that looks more like a mole in the sky—I think it's ugly, so I tear up the paper and start again. If you do something, you should do it well.

We've got a visitor coming this afternoon, Daddy told us, but that's not unusual. And now he's changed his clothes twice. He shouted at Alexander because he spilled something on his sweater, and he poured himself a glass of beer and then suddenly dumped it down the sink.

"Who's coming?" I ask.

"A friend of Daddy's named Marie. I'm sure you'll both like her."

"Marie's a stupid name," Alexander says. He's sitting playing with his Playmobil.

"Don't you say that to her, Alexander. It wouldn't be polite."

Alexander shrugs and cries "Wee-ooo, wee-ooo" as he drives his police car over the rug.

"Alexander, please don't make so much noise." Daddy sighs. "I hope you'll both behave yourselves later. Would you do that for Daddy?"

I want to do that, of course I do. I've been ten, in the double digits, for seven weeks now. But whether Alexander will manage, that's the question. He never understands what being well behaved means. I'm constantly explaining it to him, but sometimes it just seems hopeless.

The bell suddenly rings and I run to the front door to be the first. "Good day, ma'am, how can I be of assistance?" I say it especially loudly for Daddy's benefit. It sounds polite enough to count as well behaved, I think.

"I'm Marie. Your father invited me," she says.

"Come in, please. He's expecting you." I've got good manners, I know it. If I do my best, at least.

Marie has long dark hair with lighter stripes in it, as though someone dyed a few strands and forgot the rest. Her bangs have been dried into a curl that points outward to make sure she can still see properly, I guess. She's wearing a lot of makeup and she's got big eyes, which are quite pretty, I think. Her whole body is big, she's almost as tall as Daddy, but she's wearing shoes with really high heels, which is cheating of course. She's wearing a minidress that is black, white, and bright blue. Her brown leather coat is unbuttoned.

"Can I take your coat, ma'am?"

"That's very sweet." She takes it off and gives it to me.

My father goes right up to her and kisses her, not on the cheek, but on the lips. I've never seen Daddy kiss anyone on the lips, not even Mommy. She only got a kiss on the cheek, if she got any kind at all.

Marie smiles at him, a big smile, then walks over to Alexander, squats down next to him, and says, "You must be Alexander," which is kind of a stupid thing to say, I think. I don't like people saying the totally obvious.

Alexander barely looks up. He's trying to put a little man in his fire engine.

"Shall I help?" She doesn't wait for a reply but takes the Playmobil man from his hand and clicks it in. "There you go," she says, smiling again.

"You can be the fire department, I'll be the police," Alexander says. "Because there's been an accident. A car accident with my mommy—"

"Kids, let's not bother Marie. She's going to sit down with Daddy first and have a drink."

Marie strokes Alexander's head, gets back up, and carefully sits down in the biggest armchair. She's wearing blue nail polish to match the blue in her dress. Daddy gives her the glass of white wine he poured in the kitchen; she puts it down on the coffee table.

"Merci," she says with a giggle I don't understand, and then keeps smiling. Her teeth are very white, much whiter than Daddy's, buttermilk compared to banana skin.

"And you must be Mona?"

I don't reply. It's not like I can say anything, it wouldn't be polite to. Then she adds, "I heard you read a lot of books. What are you reading at the moment?"

"*Charlie and the Chocolate Factory*," I reply, "by Roald Dahl. It's very funny."

"Maybe you can read some to me later?"

I don't know whether it's just a coincidence but I love reading aloud. The teacher lets me read to the class sometimes because she thinks I'm good at it. At least, she asks me more often than the others, so I think she thinks that. I pay attention to that kind of thing. I don't tell Marie, though, because boasting isn't polite. "If Daddy says I can," I reply.

"Yes, of course, later on," he says, emphasizing the "later" part. He sits down quite close to her, the way you would sit down next to a girlfriend. "Maybe you could go and read or play for a while so that

Daddy and Marie can talk. And later in the afternoon, she can listen to you read, all right?"

I can tell this is one of those questions Daddy asks that there's only one possible answer to. It can be confusing. Sometimes he really wants to know whether something's all right, and sometimes a question is actually a kind of command, but it's not always easy to know which is which. Without saying anything, I sit down at the table with my mini weaving loom. Granny gave it to me for my birthday and it's less frumpy than I thought at first. She said I could weave a scarf for Daddy, which I haven't done yet. I'm happy that Granny has kept coming just as often since Christmas. Daddy does his best to be friendly to her, I can tell.

Alexander doesn't seem very interested at all, but I keep an eye on Daddy and Marie from behind my loom. They talk in hushed voices, most of the time I can't hear, but they both laugh all the time, like they're constantly cracking jokes. Sometimes Daddy can really be hilarious. I like Daddy when he's happy, so it's annoying I can't sit with them. I make three squares of cloth, one of them in blue, white, and black, like Marie's dress, though I don't have exactly the same colors. Maybe I'll give it to her as a present, but I'm not sure yet.

When Daddy finally gets up to go to the bathroom, he says to me, "Show Marie your book now, if you want."

I rush to the window seat, grab *Charlie*, and hurry to the sitting room as fast as I can so Alexander can't get her attention before me. "Here it is," I say proudly, even though it's not like I wrote it myself.

"Come and sit on my lap, then, you can read and I can look at the pictures if there are any." She reaches out her arms. That seems weird. Mommy thought I was too big to sit on laps years ago, and now I'm even bigger.

"OK," I say as calmly as I can before climbing onto her lap. She smells strange: a lot of perfume that reminds me of hairspray and lavender and apples. She puts her hands on my sides, and looks over my right shoulder at the book. Her hair tickles my face.

"Is this where you are?"

I nod and begin to read, making sure I articulate properly. The teacher always says that: "*Ar-ti-cu-late* properly," breaking the word down into chunks. I hope that Marie will say stop when it starts to get boring, because I can read for ages. She seems to be listening carefully because she even laughs along twice, which makes me feel warm inside. Daddy sits back down again with us. I look at him when I finish the chapter.

"Nicely done," he says. I suspect what he means is that I should stop now, so I close the book. "Mona is very good at reading and writing," he says. "You should see some of her compositions, she's almost always asked to read them out loud in class. She's very advanced for her age."

I begin to blush. I've never heard Daddy say anything like that. It makes me happy that he thinks it's important for Marie to know this about me.

"That doesn't surprise me," Marie says. "Will you read again next time I come?"

"You're coming again?" asks Alexander, who has walked over to us, his police car in his hand.

"Alexander, what did I say about impolite questions?"

Alexander says nothing and looks angry, which I don't find very well behaved of him. Daddy's staring at Marie again. I get the feeling I'm in the way, so I jump off her lap.

"Do you want to play a game?" she asks. "Just a quick one, before I go."

"I guess," Alexander replies. I run to the cupboard and get out Mastermind.

"You need to pick something Alexander can play too," Daddy says in a strict voice, which makes me feel guilty for only thinking about myself.

"Sorry, then?"

"Yes!" my brother cries, not angry anymore.

The four of us sit at the table and play. Marie smokes a cigarette, Daddy drinks a glass of wine, just like her, even though he usually drinks beer or coffee. Daddy has never played a game with us before, but now he seems enthusiastic. There's a lot of laughing. When it's not my turn, I stare outside. It's cold today, but the sun's shining all the same.

8

They went upstairs. Daddy said they were tired and that they were going to take a nap. At two thirty in the afternoon. And that we shouldn't go upstairs because we might wake them up. They'd come back down in about an hour, he said. And we could watch television if we wanted.

We recently got a VCR. Nobody else in my class has one, but we do. We've got movies too. The one I like best is *The Sound of Music*. It's funny and a little sad because the dad is very strict with his children, at first, but then it gets better when he falls in love, and then it's sad because there's something about the war, and they have to run away, which is scary, but then it turns out all right, which I like. I like to sing along to the songs in the film even though they're in English, but I can already speak some English as well as Dutch. Uncle Artie sometimes teaches me new words. Uncle Artie can speak lots of languages. I like Uncle Artie.

"We'll watch *The Sound of Music*, all right?" I ask Alexander, and I want it to sound like the kind of question when you're sure the person will agree.

"I want to watch *Robin Hood*."

"But we watched *Robin Hood* last week, when Daddy had to spend the whole afternoon on the phone in the kitchen."

"*The Sound of Music* is boring," Alexander says, making the *o* very long.

"But those kids and all those songs—you like them too, don't you?"

"No, I don't."

"We could flip a coin." I take a coin from the change jar on the side table next to the door.

He hesitates for a moment, straightens his sweater, and then says in a serious voice, "I'll take tails."

I throw the coin up in the air, it flips over a few times, falls onto the floor, heads up.

"Ha, so *The Sound of Music*. You can either watch or play with your Playmobil," I say in a happy voice as I go to find the tape.

Alexander stays standing there, stamps his foot on the floor in anger, and shouts, "It doesn't count. The coin has to land in your hand. If it falls on the ground, you have to flip it again. That's the rules."

Alexander can't stand losing. I don't mind letting him win now and then because he's the youngest and I have to remember that, but now he's overreacting. He's sort of right about that rule, but we didn't say it beforehand, so it doesn't count.

"You have to learn to be a good loser," I reply. Alexander starts to cry, not because he's sad but because he wants to get his way. "Crying is for babies," I say, putting in the tape and pressing "Play." He stands in front of the television so that I can't see. "Alexander, don't be so annoying, or I'll tell Daddy on you."

"Daddy's asleep and we're not allowed to bother him." When he's being a pain, he always squints his eyes in this totally annoying way. I go over and push him away from the TV. Alexander falls to the floor. What a baby, it was only a tiny push. He begins to really scream now.

"Stop it. If you don't, Daddy will come down and then there'll be trouble," I say.

Alexander scrambles to his feet, storms over to me with a super angry face, and before I see it coming, bites my arm like a dog. I scream, more in surprise than pain. He stops and darts back.

"What are you doing, you idiot?" I've got teeth marks on my arm, it looks a bit bluish red, and there are tiny drops of blood. "Blood!" I cry. The teacher once told us that a dog bite can be really dangerous, that you can get a sickness from it I forgot the name of. Would it be the same with a brother? "Dumbass," I say. He looks really shocked, but I'm not going to be kind to him. I swallow until my tears stop wanting to come. "I'm going to tell Daddy it's your fault I had to disturb him."

"I'll tell him you pushed me. It really hurt. And you cheated." He cries in a whining way now, like a toddler, and sits down on the floor.

I run upstairs and throw open the door, crying, "Daddy, Alexander—"

Marie is sitting on top of Daddy without any clothes on. I can see her back and her right breast. All of it naked. She lets out a shriek, ducks down next to Daddy, and they pull the covers over themselves. "Goddamn it, Mona. What did I say?"

I stand there frozen in my tracks. I hold up my arm to show what my evil brother has done, but Daddy doesn't seem to see.

"Go back downstairs, for god's sake, and close the door behind you."

"What did Daddy say?" Alexander asks nervously.

"Daddy and Marie are doing sex."

"Sex?" Alexander repeats.

"You're too little to understand," I snap, knowing how much it will annoy him.

He doesn't dare say anything back. What should I do now? What if I'm getting a terrible illness from that bite? I go to the telephone and look up Uncle Artie's number. He'll be able to help me. I let the phone ring at least twelve times, but he doesn't pick up.

"You better hope I don't die," I shout to my brother. He looks sad. Then I fetch a towel, wrap it around my arm, crawl into the armchair, and put on *The Sound of Music*. Alexander sits down on the sofa next to me without a word.

On the TV, the children march down the stairs, the dad blows a whistle, and they all stand in a row, like they're soldiers. The girls and boys don't look happy, though. Their father isn't kind, but I can't help thinking he would certainly do something if one of them bit another. I turn up the volume.

9

Ellen asked me how it feels to have a new mommy now. She gave me an Easter egg from the package she'd brought to school. We didn't get any Easter eggs at home this year. All of a sudden, she asked that, on the playground. I wanted to know why she thought that. She told me she'd heard her mom tell her dad that it was a little soon for Vincent to have another woman already, but it might be good for us because we'd get a new mother. I like Ellen's mom. When she laughs, she holds one hand in front of her mouth, and when she puts on her shoes she uses a spoon, the kind you eat with. She loves dogs, brown clothes, and Ellen. But I don't like her saying things like that to Ellen's dad, who I like as well.

I replied that I didn't have a new mommy, just a Marie, and that she didn't come over that often. I hoped Ellen would stop asking questions and she did.

This morning the teacher was talking about Jesus, who rose from the dead to save us. She sounded very serious when she said it. She said he'd risen from the dead. I thought it wasn't very fair of God to only let his own child come back from the dead.

"What do you think happens when people die, normal people who can't rise up again?" I ask Ellen during art.

"Daddy says they become stars in the sky. Like my grandad and my cat, Mitsy, she's a star now."

A star, I think. They're just stuck there. I don't want to think of Mommy as a star. I don't say this to Ellen because she seems happy for her grandad and her cat.

To be honest, I'd actually find it creepy if Mommy was still around in some way. I heard someone say that on TV once: that the souls of the dead watch over you. I don't think it can be true because how could she watch over me and Granny and Daddy and Alexander and her sisters and my cousins while we're all in different places? But I can't know for sure either. The man on TV did look smart. If it's true, can those souls also know what you're thinking? Because how can they really watch over you otherwise? But even if they can only see and hear what you're doing and saying, and Mommy is one of those guardian spirits, I think she'd be really, really angry with me a lot of the time, and you don't want to make Mommy mad, not even as a spirit.

I draw a cat and a dog under a sky full of stars and it almost looks all right, I think.

Could something like a new mommy exist? Actually, you call that a stepmother, like in *Snow White*, but hers wanted to poison her because she was prettier than her stepmother. Luckily I'm not prettier than Marie. Marie is the prettiest woman I know. Or at least prettier than my aunties and the teachers at school and our neighbor, but well, she's sixty or eighty or something.

Daddy said we can't say anything to Granny about Marie, he said it would make Granny sad, and we don't want that, do we? He said he'd tell her when the time was ripe. That's a stupid expression. *Ripe* is for cherries on a tree, or melons in a fruit basket, or a zit on my cousin Emilie's chin, and then it means "ready to be squeezed." That's what she said and she showed me once and it was disgusting. I hope I never get a zit, but Emilie says that zits mean you're growing up and I do want to grow up. I don't know when Daddy will think that the time's ripe to tell Granny, but I hope it's soon because I'm always worried I'm accidentally going to say Marie's name when Granny's around, and I've got enough stress in my life.

When Daddy's with Marie, he usually seems happier. Sometimes he's angry with us, when we want to show or ask Marie something, for example. And the two of them disappear upstairs a lot, I know what for now. I always feel a bit nervous then because I'm worried something terrible will happen and there'll be nobody I can go to for help.

When it's just Daddy and us, I sometimes worry he'll die too. Like he'll be lying on the floor in his office and we'll only find him hours later and he'll have stopped breathing and gone a bit cold. Dead people are cold, I know that. And then Uncle Artie won't pick up the phone and I don't know what will happen to us.

I'd like to be a grown-up, urgently in fact. I'm now already ten and a quarter, but I mean really grown-up. Then I'd know everything. And I wouldn't have to knit when the teacher says we had to knit. Wouldn't have to go to sleep when Granny or Daddy or the babysitter says I have to sleep, while there are books waiting for me underneath the covers, next to my flashlight. I could decide when I wanted to eat candy, entirely on my own, without having to ask. I could choose never to have sex because it seems like such a strange thing to do. Love, that would be fine, because people live long and happy lives when they have love, at least sometimes, but all the things that come with that, I wouldn't need them. And of course, when I've found love and the person dies, it will be sad, so perhaps it'd be better not to get married when I'm older. I'll have to think hard about that.

10

Granny took us to Emilie's birthday party today. Emilie is a Gemini because her birthday is May 23. That's a nice sign to have because then you're a twin and never alone. Daddy had to work, he said, even though it was a Saturday. Granny was supposed to bring us home after the party, around nine o'clock, she thought. But nearly everyone had left by seven thirty, so we left too.

Granny parks the car in the driveway, and Alexander rushes to the front door, shouting, "I'm going to ring the bell."

"No need, I've got my key."

Granny comes inside with us, through the hall into the living room. Sad music is playing, loud. I open the door and see them right away, sitting there on the sofa. Marie with her legs folded over Daddy's. I want to shout: *Run away! Hide in the garden or in Daddy's office or in the cupboard.* But it's pointless because Granny's standing behind me and she can see exactly what I can see. Daddy springs up at once, like he's been stung in the ass by a wasp. Marie's feet fly up into the air and she ends up lying down a bit clumsily before she can get up again. It would have been funny, if it wasn't all so unfunny. I look at Granny, who isn't saying anything.

"Um, this is—wow, you're back early. Well, this is Marie."

Marie stands up. We stand there not moving, Alexander and me, like a shield between Granny and Daddy and Marie. She comes over to us, gives us a kiss, and holds out her hand to Granny.

"Pleased to meet you, ma'am." Marie's got good manners too.

Granny doesn't respond immediately. Marie holds her hand out for a while before Granny finally shakes it briefly.

I should have told Daddy, I knew something like this was going to happen. Mommy always said you shouldn't lie because "the truth will out." Though that's not entirely true. For instance, I once said that I was home late from school because the teacher had asked me to help clean up, only I was actually with Ellen, stealing candy from Mariette's shop. She's so old it takes her ages to get to the front, so you can put some in your pockets before she gets there, and then you buy a little more candy and you're off. We don't think Mariette's very nice, though, so it's OK, we think. But this time Mommy was right.

"I wanted to tell you this week, Josée, but there was never a good time, and I thought—"

"You should be ashamed of yourself." Granny glares at Daddy. When she looks at me like that, I do everything she says. Her expression reminds me of Mommy's. "It's only been nine months since Agnes—"

"Yeah, maybe it's a bit—"

"I don't want to hear your pathetic excuses, Vincent. It confirms everything Agnes ever said about you. And—"

Then Marie walks off, so suddenly that Granny stops talking. Alexander gives me a bewildered look, but I don't know what to do or say either. Daddy sits back down and stares at his knees. "Let's talk about it later, just the two of us. I understand that it's not easy for you. It's unpleasant that you had to find out like this, I—"

"Oh shut up, you sanctimonious pig."

"Josée—" Daddy tries. He moves closer.

"I won't set foot in this house again. Figure it out on your own."

Then I take hold of Granny's hand. She can't just leave us, can she? She can't let us down? I get that she's angry with Daddy, and maybe with us too, because keeping quiet about something is also a kind of lying. But angry people can calm down again. And we're her grandchildren, aren't we? I look at her. I see her large bosom, the gold chain with the medallion she always wears when there's a party, and above it her small face with all those tiny wrinkles. She keeps staring at Daddy for a while. Then she turns her back and says, in a strange, official tone, "Bye Mona, bye Alexander, I'll see you again." She marches out of the room. Even though the music is still playing, I hear the front door slam.

Daddy immediately goes to the bathroom to see how Marie is. I go into the living room because the window overlooks the driveway. I crawl under the curtain, which hangs heavy around my shoulders and smells like dust and Sophie's coat. I can see Granny putting on her seat belt. Then she turns on the headlights, even though it's not that dark, and looks back so that she can reverse into the street. She pauses for a moment and I begin to wave, but she's not looking at the house anymore. She just drives away. I stay there for a while. There's nobody else outside. I wonder why everyone always leaves me.

11

"Kids, wouldn't it be fun if we got married?" Daddy has a big smile, Marie lays her hand on his leg. This is absolutely a question where there's only one right answer.

Alexander rocks back and forth. "Will there be a big party? Will I get new clothes?"

I think: *throwing water balloons, like Ellen and I did yesterday in her garden, that's fun, or a pillow fight with feathers flying around and not having to clean them up after.* Or the teacher being sick and the class being allowed to quietly do something useful the whole afternoon.

"When would that be?" I say it in a cheerful voice, I think.

"End of August," Marie replies. "The weather will hopefully be good, and we can have a nice outdoor party, and you'll get new clothes, both of you." She beams as she says it, probably because she'll get new clothes too. *Late August,* I think. Mommy died on August 20. Wouldn't Daddy find that strange?

"Mona is so delighted, she's lost her tongue. Right, Mona?"

"Yes," I say, nodding. I push up my sleeves and then pull them down again over my wrists.

"Maybe you could write a poem and read it in the church? You'd like that, wouldn't you?"

Marie knows how much I like that kind of thing. For God knows how many people, perhaps a thousand, and me being allowed to read into a microphone, that does sound good, yes.

"I'll write a very long poem," I say.

"Or a shorter one," Daddy says. "That would also be good. Give Marie a big kiss, kids." Alexander and I get up at the same time and give Marie a kiss, each on one cheek. "Are you happy?"

"Yes," Alexander says, and he gets onto Marie's lap.

"'Course." I lean against Daddy's knee and put on a sweet face.

"And we've got another lovely surprise for you: You can both call Marie Mommy from now on. We've decided you don't have to wait for the wedding, because she'll be spending more and more time here, since Granny, well—" He makes a face like he's just told us we'll finally be getting a kitten or a puppy. "Isn't it wonderful?"

"Yes," I reply, "wonderful."

"Well, we're going to go upstairs for a rest now. You can have a Coke, if you like, to celebrate." Daddy gets up.

"Coke!" Alexander shouts as he rushes to the kitchen.

"Mona, you pour it into glasses and don't spill now, OK?"

They're on their way upstairs already.

"What about Granny? Will she come to the party too?"

"I don't know," Daddy says. His voice sounds normal, not sorry at all. Not guilty.

I go to the kitchen. Alexander has already gotten the bottle out of the fridge. I take it from him, get the glasses, and fill them.

"Are you happy?" I ask.

He shrugs and glugs down his drink, then he makes a funny sound, like Daddy unclogging the toilet, only quieter.

"What does that mean? You're not sure?"

"Parties are nice. Do you think we'll be allowed to invite our friends?"

"Maybe. You'll have to ask later."

"Hmm," Alexander says, like he's thinking we shouldn't have to ask. I refill his glass. "Are you going to call her Mommy?"

He nods. "Daddy says we're supposed to, so."

Alexander doesn't seem to see the problem. He empties his second glass too and goes to play with his puzzle. Maybe it's just me, but I think it's strange. I already have a mommy, even if she's dead, even though there's probably not much left of her by now. How quickly can creepy crawlies eat a whole body? The creatures are smaller than Mommy, but there are a lot of them, I think.

I think about Mommy when I smell hairspray. And when Daddy goes to a restaurant. And when I'm lying in bed at night sometimes. When I walk past the room in the basement. Or when I'm a little bit scared, even though I'm not sure exactly why. Sometimes I don't think about her. Ellen once asked me whether I miss my mom. I didn't answer her.

And now we're supposed to call Marie Mommy. That's like getting two kittens and calling them both Fraggle, or two puppies and calling them Charlie. Alexander says he doesn't really want to do his puzzle. He wants to play soccer. "Will you be the goalie?"

"No, not now, I've got something else to do."

He looks disappointed but goes out to the yard on his own without complaining. Sometimes he is well behaved. I watch him go. I'm a bit jealous of him. Not because he's a boy, and not because he's still so little, and not because he always picks his nose and is a bad loser, but because everything seems easy for him. He accepts things as they come.

That evening I'm lying in bed. I pull the covers up to my chin, they just smell of sheets. I can hear the sound of the TV downstairs, and a bird nearby cooing, and now and again a car driving past. I try to fall asleep by lying very still with my eyes closed, but it doesn't work. Then I begin to think, because my mind does that on its own. I think of birds eating worms, and worms eating dead people, and dying, and that it can happen to children sometimes. More than just sometimes in Africa because they're all starving there, which is because of us here, the people in this part of the world are being too selfish, that's what Uncle Artie says. I'd like to share my food with the children in Africa, especially when it's Belgian endive, or when Marie has cooked pork chops that are so dry and chewy you could beat a small animal to death with them. Daddy said that when Marie couldn't hear him. Secretly I thought it was very funny of him.

I wonder what we'll eat at the wedding and whether there'll be a big cake like in the movies, with circles that get smaller and smaller, and a heart on the top or something. Those kinds of cakes probably don't exist in real life. In films, people are always saying "I love you," even mommies and daddies say it to their children and that doesn't really happen in real life, at least not in our country. I can still remember the way Mommy—I almost think about something, but then I stop because I don't want to think about Mommy again tonight.

I lie in my dark bedroom and try to just listen to the sounds. The wind outside. A door closing downstairs. "I'm not alone," I say out loud, and then again. I don't know if other people get this too, but sometimes it feels as though something's biting my neck. It holds on tight and won't let go. That sometimes is now.

12

Normally Marie comes to us, but today we're going to pick her up and all go to Uncle Artie's together. I think Daddy wants to because he's driving the new car for the first time. He bought another Citroën DS, a sky-blue one. This time it's even got a roof that can come off, which is really special. That makes it remind me a little less of the old one, the way it looked after what happened, with everything inside.

Marie lives with her parents. They're called Fernand and Therese, Marie told us. Her dad is a cardiologist, which is a doctor who treats hearts.

Granny went to a cardiologist once because she was getting heart palpitations. I think I get heart palpitations sometimes too. When I'm lying in bed and I put my hands over my ears, I can feel my heartbeat racing away there. I don't think this is normal. Maybe I can ask the cardiologist what the problem is.

Marie's parents live in a really big house. It's white and tall and wide, with a black roof and an enormous garden full of old trees. Daddy pointed it out to us once as we drove past. We're sitting in the open-topped car, waiting. Alexander's wearing a hat and I've got a scarf around my hair because there's a lot of wind when the car's moving, and otherwise we'll get sick, and Daddy can't be having that—sick children—we have to understand that.

Daddy rings the bell; he's wearing a leather jacket he bought with Marie. It looks really cool. Then I see Marie come out with her parents right behind her. Daddy has never met her parents and I think he's a bit nervous about it. After a very quick chat, Daddy and Marie come toward us. Her parents stay standing at the door.

"Wave," Daddy hisses as he opens the car door.

So Alexander and I wave and smile as sweetly as we can. Marie's parents don't wave back.

Alexander stands up in the car, he probably thinks they can't see him well enough. He waves and shouts, "Hel-lo, Mommy's parents." They turn their backs on us and go inside. The door closes behind them with a slam. *It must be a heavy door,* I think. I'm still waving, I realize, which is accidental.

"They didn't wave back," Alexander says in a small voice.

"They will," Marie said, "but first they have to get used to it."

"To the new car?" Alexander asks.

"No, to the fact I'm going to be your new mommy."

"Oh, that." He sits back down.

Daddy starts up the car without saying anything and turns onto the road. What a shame it's just a short drive to Uncle Artie's. The sun is shining brightly, which feels lovely and warm, and the wind blows in my face. I lean my head back and look up at the sky. There are a lot of birds and not many clouds. I can't hear the birds because the car is making too much noise. And Daddy and Marie are also shouting to each other above the racket, but I'm not listening. I don't want to hear what they're saying, not this time.

I wonder what kind of people don't wave back at children. I try waving at the couple in the car next to us and the mom raises her hand immediately. I hope we won't have to start calling them Granny and Grandpa. It's true I've never had a grandpa—Daddy's parents died before I was born, and the grandpa that goes with Granny on Mommy's side died when I was a toddler, of a heart attack, just like that, all of a sudden, collapsed in the bedroom while he was putting on his pajamas—but I'd rather have no grandpa than one who isn't nice. When Granny told me about Grandpa, I wanted to know if she was shocked when he suddenly fell to the floor, but she said she'd rather not talk about it. I know there are all kinds of things adults would rather not talk about. I get that, but at the same time I don't. I like talking more than anything else. The teacher wrote on my report, "Mona is the chatterbox of the class." I don't think she meant it as a compliment but still it made me laugh and Daddy too, in fact.

13

As we wait in front of the church, I can't help but think that we haven't been here since Mommy's funeral. Mommy is lying behind the church, on the right, almost underneath the big beech tree. We never go to the grave, but I don't mind because I don't like seeing that she's buried. I shouldn't think about her, I tell myself, not today, because today we are celebrating Daddy getting married to Marie.

Uncle Artie takes us inside and sits down with us in the front row. He looks handsome in his black suit and shiny shoes. Daddy looks all right too, as handsome as he can be. Marie makes a beautiful bride, that's what Uncle Artie said to her. She's wearing a yellow dress, quite short, and white shoes with really high heels. Her long legs look very brown, she's been sunbathing in the garden a lot. The outfit is from a very expensive shop, Marie said. I never want to get married in one of those white dresses with tons of fabric when I'm older, they're too princessy for me. But maybe I'll never get married. Marie's not wearing white because of Daddy already having been married once. I overheard Marie saying it was a shame, but Daddy said she had to understand it would be better to wear something fitting. "Fitting" was funny, I thought, because it's better if your clothes fit when you're getting married, even though I knew that wasn't what he meant. That was when she said she'd go to the most expensive shop to buy her outfit. Marie likes the word *outfit*—she uses it a lot. She's like Mommy in that way. But not in any other way, I suspect. But maybe that's only because I don't know her well enough yet.

We have to sit at the front and wait; the couple will walk from the back up to the altar while classical music is playing. It won't be "Here Comes the Bride" like in the movies, Uncle Artie said, which is too bad. Mass is really boring. I kick my legs back and forth, first to the right, then to the left, and then again. Alexander seems to find it annoying because he pushes his knee against my left leg and makes the same face Daddy does when he's angry. I'm not allowed to come forward until just before the communion. I don't know when that will be, but the preacher will announce it. This is annoying because it means I have to listen to what he's saying. Just as I'm thinking this, he says, "And now their young daughter, Marie, will come forward to read a poem she wrote herself."

I get up and walk solemnly toward the lectern, that's what it's called, Uncle Artie told me, and in the meantime, I feel in my skirt pocket for the rolled-up paper with my poem on it. I feel and feel but I can't find it. I stop, it's a very small pocket and I've only got one of them, the piece of paper must be in it. I turn my head and try to look into the pocket, which doesn't work, of course. I see all the people in the church sitting and staring at me. What should I do now? *Don't panic, don't give up, that's the most important thing.* I go forward, take the microphone, clear my throat like grown-up people do, smile, and say, "Dear everyone, I've lost my poem, it seems, and I'm sorry about that. But I wish Daddy and Marie lots of luck, and let the champagne flow." The people in the church laugh, which gives me a good feeling all the same. Or at least less of a bad feeling.

When I'm back at my seat, Uncle Artie squeezes my shoulder. "Well resolved, sweetheart. Maybe you can read the poem at the party later. The two of us will go back to the house and pick it up. You've got a rough draft or something, don't you?"

I nod gratefully. Uncle Artie is kind. Then I realize that I said Marie and not Mommy, and I feel really bad about it. It's the kind of thing that would really disappoint Daddy. I feel like crying but don't—that would be really inappropriate on a day like this. Unless you cry from happiness, but only old people do that, I think.

Alexander pokes me and whispers meanly, "You'd forget your head if it wasn't screwed on." Mommy used to say that to me. Does it mean Alexander is thinking about her too? I don't ask him, the pest. I look at Daddy and try to see if he's angry because of my goof, but Marie's head is in the way. She looks serious, and then all of a sudden, she smiles at something the preacher says.

Later, at the party, Uncle Artie lifts me onto the table of honor, still wearing my shoes, and asks for silence by tapping a glass of water with a knife. There are fewer people than in the church and I don't have a microphone, which is a shame, but I speak in my loudest voice and try to articulate properly. I see everyone looking at me right up to the end. I think the people can understand me because when I finish, they all clap, which feels amazing. Even Daddy. Daddy still hasn't said anything about my screwup, so I hope he's forgiven me a little.

The party still isn't over but Uncle Olivier is taking us to Granny's. We have to leave because it's already late. I don't think twelve fifteen is too late, I could stay awake until four or even five, I'm sure of that. But no one ever asks my opinion about stuff like that.

Granny wasn't at the party. Daddy said she was invited but chose not to come. Sometimes we go and visit her, just me and my brother, at her house. It smells funny there—I'd forgotten about that. Like the chest of old clothes at Ellen's for dressing up, and also like soup and fried onions.

Granny isn't always kind, but she's done so much for us and she must be feeling lonely and sad now. She doesn't say so, it's just what I think. Of course she's still got Auntie Rose and Auntie Emma, but she must miss her daughter, and us now too since she used to see us so often. That's why it's good we're going to stay with her for ten days while Daddy and Marie go on their honeymoon. I'd rather have stayed at Ellen's, which her mom said would be OK, but then what was Alexander supposed to do? And I also would like to have stayed at Uncle Artie's, but Daddy didn't want to ask him because he's not very good at looking after little kids, Daddy says, which I think is a load of crap, but oh well.

We've never traveled to another country. Daddy and Marie are going to the Côte d'Azur, which is in France. And they've got a hotel there with a big swimming pool. Marie showed me some pictures in a brochure. It looked wonderful, like it was built for sheikhs and kings and queens. They're going to have a glorious vacation. They'll have a lot of sex as well because that's what you're supposed to do on a honeymoon. Ellen told me that. Ellen imagines that they'll make a baby brother or sister for us, at least that's what she heard her mom telling her dad, but I hope they won't. Tiny babies cry at night and wake you up and then always sleep during the day so you can't play with them. What's more, a child is a big responsibility. I heard Granny say that once and I think that two are enough for Daddy and Marie. Plus, if Marie gets her own baby, she'll probably only love that one, or at least love it more. And I'm worried that, if she does have a baby, it'll be a boy and one brother is more than enough for me.

I told Alexander he doesn't have to worry because I don't think a little brother or sister will come along. I told him, "They've already got their hands full with us." He looked at me like I'd said we were going swimming in a pool of crocodiles, and then went on playing.

14

Uncle Artie takes Alexander and me to the airport to pick up Daddy and Marie. My brother is more excited about it than I am, excited about seeing airplanes close up. He goes wild in the car, I have to tell him to shut up several times. If he's not careful, Uncle Artie will never take us anywhere again, I tell him.

I think it's kind of bizarre that the four of us will be going home together and then it will stay like that forever. Unless someone dies. Marie has been spending a lot of time at our house over the past months, but she's never stayed over and sometimes we didn't see her for an entire day. Daddy was usually at work then, but I felt more normal. It's not just about Marie—it's also Daddy, who always wants everything to be perfect when she's in the house. I like things being perfect too, but Daddy likes them even more perfect. And he said to us even before the wedding that he wants us to always be good in the future, and we're to think before we speak, before we say anything to Marie, because she has to be happy with us. I realize it would be really difficult for her if there were naughty children, especially because she's so sensitive. That's what Daddy said. Alexander said he didn't know what *sensitive* meant, which was dumb of him, I thought. I just wondered what I can and can't say, but Daddy looked so concerned by Alexander's comment that I didn't ask.

Suddenly we spot them. Daddy's pushing a cart with two big suitcases on it and a little one at the front. Marie is walking next to him. When they get a bit closer, Alexander shouts out, loud enough for everybody to hear, "Mommy, are you expecting now?" I want to sink through the floor. Uncle Artie just stands there laughing and ruffles Alexander's hair like he's done something brave. When they've reached us and we've given both of them a kiss, Daddy smiles at us. He doesn't reply to my brother's question, which worries me. Marie is browner than when she left and she's got a new pair of sunglasses. I notice them at once, really big ones.

"Nice glasses," I say.

"Yes, aren't they?" she replies. "A gift from your daddy."

Nothing else is said. I wonder whether Marie gets money to buy the things she wants, the way I get an allowance, since she doesn't have a job. Maybe she gets money from her parents. They've got a big house, so they must be rich.

Daddy chats with Uncle Artie as they walk back to the car, and Marie takes Alexander by the hand and begins to ask him how things were at Granny's. My brother always acts sweet to her these days, so I understand why she likes talking to him. Everyone likes him better, I think, maybe because he's the youngest. Maybe not.

It's pretty quiet in the car. Uncle Artie asks the occasional question about their trip, but they don't say much. If anyone speaks, it's Daddy; Marie sits silently in the back. Alexander tells her stuff from time to time.

I wake up. The clock says 1:03. I can hear voices downstairs. It would be exaggerating to call it shouting, but they are talking louder than normal. I go to the top of the stairs so I can hear better. I tiptoe down a few steps, very quietly, but if they open the door now, I'll have nowhere to hide, so really I'll have to go back to my room soon. I catch little bits of what they're saying. Daddy calls Marie "creature" as in "you poor creature." And Marie calls something the biggest anticlimax of her life. I don't know that word, I'll have to look it up. I say it five times so that I don't forget it: *anticlimax, anticlimax, anticlimax, anticlimax, anticlimax.* Maybe they're angry with each other because they're tired from the trip and traveling by plane and all that sex. When Alexander's tired, he's horrible to me. I tiptoe back upstairs and get back into bed.

Mommy and Daddy used to argue a lot too. Maybe it's normal for people who are married.

Next week, school's starting again. Ellen and I are worried we'll end up with Miss Beavering. She's very strict and she's got gigantic teeth, particularly the front two, you can always see them poking out a bit, even when her mouth's closed. That's why we call her "the Beaver." I think it's a pity that she got those teeth with a name like that, but that doesn't make her any nicer, of course.

I turn onto my other side. Daddy and Marie are still arguing. They get louder and louder. I try to think about something else, not about calamity, not about arguments, and not about the fifth grade, otherwise I'll never get to sleep.

15

It's a Wednesday afternoon, which means Alexander and I are at Granny's. It was decided at the start of the new school year: every Wednesday afternoon, which is a half day, we go to Granny's. She picks us up from school and drops us back home again at six. "Marie can have some time to herself and you can see Granny. It's a win-win situation," Daddy said. I thought "win-win" was the wrong thing to say because it's sad that Granny won't come to our house anymore and that Marie wants us out of the way. Maybe that's one of Daddy's talents, seeing the good in things instead of the bad. Sometimes, anyway.

Uncle Artie was talking about that—about the glass half-empty and the glass half-full, both of which are true, but a glass that's half-full of Coke makes you happy because there's a lot left, while a glass that's half-empty can be sad because it's almost finished. So you can decide for yourself whether to be happy or sad about things, depending how you look at it. Since then I've been trying to look at things in a good way, not a bad one. Sometimes it's tricky, though.

"I need to make covers for my schoolbooks," I tell Granny. "I haven't done it yet and the teacher mentioned it this morning."

We've finished eating and I help clear the table. Alexander doesn't, he's lazing around as usual. And Granny doesn't say anything about it.

"Do you have any paper to cover them with?"

I shake my head. "Alexander doesn't have any either."

"I don't," he cries, as he sits there breaking the rinds from the cheese into tiny pieces. "I want the paper that Jeremy's got with race cars on it."

"No one at home got any for you?" Granny asks, a question which of course she already knows the answer to. I shake my head again.

Granny looks at me like she's just put something nasty in her mouth. "Daddy didn't and she didn't either?"

Granny never calls Marie by her name. Once Alexander accidentally said, "Mommy doesn't think so," and Granny doubled over and went to the bathroom and stayed there for a long time. I've decided I can call Marie Mommy and that my real mommy's called "my mommy" from now on, just inside my head where no one's bothered by it. It's a mind trick, but still.

"Sorry," I say to Granny. I should have kept my mouth shut about the paper.

"No, you don't have to be sorry."

I understand what she means, but Alexander doesn't or he hasn't been following because he asks, "Are we going to the store, Granny? Can I have the paper with racing cars? And can I have new felt pens too? Mine don't work very well." That boy always finds a way of making things even worse.

"You shouldn't ask that," I say. "It's not polite." I smile at Granny to make it clear that I'm trying my best to steer Alexander in the right direction.

She doesn't respond at first. She putters around a bit in the kitchen, piles up all the dishes, takes off her apron, and says, "Come on, then, coats on, we're going."

Granny helps us cover all the books we have in our satchels. There's even enough paper left for the books we left at home. And at the end of the afternoon, she plays a card game with us. Alexander wins. "I'm the best," he cries. Actually, I let him win. I gave Granny a few meaningful looks so that she would realize, but I don't know if she understood. She was very quiet.

When she drops us off at home, at six on the dot, she gives Alexander another kiss and clutches my face between her hands. They feel cold, as though she's just made a snowman without wearing gloves. "Ask her whether she'll help you cover the rest of the books, won't you, so the teacher won't gripe tomorrow. And tell her I was happy to buy that paper for you." Then she kisses me on my left cheek.

"Yes," I say, thinking what a strange word *gripe* is and also that I'm not going to pass on her message. In the same way that Granny doesn't like us talking about Marie, Daddy and Marie don't like it when we mention Granny. We always have to be really careful what we say.

I turn around at the door to wave at Granny one last time. She's still there, in her car with the engine running, but she doesn't look at me. She's looking through the big window into the living room. I hope she doesn't notice we've got a new sideboard and there are different curtains. Marie wanted them. She also wanted a new table with new chairs and a new bed. It had to be her house too, Daddy said, and we went to buy the stuff, even before the wedding. Alexander and I were allowed to go along. It took ages and we had to be quiet and well behaved. In the end nearly all the stuff they picked I thought was ugly. Only the chairs are OK, they're orange and white, and orange is a pretty color. Apart from that, I prefer it when things stay the same. But well, it's not up to you when you're a kid. Other people always make all the decisions, even the ones that have to do with you.

Every time I come home, it takes a while to get used to it. I haven't told anyone because it would seem ungrateful. Lots of children don't get new stuff in their homes. And ungrateful children are the worst, Mommy always said.

As we eat sandwiches with Marie in the kitchen—Daddy's still with his patients—Alexander says, "Granny bought me cool paper to cover my books. And she covered all the books in my bag, but you have to do the other ones."

"All right, then, tomorrow," Marie says.

"No, it has to be tonight," Alexander says, taking such a big bite that all the smoked meat in his sandwich disappears into his mouth in one go. "Otherwise, my teacher will get angry about it."

"I still have to bake three cakes this evening for the charity event my mother is organizing. Are there many books left to do?"

"Yes."

Now Marie sighs. "All right, if need be, I can get the cakes from the bakery. But my mother will be disappointed," she says, sighing again.

"It's sigh-day today," Alexander says.

"What do you mean?" Marie says. Her voice shakes a little.

"Nothing."

"Granny sighed a lot today," I say in an attempt to shift the guilt onto someone who won't be bothered by it. For a moment, it's as though she's going to cry. We sit there quietly and stare at our plates. Not saying anything is actually the best approach. And wolfing down your sandwiches and drinking up every last drop of milk. The only sound is Marie's knife on her plate. When she doesn't look like she's going to eat anything else, I ask, "Is it all right if I clear the table?"

"Yes," she says, before disappearing into the dining room.

I order Alexander to go and help her. For once he doesn't make a fuss. We fetch our books and lay the roll of paper next to them. I count the books—there are still eleven left to cover. Granny did most of them. Marie sits at the big table smoking a cigarette, she sucks on it hard and the glow of the reddish-orange ash makes her face even prettier. I don't know whether we've done something wrong.

"Here they are."

"Thanks." When she's finished her cigarette, she moves to the middle of the table and gets to work. Once Alexander's first book is ready, Marie calls him. "That's one," she says triumphantly.

Alexander picks up the book and says, "It's crooked," before adding, as quick as lightning, "but that doesn't matter, of course." I thought that was clever of him.

We have to go to bed early that night. I offered to help with the cakes but Marie didn't want that. We didn't see Daddy.

When we give her a kiss before going upstairs, she gives both of us a hug, one in each arm, and presses us close to her. She smells of Nivea, the little blue pot that's in our bathroom now. Being held is the nicest thing there is. That and being allowed to eat candy when it's normally not allowed, or being allowed to stay up late, or playing with Ellen's mom's makeup—she's allowed to—or being given a new thick book to read.

"You know that Mommy loves you very much? Very, very much."

We nod. Then she lets go. I think: *It's just like a movie, except she didn't say it in English.*

16

So, we did end up in the Beaver's class. There was a 50 percent chance and of course we had bad luck. Fifth grade was bound to be a disaster, that's what Ellen and I said to each other at the start of the school year. And we were right.

It happens on a Tuesday morning. The teacher gets mad. Our class is much too noisy, and anyone who says another word will be drawn and quartered. She says that: "drawn and quartered." I can see that she's really angry so I stay silent. But when the teacher turns to the blackboard, Sophie, who has always been a daredevil, whispers, "Another word." The class giggles, including me. Then the teacher, her back to us, says, loud enough for it to be heard in the neighboring classrooms, "Mona, two pages of lines for tomorrow: 'I must learn to hold my tongue in class.'"

"But, miss, I wasn't the one who—"

"It's always you." She doesn't even look at me.

I look around and everyone pretends it doesn't have anything to do with them. Even Ellen keeps on staring at the teacher as she plays with the lucky charm attached to her pencil case. I don't have a lucky charm.

"No, it wasn't, it really—"

"Don't finish that sentence, unless you want me to make it four pages. If necessary, consider it a punishment for all the times you got away with it. Open your exercise books to page seventeen."

I could cry, but I don't. I'm very good at not crying, which is one advantage. The Beaver is famous for this kind of nastiness. It's true that I talk in class a lot, but never when the teacher is about to lose her temper, I know better than that.

When I get home, I go straight to my room. Sometimes we get a four o'clock snack if we're good and usually I don't want to miss that, but today all the snacks in the world can go to the children in Africa or wherever they're hungry, as far as I'm concerned. Injustice is the worst, I think. Along with not being able to get to sleep for ages, and being frightened, and having to be on your own in a dark basement, and everyone dying.

Marie comes in while I'm doing my homework. "You went upstairs so fast. Here, I've brought you some warm pudding, vanilla, your favorite." She gives me a wet kiss on my cheek. I don't dare wipe my cheek. She sits down on my bed. "So how was your day?"

I want to tell her, but I'm worried I might cry and crying isn't appealing, so I just say, "Good."

"I had a good day too. Mom came to visit." I smile at her because I can't think of anything to ask about her mother. "And Monique, a friend of mine, called to tell me she's pregnant. That's nice, isn't it?"

"Yes."

"What's the nicest thing you did today?"

"We were allowed to play basketball and my team won. I scored twice."

"I wasn't any good at sports as a kid. Well done, you."

It might be because of the pudding, but I feel really warm inside.

At six fifteen, Daddy calls me down for dinner. He's finished work early. I'm writing a story about bad teachers who turn into slugs and about a girl with magic powers who can make anything happen she wants.

At the table, Alexander talks nonstop about Jeremy, who brought his tortoise to school. He wants a tortoise too, and tortoises this and tortoises that. I don't listen. After a while Marie interrupts him to tell Monique's news to Daddy. She says she's very happy for her friend. Daddy just says, "Oh lovely." And then he asks Alexander another question about the tortoise.

"You're so quiet." Marie turns to me.

"No, I'm not."

"You are. And you don't even like the horsemeat I got especially for you. You haven't eaten any of it."

I don't know why she thinks I like horsemeat. Daddy likes it. But horsemeat makes me think of the animals, and even though they're a little bit scary close up, they're very pretty, and they have forelocks, which are a kind of bangs, and knees and muzzles, and they're called "noble animals." I don't say any of this. "I'm not hungry right now. Maybe later."

Daddy is putting some horsemeat onto his bread and asks, "How was school?"

"The Beaver's horrible," I reply. It just slips out.

"Oh? But you were so happy earlier. Her team won at basketball, Daddy." I don't know why she calls my dad, who isn't her dad, Daddy, especially when she's not even our real mother.

Then Daddy asks, "Why is Miss Beavering horrible?"

"Yes, I'd like to know the answer to that too."

I don't know what to do. If I tell them about the unfair punishment, Marie will be offended that I kept it from her, and if I don't tell them, it will be a kind of lie.

Then Alexander chimes in. "Miss Beavering is mean, everyone says that. She's like Mr. Van Hulle. It's a shame you have to have her."

I don't know whether it's because I've been holding them back the whole day, or because of my brother suddenly being nice to me, but they come, the tears.

"It can't be that bad, can it?" Marie says. "You're always happy to go to school. You were happy earlier. There's no need to put on the amateur dramatics for your mother."

Daddy says soothingly, "Hey, my big girl, what's all this?"

I can't say anything because I'm sobbing too much and because, if I don't watch out, snot is going to run out of my nose. So I get up. I want to go get a paper towel, but Marie stops me.

"For god's sake, tell us what's the matter." She sounds more angry than worried and I cry even harder, which makes me need the paper even more, so I tear myself free and rush to the kitchen. I'm just in time to tear off a square and wipe my nose.

"What the hell am I doing wrong?" Marie cries. "No one trusts me here. I'm doing my best. I don't know what more I can do." And then she begins to bawl, much louder and with more tears than me.

I stop crying from the shock. "No," I say, "I just had to wipe my nose."

She hardly seems to hear me. In the meantime, Daddy has gone to stand behind her. He rubs her back and looks at us. He nods at me.

"It's just that I got punished today for something I didn't do."

She still doesn't react. Alexander climbs onto her lap and gives her a kiss.

"We do know how much you do for us. So much." I say this in a serious voice. "So much." I look at Daddy, but he keeps looking down.

"The children are very grateful."

She seems to calm down, sobbing less. Then Daddy takes her into the next room.

I clear the table and, a few minutes later, Alexander and I go into the living room. Marie is sitting in the big armchair.

She says, "I'm only trying to do things right, you know. Really. But I'm not used to all of this. I hope you can understand."

"Of course," I say.

"And I don't need a tortoise," Alexander says. Once again, he hasn't understood any of it.

Marie's face is red from the crying. She looks awful. I feel bad for having made her unhappy when she's trying so hard to do her best.

That evening I'm already in my bed when Daddy comes into my room. This doesn't happen much. He sits down on the edge of the mattress and looks serious.

"Sorry for what happened earlier," I say.

"Never mind. You just have to be more careful. Mommy's not as strong as you are. And for her it's a really big change, to go from living with her parents to having a family with children. It can be too much for her sometimes. Do you want to help her? Be a big girl and be sweet to her. Don't say anything that might upset her. Can you do that for Daddy, do you think?"

"Of course." I feel proud that Daddy is confiding in me, that he needs my help.

"My sweet daughter," he says, pinching my nose and giving me a kiss on the forehead. "And now under the covers with you. Chop, chop."

I let him tuck me in. I always enjoy that, even if I'm too old for it.

When he's gone, I solemnly promise myself never to make Marie sad. I want Daddy to be able to count on me. He's had such a difficult time, and sometimes he and Marie argue, and he shouldn't have to deal with this kind of nonsense on top of it. I get my flashlight from under the bed—it's always there, along with a book for when I can't sleep.

I get out my notebook and write in a blue pen in my nicest letters: "Im will by happy evryday." It sounds better in English than in Dutch. I put it in the drawer of my bedside table. It's a resolution. Like a New Year's resolution, but it's all right to do it in October too, I decide. Everyone likes happy people. Happy people never make others unhappy. That's what I think.

17

"Stunning." Marie claps her hands when I come out of the changing room. She's brought me to an expensive store so we can pick out some new clothes together because I had such a good report card. "Do you like it?"

I look in the mirror. It's a short red-and-white gingham dress, a cute collar, and two pockets with the checks running in a different direction. I look eleven, even though I won't be for another six weeks and four days.

"It looks wonderful on her," the saleswoman says, straightening something on my dress that was already straight, but that's what they do in expensive stores, I think. We never came here with my mommy.

"Want to try the other one?"

I nod. I go back into the changing room and take the other dress off its hanger. New clothes smell like the fabric, I think, or like a smell that is trying to be flowers but doesn't come from flowers. This one is blue with a pattern of white clover. It's a little longer, tight at the top, and pleated at the bottom, as if it has a separate skirt.

"Oh," Marie says, covering her mouth. "Even better, this one. Don't you think?" She looks at me in the mirror and puts her hands on my shoulders.

The saleswoman says, "Those colors look pretty with her eyes and her hair."

"Don't they?" Marie coos. "Everything suits this princess." She pinches my cheek. It hurts a bit but I don't mind.

"What do you think?"

"This one," I say with a smile.

As Marie pays at the register, the saleswoman hands me the big bag. I hang it over my shoulder. I'm proud I can walk along the street with it. Marie looks at me. When she's happy, she smiles so big you can see her gums.

"Thank you," I say when we're outside, and I give Marie a big kiss.

"Are you happy with it?"

"Yes, of course, very." I give her another kiss, just to be sure.

"And now, should we have pancakes or ice cream? I'd love a coffee, actually."

I beam at her.

"Are you having fun spending time with your mommy?"

I nod. I feel very grown-up, the two of us like this. Alexander would be jealous, I know that for sure.

18

I jolt awake. I had such a scary dream. I was walking in a forest of bare trees and the clothes of dead people were hanging in the branches. They hung there like the men and women were still in them, even though you couldn't see them. I was all on my own, frantically searching for something or someone I couldn't find. The sky was dark gray, my hands were cold, my nose and feet too, and the mossy ground felt slippery. And I was very, very scared because someone was following me. I don't remember anything else after that.

I rub my eyes and sit up in bed. The house is quiet. I want to forget the nightmare as quickly as possible. But some dreams stick to the roof of your head. I try to think of other things but can't really. I'm thirsty. I make saliva in my mouth and swallow it. It doesn't help. Do I dare get a drink from the fridge? I'm not allowed to. Still, I get out of bed and walk barefoot to the kitchen downstairs. I look for a glass and take the very big one Daddy uses for beer. Nighttime thirst is always worse. I fill the glass with water and I drink with greedy gulps and burp. *It's good no one can see me,* I think, burping again.

As I'm putting the water back into the fridge, I hear a sound, like there's someone on the stairs. I turn out the light and hide in the bathroom next to the kitchen, the glass still in my hand. *Don't turn on the light.* If they catch me, there'll be trouble. I close the toilet lid and sit down on it. The tiles feel cold beneath my feet so I pull up my knees.

Somebody comes into the kitchen. The fridge opens, I hear rummaging, the fridge closes again. Things are put on the table. Then the pantry door squeaks, the sound of boxes and jars and bags being picked up and put down again. Someone going back and forth. Finally, the door squeaks again and I hear it latching. A chair is pulled out from the table, someone sits down and moves the chair closer. What's going to happen now? It's one in the morning or something.

I hear bags being torn open, tapping on a plate, a kind of puffing, chomping, coughing. I try to breathe as quietly as I can, but I'm also really curious. I slide quietly from the toilet and look through the keyhole. I see the side of Marie's face, her shoulders, part of her upper body and part of her arms, part of the table, the wall with the yellow wallpaper, the coffeepot behind her on the windowsill. She picks up a can of whipped cream, shakes it, holds it diagonally, and squirts into her mouth. *Oh, I should try that sometime.* Then she picks up a jar of chocolate spread, puts a spoon into it, and then puts the spoon in her mouth. She licks the spoon and dips it into the jar again. Then she tears open a bag of nuts and throws a handful down her throat. She chews as though she's trying to break a speed record.

Marie calls herself someone with a small appetite, and it's true when she's sitting at the table with us. She never eats everything on her plate, while we always have to. Maybe that's why she's so hungry, because all of the hunger from all the times she didn't finish her plate has gotten stuck in her body. She grabs the whipped cream again and sprays and sprays and sprays. Her forehead shines a bit. Soon the whole can will be empty, no doubt about it. Then she eats another spoonful of chocolate spread. After that, the chocolate sprinkles. She opens the little valve on the box and pours it down her throat; some bits fall on the table and on the floor. I wonder what would happen if Daddy found her like this.

I hope it won't take much longer, because I'm getting cold. I sit back down on the seat, as quietly as I can. I think about what I'd eat if I was allowed to have anything I like: chips, fries with four different kinds of sauce, mussels, cherry tart, chocolate mice with praline filling, ice cream—just straight from the tub with a spoon—but I'd stop just before getting a tummy ache.

Suddenly I hear the chair creak—she's getting up. I tense all my muscles, as though it will make me invisible. She won't need to go to the bathroom, will she? Then the door opens. Marie screams, I scream. I drop the big glass and it breaks on the floor. She looks at me. A blob of cream is stuck to her nose and there's chocolate on her top lip. She's still chewing something, her mouth moves quickly. She stands frozen to the spot, she breathes noisily, shaking a little. I don't say anything because I don't know what to say. It all seems to take a very long time. And then, suddenly, she strikes out at me and the back of her right hand connects with my face. Bam. The left side of my head hits the wall. I feel her ring with the green stones graze my cheek. Pain. I touch my face, it's wet under my eye, I look at my fingers, blood. I hold my hand over it and look at her.

"Sorry," I say in my quietest voice.

I stand there, wondering whether to sweep up the glass or not. Marie's eyes are bigger than usual, at least they look it. "Upstairs, you."

I lie in bed, not daring to move. If I turn my head I'll get blood on my pillow, and blood is hard to get out. I think about the hand I saw coming toward me, the ring on her finger. My cheek throbs a little, as though something wants to get out. And I've got a bump on my head, a little one, which I can feel with my hand. No one has ever hit me before, not even my mommy. I think about Daddy. He would be furious with me if he heard about this. Will Marie tell him? And would she say what she was doing in the kitchen in the middle of the night?

My head starts pounding now, too, with all the thoughts that are in it. *Sleep*, I think, *sleep now*. I've got school tomorrow. I look at the clock: 2:21.

19

The ice is thick enough, they said on the radio. We've driven all the way here, to another country. The Netherlands shares a border with Belgium, where we live, and there's a lake here that Marie used to visit with her parents, that's what she told us. It was her idea to go ice-skating, I'm sure of that because Daddy doesn't really like outings. We never went on a single one with my mommy. We've been to the seaside a few times with Uncle Artie because Uncle Olivier had rented an apartment there, but then we stayed the night, which means it's not an outing anymore, more like a vacation. The bathtub in that apartment, the same one every year, was lilac colored, I can still remember that. And the toaster looked black on the top, as though flames had come out of it. I never ate toast there.

Alexander has gone on a long way ahead of us. Typical of my brother, he can never control himself and just go slow. I walk next to Daddy and Marie. My boots almost get stuck in the snow with every step I take, it's that deep. I love the sound of walking in the snow, and Daddy does too. He calls it *scrunching*. That's a funny word.

Someone's parked a car next to the lake and there's music coming out of it, which makes everything even nicer. Daddy spreads some empty garbage bags on the ground and then the bag with everything we need on top of them: thermos flasks with coffee and hot chocolate, and

Marie has made scrambled eggs for the sandwiches, real party food. We sit down on the plastic bags and put on our skates. Daddy has to help Alexander. I'm sure he could have done it himself, but his lordship likes to have servants. I've never skated before. I'm a bit scared. What if I fall and it really hurts? I've put on two pairs of tights under my trousers, just to make sure. Marie promised to teach me because she's good at it.

"Look!" Alexander shouts to us, as Marie pulls him forward. She's skating backward, which is quite impressive. Daddy's skating next to me, he says I can skate really well already, but I've fallen down at least eight times, so he's only saying that to make me feel better. I watch Alexander and Marie. She lets go of him and Alexander skates on. So much pride on his little face. He stays on his feet and doesn't even wobble much. He understands how it works: long movements, low to the ground, like there are sponges stuck to your feet and you're trying to polish the ice, Marie said. I don't manage to do it very well. My brother learns it much faster. While I'm thinking this, I fall down again.

More people have arrived. I'm doing better now. Still not as good as Alexander, but I can stay upright for a reasonable amount of time. Daddy and Marie have gone to the car to warm up, they said. I'm starting to feel really cold now too. I ask my brother whether he'll come to the car with me for a while, but he's skating with a boy he met here and they want to keep playing.

I take off my skates, which is a pain with all the little hooks. Alexander's boots and mine are still next to each other on the garbage bag. I pull mine on and go to the open space where the car's parked. It's like climbing a mountain, that's what it feels like as I sink into the snow with each step. I imagine I'm climbing a very dangerous mountain trail, right to the top, and if I don't make it, people will die. *Don't slow down, keep going, keep looking around because there may be enemies about.* I'm almost there. My nose is so cold it might fall off, but it will all have been worth it when I reach the top. And then I see it: the top, the car, with Marie and Daddy in it. They're talking. Marie is moving her hands the way she does. The closer I get, the more it looks like arguing. What should I do? I'm cold, but they won't like it if I join them, I'm sure. It's started to snow again. I try to catch the snowflakes on my tongue. I have to run around in circles to do so, so hopefully it will warm me up. After the eleventh flake, I start to get bored. I blow on my hands and stop moving for a moment, then I go over to the car anyway and pull open the rear door.

"Hello," I say in an especially sweet voice. "I'm really freezing." Silence in the car. "I'm not very good at it, but skating's wonderful."

"Yes," Daddy replies.

"Good idea, Mommy."

"Yes, wasn't it?" Marie stares ahead.

They don't say anything else, not to each other and not to me. It's as quiet here as it is in class when the teacher is really angry at us. I look outside through the window. Even the sky is white today. A flock of birds flies high up. I think about what I can tell Daddy and Marie or ask, but I can't think of anything. It feels like someone has laid a heavy rock on my chest. I hope I warm up again soon so I can go back outside.

20

The guests are going to come in a minute. There are streamers in the living room and in the kitchen, three balloons are dangling from a string on the front door, and Alexander made a big drawing for me. He's written **MONA 11** in big letters and, underneath it, **1-24-1978**. He drew a soccer ball on it, even though I don't like soccer, and I think people know what date it is today, but it's the thought that counts.

This morning we went to the bakery to get three big cakes, and we picked out snacks from the deli. Uncle Artie is coming, Uncle Olivier and his family, Marie's parents, her friend Monique, and the neighbors on the right too, but they're only bringing their youngest son, the others are too big, and I was allowed to invite Ellen, otherwise it would only be boys, which isn't nice for me. It's sad that Granny can't be here today, I think. Also because she usually brings a big present. But hopefully she'll still give me one when I see her next Wednesday. Birthdays are the most wonderful thing there is, along with petting small animals and lying in the grass when the sun's shining. You get lots of presents on your birthday and everyone acts nice and looks at you.

At three thirty, it's time for the cake. Marie has put eleven candles on the strawberry one. Everyone sings "Happy Birthday" and then I'm allowed to blow out the candles. I can make a wish if I blow them all out in one go. I take a deep breath. Two stay lit. I get the first plate with a big chunk of chocolate cookie cake on it. Uncle Artie asks what's the best thing about being eleven. I think for a long time and then I say, "Being one year closer to being a grown-up."

"And why do you want to be a grown-up?" the neighbor asks. "Being a child is the loveliest thing there is."

I have to remember that, I think, *so that I never say anything that dumb to my own children, or anyone else's.*

"And what was your best present?" Uncle Olivier asks.

It's a trick question, I know, because you can disappoint people. "They were all good," I lie, because the set of ink stamps I got from the neighbor is totally uncool and babyish, but of course you can't say a thing like that. Ellen has picked apple and raisin cake; she takes really big bites, her cheeks get fat as she chews, like a marmot.

"And we've got an announcement too, don't we, Daddy?" Marie says. Daddy stands behind her like they're about to pose for a photo. Everyone looks at them. "I'm having a baby. I'm not three months along yet, but we couldn't keep it quiet any longer. The due date's August 15." She giggles as she says it.

Everyone gets up to kiss and congratulate them. I look at Alexander, who's enthusiastically eating a piece of strawberry cake like nothing is happening.

"Well, kids, you must be happy too," Daddy says once everyone sits back down.

"I want a brother," says Alexander. "If it's a sister, can we give her to somebody else?"

Everyone laughs.

"Very happy," I say through the laughter.

"Let's drink to that, right, bro?" Uncle Artie looks at Daddy.

"Good idea, I'll get the champagne."

I eat my cake. Everyone is talking to each other, happy and excited. No one looks at me, not even Ellen. She's sitting next to me but having a conversation with the boy from next door. It turns out they know each other. All I can think is that I don't want a little sister or a little brother. Ellen predicted that this would happen, but I didn't want to believe her. I've got my hands full with Alexander, and now one of those crying babies with stinky diapers? Little kids are cute but not for long in your own home.

Ellen has finished her cake. "Want to go upstairs?" she asks.

"Fine," I say and follow her to my bedroom.

"So? Are you happy?" She lies down on her belly on my bed, puts her hands under her chin, and gives me a questioning look.

"I don't know."

"I'd like to have a little sister, but Mommy and Daddy have said there's no chance of them having another child."

"Yes, but you're an only child, so that makes sense. I've already got Alexander."

"That's true." Ellen looks worried and a frown line appears above her nose.

"Maybe it won't be nice, another child." I say it quietly, as though they might hear me.

"Why not?"

"Marie will be that kid's real mommy. Don't you think moms always prefer their own kids?"

"I do think that." Ellen holds her head at an angle, the ways she always does when she's thinking about something.

"And on top of that, babies can't do anything wrong yet and everyone thinks they're cute. So Daddy will prefer the new baby too, don't you think?"

"I'm not sure, but it is possible." Ellen sits up and puts her arm around my shoulder, like she's a mother or something. "Your daddy loves you, though. Just because he works so much, it doesn't mean he doesn't love you."

I don't understand why Ellen's talking about work. "What do you mean, he works so much?"

"Nothing. My mom told my dad she felt sorry for you, because you saw so little of Vincent. I once told her that I never see him when I play here, and even when I stayed the night, he was still working when we went to bed. So I thought that maybe because of that you weren't sure your dad loves you, but I'm certain he does because all dads love their kids."

I didn't say that I was worried Daddy didn't love me, so now I feel even more concerned. It's true that he works a lot, but what else can he do? He has all those patients who need him.

"Want to play with one of your new presents?" Ellen suggests.

"Yes, all right," I say.

Ellen picks something. I can hear the people downstairs laughing and chatting. Through my window I can see the boys playing outside. It's freezing but that doesn't seem to bother them. It's my party and everyone's enjoying themselves. And I'm trying not to think about things, which isn't working, as usual.

21

Alexander's going home with Jeremy after school because it's Friday and he's staying over there. I walk home alone, slowly. The crows caw and the ice-cream truck plays its tune somewhere in the distance. I've got a stomachache. I often have a stomachache these days, I don't know why. I think about things I can talk about. If I can't think of anything, Marie thinks I don't want to talk to her. Sometimes I just make up something nice that is supposed to have happened because my day is too boring to talk about. I don't consider that lying because they're stories about things that *could* have happened. I like to write stories too. I write them down in the big exercise book Uncle Artie gave me. He says I should do lots of writing because I'm good at it. I don't know if that's true, maybe he's only saying that to be kind. Uncle Artie likes to be kind.

I open the front door with my key and hang up my coat in the hall and put my shoes with their toes facing the wall because that's neat and tidy. I prick up my ears, hear nothing, and cautiously open the living room door.

"Hello, Mommy."

I give her a kiss on the cheek. She smells like coffee and cigarettes. She smokes more than she used to since she has to lie flat on her back for the baby. That's what she calls it: lying flat on her back, which is strange because lying down is flat, of course. It's really bad luck for her that she has to do that, but if she doesn't stick to bed rest, the baby might be born too early. And then it could be dead or handicapped. Marie is only allowed to get up to go pee and to shower but not for anything else. Daddy ordered a special bed like the ones they have in the hospital and it's in the living room. And Marcella comes every day now until three o'clock. After that she has to get back to her children, but soon after that we get home.

I hope Marie's feeling all right today. It's really tiring for her, of course. How would you feel if all you could do was lie in bed? I can see from her face it hasn't been that bad today.

"Can I get you anything?"

"I'm really craving some herring. Could you go to the fishmonger's for me, maybe?" I nod. The fishmonger's is a long way away, but it's a sunny day so I don't mind. "Take some money from my purse, OK?"

As I'm putting my coat back on, Marie calls me all of a sudden, really loudly. I think something's wrong and rush to her.

"Quick, here, he's kicking."

She puts my hand on her belly and I can feel movement. So strange that such a small human can already do that. I've never felt anything like it.

I smile at Marie. "He?"

"I think it's a boy, but we're going to let it be a surprise."

Marie moves my hand across her belly and I can feel my little brother or sister going crazy in there. *Maybe it will be fun after all,* I think, *once it's really here.*

"Thank you for showing me."

"Of course." I see Marie's gums. "You're going to be a good big sister."

"Yes, for sure," I say, and I mean it too. I'm not going to disappoint Marie and Daddy.

Marie asks me to buy some smoked mackerel, too, while I'm at it. Excited, I go outside, my face lifted toward the sun.

22

To be honest, I prefer small houses. Like Ellen and her parents'. Their kitchen is so small, you can only stand and cook in it, and they don't have a dining room, and their living room is packed with the sofa and the coffee table and the TV and the table and chairs and some cupboards. But everyone's always together here. That's how it feels. Ellen's parents ask lots of questions and they talk about their own lives a lot, like it's always Christmas or something. But a fun Christmas, like in the movies, I mean. I'm allowed to stay over tonight, and then we're going to the movies to watch *Grease*, which is a film with John Travolta. Two kids in my class have already seen it, and they both said it was fantastic, so I can't wait.

It was very nice of Marie to let me go. All she does is lie there all the time, worried something will go wrong with the baby. She needs help fetching stuff and so on, and here I am, off to have a nice time with my best friend. But Marie said that she always puts the happiness of others above her own, so she was genuinely happy I was going.

I think Ellen's dad is really funny. He can wiggle his ears, which not very many people can do. Ellen and I and her mom tried it and we couldn't do it. I'll have to ask Alexander and Daddy when I get home. Her dad can also do tricks with their dog, Banjo, a fluffy little white thing. It's a bit silly naming your pet after a musical instrument, but that doesn't really matter. Her dad can make him turn in circles and stand on his back legs for a long time. And he howls like he's singing a song. Banjo is a sweet dog. He always wants to stay close to Ellen. That must be nice, having someone close by like that, even if it's an animal.

We leave the movie theater. The film really was excellent, the kids weren't exaggerating. And we had praline ice cream during intermission and it was divine. *Divine* is a nice word, I think, but you should only use it for things that really deserve it. Like ice cream and amazing movies and when someone does something really nice for you.

We walk along the wide sidewalk toward the car and then suddenly Ellen takes her dad's hand and mine, and then Ellen's mom gives me her hand and the four of us walk along the street like that. Like nobody can break our chain.

"And now skip," Ellen says. She giggles and looks at her mother and then her father.

"Go on, then," her dad says. He counts and, on three, we all skip, the four of us, two of whom are adults. It must make a ridiculous sight, but we all think it's funny. Then Ellen gives her dad's hand to her mom and the two of them walk along, hand in hand. I've never seen Daddy and Marie like that.

It's late when we get back to Ellen's. We're allowed to talk a bit in bed, Ellen's mom says, but we have to go upstairs right away. In the bathroom I discover I've forgotten my toothbrush. Ellen's mom has a spare, still in its packaging, a pretty blue one. I can keep it, she says.

When we're in bed, she comes to wish us good night. She gives Ellen and me a kiss and makes the sign of the cross on our foreheads with her thumb. Her hand is warm.

"What's the cross for?" I ask.

"To protect you," her mom says.

I like to be protected.

She goes to the door. "Sleep well, sweet girls, and don't talk for too long, OK?"

"We won't," Ellen replies.

I ask whether her mom came upstairs with us just because there was someone staying over. Alexander and I have to put ourselves to bed.

"Oh no, it was just normal," Ellen says, as though it really is the most normal thing in the world.

23

Daddy is wallpapering Alexander's bedroom. Not for Alexander but for the new baby, who hasn't been born yet. This house was built when Daddy and my mommy had two children, so there are only three bedrooms. Since the baby needs to sleep a lot and can wake up easily, which could wake us up, he or she is getting their own room. It's the only option, Marie says. I don't want to share my room with my brother. But Marie says that my bedroom is very big, which is true, and they could put a wardrobe or something in the middle to make it feel like two separate rooms. I don't really understand how they're going to do that.

I asked whether I could help Daddy, and I was allowed to. Daddy hates wallpapering, he'd rather paint, to be honest, but Marie thinks wallpaper is prettier. They picked out a cute pattern. White, but not bright white, with big pale-blue stars.

I'm allowed to put the paste on the paper, and then Daddy hangs the strips. He curses as he does it because often he sticks it crooked, or there are air bubbles, and then he has to take it off and do it again. You need a lot of patience for wallpapering and you need to be handy. You'd think that a dentist would be handy, but Daddy says teeth are very different from walls. I can't argue with that, of course.

"Have you already decided what to call the new baby?" I'm waiting with the next strip, but Daddy is still struggling with the previous one.

"Marie's thinking Jean-Philippe for a boy and she can't decide between Anne-Cathérine and Anne-Sophie for a girl."

Oh no, I think, *nothing with Sophie in it, the kid might stink,* but I don't say it. "And you?"

"What do you mean, me?"

"You said 'Marie's thinking.'"

"Well, what Marie wants—" Then he stops. There's a big crease in the strip he's just hung up.

"There's a—"

"Yes, I can see it," Daddy grumbles, pulls the strip off, and balls it up. He looks at me and then throws it at my head, laughing. "Think we should call in a professional?"

I twist my mouth to the left, open my eyes wide, and shrug. Maybe not such a bad plan.

"Oh, you've got that much faith in your father, huh?"

"No, I—"

"Joke, Mona." Daddy takes the new strip of paper from me and tries again. "Maybe we should sing or whistle, that might help."

"I can't whistle," I say. I purse my lips and blow air through them, but nothing happens. "See?"

"You need to relax your cheeks, purse your lips properly, and blow the air from the back of your throat," Daddy says. And very loudly, he whistles the beginning of "Oh When the Saints," a song he sings sometimes when he's in a good mood. Like his explanation is going to help, I think, but I try again to prove that I'm doing my best to listen. It sounds just as stupid as before.

"Keep practicing." He climbs one rung higher on the ladder to be able to reach better. It wobbles a little, it's not very stable.

"Babies are always sweet, aren't they?"

"Oh, I don't know. When they cry and their diapers are full, they're not *that* sweet," Daddy says.

"Babies are sweeter than big kids, though, right?"

Daddy admires his new strip. "Hey, look how good this one is."

"Yes," I say, nodding energetically to show how much I mean it.

"Oops, I don't have a new one ready," I say as I go get one from the table. "Daddy?"

"Yes, Mona."

I approach with the new strip. He takes it.

"Nothing. That strip looks really good."

24

She was already like that when I got home. I'd walked home happy on the last day of school because I had a really good report card. I would bet it was even better than Alexander's. My brother kept on kicking a can along the street, which makes an awful sound, but instead of telling him to stop, I joined in, I was that happy.

When I opened the front door, I could already hear the sobbing. My brother looked at me and said, "I'm going to play upstairs." I didn't mind, he's only eight. I went into the living room and she was lying there with lots of pillows against her back, crying her eyes out. I asked what the matter was but she couldn't reply because all the tears and the sobs got in the way.

"Hush now," I said. "Hush."

But it only got worse. I asked if she was in pain, but she shook her head. I asked whether something was wrong with the baby, she shook her head again. I fetched water and a hanky and a nice snack, but that didn't help. I checked that she still had cigarettes and she did. Just to be sure, I emptied her ashtray. I didn't know what else to do then.

Now I've been standing here for I don't know how long. I haven't been able to mention my good report card, even though I considered it because it might make her happy. She's probably upset about something I've done. I think and think and think, I rack my brain for something

I could have said or done, or forgotten to ask, or something like that, but I can't come up with anything. But I often make mistakes without realizing. She seems to be panicking, she's having trouble breathing.

"Should I get Daddy?"

She doesn't respond, tears run down her cheeks, and she cries like wolves in the movies. High-pitched and very loud.

"I'll be right back." I go into his office, and I see three people sitting in the waiting room, so I can't bother Daddy now. I go back to the living room.

"He's very busy." She still can't speak. I don't know what else to do. If I'm not careful, I'm going to start crying too. "Lovely Mommy," I whisper, and again.

Eventually the sobbing gets slower and quieter. I hope it's going to stop completely now. Just to make sure, I say "Lovely Mommy" a few more times. Then there's a really big sob, and her whole body jerks a bit, and then she stops. Her eyes are red, her face looks terrible, her makeup has been washed off by the tears, or she didn't put any on this morning, which would be highly unusual. I've sat down at the dining room table. I look at her, she looks at the wall. When she turns to me after a while, I ask if she wants to see my report card. She doesn't reply.

"I got ninety-five-point-two percent."

She smiles. I'm about to go and get my report card out of my bag, because the Beaver wrote something nice, because even she had to admit I did well, despite talking in class, when all of a sudden Marie says, very quietly, "That Daddy, eh? He's destroying me. Just destroying me."

25

We hadn't been to Granny's for a long time because we had to be around to help Marie on Wednesday afternoons. But now Daddy has brought us, on a Saturday, since he can stay with Marie. Granny hurt her foot, just a sprain, did it on her way to the store, she says. There's a bandage around it and she's using a walking stick she says used to belong to Grandpa. It looks both funny and a bit pathetic.

Today Granny smells even worse than usual. It's mainly her breath, but the clothes she's wearing, I think, are smellier than Sophie's. I try to keep my distance, but it's not that easy, because all the rooms in her house are small. I've asked whether we can sit in the garden so the smell can blow away a bit, but Granny doesn't like to sit in the sun, she says, when it's so hot. Alexander stands close to her a few times, he doesn't seem to notice such things as much.

My brother and I have shown her our report cards. Alexander worked hard too, he got 92.1 percent. His teacher hadn't worked it out, so Daddy did it for him. I asked where he ranked in his class but he didn't know. I thought it odd the teacher hadn't told him. Where you rank is the most important. Daddy and Marie think so too. They'd rather you ranked first with, say, 92.1 percent then second with 95.2. They don't say so, but I know they think it.

Granny put on her glasses and looked at our report cards for a long time, like she was studying them for a test. "Well done," she said at last, and gave us each a little money. I didn't mind Alexander getting the same amount as me with his 92.1 percent, because you should put the happiness of others above your own.

We're sitting at the kitchen table playing cards.

During the game, Granny asks a lot of questions about "her"—which means Marie—and about Daddy, and our house, and the baby on its way. Mostly I pretend not to really understand what she means, and I only tell her stupid, unimportant things. She probably thinks I don't realize she only wants to hear bad stories, but of course I do. People think that when you're a kid you don't understand a lot of things. I don't understand why, to be honest. They were kids too once, right?

Alexander takes forever to choose his next move. I notice a new picture on the sideboard, with Auntie Emma and Auntie Rose and the boys and Emilie. Emilie looks older. I've seen them twice since that one Christmas, when they came to visit at Granny's on a Wednesday, but the last time was ages ago. They said Alexander and I should come to their house to play or for a sleepover, but I didn't hear anything more about it. Everyone goes away, sooner or later.

"I won!" Alexander cries triumphantly.

"Another round?" Granny asks.

"Yes!" my brother shouts.

It's not the best card game there is, but I agree to play again anyway, and I tell Granny it's always so lovely spending time in her company.

26

"Shit!"

Marie says we're not allowed to curse, but now she herself is cursing. It was supposed to be three more weeks until the baby came, but she's having contractions already and they look painful.

She just came back from taking a shower and I heard her cry, "My water has broken." *Water that breaks, who ever thought of calling it that?* I can't help thinking. I saw a puddle on the floor in the hall and Marie made a face like she'd just seen a live woolly mammoth.

"It's started!"

"What should I do?"

"Tell Daddy, tell him he has to come now, right away."

Alexander was the closest to the telephone, so he called Uncle Artie right away because Daddy was at his house. "He's coming as fast as possible," Alexander said in his most worried voice.

We stand next to her, she moans softly.

"Does it hurt?" Alexander asks.

"No," Marie says, "it's great fun." Marie's face looks a bit white. She holds the edge of the table with both hands, sticks out her bottom, and pants. I don't know how to help. "Fuck . . . ing . . . shit," she wails, pausing after each syllable.

"Can I do anything?"

"Pray that Daddy hurries."

Since her forehead is shiny with sweat, I fetch a cold washcloth. I come back from the kitchen with it and dab her forehead.

"Don't do that, Mona, no."

I'm even more nervous than I am before a school party.

"Is this normal?" I ask. "Or is there something wrong with the baby?"

Then she groans, quite loudly. Oops, now I've upset her. I remain silent and keep my distance. I gesture to Alexander to do the same. He looks quite pale too. He keeps running to the window to check whether Daddy's arriving or not.

The panting gets worse and worse. Marie stands there rocking gently back and forth, as though the baby's already here and needs calming. Then all of a sudden, it gets better, apparently. She asks us to call Uncle Artie's house again. Alexander rushes to the phone, but just as he picks it up, I hear the door.

"He's here, he's here!" I've never been happier to see Daddy.

Alexander goes into the hall. "Hurry, hurry."

Daddy comes in and goes straight to Marie. "How many minutes apart?" he asks. It sounds very doctorlike.

"Now Daddy's here, everything will be all right," I say to Alexander, but to be honest, more to myself.

"No idea! Like I can look at the clock while going through this hell."

"I'll time it," Daddy says.

"Get rid of the children first. Those children have to get out of here."

Alexander looks both crestfallen and relieved when he hears this.

"Mona, dear, give Uncle Olivier a call, he knows you're supposed to go to his house when the time comes."

I call the number. He'll come and get us, he says. Fifteen minutes.

In the meantime, Marie is moaning again. Daddy rubs her back. "Keep it up. Everything's good."

I don't want to think about maybe having to give birth myself one day.

Marie looks terrible, more terrible than I've ever seen anyone look, except maybe that lady on TV with bad burns everywhere, even on her face. I had to look away and it still keeps me up at night. There'd been a party with candles at her house and then everything had gone up in flames. She'd escaped just in time, otherwise she'd be dead. There are different ways of being lucky.

I think I've decided that I never want to have children. The worst is still to come. The contractions are just the beginning. It doesn't get really bad until the baby wants to come out. No doubt about that. I've looked at myself down there and I've thought, *OK, I'm only eleven, but how much bigger can it get?* And a massive baby has to get through it. Ellen says that some women tear when they give birth. "And they sew it up again afterward, down there." I never know how Ellen knows things like this. She says it's because she can often hear her parents talking, and they forget she's listening in.

I look at Marie and imagine that happening to her. What's she going to shout then? She's already going crazy. Then Uncle Olivier pulls into the driveway. Alexander is already at the door, he can't get out of here quickly enough, apparently.

Late at night, past our bedtime, in fact, we're allowed to go look at the baby. It's lying in a little bed on wheels, and it's wearing a hat, even though it's summer. Alexander and I stand over its head to get a good look.

"Is it a brother?" Alexander asks.

"No, it's a girl. Anne-Sophie."

"How pretty," I lie.

"Would you each like to hold her?" Daddy asks. "Sit on that chair there."

Alexander says, "She can go first." He sounds disappointed.

I get ready and Daddy hands me the baby with a blanket around it. "Hello, little girl," I say because I don't want to say her name. She makes a sound, a kind of tiny groan, but maybe out of happiness, I think. She keeps her eyes closed, her hands clenched into fists, her lips pursed like she's expecting a kiss.

"Careful," Marie says. I nod. She turns her little head back and forth, making her hat crooked. When I try to fix it, I accidently pull it off. I almost die of fright, there's something wrong with the baby. It's got a very long head, like a massive Easter egg stuck on top, above her eyebrows.

Daddy sees me looking. "That'll go away. It was a vacuum delivery."

A vacuum? I don't want to know.

"Is she going to get a head like ours?" Alexander asks. "Or will she stay handicapped?"

"She's perfectly healthy, Alexander. It will all be all right."

"Are you happy?" Marie asks.

"Yes, she's very beautiful," I say, hoping to cover for my brother's stupidity. In the meantime, I try to put her hat back on using one hand, which I can't manage. I hope Daddy's right. It would be hell having to go through life with a head like that. Isabelle gets teased in class and she's only got red hair, apart from that she looks totally normal.

Alexander has already lost interest in the baby, he's hovering above the basket of candied almonds that Uncle Olivier brought with him. He's talking to Daddy and Marie. I don't listen to what they're saying, I just look at the little baby.

"You poor thing," I say quietly. "Being born with a vacuum, that's no fun. But everything will be all right, Daddy said."

"The baby actually needs to sleep now," Marie says, "and so do the both of you."

"Come on, kids," Daddy says. "Off you go with Uncle Olivier. You've been able to make her acquaintance now."

I put the baby back in her cot and think, *Make her acquaintance—what a formal expression.* Daddy is acting strange. Maybe he's already started loving her more than us.

"Alexander, are you going to say goodbye to your new sister too?"

"Goodbye, sister," he calls from the other side of the room, not taking his eyes off the candied almonds.

"And take some candied almonds, kids."

Only then does Alexander smile.

In the car I think that I'm going to like the baby, despite her name. I'm happy it's a girl. Alexander stuffs three almonds into his mouth, one after the other. Uncle Olivier doesn't notice. I breathe in, planning to say something, but then I change my mind. I'll have to take care of another child from now on, I can't deal with everything. I stare at the trees outside and at the dark night. I was a big sister already but now I'm an even bigger one.

27

She lies in her cradle with a red face, cheeks wet with tears. She's kicked everything off her and I see it right away: poop everywhere. Her diaper, clothes, the sheets. She stinks like a sewer. *Where's Marie?*

"Mommy? Mommy?" Nothing. "Oh, come here, sweetie." I pick her up under her arms and hold her as far away from me as I can. Her and her poop. She kicks her legs, the crying doesn't stop.

Alexander comes in. "Bleuuurgh," is all he says, then goes right back out again.

"Shh, I'm here. It will all be all right." I rock her a little, but not too hard, because I'm worried the poop will fly all over the place. Where to start? Upstairs. I go up the stairs to the bathroom. It's not easy holding a screaming bundle like this at arm's length. "Don't kick so much, baby, you'll get it all over me." Make sure I don't fall on the stairs, that would be typical of me.

How am I going to do this? A baby covered in poop in a white bathroom? I swing her up onto the changing mat—it's easier to clean than most things. I roll up my sleeves and take off her clothes. I throw them into the tub because I don't know what else to do with them. Poop on my hands, couldn't be avoided, don't think about it, just go on. Then I see a streak on her face, probably from pulling her top over her head. She's still screaming. I look for a clean bit of skin on her belly and hold her there with three fingers while I reach for the washcloth with my other hand. I stand with my legs wide but I still can't reach it. I let go of the baby for a moment, really briefly. "Stay there," I say, mainly to reassure myself. Quick, cloth under the tap, baby soap, and then quickly back to the mat. She screams like she's being tortured, her face bright red. "Shh," I try to say. "Yes, I know. It's not pleasant. But it's not pleasant for me either, if that makes you feel any better." As though she was eight and could understand me. I always do that, just talk to her normally, not in that gaga-goo-goo language some grown-ups use. I find it ridiculous. Daddy once said it was good that I said all kinds of things to her, that way she'll learn words more quickly later. I felt proud.

I try to rinse the washcloth, but I can't get it white again. Another one, a few more, that's what I need, from the small cupboard next to the toilet. She's lying still so I can get some real quick. It's a mystery to me how such a small baby can produce so much poop. And that smell! If I don't watch out, I'm going to vomit. "Soon, my face will look as red as yours," I say. I wipe the last bits clean. The crying has almost stopped. Now it's just in jolts. As though she keeps forgetting what she's doing and then suddenly remembers.

Now to do the whole body again with a clean washcloth and a lot of soap, and then she'll be as good as new. I stand at the sink, turn on the tap, wait until the water is warm enough, hold a fresh washcloth under it, and then I hear a thud. After that it's very quiet for a moment and then a very loud scream, much worse than before. I spin around, dive down, pick her up, hold her tight, hug her close to me. There isn't any blood, is there? I study her head, her body. No, there isn't. How exactly did she fall? I rock her and give her little kisses on her head. "Come on, don't cry. Please be all right, little sister, please be all right." I gently rub her hair, ouch, there's a bump coming at the back, a big one. So she fell on her head. Babies can die of that, I've heard. There's something not yet fully grown about their heads. "Please, Anne-Sophie, please don't die." I keep on rocking her. If she doesn't stop, she's going to choke on all that crying. "Sweetie, what am I going to do? Tell me what to do to make it better. A kiss on it? Sorry, sorry, sorry."

"Jesus, what's all this?" Marie opens the bathroom door and stands in the doorway in her nightgown.

"Anne-Sophie was crying because she had a dirty diaper," I say.

I hesitate for a moment. Maybe I should confess, maybe a doctor should take a look, or she should go to the hospital for X-rays, like when I broke my ankle a long time ago. But I don't dare to tell her. My mouth opens but no sound comes out.

"I can see. You're covered in it too."

"Sorry," I say.

Marie takes Anne-Sophie from me. Now she's going to notice the bump. "Go and get changed."

I run to my room, take off my sweater, and get another from the drawer. When I get back to the bathroom, the baby is quiet. She's lying on the changing mat in a clean diaper. Marie is putting pajamas on her even though it's nowhere near bedtime yet.

"Will you clean up in here? I'll put her in the cradle downstairs."

"Yes," I say, "sorry." You can never say sorry too much.

I tidy everything up and go into the living room. I run into Marie in the hall.

"Everything all right?" I ask.

"Yes, yes," she says. "I need to go take a nap. I'm exhausted from all the carrying-on with the baby."

"Enjoy your nap," I say. "I'm here. I'll look after her."

"Yes," she says, turning around and going back upstairs.

I wonder what's wrong with Marie. Some days she doesn't even get dressed, not for the whole day. Daddy says it's not abnormal and goes with "early motherhood," that's what he calls it. He says it's really tiring. It must be. I'd thought the baby would make Marie happy because wasn't that what she'd really wanted? Well, she's got a lot on her mind, with Daddy and with us and now with the baby on top. A baby who fell because of me and who might have something terribly wrong with it now.

I walk over to the cradle. Anne-Sophie is quiet and moving only a little, sucking on her left hand. She seems all right, but appearances can be deceiving. I lift up her head and feel the bump—it hasn't got any bigger. Hopefully that's a good sign. Then she smiles at me, as though nothing happened. It's handy that babies don't remember anything later when they're big enough to talk. I smile back, as big as I can, and she smiles again. She's only just learned to smile. She smiles at me the most, or that's what I thought, but Marie said she's still too small to be able to recognize people.

"Sorry, sweet girl, once again I was a champion dumdum." I move my little sister from her cradle to her playpen so I can see her better, and then she can play. Pooky Penguin is close to her, the rattle, and the plastic beer bottle that squeaks when you squeeze it. Then I get my homework and my pencil case from my bag. "You play now, all right? I have to focus on my math." In sixth grade we're suddenly getting a lot more homework. That's not that convenient right now, with Anne-Sophie.

She doesn't seem aware of anything. She babbles a bit, blows bubbles with her saliva, and throws around any part of her body she can move. A child that was about to die wouldn't do that, I hope.

I wonder whether Alexander's got any homework. He's still wandering around outside and I don't feel like shouting. It's up to him. I stare out the window, the sun is shining weakly, and then I look back at the book. *I hate math,* I think. Then I do the first problem.

I check on Anne-Sophie every fifteen minutes for the rest of the day. She cries once, but that's hunger. In the evening, Marie says, "Leave the baby alone, for god's sake. She can't sleep like that." I have to listen to Marie but that makes me even more stressed, because if anything happens to her, it will be unbearable and totally and completely my fault.

I can't sleep that night. I look outside: it's dark, there are lots of stars in the sky. They look lovely, like tiny holes in all that black. I can hear myself breathing and swallowing. I can hear a bluebottle buzzing frantically. It flies off and immediately crashes into the window again, like it wants to get out and doesn't understand why it can't. I look at the fly: it's completely alone, like most flies.

28

I still dream about dead and handicapped babies sometimes, but my sister is clearly all right.

Marie's mom is visiting. They're sitting in the living room eating cakes, the little ones from the expensive bakery. I've already had one and Alexander too, and then Marie said we had to go play because the grown-ups wanted to talk. I came upstairs but I don't feel like doing homework. I'm just sitting here wondering what they're talking about. The teacher calls me a "nosy parker." No one else talks like our teacher.

I find a test paper that has to be signed, which is a good excuse to go back downstairs. An eight and a half out of ten, could have been better, but still. I walk down the stairs in my socks, through the living room, and when I reach the dining room door, I hear Marie talking quite loudly. I stand close to the entrance, barely daring to breathe. I can't catch all of it but it's about Daddy and us, "the children"—I don't know if she means Anne-Sophie too. Then about something being "unbearable," I think. And then her mom says something quietly. I stand there thinking I should go because I sure don't want to be caught. Eavesdropping is almost as bad as, say, reading someone's diary. I don't have a diary because I'm certain someone would find it if I did. I do write letters, for example to Uncle Artie, sometimes he sends a post-card back, a real one with a stamp and everything in the mailbox. And

Granny always says thanks when I leave her a note, so I think she likes to get them, which is probably because she's very old and a bit lonely. Old people are often lonely. I often see them walking down the street on their own, and they talk a lot at the baker's, even when there's a long line of people waiting, but that's because they don't have anyone at home to talk to, I suppose. I would rather not get old, because then you get lonely and you start to shrink and I would like to be tall. I'm almost taller than Marie's mom now, at least if she didn't always wear high heels. I don't know what her mom said, but suddenly Marie gets even louder: "Maybe I should just load them all into the car and drive into the canal, then we'll be rid of them for good." I forget to be extra quiet as I run back to my room. I hope they didn't notice anything.

Sitting in my bedroom, I think about what I heard. Drowning in cold water sounds really horrible to me, maybe even worse than dying in the car in a normal accident because I think that goes really quick. They did take my mommy to the hospital, though. I try not to think about the icy cold and suffocating and dying and I take deep breaths, in and out, in and out. Uncle Artie taught me this. He said that you should do it if you have an anxiety attack, and that after a while you'll feel better. Should I tell Daddy? But then he'll know I was eavesdropping, of course, and he'll be really angry with me. And Marie will be even angrier.

I feel sorry for Marie. You have to be really unhappy to say a thing like that. Is it Daddy's fault? Or mine? Or Anne-Sophie's? Not because of her, but because babies are exhausting. She didn't really mean it, did she?

I think about the coming winter and try to remember where that canal is again. Then I'll know, when we're all in the car on our way somewhere and Marie's driving, which luckily is almost never the case, that I have to watch out if I see a canal . . .

Daddy comes upstairs. He pokes his head around my door. I pick up my French book as though I'm studying.

"Dinner in half an hour, Mona, OK?"

I nod. "Is Mommy's mom still here?"

"Haven't seen her. Why?"

"Never mind."

He closes the door again. I can't tell Daddy, he's already got enough worries. I'll just have to keep a really close eye on Marie. I can do that.

29

She wakes me up and tells me very quietly to come with her. For a moment I don't know where I am, then I sit up in bed. My hair is sticking out all over the place, I can feel it.

"Is something wrong with Anne-Sophie?"

Marie shakes her head and then says, "Come, you can sleep in my bed."

I look at her.

"Come on."

I get out of bed; the floor is cold. Alexander is still sound asleep. I follow Marie. The bedside lamp is on in their bedroom. There's an alarm clock on the bedside table, an ashtray with butts in it, her packet of cigarettes and an orange lighter, her three rings, of which two have a diamond, and a strip of pills with a couple missing already and a glass jar with more pills in it.

"Where's Daddy?"

"Gone."

What does she mean "gone"? I prick up my ears. Any sounds coming from downstairs? Isn't he going to come back up to bed and want his spot back? I'm so confused. Marie gets into bed and rolls onto her side, her face toward me. I'm standing barefoot on the woolly carpet on Daddy's side, hesitating. I look at the pillow, it's not white, there's something yellowish-brownish in the middle of it.

"Come on now," Marie says, holding open the covers.

I don't want to sleep here in this room with its strange smell. I want to go back to my own bed. I don't dare say anything, just stay standing there.

"Hurry up, it's getting cold."

I get under the heavy eiderdown, lie the way I always lie, on my side, facing the window, the same way Marie is lying. The pillow smells like Daddy's hair. I wonder where he could be. I can't hear anything inside the house. Has he left? Where could he have gone, so late at night? He didn't leave forever, did he?

Then Marie turns off the light and moves toward me. She smells of nightgowns and armpits. Then she lays her arm over me, on top of the covers. She squeezes too tight for me, and I wonder whether I can tell her. I'll never get to sleep like this. But Marie looked so sad, I hold my tongue.

"You can stay with your mommy," Marie whispers, "nice and close to your mommy."

I feel her nose in my hair for a moment. I don't want this. She breathes heavily and her arms feel like weights.

"You won't leave me, will you? You'll never leave your dear mommy."

It sounds half like a question, but I close my eyes as if I'm asleep. I don't reply, I try to forget where I am and not think about anything anymore.

30

It's my ball, so I always get to decide what game we play. That's the way it's been since last year. We used to go home for lunch when my mom was alive, but since Marie came along, I've been staying at school all day. I asked if she wanted me to come home to help with Anne-Sophie, and she said she'd think about it. My favorite game is Dead or Alive. You have to make two teams and try to get everyone on the other team out. You choose an opponent, say her name, and then throw the ball. If the other team can't catch the ball and it falls on the ground, the person whose name you said is out and has to go to the side. You do that until the whole other team is out.

I'm thinking about how to divide up the teams fairly when suddenly Nadine says she wants to play crab soccer or dodgeball or horsey-horsey.

"No, we're not doing that," I say, assuming the discussion will be closed.

But she carries on, saying how cool it would be to play something else for once and that dodgeball is really fun, they played that at the youth club and . . . She blabbers on, typical Nadine. To my surprise, a bunch of kids take her side. And before I realize what's happening, we're playing dodgeball. It's the dumbest game in the world. I bring the ball to school every day, I make sure we get good at certain games, and this is the thanks I get. Ellen isn't happy either, I can see that from her face, but she doesn't say anything.

I can't concentrate in class. I'm not sure why. Three kids are about to give talks. Nadine's one of them, she's going to talk about Spain. She's very proud of all the pictures she's collected. Her family went there last summer and her mom had the photos enlarged. This morning she was rubbing the green folder containing all her material with a look of pride. But she won't let us see inside, it has to be a surprise. I wish we could go to a far-off country on vacation; there'd be palm trees and lots of blue water to swim in and animals we don't have here, like snakes or crocodiles, even though I'd be scared of them, but not that scared, I think.

The bell rings. Recess. Everyone rushes out of the classroom. I hang around a bit, pretend to be looking for my apple, and then, while the teacher's wiping the board, I get Nadine's green folder from her bag, put it into mine, close it up, and head out.

After recess, the teacher says, "Nadine will give the first talk. She's going to tell us something about Spain, I believe?"

Nadine grins broadly, which she's good at because she's got a mouth full of big teeth. She puts her bag on her lap and looks for the folder. She wriggles her hand between the various books, her movements become faster and faster, and then she looks at the teacher in shock. "I, erm—" She starts to empty her bag.

"What's taking so long, child? We are waiiiting," the teacher says.

"My pictures." Her voice shakes.

"Good preparation is half of the work, hurry up."

When the entire contents of her bag are on her chair, she peers into her empty bag and begins to cry. "I don't have it." She looks as if someone just told her she'll die of a dreadful disease before the day is out.

"How is that possible?" the teacher says. "You knew it was your turn today."

"I put it in my bag, I know I did."

"Yes, yes," the teacher says with a sigh. "Incomplete. Well, that's a two-point deduction to start with. Make sure you're prepared to give your talk tomorrow. Next person, then: Sophie, come to the front."

That's that, now neither of us can concentrate, I think.

31

"What score did you get on your last report card again?" Marie calls
to me from the room with the grand piano, where she's sitting with
Angelique, a friend of hers. I had to come with her to play with
Angelique's daughter, Marlene, even though I don't like her very much.
Marlene loves Barbie dolls; she's only ten, after all. She's got a ton of
clothes for them and also a kind of house and a car, both pink. Nothing's
stupider than Barbies and pink. "Come in here, I can't hear you."

I go to them. There's the softest carpet everywhere, like you're floating instead of walking. Marie's friend has a diamond bracelet on her left
wrist, and she's wearing a very long dress that's a pale kind of green. She
smiles at me. She has a brown mark between her nose and lips and she
smokes these weird, thin cigars. Marie pulls me onto her lap.

"Tell us. What was it? Ninety-seven percent?"

"Ninety-four-point-four."

"Mona is so clever. She gets that from her father." Marie runs her
hand through my hair and places a lock behind my ear.

"You've been very lucky with your stepchildren," Angelique says.
"Hilda's are real devils. The hell she's had to go through already." Then
they both laugh, really loud.

"They're just like my own children," Marie says. "I love all three of
them. I make no distinction." Then she gives me a kiss on my right cheek.

Anne-Sophie begins to whimper.

"Do you want to?" Marie asks. I get Anne-Sophie from the stroller. She quiets down right away. "Mona's fantastic with babies too," I hear Marie say.

When I get back to the playroom, Marlene has put new outfits on three Barbies. She shows them to me. I sit down on the carpet, and just as I'm lifting Anne-Sophie to switch arms, a big gush of sour milk comes out of her mouth. It runs down my sweater and my skirt, and even gets on the carpet. The baby continues smiling happily. I ask Marlene whether she's got a cloth. The girl stares at me as though I've just asked her to give me all her Barbies. Then she says, "Boy, that stinks."

We're in the car. The traffic's crawling because it's pouring rain. Marie lights a cigarette.

"Can I open the window?" I ask.

"It's cold outside," Marie replies. She honks at a van in front of her. To be honest, I think cigarette smoke stinks, even worse than Anne-Sophie's sour milk. Marie honks again.

"They're all stuck," I say.

"Really? I hadn't noticed." She smiles.

From the back, I lean into the front seat and push the tape into the tape player. The second song is "Thank You for the Music" and I like to sing along to that and Anne-Sophie likes it when people sing to her. I take a deep breath and join in. Anne-Sophie watches me really closely—she's super cute when she does that.

But Marie turns the music off. "Sorry, it's too much for me. Angelique can talk the back legs off a donkey." It's silent for a moment, then Anne-Sophie begins to cry. "Maybe you're spoiling her too much. She whines a lot when she's in her bed or in the stroller or the car seat, don't you think?"

"Her belly is hurting, she was sick earlier."

"Oh, that's that disgusting smell," Marie says.

"No, that's your cigarettes," I say. It just pops out, I do that sometimes.

"Sorry?"

"Joke," I try.

I see Marie looking at me in the rear-view mirror. I rub Anne-Sophie's belly, but she's still screaming. I unfasten the straps on her car seat so I can put her on my lap. The car's practically stopped anyway.

"You're not going to take that child out of her seat, are you? Once she understands she'll even get picked up in the car—" Then the traffic starts moving and Marie doesn't finish her sentence.

Anne-Sophie looks at me in confusion with those big eyes of hers, her little mouth half-open, as if she's wondering whether to keep crying or stop. *I have to,* I think, *just for a moment.* The traffic stops again, and Marie turns around and sees Anne-Sophie smiling on my lap.

"Who's the mother here?"

"I'll put her back in her chair in a minute, just one—"

"What is this? Are you trying to ensure Anne-Sophie prefers you to me, is that it?"

"But I—"

"No buts."

Marie honks again. I strap the baby back in her seat, then look out the window. I like watching pouring rain. The streets and the sky and the houses are all blurred, like in watercolor paintings. I suddenly remember that time in the summer when Uncle Artie went outside to dance in a big rainstorm. His clothes stuck to his body and his hair looked really crazy. I would like to see him again, it's been a while. Since Marie has been living with us, he doesn't come around as often as he used to. Anne-Sophie grabs my finger and pulls it toward her mouth. "No, that's dirty," I say very quietly. She looks at me and smiles. She's still so little.

32

We learn about All Souls' Day. The teacher says that's when people honor their dead. For example, they visit their loved ones' graves. And then she says, "Like Mona, for instance. She'll be going to the cemetery to visit her mom, right?" I nod because I don't dare say that we never go, not even on November 2. We never went before and we certainly don't now because that would be insulting to Marie. I suddenly realize that I haven't thought about my mommy for a long time. Then I feel guilty. I don't tell the teacher that we never go to church either because she's very religious. She wears a chain with a cross on it and begins every day with a prayer. We have to be quiet and keep our eyes shut. The teacher says that praying is talking to God. But why does she always say the same thing, then?

During recess, Ellen says she's probably going to Saint-Bavo's next year for seventh grade. I feel like I swallowed something too big for my throat and it's stuck there. Daddy and Marie think I should go to Saint-John's because the Latin instruction is apparently the best. How can they know which is the best? They didn't go there. I don't want to go to a different school than Ellen. But even if we went to the same school, we wouldn't be in the same class, because Ellen doesn't want to take

Latin. She says it's a dead language that nobody speaks and she doesn't see the point of it. Daddy and Marie think I should at least give it a go and then maybe switch if I don't like it after a year or two. But Daddy says that since I love writing and reading so much, I'm certain to enjoy it. He always wants the best for me, so I say yes. I don't think Ellen will mind as much as I do, our not seeing each other as often. I'm not sure but that's how it feels. She asks if I want to jump rope with her. I say I don't want her to go away. This makes Ellen laugh like I've said something really dumb. "I'm not going away. Just to a different school." I try to smile too, but I don't manage very well.

33

I'm woken up by the front door slamming. I hear a car start up. I sit up quickly. They've abandoned us, the three of us in this big house. I always try to stay awake for as long as possible because I've been afraid of this happening. I breathe deeply in and out. This time it doesn't help. Alexander is asleep. I check on Anne-Sophie, she's got one arm outstretched and the other's next to her head, fist clenched. It's like she's stretching, which is very cute.

I creep down the stairs and stand as close as I can to the living room door. I listen and listen, but all I hear is silence. I hesitate, then open the door anyway and see Daddy on the sofa. He's sitting with his head in his hands. He doesn't look up until I close the door behind me. He smiles, in a tired way.

"Mona, dear, you're not asleep? It's so late."

"No, not yet," I lie, moving closer to him. "What happened?"

"Nothing, sweetie, nothing."

If there's one answer in the world that I hate, it's that. "Why did Marie leave so late?"

"Marie wanted to go for a little drive, clear her head. Grown-ups need to do that sometimes, but she'll be back soon. Nothing to worry about."

"Where's she driving to?" I think about the canal. I remember what she said about Daddy: *He's destroying me.*

"I don't know, just around, I think. Come on, get back to bed. You don't want her to come back and discover you're not a good girl."

"Yes, but—"

"It's late, you really have to sleep, child. You have to get up early tomorrow." He sounds annoyed when he says this, or maybe just tired.

"But Daddy, shouldn't I stay here to comfort you?" *He looks so unhappy*, I think, *so completely alone.*

Then he smiles again. "No, everything's fine."

I don't let him brush me off. "Why's Marie sad?" Sometimes it's like he's not happy to be telling me things.

"Marie wants the moon on a string." I keep staring at him. An answer like that doesn't help much. He rubs his thumb over the palm of his other hand, like he's trying to comfort himself. "Everything will turn out fine," Daddy says.

As if I didn't know that some things don't turn out fine. Like the second-grade teacher's husband who died, I don't know what of. Or like Sophie's hamster that she brought to school last year. It's really sick now and Sophie's afraid he's not going to make it, and Nadine said, "Oh, then you'll just have to buy a new one," which wasn't nice of her. Or like hunger in Africa, I don't think that's just going to go away because our country and other countries have already sent lots of sacks of food. People are still dying there.

"Come on, you really have to go to bed."

I walk to the stairwell door, grasp the handle, look back one more time, but Daddy's already gotten up. I can only see his back as he walks toward the kitchen.

In my bedroom, I think about Marie and the canal. I wonder how I can help Daddy.

Just to make sure, I stay awake until I hear Marie come home. She's been out for an hour and sixteen minutes. That's a long time when you're just staring at a clock. A very long time.

34

I've counted twice: I've got 716 francs in my piggy bank. A loaf of bread costs twenty-six francs, and a big bottle of milk, twelve. I could take all my clothes and books with me and some games they don't have yet. Seven hundred and sixteen francs won't be enough for Ellen's parents to pay for my food if I go and live with them, but they'll get the message that I'm trying to help. And I can do chores in their house: dishes, laundry, walking Banjo, cleaning if necessary. And Ellen will never get bored again because I'll always be there. And then I'll write stories especially for them and put them on their pillows to read before they go to sleep, maybe they'd like that. Do I dare ask? Maybe check with Ellen first? I try to imagine how they'd react. Maybe they'd be happy? But maybe not, of course. They're probably happy with just one child because Ellen is so sweet and kind and good and everything, much more than I am, so yeah.

35

Zero out of ten, I've never gotten that before. For a moment I think it must be a mistake, but it is written there clearly in thick red pen: zero, and underneath it a slash and a ten. The teacher has written something next to it, two words I can't read.

"Miss? What does it say here?"

"First raise your hand, wait until I give a sign, and only then speak, child. How often do I have to repeat this?"

I raise my hand, but the teacher makes me wait a long time. I support my right arm with my left hand.

"Yes, Mona?" she says, like she's surprised I want to ask something.

"I can't read what you wrote on my essay." I don't dare say, *Next to the zero out of ten.* I'm so embarrassed I could die.

"Bring me your paper." I go up to her, and before she even looks at it, she says, "Don't lie, exclamation mark. That's what it says." She lays the paper back down on her desk and looks away from me, at the wallpaper or the ceiling.

"I didn't lie, though!"

"The essay was supposed to be about your favorite food, but that doesn't mean you can come up with something fanciful that doesn't even exist. Eh, Mona?"

"*Moules parquées* does exist," I say indignantly.

"You need to write a new essay, unless you persist in lying, of course, in which case we'll go with the zero."

I don't dare say anything, and return to my seat. It's been three years since I had a nice teacher, so I'm used to it, but there's nothing worse than not being believed.

"Did someone say something?" the teacher asks, looking right at me.

"No, miss."

"Now, all of you take out your grammar books."

I can't help thinking about the raw mussels I tasted for the first time last weekend. Uncle Artie made them as an appetizer. There was a little party at his house, which was fun. Alexander didn't want to try one. "I don't eat slime," he said. But I tried them because Uncle Artie said they were delicious with a sprinkle of pepper and a dash of lemon, and you should try everything at least once, Daddy says. I even asked Uncle Artie how you spell *moules parquées* because I already knew about the assignment. To be honest, I thought it was a stupid title, the one the teacher came up with: "My Favorite Food." As if you can write a good story about that. But then I was happy because no one else would have the same food as me.

At home I'm busy writing a new composition about meatballs in tomato sauce with mashed potatoes when Daddy asks what I'm doing.

"Writing a new essay," I say, making my voice soft and putting on a sad face because I'm hoping Daddy will notice something's wrong.

"What do you mean, a new one?"

"The teacher gave me a zero because she didn't believe *moules parquées* existed."

"What kind of a teacher is she?" Daddy says. *Good,* I think, *he's as angry as I am.* "A person can be uncultured, that's up to her, but to punish a child for it? I won't have that." He pulls the paper from my hands and tears it in two. "What time are you leaving for school tomorrow?"

"Ten past eight, same as usual."

"Come get me. I'll go with you and tell the teacher what I think of this."

I've never seen him like this before.

"But Daddy—" I splutter, worried the teacher is going to get even angrier with me.

"I will be polite and behave myself, Mona, but I won't let this happen." He strolls to the kitchen like he doesn't have a care in the world.

In the morning I feel the stress all over my body. I'm curious what Daddy is going to say to the teacher and what the other kids will think when they see me turn up with my father. It's never happened before, so they'll wonder what's going on.

I've changed Anne-Sophie's diaper and she's lying happily in her playpen. The lunchboxes are prepared and are in our bags. Alexander has eaten two slices of toast and drunk his apple juice. I'm ready. I go back into the hall to listen. Daddy is probably still in the bathroom. I can't hear anything. I go upstairs; we have to hurry up or we'll be late. The bathroom's empty and I don't dare go into the bedroom in case I wake up Marie. Then I think, *Daddy's probably in his office going through some paperwork or something.* I go into the waiting room and knock. Nothing. I knock again, harder. Then I open the door—no one. I look outside, no one.

"Come on, we have to go," Alexander says. He's right.

"Daddy," I call, but not too loud because of Marie. I wait a moment but nothing happens.

As we walk down the street, hurrying because we're later than usual, all I can think about is that zero. I was allowed to write a new essay, but if I didn't, my teacher said, zero would be my final score. Can I think of an excuse? That Anne-Sophie threw up milk on my essay this morning? Something like that could actually happen. I let out a loud sigh.

"What's the matter?" Alexander asks.

"None of your business," I snap.

I don't see Daddy again until we're at the dinner table. I wonder what his explanation will be, but apart from "Would you pass the salt?" he says nothing to me. I'm angry but that isn't being nice, being angry, and I know that. I say nothing and clear the table. I scrape the rest of the meal from the pot with a spoon, which makes an irritating sound.

Later, Daddy lets me stay up to watch a whole movie. Maybe that's his way of saying sorry? The movie's not that great, but I love staying up late. It's raining very hard outside and there's a strong wind, just short of a storm, but almost one.

"Do you know what I'd like?" Daddy says, apparently not enjoying the film much either. "Fries. What do you think, Mona? Shall we go and get some together, the two of us under the umbrella?" Daddy loves standing outside under his umbrella in bad weather. Sometimes he just does that in the garden, even though he doesn't have a reason to be outside. I think it's a bit strange but also funny.

"Yes!" I say.

"At this time of night? I think the French fry stand is already closed," Marie says.

"At ten thirty on a Friday night? I don't think so. Shall we go see?"

I hurry out of the room, pull on my coat and shoes, and look for the big umbrella in the hall.

"Will you be able to sleep if you eat fries this late?"

Daddy doesn't reply and buttons up his coat. As we walk along the street together, he puts his arm around my shoulder, just so that we stay closer together and neither of us has to get wet. He never does it otherwise.

"Listen to the wind," he says. "Isn't it great?"

I can mainly hear the sound of cars on the road and the spatter of rain under their wheels, but I reply, "Yes, excellent."

I order a large at the stand, which I'm not normally allowed to do, but Daddy doesn't say anything, and I order mayonnaise too. The man standing behind the deep fryer swishes a big glob on top. Daddy gets tartar sauce with his.

"Doesn't Marie want any fries?" I ask.

"No, Marie only likes healthy food, you know that, don't you?" He winks at me.

I wink back and grin as though we've just shared the biggest secret in the world. Daddy gets the fries wrapped up and then we head back home. I'm allowed to carry the bag.

When we're walking side by side, I say, "Daddy?"

"Yes, sweetheart?" he replies without looking at me.

I want to ask whether he just forgot this morning because he was tired, or if he changed his mind and decided the teacher was right. But then I think about how sad he might be, or angry even. He probably didn't mean it in a bad way, so I say, "I think this has been the happiest night of my life."

"Really?" he says.

"Really," I say.

We carry on walking through the rain and I wish things could stay like this forever. We'd keep walking to the end of the world, across every country, without ever getting tired, without ever having to sleep or eat anything other than fries, or go to school or work or ever have to write essays about food. Just walk on and on, Daddy and me.

36

It's my fault, that's the only thing I'm sure of.

"But where did she go?" I ask. I picture the canal and a car containing Marie and Anne-Sophie sinking in it.

"She's staying with her parents. Don't panic, Mona. She just needs a few days' rest."

Daddy always acts like everything will be all right, it's a horrible habit of his. Alexander asks what we're going to eat. Typical Alexander, thinking about food. Does Daddy really think everything will be all right, or is he just putting on a brave face for us? Of course he doesn't know how difficult I make things for Marie. I haven't looked after Anne-Sophie as much in the past few days. Yesterday, Marie had to complain about the mess in my bedroom yet again. The morning before that, she was unhappy because I didn't give her a kiss before I left for school, which proved I didn't love her. Her voice shook when she said that and she looked really sad. I told her of course I loved her. And then there are all the things she doesn't talk about, because Marie reminds us often of those: that she puts up with a lot without complaining, while there's so much that bothers her, because she's so self-effacing, putting everyone else first. And that's the truth, I think, because she wants to spare our feelings.

Daddy cooks a tomato omelet. He puts the eggs on a dish towel instead of a placemat. Everyone takes a slice of bread, even though we already had sandwiches for lunch. Alexander dips his in his egg but it isn't even a soft-boiled egg. He gets a bit on the table. Luckily we aren't using a tablecloth tonight.

Daddy doesn't touch his egg. He doesn't look at us, just stares out the window. He sits there like he's frozen to the spot. I haven't seen him so unhappy for a long time. Not since my mommy died, I think. That's quite a long time ago now. I've forgotten what her voice sounded like. Even the way she sounded when she was angry—I never thought I'd forget that.

I wipe my plate clean with a crust. I take a sip of water and choke. I start to cough really hard, so hard that my eyes almost—only almost—fill with tears, just from that, the coughing.

37

Marie and Anne-Sophie still haven't come back. One thing is certain: we can't go on like this. Daddy's in his office. I ask Alexander which movie he wants to watch and put it on. I tell him not to bother Daddy unless there's a real problem.

"Where are you going?" he asks with a finger in his mouth.

"I'll be back soon."

I get my bike and ride to Marie's parents' house. It's way, way too big for just two people. They probably want Marie to live with them, and Anne-Sophie. Unless they have a problem with crying, of course. Or maybe she'd cry less in such a beautiful house. Or maybe Marie is happier there and that makes the baby happier too. I bike so fast the air hurts my throat.

When I ring the doorbell, my legs are shaking. It's like the time I had a fever. Marie's dad opens the door. The cardiologist is a very large man with a wide mustache and a bald head. He and his wife rarely come to our house, only if there's a party or something. I ask very politely whether it's possible to speak to Marie for a moment. He lets me in without saying much. Marie is upstairs, second door on the right. I can hear Anne-Sophie making little sounds in the room next to the hall, but I walk to the stairs and go up. The second on the right, this must be it. I listen at the door, nothing. Then I knock three times.

"Yes."

"It's Mona," I say as I open the door, so as not to frighten her.

Marie is sitting on her bed smoking a cigarette. The ashtray is made of copper and is full of butts. She's dressed, she's not in a nightie or a robe, which is a good sign, but then maybe not, because it might mean she feels better here than at our house. I look at her, hoping she'll be the first to speak, but she just stares at me and then at the ashtray when she taps her cigarette into it.

"We miss you," I say very quietly.

"That's sweet."

I'm glad she's talking. Has she been crying? It's hard to tell. "Daddy keeps saying how sweet *you* are." I'm lying, but I think it's all right to lie now. It's for a good cause.

"Oh."

"Yes, and me and Alexander think so too." Then she smiles, a small smile. "We wondered when you were coming back."

Marie looks out the window. "Did Daddy send you?"

"No, he doesn't know I'm here."

"Hmm," she says. That doesn't sound as hopeful. And she doesn't answer my question.

"A little vacation at your parents' house can work wonders." I smile at her.

"Oh, so you think I'm on vacation here?"

"That's not what I mean, but you know, after all the tiredness with the baby and everything." Marie says nothing again. "I got a nine out of ten for my talk about gorillas. Now there's not much homework at the moment." She doesn't respond. "I can help out a lot with Anne-Sophie."

"I didn't ask you to help, did I?"

"No, of course not, but I like to. I like to help. Because I love Anne-Sophie." Marie stubs out her cigarette and lights a new one immediately. "And you too, of course." She looks outside. "Will you both come back and celebrate my birthday at home with all of us? It's only fifteen more days."

"Mona, I—" And then she just sighs. The cigarette burns away in the ashtray. "I really don't know what I want to do at the moment." She doesn't look at me as she says this.

"But you are coming back, aren't you? One day, I mean, soon. But soon could also be in three weeks' time, for example. When you're fully rested. Not that it's restful here, you're not on vacation, I mean—"

"Oh, Mona, love."

That's what she says. It's all she says. And I look at her and I don't know what else I can do and then I do it. I hadn't planned it, but my head felt like it was bursting open and—I don't know. I take her cigarette from the ashtray and put it out on my left arm. It happens faster than I can think.

"Mona!" Marie screams. "Have you lost your mind?"

I hear footsteps on the stairs. It feels very hot and now it begins to burn, really burn.

"See? Now I've had my punishment, won't you both please come home?"

I begin to cry—from pain or fear that she'll stay here, I'm not sure which.

PART TWO

1991

1

The whole morning is out there already. The wind is almost gale-force, and here, in bed, everything is still. The air is thick, time lost. I should get up, right now in fact, but sometimes it's hard to get started. A strip of sunlight slips into the room between the wall and the blinds—the ones I bought are too narrow. It shines on my right big toe as though the toe is emitting light, like in *E.T.*, only in a downward direction.

My toes are horribly ugly, the big toes as well as the little ones: too short, too wide, too curly. I've heard I've got my mother's toes. I don't know if that's true. Strange how even people who are important to you crumble into pictures, into a few memories I'm not even sure are mine. Maybe it's only that one photo that makes me think this—I've got it in a box somewhere—or the story they told me. We know very little about how reliable our memories are.

I hate feet. I stay as far away from them as possible. Getting a freshly washed toddler's foot into a sandal is just about doable, but once they're eight or older, I begin to find it difficult. And don't get me started on adults poking their bare feet in my direction.

I've got more of them, irrational dislikes. Filling up the car with gas, for example, especially if the mechanism isn't working, which is usually the case, that little clip so you don't have to keep pressing the handle. Or parking in parking garages. Pumping up bike tires, transferring money, licking stamps and envelope flaps. People who use air quotes when they're talking. Dogs that pant heavily in the summer with their tongues hanging out of their mouths. Drivers that honk their horns when they know it won't help. People who smack their lips when eating and deny it when you complain. People who are total perfectionists, but deny it. The sound of vacuum cleaners, and the smell. The smile I gave that woman with the perfect eyebrows, fully aware she'd said something very unkind about me two weeks ago. Sly digs, very thick winter coats, expectations that aren't met, and sometimes expectations that are. People who are crazy about sports (admittedly, only because I'd like to be one). Questions there's no answer to. Not being able to forget what you really want to forget. Drizzle, boring books in German, toilet seat covers in cheerful colors. Vests, people who suddenly hang up on you, jokers, gossips, know-it-alls, bodybuilders, doubters, tailgaters, grinding discs, waiting times, line jumpers, people who get aggressive toward line jumpers, cowardice packaged as given-the-circumstances-this-is-the-best-option, exotic fruits you don't know how to eat. Saying goodbye. Vomiting, both the sound and the smell, tiaras, noisy wall clocks, drafts, draft guards, bicycle clips, packed rooms with cramped seating, uniforms, platitudes, stories about skin conditions, hand dryers, bracelets, toe rings, debt collectors, forms, useful gifts, squeaking windshield wipers, bike thieves, salt-of-the-earth types, women who always know what they want, cheapskates, frosting on cakes, Earl Grey tea, and lime tea. Not daring to be angry when you actually know you have a right to be, even if briefly. Goldfish from the fair when you were a kid and the fact that they always died. Not being able to cry even though you think it will help. The expressions *children are easily pleased* and *every man to his trade*. My own hesitancy, my fits of sneezing, my helplessness, my big dreams (sometimes), my own weaknesses, my need for stability and love, a lot of love. Fanny packs, men in cutoff pants, registered mail, which I never pick up on principle. And I hate principles, they release you from the need to reflect, and I don't think existence is meant to be like that. What I do think: you are also determined by all the things you're *not*, just like everything you've lost.

I get up, go to the bathroom, and look in the mirror. My hair's unfortunate, there's no better word for it. I shower for a long time; water rinses everything away: sleep, dreams, anxious thoughts, the things I can't do. I'm twenty-four and I feel like I've been sleep-deprived all my life in some way or other.

As I eat a soft-boiled egg, I put on a CD. *The music sounds so lonely,* I think, maybe also because it's playing softly on the stereo hidden away in the corner. I go back and turn it off. A person should know what they can handle on a given day. Then the phone rings. I see "Home" on the little screen of my new phone—that's what I've labeled Dad and Marie. *I have to pick up,* I think. I stare at the phone and don't pick up. *I really have to pick up,* I think. Immediately. I take a step closer, reach out my arm, then it stops. I sit down again. I drink my coffee black, like a hero. I turn the corners of my mouth up into a smile. Scientists claim that it's impossible to think about unpleasant or bad things while you're physically smiling, even if it's not a genuine smile.

I live in an apartment on a narrow alleyway, which means that life on the other side of the street is very close to mine. There's a man sitting reading a book behind one window, his fat calico cat on his feet. Either he's reading slowly or he's fallen asleep, the book's been open to the same page for so long. The man with black curly hair is up on the roof, and that woman who always wears beige is sitting at the table with her two children. I can't see what they're eating or how much they're talking, but it looks like a happy scene from here, a real family, like my younger brother will have soon. It's a funny feeling—I'm still so young and he's going to be the first of us.

I have to go outside, I think. It's Saturday, springtime, the sun is shining, and they say exercise is good for you, and fresh air and so on. I put on the coat I'm still not sure I should have bought, and leave. I walk along empty streets, past water that's the color of rocks, trees, sun, past squares and people sitting on benches chattering. And then, in the middle of the busy shopping street, I stop in my tracks, just like that, on the slippery cobblestones, feet together, arms close to my body, for at least eleven minutes. If you stop, no one can see that you're lost.

2

A dingy café filled with old men. A confusion of clumsily painted pictures on the wall, sad-looking drawings, pasty figurines on racks, mirrors, tapestries, all of them featuring clowns. The manager is a collect-o-maniac, either that or he wishes he worked in a circus, also possible.

Marcus Meereman is late. This is normal, of course, considering that he's one of the most important theater producers in the Low Countries. I almost died when I got a phone call from one of his employees to say he was looking for a new dramaturge and did I want to talk to him. So flattering. I've been working for my present company for only two years.

Twenty minutes after the agreed-upon time, he wanders in, orders a vodka-orange at the bar, and only then does he look around. I raise my hand as though I'm a schoolkid who wants to ask a question. He doesn't apologize for being late, just asks whether I want another drink. I shake my head, take another sip of my chamomile tea, and realize how frumpy it must look, beside his vodka-orange. Job interviews in bars only mean extra stress.

Marcus is a very tall man with strong shoulders; dark, shoulder-length hair; deep-set blue eyes. He's got a scar above his right eyebrow, which makes him look a bit tough; he's wearing an eccentric jacket and pointy shoes; he's got a ridiculous amount of charisma. He sits down opposite me, runs two fingers along his nose, and says, "Well, Mona, I've heard good things about you."

I smile with everything I've got. I don't ask who he heard this from, I seriously can't think of anyone who could have said it.

"And what's a dramaturge to you, then?"

"Hmm," I say, "no one knows. Not even us dramaturges." I grin, Marcus looks at me impassively; he's expecting a real answer, it seems. "The director is responsible for the acting and the actors, and the dramaturge the text, and in an ideal situation, the two come up with a concept for the production together, which they oversee and fine-tune in consultation with each other to get the best results." Marcus takes a big sip and says nothing. "Naturally, the director's is by far the most important role." This sounds gauche, I can't help thinking. I scratch my head, even though I don't have an itch. "Perhaps the greatest skill is knowing when to remain silent. Constantly trying to prove you've read difficult books is just exhausting." His expression remains guarded. I hope he's not expecting more than this.

"We're going to do Chekhov next. We're not doing just one of his plays, I want to make a collage of different texts, which is why we'll rehearse for five months, much longer than normal. There are five actors."

"Sounds fantastic."

"We begin in three weeks. Can you make yourself available? And get up to speed very quickly?"

"If I explain things to my director, I suspect he won't want to deny me this opportunity. Our next production isn't for another three months, there's still time to look for a replacement."

"What does that say about your sense of loyalty? Just leaving like that?"

"Nothing. It just means I'd jump at the chance to work with you." This makes me sound like a real ass-kisser, but it's the truth.

"Does this interest you, such a big production? Of course, in this case, the dramaturge will have a greater responsibility than usual. I expect a lot of input from you: finding texts, translating and adapting them, helping me think about the composition of the show."

"The more the better. It's not my goal to be intellectual wallpaper."

"What's your favorite line from Chekhov?"

"It's from *Uncle Vanya*." I'm so happy he's chosen my favorite playwright, I don't even have to think about my answer. "As you know, Sonya is head over heels for the doctor. Everyone's noticed, except the doctor himself. In the end, her stepmother tries to intervene: 'You know what? If you let me, I'll talk to him . . . I'll do it carefully, only hints . . .' And then Sonya replies, and here it comes: 'No, it's better not to know . . . At least there is hope.'"

"Hmm," Marcus says, a vague smile showing on his face for the first time. "And what does that say about you?"

"Everything, probably," I say as airily as possible.

"Will you at least have a drink with me now?" he asks then.

"A pint of beer," I say.

He slams his fist three times on the table, like a round of applause for my drinking.

3

There's a party. We don't start rehearsals until next week, but Marcus feels the first stages have gone well. One of the advantages of working in theater is that any reason for a party is good enough, even no reason at all. Marcus has invited people who are connected to the company in some way. He struts from one group to the next. The music is loud, there's drinking, smoking, laughing, noisy arguments, and intimate chats. I move around between actors who are my heroes and try to act as though I belong here, as though I find this normal. I'm just heading for the bathroom when Louis stops me. He's an author whose books I like, and he'll be writing a play for Marcus later this season.

"Such dreadful music. Why don't you come outside with me? I'll share my cigarette with you."

I don't tell him I've actually given up smoking, just follow him upstairs to an improvised roof terrace. He lights the cigarette, sucks on it greedily, and then gives it to me. We stand there and smoke. We've never met before, yet we dare to just stand there in silence, which I find quite unusual. We study the late light falling across the housefronts, the church steeples in the distance, the confusion of roofs around us, the square at the front of the building, and the canal between the long rows of plane trees on the neighboring streets. Pigeons walk in circles, cooing noisily, like they're trying to impress us.

"If you're as fierce as the look in your eyes, then you're the only person I want to talk to tonight." He says this with a smile that confuses me because it might be scornful, but it could also be genuinely inviting.

"If you tackle life the same way you dare to stay silent with a stranger on a rooftop, maybe I feel the same." I stare at him from under my eyebrows.

He takes his cigarette back from me. The palm of his hand touches mine. He takes a drag and passes it over again.

"Which play are you acting in this season?"

"I'm a dramaturge."

"Oof," he says, and then has to laugh.

"Well, someone has to do it." I laugh along, trying to gauge his expression at the same time. Perhaps he's a man who always has a slightly mocking twist to his mouth, I find myself thinking. There's a lot of irony in his novels.

"If I asked you to come with me now, would you?"

"Where to?"

"Oh, I wouldn't tell you. Would you come?"

"Would you ask?"

He just looks at me, not answering. Then Marcus and Sasha, an actress from the cast, come out onto the terrace. Marcus is wearing a dramatic scarf and carrying a glass of whiskey. He looks at me and says, "I thought you gave up smoking?"

"I did," I reply, grinning at Louis.

Then Marcus immediately begins talking away about Louis's latest novel and how it's such a delicious fuck-you to prevailing capitalist norms, and how the omniscient narrator was such a daring choice. I see Louis frown and I go back inside where Jolene and Joris, two actors, wave me over. I've been friends with Jolene since I worked with her two years ago, I'm so glad she's part of this.

As I'm about to leave at the end of the evening, Louis stops me, just in front of the door. He takes my hand and plants a kiss on it. A bit of theatricality suits him, I think. "I'll find you," he says before spinning on his heels and disappearing.

I walk home. The night is still reasonably warm. I'm happy I'm on foot because slowness helps me to reflect on what just happened. *Nothing, probably,* I think, *it's my life, after all.* Yet I smile as I put the key in the front door. Maybe I'll sleep well tonight for once.

4

"So, don't forget, Charlie and I have supposedly known each other for a year, OK?"

Lying is a national sport in our family. We learned it when we were little and it's gotten into our bodies, like blood and water for other people. Daddy, who wanted to protect Marie from any rancor or possible calamity; Marie, who liked nothing better than to share secrets with us and then demand our loyalty. All of this to keep the so-called peace.

Alexander is talking even faster than usual. He's ironed his shirt, which he does only on holidays. He wraps his arm around Charlie's hip, she kisses his neck in response. It's all moved really fast, it's true, but those two have taught each other what love is. That's how it seems, anyway, and I'm happy to see it.

"Oh yes, and better not kiss me inside, my parents are rather old-fashioned about that."

Alexander always talks about his "parents" and about "Mom" when he means Marie, even when she's not there.

Daddy is standing in the doorway waiting for us. "Come in, come in!" he shouts, as though he has to drown out the sound of seven cars racing past. When we're inside, he offers Charlie his hand. "They're getting prettier and prettier, my son's girlfriends." He gives her a big smile; Alexander pulls her closer.

Marie comes in. "What would you like to drink?" She's wearing a new dress, dun colored, constructed out of brownish wool, a kind of a sophisticated straitjacket. There should be laws to forbid such things, laws to protect people from occasional poor taste for their own sake and for the sake of the people obliged to witness it. All the same, the beautiful girl shines through in the older Marie, whatever she wears. "Oh, I'd heard we'd be meeting Alexander's newest girlfriend. Remind me of your name?"

"Charlie." She holds out her hand.

"How unusual!" Marie says.

Alexander compliments Marie on her outfit. I ask my dad whether there's any coffee.

"Coming right up. Alexander, Charlie? Am I pronouncing it right? Char-lie?" As if there are thirty-seven different ways of saying the name.

"Oh, I'll have a glass of wine," Alexander says.

"At this time of day?" Marie purses her lips.

"Good idea," Charlie says. "I'd join you in any other circumstances." No one picks up on her implication.

"I've got a good Chablis," Dad says, growing enthusiastic himself now. "I'll open that. Anyone else for a glass? It's a festive occasion, isn't it, Mommy?" It seems like Dad's prompting Marie, but when she doesn't say anything, he simply goes to the kitchen.

"All right, I'll have one too, then," she calls after him. Consistency is the last resort of the unimaginative, Oscar Wilde said a long time ago.

"Not you, Mona?" Dad calls from the kitchen. "Come on, a glass of Chablis?"

"All right, a small one, then."

Everyone is still standing up, as though we've never been here before.

"Sit down, please. Vincent will be right back."

Alexander sits down in the middle of the biggest sofa and gestures to his girlfriend to join him. "Where's Anne-Sophie?"

"Lesson at music school," Marie says. "They really push the children there: two theory lessons, one lesson on an instrument, and one on the history of music. Well, as long as it gives her an excuse not to have to spend time with her mother, eh?" She laughs then, a high-pitched cackle. "Joke. Her teacher says she's very good, actually." Then she calls out to the kitchen, "Bring the good pralines too. The good ones, not the normal ones, they're in the top right of the fridge in the gold-colored box, and put them on that pretty plate, you know the one." Then she turns to me, runs her hand down my cheek, and says in a conspiratorial manner, quieter but still loud enough for everyone to hear, "You were going to start using that Chanel product, weren't you? Like I suggested? I can feel the difference and that dull appearance is gone." I haven't started to use anything, but I still smile at her gratefully.

"Well, Charlie, tell us something about yourself."

Alexander's left knee bounces up and down. "Charlie's a fashion designer. She's worked in Paris and Berlin, and now she wants to start her own collection."

"Oh, she wants to do that or she's doing it?"

"I'm doing it," Charlie says to stop Alexander from speaking for her purely from nerves. "The first reactions have been enthusiastic." She looks cheerful, with a hint of a deep-down confidence. Some people can do that—simply believe in who they are and what they do.

"And how old are you now, might I ask?" Marie says.

Charlie is indeed visibly older than Alexander, who is twenty-one. His knee begins to bounce even faster.

"I'm thirty-two." Charlie glows as she says this.

I loved this woman immediately, right from the first time I met her a few months ago. Alexander had sounded enthusiastic, but he was always like that at the start of every relationship and normally got fed up with them after three weeks. This time, though, I noticed that things were different, not because she was older but because she seemed to understand the way life worked—life, and what made him tick, that too, and she wouldn't just be swept under the rug. It made me jealous.

"Ah, eleven years older than Alexander, then. Ah." A silence falls.

"How many years is Vincent older than you, again?" Charlie asks Marie.

Touché, I think. Nine years, in any case.

"The man being a bit older, well, that's different, of course. But anyway. Fashion?"

"Yes." Charlie nods.

"I've made clothes myself in the past. And for the children when they were little. Did a lot of knitting too, crochet, embroidery, tried that too, but well, it was just a hobby for me."

"Same here, only I hope to be able to make a living from it."

"Hope's a fine thing, yes."

Dad comes in with a tray with a coffeepot, four big glasses of white wine, and some pralines in a dish. He puts it down and Alexander immediately takes a praline.

"Oops. You didn't remember the good plate for the pralines, then? The one with the bunches of grapes along the edge?"

"Um," Daddy says, "I could only find this one."

"What a pretty dish," I say, "stylish."

Dad nods gratefully and takes a praline as he sits down. He looks at Marie, smiling; she stares at the "wrong" dish with a frown on her face.

I eat three pralines one after the other, murmuring now and then in an approving fashion. I look at Alexander and Charlie. There's something Jane Birkin-ish about her: big eyes, full lips, small nose. Alexander looks older than twenty-one with his beard; I wonder if that's why he's grown it. The two of them will surely produce beautiful children.

Suddenly, Alexander jabs his foot against mine as he says, "Almost a year now, or thereabouts."

"Yes, must be something like that." I hadn't realized we'd gotten on to this important topic of conversation.

"What?" Marie says, looking at me. "You've met her already? Before us?" Marie takes small sips from her glass, like people do with hot tea.

"Maybe more like ten months, and I've been busy. I can't introduce you to just anybody."

"Oh, so you thought she was just anybody?"

"Of course not."

Hopefully he'll shut up now, I think, *otherwise he'll only make it worse.*

"Yes, of course you're busy, son. A medical degree is nothing to sneeze at." Then Dad turns to Marie. "He passed his first three years with flying colors, if only his grandfather had been alive to see it."

Alexander gives me a questioning look. I simply nod.

"There's actually a good reason we're sitting here now. I have some fantastic news." Alexander gulps so loudly we can hear it. "We're expecting."

My brother asked me to come here with him—he was that scared of telling them. But it's like I told him: I can't do anything to help.

A silence follows, not a polite one. No one looks at Dad, everyone looks at Marie.

"You knew about this too, I take it," Marie says to me.

I nod. It seems something is expected of me now. This house is always so full of expectations, the trick is to sense them and deal with them, but I can't think of anything concrete to do or say. Dad rearranges himself on the sofa, clears his throat, but then remains just as silent as everyone else. Marie purses her lips, as though trying to hold back all the things that come to her spontaneously.

"We're very happy," Charlie says.

"I get that you would be happy." Marie doesn't look at Charlie.

"But you've got so much studying left to do, son," Dad almost whispers. "How's that going to work?"

"Yes, so that's the second piece of news. I left the program. I know what you think, but I've reflected long and hard. I've never dared to tell you before, but medicine isn't really for me."

"But, son—" Dad's voice is getting quieter and quieter.

"My grades were good, while so many students drop out each year, so I carried on. Also because I know how important it was to you both. But to be honest, my heart wasn't in it. I don't want to study for a decade just to spend my life with the sick and dying. I don't want to spend more time in hospitals than in my own house."

"But what are you going to—"

"I've already found a job, at the Museum of Modern Art, right near our apartment. Marketing, developing small projects. They thought it was very interesting that a person with my CV would apply, and after the interview they decided to give me a chance. I'm starting in three weeks, shadowing a man with a lot of experience. I'm going to learn so much, and I think I'm going to be happy there."

They couldn't have looked more shocked if he'd just told them he was going to jail for stealing a truckload of zucchini. Marie's mouth is still hanging open, but she doesn't speak.

"But, son, why?"

"Because I want to see my child grow up. Because acting like the-world-needs-me-constantly-and-so-I'm-always-busy-busy-busy isn't a very interesting way to lead your life, as far as I'm concerned."

Dad smiles, like he always does when anyone says anything that hurts him.

"Coffee, anyone?" Marie doesn't wait for a reply but gets up and trots to the kitchen for mugs, her heels clicking frantically on the parquet floor. She walks the way women on the catwalk do, in a straight line, decisive, elegant, back straight, neck long. It's every woman's duty to be elegant, she believes. "Will you come and help me, Vincent?" My father stands up, shrugs apologetically, and follows.

"That went well," Charlie says with a laconic kind of laugh.

Alexander looks perplexed.

"We hardly expected anything else, did we?" I try to make it sound like a consolation.

We've never learned how to handle this—disappointing them. We do it constantly, particularly me. Sometimes I picture myself through their eyes and see a girl with hair that's too short, a face that's too long, patchy eyebrows, and breasts too small and hips too wide, not the graceful beauty they'd hoped for. A life too messy and an apartment too small and in the wrong neighborhood. A nightlife too turbulent to lead to anything. Career decisions that don't show enough ambition, not the fantastic career they'd dreamed of for me. Not enough money to be able to easily do, and not do, what I want. Too many acquaintances I call friends. Too little time for my parents and too much for myself. A character too difficult for love. Too much of a thinker to be happy. Too weak, too probing, and too sensitive for the world that *is* hard, that's how it is and they know everything about it. I can read their minds.

Alexander had to compensate for the both of us. Us, the children Marie had gotten for free. If she'd been able to invent us herself, she never would have conceived us as we were. For a long time, it had seemed as though Alexander was going to work out, until now. I wonder whether this doesn't give me a perverse kind of pleasure somewhere in the darkest depths of my mind, there with all those things that aren't allowed to exist, that you won't let exist.

They're gone for ages. Alexander talks to Charlie in muted tones. I eat another praline, which brings me to the edge of nausea. Then the door handle moves, our heads turn, we hear pinched voices through the crack, loud whispering. It's unintelligible, which I'm glad about on my brother's behalf and also on Charlie's. Then the door opens completely. Dad walks toward us, apologizing with his face contorted into emphatic creases that Marie cannot see. Marie remains in the kitchen for a while first, her back to us. She blows her nose on a piece of paper towel, and only then does she come. Her makeup has been partly rubbed away but she leaves it like that. If you look at it objectively, it can be said that she cries a great deal and that's because everyone is *always* against her—that's how she sees it and that's how she experiences it. Some people are so attached to their expectations that it's almost impossible for them not to be fulfilled.

"Sorry for getting emotional, folks, but I'm finding it difficult to process that you're doing this to me, Alexander. You of all people." She blows her nose one last time. "But all right, it will pass. Let's talk about something else." She lights up a cigarette and allows her hand to dangle nonchalantly. She even smokes with refinement. She blows the smoke shamelessly into the living room and says, "Charlie isn't even three months gone yet. Anything can happen."

"Excuse me?" Charlie says. She looks at Alexander, probably hoping he'll respond. But he just looks insulted and searches for words he apparently can't find.

"Oh no, I don't mean anything by it. I was just thinking out loud, because that's just a medical fact, you can't be entirely sure, but *of course* I'm hoping it will all go really, really well for you. That goes without saying, obviously." There's a silence. Thoughts float around the room. "It's your life at the end of the day. I mean—everyone makes choices, and as a mother, the only thing you can do is back them, ultimately."

Alexander goes and stands next to Marie's armchair and lays a hand on her shoulder. "Sorry, I didn't mean to hurt you."

Charlie looks baffled.

"I'm sure it will be a beautiful baby," Marie says, smiling as she puts her cigarette back in her mouth.

Dad looks at me, his head at a slight angle. I know it means I have to think of something reassuring to say. "I think it's going to be a little girl who loves to go shopping with her grandma."

"I'd rather drop dead than be called Grandma, it makes me sound about ninety-three and ready for adult diapers."

"We'll think of something," Alexander says.

"I'm sure we will, kid."

I've been falling out of a window my whole life, that's what it feels like. Do other people have that too?

5

It's a day without mystery. The light is sharp edged, the sky translucent. I sit on the sofa, eating a roll with crab mayo. I never sit down at the table for a meal because the emptiness of the seat opposite mine would suddenly become so real. I think, *Don't spill on the sofa, you'll never get the grease marks out.* In the meantime, I take a big bite, and a lump of crab with grated carrot and mayonnaise falls onto my russet-colored skirt. Then the phone rings. I hastily scoop up the spill using both my hands, hurry to the kitchen, dump it in the sink, wipe my hands on my newly washed dish towel, and then run back to pick up my phone. It isn't until I'm holding the receiver to my ear that I realize I'm going to have to say something. I try to push the half-chewed-up mouthful into my right cheek.

"Mona here."

"Do you always answer the phone with your mouth full?"

"Only when it's you." It's Louis. Hadn't been expecting him. I hold the part of the phone you're supposed to talk into in the air so that my turbo chewing isn't audible. I swallow much too much at once—that's noisy too. *It's lucky that shame doesn't make any sound,* I think.

"I want to have breakfast with you, the day after tomorrow, in that café on the square, just near the theater, you know the one. Nine thirty. See what you're capable of on an empty stomach."

"Oh lovely, his lordship is planning a test."

"His lordship has a busy schedule and I don't want to wait too long to see you, that's the long and short of it."

"How can I resist such charm?" I feel myself smiling, but stop immediately, as though he can see.

"So we'll see each other there? And you'll wear your sexiest outfit, OK?" I can hear the smirk in his tone.

"At the very least," I reply.

Then he hangs up. I raise my arms in the air, like a child who has scored a goal. I throw the half-eaten crab roll in the trash. Food is a solution for people who have nothing to celebrate.

I've put on a pair of black pants and a thin dark-blue roll-neck sweater. Louis won't know that Yamamoto uses this color combination, but I suspect he'll appreciate the joke of wearing clothes that provide coverage from head to toe, after the promise of sexiness.

I don't want to be first, so I arrive ten minutes late. No Louis to be seen. I pick a table by the window. I look outside, don't see him. Three minutes pass, and then four, and then another three. *He won't come,* I think. *Why would a man like that be interested in me?* Perhaps he thinks that, as a dramaturge, I determine which writers will be given commissions in the future, while of course those things are up to Marcus. *Stop thinking like that,* I tell myself. *Don't be nervous, otherwise you'll start sweating, and when you sweat, you stink. I'm sure I stink,* I think. *Maybe I can pop to the bathroom to give myself a smell check.* That woman with the beautiful full lips and glowing skin is giving me funny looks, maybe there's some encrusted snot on my nose or something. I touch it, seems all right. *I can smell myself even without the sniff test,* I think. *What a disaster. Why on earth didn't I slip a bottle of perfume into my bag?* Maybe there's still some in there from last time. I lift my enormous handbag onto my lap and rummage around in it. Just when I've got a used tissue in one hand and a piece of paper wrapped around old gum and a topless lipstick in the other, I hear Louis say, "Sexier than I ever could have imagined."

The waitress comes to our table and Louis orders the champagne breakfast for two without even asking me. He smiles. There's no pretending otherwise, he's not a good-looking man. Skinny legs, bit of a paunch, pasty skin, receding hairline, mousy hair, old-fashioned glasses, and the third tooth on the left is noticeably crooked, a dissident in a cream-colored row. He's got quite a few sun spots, not just on his arms but also on his face. But I'm not that interested in a man's appearance. When girlfriends coo about an ass strutting past, I haven't even noticed, and while they're six-pack spotting on the beach, I'm looking at women with better legs and breasts than me. That's how it's always been. And then there's the way Louis speaks, just as beautifully as he writes, and the way we talk as though we've never done anything else. We discuss Max Frisch, Richard Powers, and Peter Handke—his heroes—and his dislike of Harry Mulisch. When I tell him Mulisch came out with that irresistible retort, spoken to the critic who interviewed him after giving his book a bad review—"But I'm sure you'd have rather written my shitty book than your shitty article in the paper"—Louis admits that this was a rare, spirited moment that proved the writer's intelligence. In general, he embraces critics as long as they are as clever as he is, he tells me, laughing. We talk about Chekhov and the Soviet Union, which is on the brink of collapse, about the girl over there's earrings, whether we believe in God, the perfect cheese soufflé. We eat croissants and a crusty baguette with cheese and fig confit and I have to blush when he comments that I'm probably someone with a lot of love to give, that he suspected that already, back then, on that first night. I don't think he's accidentally pressing his knee against mine, it's happened twice now, but then I doubt myself a moment later.

He kisses me goodbye, just next to my lips. He smells of fabric softener and cheese. As he leaves, I tell myself: *If he looks back, it's a good sign.* He doesn't look back.

6

It's the first day of onstage rehearsals. Until now, we've only sat around the table and read and discussed the script, but Marcus wants to see a few scenes. Joris and Quinten are first up—they've written a Chekhovian-style dialogue. A daring choice, if you ask me. I sit down next to Sasha on the floor, crack my fingers, and straighten my back. I'm curious.

"All right folks, quiet down now." Marcus raps on the table. "Let's get started."

"Great," Joris says, at which point both he and Quinten drop their pants. They stand there staring at us with a stupid expression. I try to keep looking at their faces but it's not easy, because around three feet from me, at eye level, two dicks are dangling against two hairy scrota and that's not something I get to see every day. As I try to think of something dramaturgically clever to say about what they might have meant by this, Sasha bursts out laughing. The actors' faces remain impassive for a moment, but then they join in. There's collective laughter as they pull their pants back up.

"Right, now let's be serious," Quinten says, clearing his throat theatrically. Marcus only grins. I wonder what I'll say if someone like the baker asks me how my day was, which makes me chuckle inside.

The actors act, and it's not really finished yet, their scene, but it is funny and I see something in it. Marcus asks me to comment explicitly on what I've seen. My last director only wanted to hear my ideas once others weren't around. Marcus's request makes me nervous and happy at the same time. As passionately as I can, I praise what I liked and give warm feedback on what could be improved. Joris says my feedback is useful and Marcus mutters something that seems like approval, at least from afar. I relax again.

After this, Sasha does a piece with Joris and Jolene does one with Dave. Marcus is his flamboyant self, he hurtles back and forth, shouts while they're acting, preaches fire and brimstone and gives gentle guidance at other moments. I watch the scenes get better and better; I see players finding themselves. *Careers don't get better than this,* I think. *Look at me now. I can even pay my rent.*

When we stop rehearsing, Marcus says we should be proud of ourselves, and then he shouts out enthusiastically, "Pub?" Aside from Joris, everyone comes along. On the way, Marcus walks next to me to discuss a few things and I act as though this is the most normal thing in the world. Life is good today.

7

"What do you think of the business with Alexander?"

We're in the car. Marie is at the wheel, I'm next to her, and Anne-Sophie is in the back. Marie turns off the music and looks at me instead of at the road. The rain blows despondently against the windshield, the wipers squeak each time they swing back and forth. She turns on her headlights. It's three in the afternoon but she'd rather not take any risks.

"Well, he's quite young, of course, but—"

"Quite young? Twenty-one. Mona, dear, he's just a pup. And he's already in the stranglehold of an older woman."

I can't help laughing at her choice of words. Anne-Sophie joins in.

"Oh, you two find it funny, do you?"

"No," Anne-Sophie says immediately.

"I realize you and Dad are concerned, but they seem happy together, don't you think?"

"I agree," Anne-Sophie says, either because she really thinks this or because she thinks she has to back me up.

"Being head over heels is different from starting a family, you know."

"Yes, maybe that's true," I say.

"And how long's it going to last between the two of them? We're talking about Alexander, aren't we? I can't even count all the girlfriends he's already had in his short life."

"Since Magalie, I think about—" Anne-Sophie counts on her fingers.

"I don't want to know, but he's consistent about one thing: he gets tired of them all."

"He was sad for a long time when Nora dumped him, and they were together for several months." My sister adds a touch of drama to her voice.

"*Dumped*! What a word, Anne-Sophie," Marie says, looking back as she drives.

"Those ex-girlfriends weren't that great, were they? Not even Nora. Did you like her?" I turn to my sister.

"Hmm," she says.

"They had to be pretty enough to talk their way into his bed, that was all."

"Talk, talk," Marie mutters.

"Charlie's finally someone with a real personality, a smart woman, one who—"

"Already bosses him around and has made him give up his chance at a good future and a wonderful career. And why, do you think?" I know she's not expecting an answer, so I only look at her. "She felt her biological clock ticking and thought, *A handsome, clever young man from a good family, I'll catch this one before my eggs run out.*"

"She's thirty-two, not forty-two."

Anne-Sophie represses a giggle in the back seat.

"You're acting as though this is just a minor detail in Alexander's life. His whole future's going to be defined by it, you know."

The car behind us honks. Marie shouts into the rearview mirror, "Yes, ma'am, yes. It's raining and we're all stuck in this traffic. What can

I do about it?" Anne-Sophie looks back with an angry expression to prove her solidarity. "People complaining, I really can't cope with that."

I look out the side window. Alongside me a large man is talking to the dog sitting next to him in the passenger seat. What could he be saying? I look at my sister and point at the man; she smiles. Anne-Sophie doesn't have the classical beauty Alexander has, but there's something that makes you want to look at her. She has flaxen hair and dreamy eyes. She's very serious-looking for her age, and introverted when it comes down to it. I never would have expected it, as a child she seemed much more outgoing.

"Do you know whether they're going to get married?" Marie asks.

"I haven't heard any talk about that."

"Great, so this cardiologist's daughter is going to have a bastard for a grandchild. Who'd have thought it?" It's 1991, but to Marie the world has remained the way her parents once decided it should be. "What do *you* think about it?"

"You know what I think."

"Maybe I do, but I want to hear you say it."

"Love isn't about having the right papers is what I think."

"That's what I think too," Anne-Sophie says.

"You thinking Alexander's too young to have a baby, I can understand that, but whether they're married or not is irrelevant."

"Well, you agree with your mother on one thing, at least, Mona. Fortunately, you have more common sense than your brother in that area." Marie looks at her youngest daughter in the rearview mirror. "And I hope *you'll* learn your lesson from this."

Anne-Sophie says nothing. I think about Charlie, the way she stuck out her belly to look more pregnant and then had to laugh about it; about Alexander and his mushy look as he stood there watching; about Dad at a loss for words. I think about Louis, who I haven't seen or heard from in nine days. I must have been a disappointment at that breakfast.

"Tell me, how are you liking your new job?"

"It's great."

"I still don't understand why you changed jobs. The new one doesn't pay any better, does it?"

"No, but he's one of the greatest directors we have."

"So why doesn't he work at one of the big theaters?"

"Because there's about as much life in the big theaters at the moment as in your average raisin. The interesting stuff's happening where I'm working now."

"Plus, Marcus Meereman is really handsome," Anne-Sophie says.

"How do you know what he looks like?"

"He was in the paper. There was a photo."

"And you *already* have an opinion about men's looks? That spells trouble!"

I look at Anne-Sophie and make a funny face. Sometimes I forget she's thirteen and the things that used to make her laugh no longer work. She tries a small smile, solely to please me.

"Yes, yes, it's all quite something." Marie sighs as she throws the plastic wrapper from her cigarettes out the window. "And I still find it a strange world, the theater. You can't be learning anything of any use there, if you ask me."

I want to reply *Yes, yes* in turn, but I don't.

"Can I come to the play you're making?"

"Helping to make, Anne-Sophie, just helping."

"Can I?"

"We'll see," Marie answers for me.

That evening, Alexander calls me.

"Say, sis, did you tell Mom you agree that I'm much too young to have a baby?"

8

I never do this, actually, visit graves, not my mother's and not Granny's. But today, I don't know, there was something going on with the birds, seagulls I suspect, even though I don't know anything about birds. The few I can identify are the ones my father once taught me. The birds from this morning, they cawed and crowed, there were lots of them all of a sudden, a flapping cloud behind my apartment building. It was as though they'd felt the end of the world approaching and thought: *We should let the people know.* It was that disturbing. I decided I should go outside, do something. And then I discovered I'd biked all the way to the cemetery. Sometimes we sense what we need to do without really understanding it.

Granny is buried between Grandpa and her sister, between a heart attack and a brain tumor. My granny was a ship that seemed like it would never go down, with her robust body, her strong arms, her parchment skin that looked pretty much the same for almost twenty years. She'd grown old early, or had remained well preserved, depending on how you looked at things. And yet suddenly, when she was seventy-two, she was found dead on her kitchen floor: a brain hemorrhage. She'd lain there for almost three days, on those black-and-white tiles, facedown. It wasn't until Auntie Rose found it strange that Granny wasn't picking up her phone that they went to take a look. I was glad she didn't have a cat. And I felt guilty I hadn't visited for a month or two.

I can't say that I missed her much. I felt bad about that because what does it say about me? Granny was the kind of woman who made it hard for people to love her. She baked cakes, sure, she bought birthday gifts and sent cards at Christmas; she told us about the trials and tribulations of family members who were still alive, about the past and her own mother and how she'd hit Granny when she was disobedient, a rap across the fingers with a ruler, which was normal in those days, but it hurt all the same. She told us this often, always that same story, in always the same words, to give the impression she'd found it normal herself. It's in the emphasis that something *isn't* bad, that it *doesn't* frighten us, that it *hasn't* made us sad, that we often betray the force of our true emotions, even though we believe the shadowy self-deception while we're formulating it. Anyway, that's what Charlie said recently when Alexander assured her that his mother's death hadn't affected him. I find myself still thinking about her words.

My mother's grave is a few rows back from Granny's. There's an ugly, weathered gravestone. HERE LIES, and then engraved underneath it in slightly larger letters: AGNES DE TENDER, and under that: 11/7/1941–8/20/1976. There's no verse, no cross, no palm branch, no photo like on many of the other graves I see here. She's lying almost directly under the beech tree and that's nice, of course. Well, the bones that are left. Apparently, it takes about ten years for all the flesh and fat to break down, so they've been gone quite some time.

I stand there looking at the concrete evidence of her passing and feel nothing. Or maybe everything, it's hard to say sometimes. Her death was so unexpected. She left and never came back.

I couldn't cry at the time and that's always stayed with me. Tears were for weaklings and you had to save them for your pillow, that's what my mother said, in more innocent times. Would she have felt this she was applicable to her own passing?

Even today, it's still not possible to talk about her. Daddy says it's too painful for Marie, as though it could prove she's not a worthy replacement. The photos have been put away in a greenish box at the bottom of that heavy oak cupboard in the dining room, and there's also a metal case with a few of her belongings. I wouldn't even know where to look for it. I wonder whether Dad sometimes gets it out when he's alone.

Once, when I was twelve or thirteen, it was an evening after a party—with free-flowing alcohol, I'll bet—he told me that sex with my mother was much better than with her. There was something apocalyptically dark about the look in his eyes. Suddenly Marie became *her*, the vague word that was usually used for my mom if mentioning her was unavoidable, like a stranger who comes along and begins to stir a pot that has been sealed for centuries. I didn't respond at the time, but I've never forgotten it.

There's a lot I have forgotten. I've got very few real memories, all in all. Louis once said that it's often better not to want to know, and I wonder if he's right. My life not feeling like my own can really upset me sometimes.

I've never really missed my mom, that's how it feels to me. I don't know whether it's even possible, a child still missing its mother if she dies so young—or might there be exceptions? I don't think I've ever met a harder woman than her. Well, I wasn't an easy child, I guess. I was bossy, constantly chattering, oversensitive too. I think I unintentionally provoked her now and then, as though I had to fight her. Maybe my image of my mom is colder than strictly necessary; Alexander is much milder when he talks about her. Of course, he always stayed just out of range, but as far as I can remember, he never ended up in the basement. I should ask him sometime. He was very good at making himself invisible, and he was always easy, like it wasn't hard at all, his smile ever ready, always prepared to make minor sacrifices to keep the peace. When the adults were looking. He was cleverest of us back then too.

Just beyond the beech tree, there's a woman polishing a double gravestone. She's scrubbing away on her hands and knees like she's going to eat off it. She's got two pots of flowers with her, those little pink and blue ones, a bit of life to put among the dead, that's nice of her. *It must be her parents' grave,* I think. *She must have loved them a lot.* A better daughter than I ever was. I've never been able to tell anybody that I don't miss my mother, that I couldn't cry that night, because in addition to a quiet kind of sorrow, I also felt a sense of relief. In the morning I looked up at the sun that was high in the sky and thought: *It's a new day.* Honestly, I missed my dad more because the absence of a person who's standing right in front of you is more intense, it seems. It puzzled me.

I bike home again, my head full of vague thoughts. As I pass the café by the theater, I slow down. A quick glass of wine. Just one wouldn't hurt, would it? Then I hear Marcus calling. I see him sitting on the terrace, there in the corner, he's waving me over. *I can't,* I think, but now I have to. *Just the one, don't stay long.* I stop, lock up my bike, and walk over to him.

"What's the matter with you?" he asks, even before I've sat down. I'm a little amazed he's so good at reading faces.

"Strange day," I say, smiling.

"Tell me."

"Oh, it's not that important." I wouldn't know where to begin, to be honest, and certainly not with him.

But Marcus continues to look at me—he's one of those men who won't take no as an answer on principle.

"I went to my mother's grave," I say, with some gravity in the hope that this one line will suffice. Most people don't like talking about mortality or other such doom and gloom.

"Oh, has she been dead for long?" Marcus isn't most people. I should have expected this.

I nod. "Died when I was nine. Car accident."

"Awful." Marcus takes a cheese cracker from a china jar on the table. "I go to my father's grave at least once a month. I talk to him—that kind of helps."

"Was he a nice father?"

"A bastard," Marcus says, "but that doesn't mean you don't miss him any less, apparently. Maybe more even, because you're obliged to miss what you never had enough of." He puts the cracker in his mouth and then immediately takes another one.

So that's possible too. I almost want to tell him what I was thinking just now, but I take some cash from my purse and ask whether he wants a drink.

9

I can get through this, I think, when I see his head coming closer, eyes closed, mouth already slightly open. I wonder why I'm thinking this now; I was so happy when Louis called me to meet up again. He was going to kidnap me, he'd said, sounding excited. I was happy he wanted to make an effort for me. I'm glad he wants me and that he wants me here and now, no mistaking it.

He brought me to this beautifully renovated 1960s manor house in the middle of the countryside. A lot of right angles, large expanses of glass with a view onto the garden and a stretch of water upon which boats sometimes sail past. Louis is staying here to write while the owner, a friend of his, is abroad for six weeks. He'd prepared lunch for us. The table in the open kitchen was laid with proper napkins and beautiful, stylish cutlery. There were three kinds of bread, real butter and olive oil, a couple of different types of fish, Ganda ham, and slices of tomato and onion in rings cut too thick. He can't cook at all, he said, but he'd done his best for me. He poured chilled Meursault and put the bottle in a real wine cooler where it tinkled against the ice cubes. We ate and talked. He ate fast, I noticed that. They say that the speed with which you eat matches the speed of your thoughts.

"Does that old-fashioned boat out there belong to your friend?"
Louis nodded.

"Then don't we really have to—"

"That's the wonderful thing about my life now," he interrupted me. "I don't have to do anything, or at least very little." He grinned from ear to ear, rolled a slice of smoked halibut around his fork, and shoved all of it into his mouth, as though he was trying to make further conversation impossible.

"Come on, we can't pass up such an authentic Jane Austen moment."

Louis carried on chewing, adding a piece of bread to his mouth.

"The ultimate chance to prove yourself as a gallant gentleman with a knack for romance." The more reluctant he became, the more I pushed. It was a reflex.

When he stepped into the boat, it began to wobble dangerously. I sat down at the far end, and he looked thoughtfully at the plank that served as a seat, wiped his hand vaguely over it, as though worried his fancy clothes would get dirty. He sat down, waited until the boat came more or less to rest, took an oar in each hand, and looked at them, as though they were the most complicated instruments ever and only serviceable by someone with a degree in rowing. He moved them around in the water with no sense of rhythm or direction. We kept drifting toward the bank. I couldn't watch anymore.

"Shall I take over?"

He nodded gratefully and I took the paddles from him. Laughing, he posed like a young maiden: thighs together, hands on his knees, the opposite end of the spectrum from manly and sexy.

And now, floating around on this quiet water, his face comes closer. His movements cause the sloop to rock, but he keeps coming. His right eye is bigger than his left one, I only notice this now, and his breath smells of the smoked fish he had for lunch, but I'm going to kiss him. Louis is clever and charming and funny, and I don't think appearances matter, so I let him come closer and off we go. He kisses like he hasn't been able to kiss anyone for seven years, more frenzied than eager, more uncontrolled than passionate, and there's no proper conclusion to it. No smacking sound to seal the kiss. He just disappears, tongue and all, back the way he came, abruptly. I don't know how it's possible, maybe it has to do with the unstable boat. He pulls his head back, looks at me, and smiles a bigger smile than I've ever seen on his face. I smile back. He puts his hand between my legs, where there isn't much space because the oar handles are there too, and here comes that mouth again.

"Gently," I try.

Louis is fourteen years older than me, but for a moment I feel like a teacher with a student who still has everything to learn. The second kiss proceeds in a more controlled manner on his part. Maybe he can improve, practice makes perfect and all that. Maybe it was a mistake all the same. I lay my hand on his hand and move it down a bit, more toward my knees. He runs his fingers through my hair. Then I pick up the oars again.

"Shall we go back to dry land?" I ask, as though I'm trying to oblige him, the water hater.

He looks a little confused, strokes my cheek, and says, "All right, then."

We got cold out on the water. It's only spring, and the air cools down fast. I want a hot drink, but he pours a glass of red wine and suggests we sit in the living room. I say I adore the view right here in the kitchen. *Tables,* I think, *and hard chairs.* They're better than sofas with voluptuous cushions.

We talk, we're good at that, and then the conversation turns to his brother. Louis was eighteen when he died, apparently. Although I have a talent for asking for more, I simply nod and listen.

"I'd just spent six months studying abroad. I came home, happy and not happy, the way it goes with those kinds of adventures. My whole family was standing at the door to welcome me back, all except my brother. He was ill, I knew that of course, but he was supposed to get it fixed. He was the bear of the family, the sportsman, the invincible member of the gang. His letters had explained all the steps taken in his treatment, and I'd been optimistic. From a distance. And all of a sudden, I see him sitting, well, lying more like it, in the armchair. If they'd shown me a photo beforehand, I'd have said, 'I don't know that boy'—that's how much damage the cancer had done." Louis takes a sip and stares at his glass. He makes the wine dance as though this dash of happiness can help him. "I barely dared to look at him, afraid that my brother would see what I was staring at: death itself, which he clearly didn't feel ready for. His body did, perhaps, but not his mind. I knew this from his letters and what my parents had told me. I embraced him, delicately, like he might break. After that, I fled upstairs, claiming I had to take an urgent shower after my long trip, but really it was to pull myself together." There are ravines in Louis's eyes, gravel, swamps. As though they want to say *Save me,* as though he believes I can. And I, I stay with him. "Three months and six days later, he was dead. It was very quiet after that." He puts down his glass and takes my hands in his and it actually feels nice.

When he brings me home later and we're sitting in the car in front of my apartment, I'm the one who kisses him, because I want to. Lips are just lips, this man is this man, with his deluge of words and his helplessness. *He's one person but also all kinds of things, and that's unusual,* I think as I kiss him again.

10

I'd put on a bikini under my clothes, it's best to be prepared in this kind of situation, and yet I stand here dithering. We were supposed to get ready, the man had said, and then come out. He'd pointed toward an area with changing rooms that led to showers on the other side. *Get ready*, that could mean anything. Nothing worse than being that one girl who's too prudish to go naked. The only thing worse is being naked among other people who are all dressed. The safest bet is often the best one, I decide, so I stick to the bikini and come out of the dressing room, walk through the locker room and out into the night. I'm the last person, the rest are all standing in a clump, just next to the sweat lodge. The only light comes from the burning torches. Only Sasha is wearing a swimsuit, she looks at me with embarrassment or relief in her eyes, I can't say which.

Nobody had to feel obliged, Marcus had said, but it would be special if we could experience this as a group—cleansing ourselves together, being brought closer to ourselves and each other, which of course meant nobody dared refuse, at least I didn't. I wouldn't voluntarily take part in this kind of ritual invented by people with too much imagination and too few useful hobbies to elevate their existence above pure idleness, not in a thousand years. But now there's no avoiding it. So I stand here, shivering in a bikini among people I actually don't know that well. I wonder whether that's an advantage or a disadvantage.

For a while I considered getting out of it with an excuse, like a terrible illness or a family member on their deathbed—the more dramatic, the more credible. I thought about that as I walked in and was hugged by a woman with a makeup-less, grooved face. She smelled of sandalwood and unwashed clothes and the knots and tangles in her hair were permanent. If they'd told me I could pick one of a hundred random women I wouldn't want to have hug me, I would have pointed her out without hesitation. It didn't get much better when a man— the boyfriend of the woman with the knotty hair, I guessed—told me what we were going to experience together. His story was emptier than mountain skies. He used words like *transformation* and *letting go* and *Mother Earth*. I expected the woman with the hair to bring out a tambourine, but that didn't happen. I repressed a yawn of boredom, and of discomfort, I think.

First we're all supposed to do the Salutation to the Four Directions, then he'll purify us before we go into the sweat lodge, he says. He runs some kind of rustling branch excruciatingly slowly over the front of each person's body, from top to bottom, and then does the other side. Once he has finished with you, you can duck through the narrow entrance into the sweat lodge and form a circle. Marcus goes first. We're standing close by and apart from him; there's not much to look at. It's dark everywhere and somehow you find your eyes inclined to follow that branch, like a child follows a finger or a dog a treat that you hold in the air and move playfully from left to right. When the man gets below Marcus's waist, I look away, but I've seen it and all the others have too, I'm certain. He's as large as you'd expect for a man with his ego. Right now, I'm relieved I'm not a man. I see people go and stand ready, one by one, I see them half-heartedly trying not to stare at whoever is receiving the treatment, and I'm grateful for this bikini.

I'm the last to crawl into the hut. It's pitch dark inside. I squeeze between Sasha and Marcus. *Squeeze*, that's the word, the circle's too big for this sweat lodge, that's how it feels. However hard I try not to touch the others, it's impossible to avoid it. I try not to think about the fact we'll be sweating like pigs soon. I don't know what's worse, my sweat touching their bodies, or theirs mine. I feel the sand and grass under my buttocks. I want to leave.

The man, sitting amicably among us, says that it's all about letting go here and we have to do that literally. This powerful ritual, as he calls it, is going to last four hours and no one can leave the hut, so anyone who needs to relieve themselves should let it flow, and menstruating women can entrust their blood to the earth. I want to know whose piss and dried menstrual blood is seeping up into my skin at this very moment. Which predecessors have shared their juices with the earth? I shudder at the thought. I want to leave.

In phase one, the focus stays on the dead; the man makes his voice sound all echoey. We're supposed to share everything we want with the group: sounds, screams, words, sentences. Everyone should react the way they feel when they think about death and dying. The last things I want to think about with my almost-naked butt in the sand and grass, with people I only really wanted to make a Chekhov play with, are my mother and my grandmother. And death in the abstract, I'd rather not go there, probably because I'm afraid of it, but please allow me that fear, it's mine, I don't need to share it, not in the form of yelping, weird noises, sweat, piss, or blood.

The temperature in the hut rises, the man starts humming some kind of primal song and encourages us to join him. It doesn't take long for Marcus to lead the way. He produces a howling scream that gives me the chills even in the middle of all this sweating. The others won't be outdone, apparently, and they too growl, roar, sob, shout, scream, and screech as though they're being clubbed to death, very slowly, by a sadist. They're actors, at the end of the day, so it's hardly surprising. I remain silent and hope Marcus doesn't notice. If Chekhov were sitting here, I'm sure he'd remain silent. Of course, Chekhov would surely have refused to come, he had a personality and stuff.

Sasha invites her dead brother to come and join us in the circle and share this magisterial experience with her. Joris expresses his gratitude at being able to be here with us because we can help him shoulder his sorrows. Marcus thunders that he is connected with his deeper self and that we should all reach for that point because it's an unbelievable gift. He uses words like *pain* and *impotence* and *broken* and *being lost* with no inhibition. In the meantime, I try to guess how many minutes have already passed. I try to daydream myself to another place, somewhere pleasant, like a proper chair or something, with all my clothes on, in good company, where people are conversing politely or remaining modestly quiet. And yet, a restless kind of anxiety, hard to put your finger on but present, prevails.

I see the shadows, feel the others. I hope no one has relieved themselves already. I'm afraid I'll have to pee soon, I've got a small bladder, always have. I'm just glad I didn't have any of the tea offered to us in the reception area. I don't understand how I've let myself get maneuvered into this situation, to be honest, but I do understand, of course. Meanwhile, the terrifying sounds are only getting louder. I want to leave.

The last phase is about returning to your childhood. The place where we were able to build up our basic confidence, the man says, the place where we felt loved and cherished, where we were in contact with our pure physicality, where we believed in ourselves completely. We can share our experiences, we can sing, whatever we want.

I hear the man's words. *I couldn't join in now even if I wanted to,* I think. I wonder whether any of the others have so many old wounds.

Since eyes grow accustomed to the dark, I can now see exactly where all the others are. Some have lain down, which only increases the chance of contact with all that fluid filth. They must have stopped thinking—apparently, they can do that. I notice that someone has really begun to stink, sweat from a skin that can't have seen any soap this morning. Luckily it's neither of the people next to me.

I listen to stories about happy children with sweet mothers and equanimous fathers. I notice that Marcus has gone quiet and a couple of the others too. I'm glad the roaring has made way for chatter and nonsense, calmer variants. I let my thoughts drift and then, all of a sudden, I start to cry violently, inexplicably. The tears just keep on coming as though my heart is bursting at every seam. I hope nobody notices. I try to keep my body as still as possible. I don't want to think about where this has come from. I want to leave.

After four hours, I crawl out of the hut, broken. I'm embarrassed that Marcus comes out right behind me and that his face is so close to my butt. God knows what that smells like after all of this, even though my bladder has held up.

Next, there'll be a sound-healing ritual and then we'll get soup and bread, this is what the man says, as though it's a reason for great joy. And we can count on another ardent hug from that lady too, I bet.

I head to the showers first; thankfully, this is allowed. I don't dare look at anyone. Most of them are silent, as though they're feeling the aftereffects, or are in touch with their deepest selves or the earth or the cosmos, who's to say?

When I'm under the shower, the tears return. I stand there trembling in a torrent of hot water. I try not to think about anything. I hope I don't get red blotches on my face.

I'm the last to leave the changing rooms. Outside, the others are sitting or lying on cushions while the man is busy with Tibetan singing bowls. I look for a corner to hide in. I hope this isn't going to be a regular part of the rehearsal process for Marcus. I don't think there's any other director in the Low Countries who would even consider it.

In the dead of night, we all go back to the cars we came in. I'm one of the drivers; Sasha and Joris rode with me. Marcus is walking right behind me. He grabs my shoulder and says, "If you dare to think about why you've become who you've become, you can change it. You mustn't forget that."

Does he dare to do that? I wonder.

11

"This is the shop I meant," Marie says, pointing at the one with a dark-gray awning. She sets off at a trot, and I try to keep up. She hands me the two bags containing the skirt and the dress she just bought and immediately starts chatting with the saleswoman. I try to keep people like that at a distance, but Marie loves sales assistants. They're paid to know what suits you, so you'd be crazy not to make use of them, Marie says, shamelessly claiming her dues.

"I'm looking for something to go with this skirt," she says, taking it out of the bag I've passed to her. The woman, who is around fifty, with angular, almond-shaped eyes and hair infused with so much hairspray that it will never hang down again in this life, is pure professionalism. She moves quickly along the racks, taking out blouses, sweaters, and tops. Marie says yes a couple of times, more often no, and then heads to the fitting room with the loot.

As she's trying things on, she talks to me through the curtain.

"So is he a well-known author?"

"He's written a couple of very beautiful novels, and later this year he's going to write a play for Marcus. I'm really excited to see that."

"Yes, but is he famous?" She comes out, stands in front of the mirror, straightens her shoulders, and turns to the side. She's got a figure many twenty-year-olds would envy. She tucks the blouse into the skirt, as though there's just one correct way of wearing it and she has to discover it.

"He is one of the better-known novelists, yes."

"But you don't find him handsome?"

"Well, he wouldn't win a beauty contest, but that's not important to me."

"No, of course not, but if you say it like that, it makes me think—" She turns to the saleswoman. "Didn't you have this one in burgundy too?" The woman with the hair carved out of stone replies in the affirmative, saying she'll see if they still have it in the right size in that color. "What do you think of this one?"

"Pretty."

"Hmm, you don't sound very enthusiastic."

"I am, it's good, really matches the skirt. Maybe even better in burgundy, though."

Marie closes the curtain behind her again. She tugs at it a few times to get rid of the gap you get in most fitting room curtains. "You hold this shut, it doesn't work." I grab hold of the stiff fabric and pull it toward the wall.

"But you are in love with him?"

"I think so, yes."

"You don't think that kind of thing, you know it."

"Yes, yes, I am, yes."

"And he's in love with you?"

"I don't know, but I assume so."

"That's a good start," Marie says, laughing. She comes out again in a black silk blouse with large epaulettes. She's turned into a triangle. "Oh well, you shouldn't expect too much of love. It's the source of much unhappiness among young people who want everything, but it's actually about persevering and plodding on and trying to make the best of things."

The saleswoman comes back and says they no longer have the burgundy blouse in madam's size, only one size larger.

"That wouldn't work at all, would it? I mean clothes should fit, shouldn't they? And that first blouse, it fit like a second skin, didn't it?" When Marie has the choice between a lot of words or very few, she never hesitates. The saleswoman takes back the blouse. "I'm glad you've got someone, Mona. I really am." She says it like I'm a handicapped ten-year-old who just learned to sit upright without assistance.

"Well, I don't have him yet," I say.

"What do you mean? Are you worried he's about to get tired of you or something? Say, I'm going to try on that top now even though I'd prefer something with long sleeves. Do you mind?"

"Of course not, we're here to shop."

"Well, I still felt I should ask. I don't want you to think we're spending too long in this shop. But didn't I tell you, they always have a collection here that suits me." She rearranges the hangers on the hook.

"I just mean I don't really know whether we're in a serious relationship now or not, or whether—"

"How can you not know?" She pokes her head between the curtain and the fitting room wall.

I don't want to look at her standing there like that, knowing she's naked behind the curtain. I turn to face the interior of the shop. "Well, like I already said, he's a very interesting man, you know. I think he could attract a lot of women."

Marie's head disappears again, I sense it. I hear clothes rustling, getting that top on seems to involve a minor skirmish. "Eh, if he's ugly, I'm not so sure."

"We'll see what happens. I'll just wait. First I'll see whether he calls me again or not."

"Yes, well, you certainly shouldn't call him yourself. You don't want him to realize how desperate you are."

"Desperate? I'm not."

"Noo-oh. But if you call first, it might look like you are. That's all I mean." Marie spins in front of the mirror in a tight white top. She stands on tiptoes. "I think I'll take the first one, the dark-green one, what do you think?"

"Yes, that really suited you, I thought."

"Didn't it? And the color wasn't so bad, was it?"

"No, nice to try something different."

"Oh, I do love shopping with you. You've really got a feeling for it, for what suits me. My little Mona." She hands me the curtain again so I can hide her fitting room rituals from human eyes. The saleswoman smiles at me as though she isn't being paid to and I smile back. I really do hope Louis calls me soon.

12

We go back outside again after the show. Louis had been anxious to see something by this young producer. He wasn't impressed; I thought it was beautiful. He lets me express my opinion before expressing his. We linger on the pavement as we come up with arguments to support our views. Suddenly, he says he wants to go home with me.

When we get there, he sucks on my earlobe and rubs my back frantically with his palm, the fabric of my sweater chafes against my skin. He breaths heavily.

"Kiss," he says, kissing me.

I feel his lips, his tongue, his nose. He tugs me toward him with a jerk and holds me tightly, as though he's afraid I might escape. He pinches my bottom.

"Should we take our clothes off?" he asks.

Without waiting for my reply, he sits down on the bed, takes off his shoes, his socks, then he gets up, unbuckles his belt, opens his fly, lets his trousers drop, and then lays them on the floor. He undoes the buttons of his shirt, one by one, first the cuffs, then the rest. He takes his time, as though he's home alone, determined not to be hurried. Then his shirt whirls down on top of the trousers and he climbs under the duvet in his underpants. His briefs are gray, once white, perhaps, that's also possible; the elastic is crenated, like the leaves of plants I don't know the name of.

"Come," he says. "Come."

I take off my dress and my tights. I keep on my lingerie and get in next to him.

"Take that off," he says. "For god's sake, take that off."

I wonder why he's saying everything twice but decide not to ask. I sit up and unfasten my bra.

"What nice breasts," he says.

He takes one in each hand and squeezes them until it hurts. Then he pushes me into a lying position and fiercely sucks on my right nipple for a long time, like he's a baby with a raging hunger. Then he kisses me again. His hands support his weight on either side of my head, his lower body pressed to mine. I wonder whether he has an erection now or not. It makes me feel a little insecure, but not too much. Too insecure and they notice and it's a turnoff, a friend once told me, and I've never forgotten it.

"Now you," I say, rolling him onto his back. I kiss his chest, maneuvering slowly downward, and pull off his briefs. He actually does have an erection, but it's not that strange I didn't feel it, his dick is so small. *Oh well, length's not that important,* I think, and slide my mouth around it, using my tongue to play around the tip, run up and down along his dick, teasingly slowly. As I try to lick his balls, he pulls my head back up. I kiss him on his lips, in his neck, and want to go back down, but he stops me.

"You don't have to," he says.

"But I want to." *Predecessors have praised me for this,* I think, *let me do something I'm good at for once,* only I don't say this.

"I want to kiss you," is all he says. He pulls my face close to his and licks my lips with all of his tongue, then he kisses me again.

There's something rapacious about it, I can't help thinking, something of a great surrender and that is nice, and warm. He pants and pinches my breasts again, then he gently kisses my whole head, each bit, kiss by kiss. He makes love to me as though I were just a mouth, and all right, a face too. In the meantime, I move my hands over his body, each time he leads them back up again to his head, his arms.

And then he suddenly asks, much sooner than expected, "Do you want me to fuck you?"

What I actually think is that it would be nice if a few more things could happen first, but in order not to spoil the mood, I whisper lustfully, "Yes."

"Do you want me to fuck you hard?"

"Yes," I say a little louder and more hoarsely, looking at him.

Then he lies on top of me, tries to push his dick into me with his hand. He misses a couple of times, but in the end, he manages. He moves, I can feel his butt going quietly up and down, but I can hardly feel anything inside. I tense my muscles, perhaps it will help. He rests on his hands, keeping his upper body at a distance, and rides me, calmly and evenly.

He gazes at a point just above my eyes and says, "Mmm, good, like that, yes, good, your cunt is good, yes, mmm, your cunt is so wet, so tight."

I let him get on with it and try to grab hold of his ass.

"No, don't," he says, as though I've hurt him, so I let go and he carries on moving to the same rhythm.

I want to turn him so that we're lying on our sides, which I find more intimate. He moves with me but his dick slips out, he laughs a bit.

"Bit difficult like that," he says, and without any questions, he returns me to my back and slides it into me again. He pumps uniformly, looks at me, smiles, and then it's already, "I'm going to come, I'm going to come. Can I come? Are you already there?" Then he shudders gently, freezes for a moment, his eyes close, he groans softly, floats there for a moment, that's what it looks like, and then withdraws and collapses next to me on his back. "Wonderful," he says blissfully. He strokes my upper arm vaguely, his breathing calms, and then he yawns. "Better watch out I don't fall asleep," he whispers. "I'm so tired." He pulls me toward him, and a few minutes later, I hear him snoring softy.

When he wakes up again twenty minutes later, he suddenly says, as though we were in the middle of a conversation, "That was wonderful, wasn't it? You're delectable."

"Hmm, yeah," I say, "and I think a lot more is possible." I emphasize *more*, trying to stay positive, and fix my eyes on his. I learned this with my last boyfriend: Don't wait to give a guy feedback on the sex or you'll be irrevocably stuck with it for years to come. You only have to say once that it was good as it was and he'll keep on doing it; give him the impression just once that you don't mind if he doesn't lick you if he doesn't like it that much, and he'll settle into that.

"Wonderful," Louis says again, his eyes closed, as though he's temporarily forgotten all other words.

"Maybe I should add, though," I say, consciously keeping my tone light and playful, "that I can't come like that." I'm not sure whether he's understood or not. It remains quite an unclear game, certainly in the beginning, when bodies are still unfamiliar to each other.

He says nothing.

Sometimes the path of absolute certainty is the only right one to take, I'm forced to think. "I don't have vaginal orgasms. But the other kinds, on the other hand . . ."

At which point he leads my hand to my cunt and says, "You take care of that, then, you horny bitch, you sexy wench, the slut that you are." He begins to suck on my left nipple mechanically as he clutches my other breast.

I feel my hand lying limply on my own cunt. "Let's just try to do it properly next time," I suggest.

"That's even better," he says with something of a relaxed sigh. He immediately lets go of my breast and grabs hold of me eagerly, as though he'd climb into me if he could. "You're a beauty," he says, "I think I love you a bit already." He presses his nose into my armpit. "I like your smell too."

I smile at him, he smiles back. It's sweet, the way he says that, he feels close and that really is the case. I lay my arm across his chest, my forehead on his biceps, and stroke his shoulder, his neck.

"Everything will be all right," I say.

"Everything is all right," he replies, kissing my hand.

13

Joris makes himself a coffee, which means noise. The espresso machine has been moved into the rehearsal room at Marcus's request. You can hear the beans being ground, and then the whine of the steam. Marcus is on the other side of the room, talking to the production designer; rehearsal has yet to officially begin. All of a sudden, he breaks off his conversation and bellows through the room, "Christ, Joris, what's your problem?" Joris looks startled, confused; he points at the coffee machine and can't do anything other than wait for it to finish, there's no stopping the thing. Everyone falls silent, which happens spontaneously. "A little bit of quiet while we prepare ourselves mentally would be nice," Marcus says. He reminds me of my math teacher when I was thirteen, who was also a large, broad-shouldered man. He consistently spoke to us as though we were only in this world to taunt him.

Marcus has been so happy recently, the sweating and sound healing seemed to bring him to euphoric heights, all of us together, one family. Now he looks around in irritation, sits down in his typical lotus position, and says he wants to start with one of Sasha's monologues, a Chekhov story she adapted herself; I helped her a bit. She takes off her jacket and stands in the middle of the room. Marcus nods to indicate that she can start. We watch from the table. She's hardly spoken five lines when Marcus interrupts her.

"What's the point of this?"

Sasha smiles shyly. "This is the story I wanted to—"

"I know what it is, I was asking about the point of it."

"I chose it because I love the atmosphere: all that impotence, the turbulent unrest, the feeling of not knowing where to go, with yourself, I mean."

"Why don't I feel that, then?"

I think: *Because she's only been talking for thirty seconds,* but I don't say it.

"Should I start again?"

"Please, yes." Marcus sighs and kicks off his shoes.

Sasha starts again, but he keeps on stopping her, about nine times in total, and then he allows her to continue to the end uninterrupted, just once. When she's finished, Marcus stands up and paces around the table. Sasha stands there, frozen, as though she doesn't dare sit down. Everyone looks at them, no one speaks. Then he sits down again and says, "You're as boring as watching paint dry." Sasha looks away, folds her arms in front of her body, and stands with her legs crossed. I expect her to reply, but she just goes out into the hall. No one reacts and no one gets themselves a coffee. Snakes slither through the room, a thunderstorm presses against the ceiling. Joris sits staring at the fruit bowl, takes a pear, looks at it, and then puts it back again. Jolene chews the end of her ballpoint pen, Frederik fiddles with his beard. I imagine myself outside in the fresh air. And Marcus, Marcus looks impervious to everything, his face reinforced concrete.

When Sasha comes back in, he sputters, "Right, so we can finally continue. I suggest we gather around the table for the rest of the day. Mona, have you thought of a way to structure the texts we already have?"

My breath falters. I haven't. It feels like someone has taken bites out of me and it's only a matter of time before I fall apart. Things keep changing every day: people get rid of bits of text and come up with new ones and sections are revised. It had seemed too soon for the big inventory.

Stone-faced, I reply, "It'll be ready tomorrow," as though this is the desired answer, that's how I make it sound. I can feel my heart beating in strange places. Marcus is drawing on a sheet of paper, they look like phalluses from where I'm sitting, but that might be my imagination. He frowns, which makes his eyes smaller, and the corners of his mouth point down gloomily, then he looks at me and I brace myself.

"I have high hopes."

After the rehearsal, I hurry back home. The rain chases me toward the buildings, a man with angry buttoned-up-to-the-neck clothing scurries along the street, a woman in a fluorescent-orange waterproof outfit bikes past, bent over as though she's trying to pick something up from pedal height. *Yes, that's how I feel too,* I think. The rain streams onto my face and my clothes grow heavy from the damp.

I wish I was somebody, I think. *I wish I could do everything, or at least the things others want me to do. I wish I had the self-confidence of that kid over there with big ears. And the joke that just made that woman with the hair, the one at the window, burst into laughter. I wish I had a lion's courage. I wish I had shiny good luck and true love that's out of this world. I wish for bravery for me and everyone else who needs it. I wish I was brilliant at what I do. I wish I could give him what he longs for. I wish I had a father I could help more. I wish I had a mother. I wish for the mist above the mountains, for unforgettable things, and to be irresistible, that too.*

When I get home, I work for another three hours. I sketch out a running order on a piece of paper, arrange the fragments, and bundle them together. Then I don't dare to look anymore and stuff it into my bag. I take a long shower and put on my new skirt and the see-through blouse and the shoes with the big square heels. Then I try to call Louis but can't reach him on either of his numbers. Where can he be?

I look around and notice the mess in the kitchen. I didn't clean up after cooking. I see the junk on the table, the papers and the books dotted on the floor around the sofa. I pick up the phone again and call Jolene. Jolene is almost six feet tall, with long red hair, green eyes, and pronounced cheekbones. When she's on stage, everyone looks at her, not only because she's so unbelievably beautiful but because she can act so unbelievably well too. When she picks up, I blurt out, "Getting drunk is the solution, I think."

She bursts out laughing and shouts into the receiver, "Give me ten minutes and I'll be over."

We go to the bar, the one we almost always visit before and after rehearsals, on quiet nights and on wild ones. We know at least three-quarters of the people in there, so before I know it I'm chatting in a circle of nine people, a glass in my hand. Jolene's got something to do with this, I'm not stupid, but still. I drink and drink and I drink another, and I join in the arguments. I raise a toast, I can't help laughing at the hilarious story of what went wrong at one particular premiere, and I think this is what the poet Hendrik Marsman meant when he wrote that he "wanted to live a splendid and thrilling life." And I wish Louis could see me like this, that too.

14

"Literally," Anne-Sophie says, "she said that it's proof I don't love her." She picks at a scab on her elbow, her left hand points away from her, her head tilted so she can see what she's doing. "Another five years and I can leave home and go to college," she adds in a businesslike tone, as though she's just counted up the cash register and is announcing the total while she neatly makes a note of everything. She was born an adult because that helped. She continues to pick at the wound, which starts to bleed again.

Anne-Sophie is a special child, I've always thought that. Her ideas are clear-cut and not all of them square up with the dictates of puberty. She rarely shows her emotions, but she is very emotional, and tempestuous, I'm certain of it. She likes to talk, in the right situations she does, and she's smart in a worldly way. She often seems so alone and she can be very suspicious, which is unusual, I think, in such a young girl. Perhaps she already understands a lot, though she doesn't let that show at school—her grades are far from impressive. Lack of concentration, apparently; it's not for a lack of intelligence, if you ask me.

She goes into the kitchen, gets some tissues out of her backpack, and dabs at the wound. She studies the red on all that white, the tip of her tongue sticking out of her mouth, a little girl again momentarily.

I've let her down, not seriously perhaps, but that's what it feels like. I left for the city. I was eighteen and had been ready for university for a long time—I mean for life elsewhere, for a flight away from the old, the volcanoes always on the point of eruption, the hidden swamps that sucked you down, the frozen ponds where the ice was never thick enough to cross safely. I left for the city and I left her behind. I left Anne-Sophie to her own devices when she was only seven. I said she could always call me. I wrote down the phone number of my dorm room on three pieces of paper in case she lost one, and then a spare, but she never called. In the early years, I'd go home on the weekends like you're supposed to, and I did see her, of course, but I also went out a lot. Returning to something you wanted to leave behind is harder than always having been there.

These days, Anne-Sophie comes to stay with me a couple of times a year. I take her to theaters and the movies, out to see obscure bands, to cafés where she drinks Coke and my friends include her in the conversation. It's not much. I try to reassure myself that if enough people see you, really see you for everything you are, and if you discover, when you're still young, that life can be all kinds of things, that this counts for quite a lot.

It's the first time she's taken the train here on her own, unannounced and without asking permission at home. I see her sitting there, that little big girl with trouble in her eyes and something grim and determined about the set of her mouth. She looks at her arm, there's blood on her pale-blue blouse, and when she sees that, she begins to cry loudly. I go to her, smooth her hair behind her ear, and ask her what the matter is.

"I don't know." She cries like infants do, with everything they've got.

I sit close to her. "There's something going on, Anne-Sophie, I can tell. Just tell me. You can tell me."

She shrugs, and sobs. It's heartbreaking. Sorrow can't be shared, I think, because words aren't enough. Arms that hug cannot take away the feeling, because understanding, true understanding, simply doesn't exist, not even between sisters who know their parents' expressions, and the sound of hearts being torn to shreds, the suffocation of the stuffy air of dining rooms and living rooms and kitchens where many words are used to avoid talking to each other.

I stay with her, I let her cry, I've got time. Outside, the bells of the little church nearby ring. I've often wondered why it sounds as though calamity is around the corner, a calamity everyone knew about beforehand, the wind and the trees and the children and the barking dogs in the distance, everyone except me.

Anne-Sophie wants to go get some food, yes please, she is still sobbing a bit as she says this. I let her choose, she wants to get Italian, she loves pasta and I know a cozy little place she's sure to like. Comfort can take so many different forms. I'll drive her home afterward. I should call Dad now to tell them not to worry, I'll think of a reason to explain why she came to see me.

I'm relieved my father's standing in the doorway waiting when we arrive. Anne-Sophie rests her hand on the arm I'm using to put the car in neutral, and she looks at me.

"You can tell me everything, you know, little sis."

"Five more years," she replies.

"Which really isn't that long at all." I smile because I can't think of anything better. Then she smiles too, because smiling is sometimes a kind of crying too.

"I'm here for you," I say. *That's too easy,* I think, and then we get out.

Daddy is already gesturing to us, finger to his lips, be quiet, then he uses the same finger to point upstairs to the bedrooms. We say nothing, kiss him one after the other, and slip into the living room.

"Have you done your homework?"

Anne-Sophie nods. "On the train."

"I'll pay you back for the ticket." As though he feels comfortable in his powerlessness. "Have a quick drink or whatever and then hurry to bed. It's much too late for a school night."

"Is Mommy already asleep?" Her voice becomes shrill as she asks this, her gaze fixed.

"Yes, she went to bed a while ago, she was"—he hesitates for a second—"tired."

I picture Marie taking a Xanax and saying, *The pills aren't good for me, but well.* Anne-Sophie returns from the kitchen with a glass of milk, looks at me with an expression that worries me, says good night, and then disappears upstairs.

"You have to go, I guess? Rehearsals tomorrow, or . . ."

Why does he ask it like this? Is that what he wants? For me to run off so that he can watch the TV shows that relieve him of the need to think, so that he can forget that his youngest child just got onto a train to go and get help, so that he can ignore the fact that he's the father of children who expect something from him, as all children do, even when they know better, even if they never say it. Or has he just formulated it that way so that I don't have to feel obliged to stay, which isn't very subtle either?

"I could stay for a drink if you'd like." I say it as neutrally as possible.

He smiles and goes into the kitchen. "Beer or wine?" I choose beer, he shuffles to the fridge, looks behind the jam and mayonnaise and jars of gherkins and pickled onions and yogurt, everything bought in large quantities as though war's about to break out. He picks up a bag containing eight apples with one hand and uses his other to feel around in the back corner. He finally manages to wangle a single bottle of Duvel from behind the confusion of foodstuffs. "Shall we share, then? You still have to drive."

"Fine," I say.

I see him bending over and it occurs to me that my father's got a lot of hair, certainly for a man in his fifties. If he dressed in a more interesting way, you might think he was a painter or some other artistic type. He's got wild hair, a ruthless look in his eyes, and strong hands, too large and coarse to be feeling around inside people's mouths, to be honest.

He pours out a perfect Duvel and only remembers then that we were going to share it. He looks for a second glass, more or less suitable for beer, transfers part of the contents, and spills on the pink tablecloth covered in piglets, one of them eating a string of sausages, which I find perverse of whoever designed it.

"Phew," I say, "*that'll* have to go in the wash."

Dad grins—sharing minor irritations forges a bond, we always found that.

"Let's sit there," he says. He keeps the Duvel glass for himself and gives me the other one.

The TV is still on in the living room, the sound muted. *Raging Bull*, he's seen that a few times, I'm sure. Dad often does this—watches the same films again, as though the reassurance of knowing how they end gives him a feeling of well-being in this restless, unpredictable life. He doesn't turn off the TV when we sink down into the cushions of the sofa. The bulky piece of furniture is a kind of vague brownish-green color, the color of food that's been in the fridge too long, of the curtains in retirement homes they can't afford to replace, of moss on rocks near water.

"Why don't you buy a new sofa?" I ask.

"Is there something wrong with this one?" He looks at the sofa in surprise, then at me, and then he focuses on the TV again. "Mom wasn't very happy about her youngest just getting on the train to go see you."

"No," I said. "Anne-Sophie was struggling with a few things. Sometimes I think there's something the matter with her."

"Marie will call you, I suspect." Dad gulps down his beer.

Few people can affect my mood like my father can. He doesn't have to say anything, do anything, it's the directionless grief in the way he silently stares, I think. Is this all because of my dead mother? That one desperate night? Sometimes I think he was already the damaged man he is now even before that. He was already eaten up by gloominess, sadness, and God knows what other kinds of old wounds. I remember arguments between him and my mother. I remember how often he hid away in his office, always blaming it on too much work. I remember the way he listened to Bach, his eyes closed, and the way that could make him smile, as though he was only happy in a world without us. I would like to ask him about this, all of it, but I don't. I leave him in his fortress, the place he's been locking his dead heart away all these years.

I sometimes think Dad loves me most of all. Alexander has a father-son battle to fight with him, which has been going on between the two of them for years. And Anne-Sophie came too late, a present to Marie, who was desperate for a child of her own, but not a child he truly wanted, I fear. Of course, I hope for my little sister that this isn't true. I also believe that he thinks I'm his most kindred spirit and if that's the case, I'd feel proud, which is nasty of me, I do realize it.

Dad was pressured by his own father into becoming a dentist. What if he'd been allowed to choose? He performed in amateur theater productions in his younger years. When he talks about that, his face glows in a way I rarely witness. Dad likes me to ask about it, about those stories from the past, as though there's more life in them than in the here and now. He remembers a collective laugh from the audience that lasted so long he began to count the minutes, that's what he says, and that afterward, a woman came to tell him she'd wet herself, it was that funny. Dad recounts this as a happy moment, not as something indecorous he is sharing without permission. Maybe he's jealous of my career, maybe that's why he doesn't openly support it, or maybe I'm just hoping that.

Dad's half glass of Duvel is finished, I pour some of what's left of mine into his.

"Give Anne-Sophie a bit more freedom. More time for her music. She needs that."

"Like I have any say in it." He doesn't look at me as he says this, just at the silent images on the TV. Life is always elsewhere for him.

15

Even though the street stinks of urine-soaked doorways, and there's a lot of noise outside day and night, their house is really nice. It's a narrow little place where every wall is crooked, with wooden beams on the ceiling, an old tiled floor, and at the back a little courtyard, shaded by the neighbor's tree. And what they've made of it, all those odds and ends they've effortlessly brought together to produce an interior with character. I don't come often, but I enjoy being here when I do.

"The playpen or the crib?" Alexander asks.

"The playpen. I can do less damage to that, I suspect."

"It's a calculated risk," my brother says, passing me the box with a grin. "If you break it, you'll have to buy us another, one we don't have to assemble ourselves."

"You know how clumsy I am, don't you? I only promised I'd try."

"Well, you're more capable than you think." Charlie laughs. She's radiant, even though her belly has gradually turned into a basketball. She clutches it as she sits down, as if the child might fall otherwise.

"Are they still bringing up my great failing as a son?"

"Oh no, it's not that bad," I lie. It's better to keep to yourself admissions that don't help the other person. "Is it bothering you?"

"Yes," Charlie replies, kissing his neck. "I try to make it clear to him that he has a right to his own life. He should set boundaries, he won't harm anyone by doing that, but I don't think he understands." Her words sound as caring as they are assertive.

"They're still our parents, though, eh?" I say.

"In my world," says Charlie, "that's a title you have to earn."

"What do you mean?"

"Do I really have to explain it?"

Yes, I think, but I don't dare say it. Charlie's older than us, and sometimes it feels as though she's started a whole new second life and has already learned everything from her first one.

She seems to pick up on my uncertainty. "Tell me, then. What do you think when you look back on your childhood?"

"Well, it wasn't always great, but Alexander and I came through it reasonably OK, didn't we?" I laugh. "I do worry about Anne-Sophie, but well, she's at a difficult age, she—"

"Don't start talking about Anne-Sophie. What did you struggle with?"

"Oh, well, I got through everything, so there's no point sitting in the corner crying about what—"

"What was difficult for you? Dare to say it for once, Mona. You can, you know, it's just us." Charlie rubs her belly and looks at me with gentle eyes.

"Our real mother, well, she could be very strict. She wasn't your typical maternal figure, let's say." I glance at Alexander. He was younger when she died, and he was also her favorite. He's staring at the instruction booklet. "And well, then she died and then we got Marie." Charlie says nothing and looks at me, encouraging me to go on. "Marie's a little unusual, of course, you have to watch your step with her, but in her own way, she was—"

Suddenly, Alexander bursts in, loudly and angrily: "Why do you always have to talk about Mom like that?"

He means Marie, I realize.

"But I was about to say—"

"No, no buts! You always do that. You sympathize with everybody, but not with her . . . I'm not going to say she's perfect, but have you ever stopped to think why she acts like she does? Imagine it: just a young girl, seduced by Dad, who put his best foot forward for a few months, until he'd ensnared her, and then he withdrew completely. Do you remember when they came back from their honeymoon? The look in Mommy's eyes, I can still see it, so much disappointment there. It wasn't until years later that she told me that, on the first evening of their trip, he was already paying more attention to the bartender than to her, not to mention the waitress and the gardener and the man who cleaned the swimming pool. But she came back, and she was saddled with two children she hadn't asked for and had to look after, practically on her own."

I find it hard to listen to Alexander saying all those things, possibly because they're true.

"Why do you think that Dad 'withdrew,' as you call it?"

"Because he's the biggest egomaniac I know."

"So, the way Marie was, the way she acted, didn't have anything to do with him being like that, according to you?"

"You're not going to claim you don't remember, are you? The way things were all those years? The way he cursed, how everyone always had to do as he pleased, how he undermined her self-confidence in a hundred different ways . . . Do I need to go on?"

"Do I need to make a list like that about Marie?"

"Oh," Alexander said, knocking a plank of the crib into place with his hand.

"Can't you break free from that argument about who's the most to blame?" Charlie says as she runs her hand through Alexander's hair. "You both always talk about other people, never about how it affected you, and that's the issue, isn't it?"

There's silence. The radio plays a song I don't know.

"This one like this, then?" I ask Alexander, showing him a plank and a pin. The question is mainly intended as an act of reconciliation.

"I think so, yes," Alexander replies tersely. He scrambles to his feet, paces around the room as though he's lost something he needs to find urgently, and then he stops, right next to me. "Do you think I'm too young to be a father?"

"Not to be the father of Charlie's child."

He stands there motionlessly, as though he can't move while he's figuring out what he makes of this. Then he says, "Thank you. I think."

"You make a beautiful couple."

Alphaville's "Forever Young" begins to play on the radio and Alexander turns up the volume. He lip-synchs theatrically, falls to his knees next to Charlie's chair during the chorus, and kisses her ear. She laughs and he laughs back.

Recently, I'd been thinking how nice it would be if you could photograph happiness so you could show it to others, or yourself, at moments when you're struggling to believe that it actually exists. This sight, here and now, of the two of them, would come close. I wonder whether I'll ever experience a moment like this. I can't actually imagine it, I realize. I have no idea why exactly.

16

He hasn't called, not my home number and not my work one. He hasn't called for three and a half days, after we'd gotten into a rhythm of seeing or speaking to each other most days. I had theater tickets, I considered staying home since perhaps he'd call, but that was going too far. I had a quick glass of wine after the play and then I practically ran home.

Now I'm inside, I go to my telephone and stare at it for minutes on end, as though it might talk and tell me that Louis has called three times already. I check my answering machine even though the light isn't flashing and so I know there aren't any messages. I check my mailbox, you never know, he might have put a note in it, like he did that one time, but it's empty.

Just as I'm brushing my teeth in the bathroom, the phone rings. I sprint to the living room, almost tripping over an extension cord from the table and the wall socket that is awkwardly in the way. It's Marie. I hang up with her as quickly as humanly possible without being rude so that I can keep the line free. I notice toothpaste on the receiver, but I leave it. Otherwise, I'll have to take the phone off the hook again, and then it would be just my luck that Louis would try to call at that exact moment. I go back to the bathroom. I look in the mirror, I look terrible today. I'm an egg timer ready to go off, ticking and quivering as I wait for release.

I don't know if other people get this too, but I can really brim over. All that love, gushing over the edge, and all I want is to be able to pour it on someone. Or is it something else, this feeling?

I've just sat down on the toilet when the phone rings again. I clumsily wipe my bottom and shamble to the living room with my panties halfway down my legs. As I pick up with my right hand, I try to pull my panties back up with my left.

"Hello, Mona speaking."

"Hey, floozy."

"Hey, it's you." If you ask people what's the best feeling you can have, most of them will say being in love or having an orgasm, but I know differently. It's relief: being afraid, waiting, and then the moment of salvation. "Been writing a lot?"

"No, not really."

So why hasn't he called me? I tell myself not to ask, he won't like it. "Why didn't you call?"

"I was busy."

"Oh, right." Who's so busy they don't have five minutes to call? And busy—what with? Making a list of reasons I'm not fit to be his girlfriend? Or rereading that Max Frisch book he must know by heart by now? Or seducing different, better women? I bite my lip. He's oblivious to this, luckily.

"I had lunch with Marcus to discuss the script he commissioned from me. That was nice."

"Yes. Marcus is looking forward to reading it." I try to sound enthusiastic.

"And I did my taxes because I was much too late submitting my return. And I prepared for that panel discussion about cultural policy and the media, and I revised my contribution to that literary magazine—well, it was mostly just a question of giving it a close read. To be honest, it turned out really well. I also went to my sister's yesterday for that thing I told you about. I really have been quite productive these past few days, I realize now."

Everyone has their own definition of productive. At the same time, how could I have forgotten that he had all that to do? He'd told me about it, after all.

"Is everything all right? You're quieter than usual." He says it with something warm in his voice, which moves me. He's worried about me, see, concerned, which people are only when they care about you. People can love you and still not call for three and a half days.

"I'm fine. I saw a bad play—that always makes me quiet." I laugh as I say it. Then I chatter away, telling him about my days and asking for more details about his.

When I sense he's getting ready to hang up, I ask, "Will we see each other tomorrow?" I try to make it sound nonchalant.

"Tomorrow's going to be tricky, but let's have dinner the day after. Why don't you pick a place and make a reservation?"

"Fine."

"Hey, pretty lady," he says as though he can hear the disappointment. "I'm looking forward to seeing you and your lovely tits and your fantastic body."

"Flatterer."

"If what I say is true, it's not flattery."

I can't help smiling.

"I dreamed about you last night. I've forgotten what it was about, but when I woke up I had to jerk off."

"Dirty old man."

"Yes, but your dirty old man."

"You're sweet."

"You're sweeter."

"That's true." I laugh loudly as I say it.

"Someone has to be." Then he kisses the receiver. I kiss mine back. When he's hung up, I breathe in and out deeply about ten times. I feel so much better.

"Stop always being so paranoid, you dope," I say out loud. Who knows, maybe I'll listen to myself then.

17

I asked what he wanted to drink. Did I have any good whiskey? he said. I always have to reply to that one in the negative. I remembered the three bottles of good red wine Louis had brought recently. He'd have to make do with that. He wasn't exactly enthusiastic.

Marcus has never been to my house and now he's here. I feel honored and a little unsettled. I wish I could fast-forward this evening, like a song that always makes you feel ridiculously emotional because it reminds you of that one time. And I also don't want to fast-forward, of course, because this is just the kind of moment you live for.

When I return with the glasses, Marcus says, "Please take a seat," in my house, from my armchair.

"Thank you," I reply, laughing. He doesn't join in.

Marcus is wearing a magnificent suit, bright blue with eye-catching buttons. It fits him like a glove, his shoes shine, his shoulder-length hair gleams, his stubble is perfectly trimmed, his eyes are full of dark promise. He's not fashion-model handsome, but he is unmistakably sexy and he knows it. He rolls a cigarette and asks me if I want one. I pass.

I continue to feel in awe of him. I can hardly tell him I was late because I couldn't find my keys or because a friend of mine is in the hospital with a burst appendix, or that I heard an amazing song on the radio and I wanted to know who it was by—it's as though Marcus is too far removed from this world to share in banalities. And now he's here and all that occurs to me are banalities. I feverishly rack my brains for something better, but then Marcus starts talking himself.

First he talks about the production in general, the premiere is slowly getting closer, then he talks about Jolene, how disappointed he is in her. Doesn't he know that we're friends? Is this a test? Doesn't he think she's a good actress? The rest of the world sure does. Should I defend her now? Will it make Marcus doubt my general professional opinion? If I say nothing, am I a coward? Should I tell Jolene what he said? Or would that be an act of betrayal toward them both? Marcus keeps a close eye on me, but he doesn't pause to take a breath, so even if I wanted to, I don't get the chance to contradict him or add anything. Then he wants to know what I think of Sasha's breasts. He asks casually, but seems to really expect an answer.

"I think they're good," I say, or stammer more like, after which I could sink through the floor for having put it like that: "I think they're good." To be honest, I don't really have much of an opinion about breasts. Yes, mine are too small to be counted in an ideal world, Sasha's are bigger, so they're good. I've never seen her naked. Marcus has, perhaps, or he'd like to. Why's he asking me this?

The CD has finished, I get up to select a new one. That's stressful too, I better not choose something he sees as representative of bourgeois narrow-mindedness or the bad taste that goes hand in hand with it. As I stand with my back to him, I hear him putting stuff down on the coffee table. It isn't until I sit back down that I see he's laid out two lines of coke on a little mirror there. I only recognize it from the movies. I gawk like I'm studying two lines of snot that Marcus has pulled out of his nose like a trophy. Then I smile at him, fearful that he can read my thoughts.

"Want some?"

I can't tell whether he thinks I should say yes or no. If I say no, that's more coke for him, but he probably has a large supply. If I say no, I'm the frump who doesn't dare, afraid of her liberated self. If I say yes, it might sound cool but then I'll have snorted coke, which I actually don't dare to do. He works away the first line with a rolled-up thousand-franc note, there it goes, whoosh, up his left nostril, and then the second one disappears up his right. *Phew,* I think, he's already decided my silence means no, dilemma over. I go back to the sofa and sink deep into the cushions as he rubs the last traces across his gums.

"Well?" he asks then, holding up a folded envelope of paper, ready to cut me a line if necessary.

"Maybe later," I say. The perfect cowardly answer, the dull compromise, unparalleled mediocrity: not now but later, maybe then. Yes, I am brave enough to try it, you know, only not now, later. I hate myself even more than usual. I try to keep smiling. He says nothing, which hopefully means he doesn't care either way.

Then he tells me about his mother and how she hates him and he hates her, and how they're stuck with each other for life. He thinks she has a mental illness, only he doesn't know which one. He sometimes wonders whether it might be hereditary. As he sits there giving examples of all the things she did to him, a long time ago, he snorts two more lines. He doesn't ask me if I want any. He must have realized what an appalling lily liver I am, either that or he's only concerned with himself at this stage of the evening, it's not clear. He wants to know whether I can fetch another bottle of red wine for him.

His story becomes more heated and more disjointed as the evening progresses. I probe deeper and try to sound reassuring. He discloses family tragedy after family tragedy in great detail and then suddenly starts to cry. His face is wet, his nose runs. I get him a paper towel, he doesn't use it. He lays his head in my lap and asks me to please comfort him. I wonder, awkward and disconcerted, what comforting might mean when there's a man who's practically a stranger lying on your sofa with his dirty shoes against the armrest and his head on your belly. I run my hand through his hair, which seems to calm him—he goes quiet. He lies there without moving, breathing deeply. I just hope he's not going to fall asleep like that.

I have no idea what the time is, but it's late, it must be. I'm too annoyed to feel really tired, but my whole body is claiming the opposite fairly stubbornly. I search for the right words to kindly suggest he go home, no hurry, I don't want to sound like someone's mom. Then he shoots to his feet, goes to my kitchen, holds his head under the tap, uses a dish towel to dry his hair, and says, "Come on, we're going out." He holds out his hand, like a father would to a three-year-old.

I stand there staring at him and can't find the words to elegantly tell him this is the last thing I want to do.

"I was actually thinking of going to bed." He looks at me angrily. Maybe anger is only inverted sadness, I can't help thinking, but I pluck up the courage to say, "I'm sure you know tons of people you could call who'd be happy to party into the early hours with you, don't you?"

"I want to party with you," he says, looking at me with those eyes of his.

There's something of a threat in them, or maybe I only think that. He goes back to my coffee table, sits down, and snorts another two lines.

"Yeee-haa!" he shouts, running his hands through his wet hair. Then he clutches me by the shoulders and says, "You understand me. Do you know how few people there are in this world like that? I really want you to come with me so I won't feel so alone."

I've never been to this nightclub, which isn't surprising because I don't like nightclubs. The music pounds through the speakers, the floor is tacky with beer, the young man next to me reeks of sweat and bergamot. Marcus stands in the middle of the dance floor jigging around wildly.

Ever since we got here, I've been looking for a good way to leave, hoping he'll forget about me if he gets swallowed up by the crowd.

Then he gestures to me theatrically, with large arm movements. The people around him are all looking at me now. I try to laugh it off, no thanks, not me, I can't dance, but then he comes to get me. He pulls me to his crotch, runs his hands under my blouse, and puts them on my bare back. He must think anything goes when you're dancing. And before I know it, I'm dancing along, because sometimes giving in means just getting it over and done with. I'm vaguely drunk, I'm sweating and feel dirty, and I'm worried he's going to be repulsed by me.

I return to the side of the dance floor, see Marcus disappear toward the bar and return with two whiskey Cokes. He lays his face on my shoulder in order to be able to shout into my ear: "Your dancing is horny." I can't imagine what was horny about my awkward teetering with my too-skinny long legs, but I smile. "You turn me on." I feel his sweat on my cheek. I want to cry my eyes out, the way he did earlier on my sofa. "You're horny too, aren't you?"

Think of a joke, now, immediately. A joke is the only thing that can save me. I think and think. "I'm very good at controlling myself." I laugh a lot harder than this dull joke is worth. "And now I really ought to be getting home." I take a sip of the whiskey Coke as a sign of my goodwill. I won't leave abruptly, I'll just calmly walk away. He can make up his own mind what he wants to do.

He takes the glass from my hands, puts it downs, pulls me to him by the hips, leans his torso back, and makes a few wild thrusts. I feel his member, which is hard. Then he pulls my body completely to his and puts his hand around the back my neck. Soon I'm really going to start feeling horny, despite everything.

"I'm going to take you. That what I think. I'm going to fuck you right here in this club, in the bathroom. Impale you on my big cock. What do you think of that?" He grins at me and does something obscene with his tongue.

I consider my options. I avert my gaze. And then, suddenly and unexpectedly, he pushes me away so harshly that I almost fall. He turns around and dances himself back to the center of the floor and the attention. I don't watch him go but look for my coat. As I'm putting it on, he appears next to me again. "And are you finally going to leave me in peace?" *What's he saying?* I nod, flabbergasted, turn around, and leave the building.

It's already getting light outside, cautiously, the streets are asleep, morning growls. I want to get a taxi, it's a long way to my house. We came here in Marcus's car. No taxis to be seen, of course, so I'll have to walk, then, in heels that are too high, and a short skirt, and tights that are too thin for this damp chill. I walk and walk and wonder what on earth happened tonight. I know it wasn't OK and yet, more than anything, I can't help feeling like the girl who wasn't good enough for her teacher.

On Monday afternoon there's a run-through on the set, not long to go before the premiere. When Marcus arrives, he gets everyone to give him a kiss as usual. When it's my turn, he just grins. He points at his lips, I give him his kiss. Then he continues with his day, which to him is just like any other.

18

"Dad, be careful!" Marie shouts as though he's on the other side of the garden, even though he's only a couple of feet from the patio, setting up a bird feeder. "He suddenly got it into his head that he wanted a bird feeder. He likes to watch the birds, he says. I said, well that's fine, go and get a feeder, then, but you'll have to hang up the seeds and stuff, I know nothing about it. He said fine. I don't know how he's going to find the time to keep going to that shop, but we'll see."

Dad has dug a hole between the rhododendrons and the magnolia. He tries to push the post deeper into the earth, panting, his butt in the air. Dad's not great at this kind of thing.

"Do you need any help?"

"No, I'll manage. But take a look, is it straight like this?"

"More toward Will and Brenda's," Marie cries. "Yes, that's it."

Dad shovels the sand back around the post and stamps the ground flat, sweating from the exertion.

"You should have seen his face when he came home with that bird thing. Nice, isn't it, to be able to get enthusiastic about nothing." Marie looks at him and holds her hand over her eyes like the captain of a ship. What's she thinking now that she's not saying? Marcus once said he'd pay good money to be able to read people's minds. I'd pay money to be certain I never ever had to know what was going on inside them, God knows what they're thinking about you.

"There we have it," Dad says. He rolls his sleeves back down and wipes the sweat from his forehead with the back of his hand. I wonder where the sweat goes to then. "It looks good there, doesn't it?" he says. "I bought various kinds of seeds on the advice of the people in the shop. They were friendly."

"Yes, the man with the mustache? He's Liliane's husband, she's very pleasant too. Worked in that chocolate shop on the square, you know the one."

Dad just looks at her, his mouth half-open, as though he's really searching inside his head.

"You know, the one with the dark hair and all that bright makeup. She sometimes wore skirts that were too short for someone with that kind of legs. But really very friendly."

"Oh yes," Dad says. I don't think he knows who she's talking about but reality doesn't hold him back, my dad.

Then Anne-Sophie arrives. She says hello very quietly and flicks me a brief smile. Dad sits down and takes a big slug of the pint of beer Marie has poured him.

"Oh, that does a man good." He puts his feet up on the other chair and looks at the garden. "We've got quite the life, eh, Mom?"

"How was school?"

Anne-Sophie shrugs and sits down on the patio steps, her back to us.

"There's still some fruit salad in the fridge if you want."

"I've got a stomachache," Anne-Sophie says.

"Oh darling, again?!"

Anne-Sophie says nothing. The first bird settles.

"Oh, that's a great tit, isn't it? With that yellow belly. Pretty, isn't it?" Dad almost chirps with pleasure.

"It's rather hard to get anything out of you." Marie studies her nails. "And she hasn't got any friends, our Anne-Sophie, that's to say, she never brings anyone home." She straightens her rings, the stones neatly in the middle. "Maybe she's ashamed of us. Are you ashamed of us?"

"Mom," Anne-Sophie says, extending the vowel.

"It's true, isn't it? I don't think it's normal, at your age."

The bird clings to the net containing the bird food. Dad stares at it, fascinated. He comments on everything he sees with a childish pleasure, like he's a sportscaster on the radio. "Listen, he's chirping a bit! And hop, more food there. He's pecking away like he's afraid we're going to take it back. Slow down, my boy, there's as much as you want." Marie looks at the bird, I look at my father, then at Anne-Sophie's curved back. "It's the simple things, eh, Mom?" Dad says.

Marie nods vaguely, her gaze elsewhere. "And that music school, that's just her and her instrument, you know. Do you think that's normal?" She looks at me and I try to act like I don't notice.

Suddenly, Anne-Sophie rises to her feet. "Sorry for existing," she roars before running off.

"Goes like that every time, she suddenly gets furious." Marie sighs and sniffs. "Was she crying?"

"Don't think so," Dad says, following the great tit as it flies off, disturbed by Anne-Sophie's tumult. "That's teenagers for you. They always act strangely."

19

In the apartment opposite, a woman is dancing in her underwear. I find a postcard from Tunisia from Uncle Artie in the mailbox. He writes that it's hot and nice there—the remaining three-quarters of the card is blank. An upstairs or downstairs neighbor, it's hard to make out which, drills a hole in the wall, and then another one. A woman bikes past outside, she's singing, as high as the birds are flying. Farther away, a car brakes so hard its tires screech rudely, but from the sound of it, no collision. I didn't go to rehearsal yesterday; dramaturges are allowed to do that. Since Sunday, I've been living in a country where people have given power to a racist party and I can't do anything about it. There are so many problems in the world that I don't even *try* to do anything about, I realize that too. Alexander told me he saw a Rothko painting at the museum where he works and discovered for the first time that some emotions are more than just being moved, that all art is beyond reason. Charlie says that everyone has a blind spot, a dash of ignorance about all the ways they sabotage themselves without realizing it. There's beer in my fridge, butter, yogurt that's three days past its sell-by date, four barely edible carrots, one egg in a six-egg carton, and an unopened packet of processed cheese. I have no plans to go to the supermarket. I'm supposed to see Louis tomorrow night, but he said he might have to do something else. In the book I'm reading, someone says it's important to keep dreaming. I've forgotten how many days have passed since I called Marie, maybe five, it could also be six, which is a lot. I wonder whose teeth Dad is working on at this moment. I wonder why he keeps doing the same thing without ever questioning it. A boy yells in the distance, like he's won something, or is cheering someone on, that's possible too. An old man sits on a wall, pressing his palms to the sides of his face as though he's afraid it might fall apart, as though he's trying to press out tears that just won't come, as though despondency is not a word but an image and then it would look like this. Sometimes the roof of my mouth itches, Anne-Sophie gets that too, but no one else, I don't think. I saw a beggar, the day before yesterday, not far from the theater, and I didn't give him anything. I wondered a little farther along if I should have given him money, but I didn't go back. I wish that, one day, all the anxiety would be gone, just suddenly, the way the hot water runs out when I shower for too long, but everywhere and for everyone. I read something by a philosopher who said that a person should try to be interesting instead of happy and I thought, *How funny he thinks there's a choice.* A girlfriend wanted to meet up, she said, "Pick a date, my schedule's open." Sometimes you recognize yourself in another's emptiness. Marcus asked us, as he sipped his coffee, how we wanted to live. *Gently,* I thought. It's not what I said to the group. Often, my thoughts grate and seem questionable.

I can't help thinking of Louis. The way he stood at my door yesterday. As though he'd been through a rainstorm in an open field for hours upon end, drenched, windblown, that was the way he stood there in front of my door. The man who always had all the words and now without out a single one. I asked nothing, took him in, let him stammer, took off his coat, and gave him my arms and a big glass of beer. I comforted him the way he most likes to be comforted, with naked skin and lots of closeness. I thought: *I like to be a sanctuary,* and I kissed him again. In bed we ate the unappetizing pizza I found in my freezer, licking the crumbs from each other's bodies. He said, "I'd really like to make you happy." I didn't worry about that conditional tense, because I was so happy to hear someone mean it. If I think about this, I get the urge to give him everything: kingdoms, the wonders of the world, infinity. I want to promise him that I'll pick him up when he falls to pieces and that I'll disappear with him, if that helps. I won't just go on believing my suspicions. I will continue to be amazed by him. I will fall on my knees for him, but then only as a joke. I will walk across seas with him, and across oceans, because I want to believe that we can do anything together. I will shelter him from tornadoes and teach him not to be afraid, if he lets me.

Today the average person will say 2,250 words to 7.4 other people, someone calculated. On this day, I will bring down that average.

20

He'd said six o'clock in the Post Horn. Louis likes old-fashioned pubs where scrawny-looking guys swill beer at the bar and talk about soccer and how things were better in the olden days. He had to give a reading of his work at a parish hall nearby, at three o'clock. He was taking the train there because his car was in the shop, and he hates trains, so I offered to drive over to spare him a return journey with two transfers.

Louis is always late, and it's only twenty past six, so I don't worry. I brought along a book, because one does learn. I finish my cup of coffee and order a pint. My hands smell like gasoline, I notice. I had to fill up the car on the way; I need to wash them before he comes.

At this point, it's a quarter to seven. Maybe I should call the venue where he had his reading. I look up the number, toss a couple of coins into the pay phone, hear it ring, and then an unknown man picks up. I explain why I'm calling, he says, "One minute please," and then Louis comes on the line.

"Oh yes, my little ray of sunshine. We were supposed to be meeting, right? What time again?" Louis hates pet names, he considers them ridiculous, and because I thought that was silly of him, romantic fool that I am, he now makes a sport of addressing me with a whole range of dubious sobriquets.

"Erm, at least half an hour ago. I'm at the Post Horn like you asked."

"Oh dear, I can't get away right now. Give me fifteen minutes, twenty max. All right?"

"Only because it's you."

I hang up and count on a minimum of thirty minutes—always good to be one step ahead of life's disappointments. I reread the same page for the third time, I can't concentrate, I don't know whether it's the book or me. I order a cup of tea, the man behind the bar breaks off his conversation with the drunk-looking customer with some reluctance. *An admirable profession, bartending,* I think. Always working late, always at the service of paying customers, not all of them likeable, always that confrontation with loneliness in all its forms. That's what I think, though maybe it says more about me.

At seven fifteen, there's still no sign of Louis. A Tim Hardin song plays on the radio, the theme song from that film *Looking for Eileen* that I saw as a student. The drunk man rocks slowly to the music, or so it seems, maybe he needs to pee. I still remember that the film was about love and that I cried a lot and there was that song, "How Can We Hang On to a Dream." The speaker crackles a bit. At the time I didn't believe that dreams could come true; I wonder whether I actually believe that now either.

After another half an hour, I call again, feeling embarrassed when I speak to the people from the organization, but I've slowly started to get anxious. After a bit of trouble, I get him on the line.

"Yes, it's very inspiring here, I can't help it. But please wait for me, I'm about to escape."

"Are you still giving your reading?"

"Yes, well, there's a kind of bar and stuff, we're having another glass of wine. I'll be with you soon, all right?" He hangs up without waiting for my reply.

When he still hasn't arrived at eight fifteen, I call Alexander. With the sordid smell of urine in my nose—the phone is right outside the bathroom—I explain what's going on, laughing about it as I always do. "Get in your car and drive home, for god's sake." Charlie has apparently been following the conversation and shouts into the receiver.

"I don't want to be the nagging girlfriend who never lets him have his fun."

"Mona, you drove out of your way just to pick him up and he left you sitting there for two hours? The arrogance of the guy. Go home, now." It's the sweetest order I've ever been given.

"Thank you," I say. I hang up and ask for the bill. "Where's the local parish hall?" The bartender explains how to get there.

I pay and leave the bar. It's so quiet in this godforsaken village, it makes me nervous. Why don't I just drive home? I know Charlie's right, but I also know how awful I'd feel. Now there's at least a chance of a happier end to the evening.

I go into the hall hesitantly, and there he is, right near the entrance, sitting at a little table with a bald man of around sixty with a poorly shaven jaw and a disproportionately large belly. They've both got a full glass of Duvel in front of them.

"Oh, there you are," I say as neutrally as possible.

"Oh yes," Louis replies, looking at me as though I'm a stranger.

"It's almost eight forty now, we were supposed to meet at six."

"I'm not happy about you chasing me all the way in here," he says, before looking at the man with the belly again. His speech is slurred, God knows how many drinks he's had.

"I, on the other hand, found it delightful that you left me waiting at the pub for so long."

He sniffs as he fiddles with his earlobe. All of his movements are slower than normal. "Wait outside, otherwise. I'll come in a minute."

I see the others looking at me with curiosity. What does *she* have to do with the great writer? Why is she making a scene?

"Hurry up," I say, going back outside.

I lean against a wall. Now that I'm standing here, waiting again, I get even angrier with myself than I already was, but I don't budge. I study the village square, recently revamped with benches and planters, cutesy in a way that irrationally pisses me off even more. Then he finally comes out, along with the rotund man, and stands in the doorway, two or three feet away from me, continuing to chat. I feel like throwing something, but I've nothing to throw. When the man finally leaves on his own initiative, Louis almost walks past me. He's drunk, I tell myself, blind drunk. I rush after him.

"Well, then."

"Yes, yes," he says. "It was a pleasure, thank you," he shouts after the man, who doesn't turn around. He hooks his arm through mine, which I find stuffy at the best of times but today is almost unbearable. Then he asks, "So, where's your car?"

"Near the Post Horn," I say, "where you were supposed to meet me three hours ago."

"Yes, you already said that." Then he begins to talk about his exceptionally interesting afternoon and the enthusiasm of his audience.

"Seven senior citizens with hearing problems who couldn't go to their lace-making class because the teacher was sick?" I ask.

"That's nice of you," he says.

"Nice of you to say sorry."

"You're right," he says suddenly, stopping. "Sorry." He goes to kiss me, aims for my lips, and misses. He can't focus his eyes, forgets what he was trying to do, and sets off again. A few feet farther, he trips over a paving stone that sticks up a half inch above the rest. A circus clown couldn't have done it any better. "Sorry," he says again, kissing my neck. "I really am." Then he grins like a child with a pie.

"You're a terrible person," I say with a sigh.

"I know." Then he kisses me again.

Once we're in the car, it isn't three minutes before he's asleep, his head against the window, his hand on my knee. I drive into the evening, past streetlamps, fields, and windmills. I glance at him and then back at the road. *I wish I was a storm*, I think, *or a squall, that would be good too, anything but this person, with this face and this heart and all this racing blood.* Louis coughs but doesn't wake up.

After we arrive, I shake him roughly back and forth.

"Oh, Rumpelstiltskin," he says, awake at once. "Oh, we've arrived. Wait, you haven't parked yet?"

"No, I'm just dropping you off so you can go right back to sleep. I'm going out for a drink. We're celebrating Joris's birthday at the bar tonight."

"Come inside with me."

I stare at him. He takes hold of both my hands.

"I love you. I want to talk to you."

"Hmm."

"Come on," he pleads. "I want to be with you, there's no one else in the world I'd rather be with." He kisses my hair. He seems completely sober again, amazing how fast he can recuperate. "Come on, babycakes, I love you." He looks at me longingly and I hesitate. "I want to discuss moving in together. I've been thinking about it for ages."

And then I say yes. He gets out and I go park the car. As I walk to his apartment, I tell myself that I must never ever tell anyone about tonight. No one. Ever. There's something peculiar about shame.

21

He sounded exhausted and happy at the same time. "Seven pounds, eight ounces. His name is Marvin." *Just the name for a child of Alexander and Charlie,* I thought.

"After Marvin Gaye?" I asked.

"After himself," he replied, and I could hear his smile through the telephone.

Louis has no interest in babies, but after more than seven months, I still haven't introduced him to my family, so a quick visit to see the mother and newborn child seems like a good idea. You don't have to stay very long and there's a lot of distraction and little opportunity for interrogation.

Marie and Dad haven't yet made up their minds about what they think of Louis in theory. They like the prestige his name suggests, one of the country's better-known writers is their daughter's boyfriend—it's nice to nonchalantly drop that into a conversation with friends. In that respect, they probably don't get what he sees in me, which is how I feel myself sometimes. They do worry about the age difference, they say, which is hypocritical given that they're nine years apart. And whether a man like that can guarantee a stable future, they wouldn't count on it.

Charlie looks stunning, even just one day after the birth. She sits bolt upright in the hospital bed in a stylish suit. Alexander is busy with glasses and a bottle of champagne, Anne-Sophie is wrapping up the last boxes of candied almonds, and Marie is standing over Marvin's cot, chattering away to Dad, who isn't listening.

Louis greets her with three kisses on her cheeks. "If it was genetically possible, I'd say that Mona had inherited her looks from you."

Marie lets out a strange cry of blushing glee, so one–zero to him. Dad shakes his hand and immediately begins to tell him something. He's trying to make an impression on Louis, I notice, which gives me a vague feeling of pleasure.

"Would you like to hold him, Auntie?" Charlie asks me.

I go over to the cot and look at this tiny human. He's already so much and not yet anything at all. I pick him up, lay him across my right arm, and sit down on the stool in the corner. He's beautiful and perfect, which can't be said of all newborns. He keeps his eyes closed, moves his little lips in a regular rhythm, the way fish do. I look at him and am reminded of Anne-Sophie. How often did I hold her like this?

Marie comes over. "See that, just like Alexander, the spitting image." I look at him and don't see anything of either parent. I don't understand how people have an immediate opinion about such things; when everything's so much smaller, it's hard to make comparisons. "Look, Dad," she continues. "Spitting image, right?"

Dad hands out glasses of champagne and looks at everyone except his grandchild. Marie doesn't insist, she's used to him not answering her.

"Oh, I was totally reminded of Charlie when I first saw him," Anne-Sophie says. "That nose and those eyes, look."

"And do you already have a good high chair?" Marie emphasizes each word.

"My mother saved my old one, a nice old chair. I've repainted it and it looks lovely." Charlie smiles sympathetically.

"Oh, but the ergonomic kind that grow with them, they're really handy, you know. And safe. Those old chairs, well—"

"He's not going to be doing much more than lying down, pooping, and eating for the time being," Charlie says. "We're not going to worry in advance about things we don't need yet."

There's a silence. Alexander and I look at each other.

"Pooping, pooping," Marie mutters, clearly not understanding how people can talk about babies using words that don't fit inside fluffy pink clouds.

I see Louis standing awkwardly in the corner, his gaze on Charlie. *He must find her much more interesting and braver and more beautiful than me,* I think.

"Here's to Marvin," Dad says, and everyone raises their glass.

"Too early in the day for me," Marie grumbles. "Gives me a headache." She puts her glass back down.

"It's Veuve Clicquot, Mom, especially for you."

"That's sweet." She still leaves the glass where it is. If the word *implacable* didn't exist, they'd invent it for her. "And how did the birth go, then? When I had Anne-Sophie, it was quite a trial. Thirty-four hours it took her to come out, didn't it, Dad? Do you remember?" It's as though she's reliving the pain of the delivery as she says this. "The nurses and the gynecologist, they said it too: 'Ma'am, how on earth you managed to persevere, we have no idea.' That's what they said, didn't they, Dad?" When Marie quotes other people, especially people with status, like doctors, she articulates exaggeratedly, each word perfectly formed, like a news anchor. "But how was *your* experience?"

Anne-Sophie joins in. "Did it hurt a lot? Did you tear?"

"Anne-Sophie!"

"A neat little cut." Charlie smiles. "And a good eight hours before I was sufficiently dilated, but then it actually went quite fast."

"And she didn't want an epidural, my tiger here." Alexander sounds more concerned than proud.

"Anything, absolutely anything, for that hunk there."

"Hulk?" Everything in Marie's face moves toward a frown.

"Hunk, handsome young fella," Alexander translates.

"Do you want to hold him?" I ask my little sister.

She shakes her head and looks upset.

"And you, sir?"

"Just call him Louis, Mom."

"Do you want one yourself?"

"Oh, I want everything." Louis grins and I give him a stern look. He adds, "Mona's still young."

Sidestepped that one perfectly, I think.

"Yes, *she* is, yes." Marie takes a breath as though she's about to say more.

"Would you like to take Marvin?" I ask. All's fair in love and war.

"Of course. Come to your nana, little Marv, pet. Yes, I'm your nana."

"We're not going to shorten his name, that's partly why we chose it, actually. It's short enough already," Charlie says.

"Oh right," Marie says.

Alexander sits down on Charlie's bed and squeezes her hand.

A nurse comes in, she has a forced smile like they all do on this wing. There's a purple rabbit pinned to her uniform, a furry broach, as though newborn babies might be able to see it. "I've come to take care of Mom. Will you all wait outside?"

Anne-Sophie goes to buy a soda from the shop downstairs. We stand in a row, leaning against the wall. There's nothing more depressing than depressing corridors they've tried to cheer up. Bilious green walls, yellowing ceilings with random cracks, smooth gray floors, and then cartoon pictures of storks and teddy bears, photos of babies dressed as sunflowers in planters, and a whole bunch of flags right at the back.

"It's a shame about the card," Marie says. Next to each door hangs the birth announcement card on a special framed little corkboard. There's one next to Charlie's room too. "I mean all that black, for a birth?"

"I think it's nice."

"Yes, there you go, to each his own, eh? Young people, it's modern, I gather."

Dad stares through the window. Louis looks at me. I suspect his eyes are asking me how much longer, but I pretend not to notice.

"The name will take a bit of getting used to too." Marie sighs theatrically, as though all the plagues of Egypt have been sent to try her.

I smile somewhat vaguely in her direction, it seems like the best approach.

"He's a beautiful-looking baby, though."

"Yes, he really is."

"Let's hope the two of them manage to bring it up decently. Raising children is never simple. And in their case . . . But I'm sure it'll be fine."

"What do you mean?" Louis almost seems genuinely interested.

"Alexander's a lovely guy, but he's so young, you know. And she's, well . . ."

"She's?"

"Well, I don't want to say anything unkind, of course, but she's not a very maternal type. What do you think?"

"What does that mean to you, a 'maternal type'?"

"Caring, warm, gentle character. Those things."

"Like you?" Louis keeps his tone utterly neutral.

For a moment, Marie wavers. She's not sure whether Louis means it or if he's making fun of her. But then she recovers since, in her life, attack has always been the best form of defense. "Exactly. Like me and most women who become mothers. Our Mona, for example, she's not a mother yet, but she's got it in her. She pays attention to others, does her best to keep the mood cheerful all the time, is eager to help, sensitive. She's an open book—to me, at least."

"An open book?"

"Yes. I know everything about our Mona. She tells me everything, we're very close, her and me." Marie looks at me, and I smile back automatically, like a dog fetching a stick. "But Charlie, we don't quite have her figured out yet."

"Inasmuch as I've understood from Mona, Alexander has chosen to follow his heart. In terms of his wife, his life, a job that makes him happy. If Charlie was able to inspire him to do that, that seems like a good sign, don't you agree?"

"Oh, so you think it's good, do you, that Alexander's no longer going to be a doctor? They do save lives, you know."

"I only write books, what do I know?" Louis is playing a game, he's good at that.

"I don't mean—naturally, what you do is also—"

Louis interrupts her with a broad grin. "I just mean that they seem genuinely happy to me. That's important too."

"If everything was what it seemed, then life might be truly pleasant," Marie says. She lets drop a contemplative pause, as though watching a procession of her own sufferings march past inside her head.

Dad takes advantage of the silence to ask Louis about the book he's working on at the moment, my father's contribution to world peace in this hallway.

"Well, that nurse is taking her time, isn't she? I'll just pop to—" Marie turns around and walks toward the bathroom without finishing her sentence.

I look at Louis and move closer to him as he explains the premise of his novel to my father. Then I look at Dad, who is listening attentively. *Maybe these two will get along,* I think and smile. Sometimes things just happen naturally, for all the right reasons.

PART THREE

2002

1

The sun is high in the sky. The steering wheel is hot, almost too hot to hold. It's still only March, but it feels like midsummer. I start the car, then turn on the AC and the radio. U2 sings that it's a beautiful day. I turn the dial to another station, where Mozart is playing, music like sweetly impending doom. I keep turning the dial, I don't like anything. The problem's me, so I turn it off.

The road is long and monotonous. The sky is an unreal blue, the fields are vast and empty; here and there, the odd cow slaps at flies with its tail. Only a couple of windmills interrupt the flat landscape. They remind me of the windmills of my childhood—at the seaside, in bright, bubble-gum colors, turning on top of my sandcastle. One time, my father attached two to the handlebars of my bike. The faster I rode, the faster they turned. He stuck one on his own bike for Alexander, whose seat was attached to the crossbar. He whooped with joy as we raced into the wind. I can still remember it.

At last I spot the exit. The hospital is on the edge of the city. The large modern wing contrasts starkly with the old part, which is reminiscent of municipal buildings from the 1960s. I can't find the parking lot, as though the world wants to help me delay the inevitable. After driving around three times, I pull up onto the grass, where you certainly aren't allowed to park. "I'm in a hurry," I say out loud, which is a total lie.

I need to find room 316. I go up to the lady at the info desk and ask her where it is. She sighs like she has better things to do than give people information, there at her information desk. I'm supposed to follow the orange line on the floor and then take the elevator to the third floor.

I press the button. Waiting always takes ages, even when it's just for a moment. When the door opens with a ping, a whole herd of us enters together. Smells mingle: peppery aftershave and sweat and mint chewing gum and new sneakers. People stand there in awkward silence as they try not to look at each other. Two stare at the screen showing which floor you're at. A man with gloomy eyes fiddles with a bouquet of flowers he's holding. A lady with extravagant hair and dark-purple lips stares at the floor, or at her shoes, her belly, it's hard to tell. Only a little boy looks at me, slightly angrily. I wonder whether it's deliberate or not. When he gets out with his father on the second floor, he sticks his tongue out. His father wraps his arm around the little guy, to be kind perhaps, or to make sure he moves along obediently.

I enter the third-floor hallway. Everything smells oppressive. There's a woman in a wheelchair waiting for someone or something. Given the expression on her face, she's been waiting for some time. I hope they haven't forgotten her. She's got red scabrous patches on her forehead along her hairline, and she smacks her elderly lips even though there's nothing to chew on. Farther along, there's a cart bearing a stock of gigantic diapers, latex gloves, and sharp needles in neat packages. Hanging from the end of it: a garbage bag that reeks of shit. *Sometimes the crudest words are the right ones,* I find myself thinking. I hurry past.

I've never understood why they leave the doors of hospital rooms wide open, as though the woman with the drooping succulent on the windowsill might want strangers to see her varicose-vein-riddled legs on top of the covers, as though that man there wants an audience as he lies openmouthed, coughing and groaning and staring at nothing in particular.

Room 316 is right at the end of the hallway. "Vacant," a sign says, but the door is shut. Who knows what's going on behind it? I press my ear to the door, hear nothing, knock three times, and then open it anyway. I see my dad lying there asleep. He doesn't look peaceful, his face somewhere between white and gray, cheeks sunken, breathing restless, his skinny legs kicked free of the sheets, and his feet—soles covered in callouses, long, dark-yellow toenails—jerking occasionally, like someone is tickling them with a feather. I don't want to sit next to him like that.

I go back into the hallway and pick a chair to wait in. A nurse marches up. She looks well into her forties, but her hair is in two pigtails, like she'd rather be in a kiddie pop band than work here, which I don't blame her for, really. She hurries into the room closest to my chair without knocking. As though being old and ill isn't enough, she shouts at the patient, loudly enough to inform everyone in the hallway, "I've come about the toilet. Can you sit on the potty yourself? Yes? Then I'll get you out of bed. But what's that, my boy? You're wearing a diaper? How did that—? Oh, you don't know. I'll just pop out and ask."

I try not to look at the man sitting on his bed waiting.

"Hey, Josefien, the patient in 312, well, he says he can go to the toilet on his own, so why's he wearing a diaper?" she screams at a colleague working nearby.

"What?" the colleague roars back.

"Why the diaper? Is 312 lying or can he really go to the toilet on his own?"

"Yes, he can."

"Oh, so it's a mistake? All right!" She thunders in again. "It was a little mistake, that diaper, I'll just take it off, that'll be better. And you go to the toilet, eh? Here, lean on my arm."

I try not to listen, but it's difficult when humanity is so loud. I think about my own death, pray for something with more dignity: flattened by a TV that's been thrown out of a window on a sunny Monday in May. Or choking on a shortbread cookie at home in an armchair after having read a mediocre page of a novel.

I go see whether Dad's still sleeping. He seems to be starting to snore a bit. He looks like he needs sleep. Waking him up isn't an option, which I feel relieved about, before immediately feeling annoyed with myself.

They said we won't know until next week. They steered us out of the room, a geriatrics specialist and a different kind of specialist who didn't introduce himself. The geriatrics doctor is called Cleavage, that's what he said, "Good afternoon, I'm Doctor Cleavage." He didn't find it funny himself. He didn't tell us his first name, it must have seemed irrelevant.

Doctor Cleavage is a colorless man, his remaining hair draped across his head, small eyes, tight mouth. His complexion is gray, as though he's trying to match the general atmosphere of the hospital.

It was the other doctor who told us, with a slight lisp, not to get ahead of ourselves. It was important to remain optimistic for the patient's morale. I found that last bit ominous sounding. Cleavage thought it important to add, "But yes, the patient is clearly in a weakened state, we shouldn't expect miracles." Then he pulled his mouth into a smile, or what was meant to pass as one, as though he'd suddenly become aware of the fact that he was talking about my father.

"He says he's got back pain too. Can you do anything about that?"

"People often don't know exactly where pain is coming from. What could be perceived as back pain could have all kinds of causes. There, too, we'll have to exercise patience until we have all the results."

"But can't you give him more pain relief or something?"

"Naturally, we'll try to keep the patient as comfortable as possible."

And without saying goodbye, they were gone.

Dad is lying there and I don't feel like seeing the people coming to visit after me, not now, not Marie, so I take the stairs and escape through the side door. I bang my knee as I get into the car, I'm always clumsy. It really hurts. I sit down, rub my knee, and look at the mother who walks past carrying her small daughter while they have a serious conversation about the colors of the cars. I watch them go. Sometimes I'm the strongest chick in the whole world, sometimes I'm chicken liver.

2

"These are occupied," the lady says quickly, her expression suggesting she's under siege by enemy troops. With the aid of a large umbrella, a big shopping bag, and two children's sweatshirts, she has managed to appropriate a total of seven chairs.

"I just wanted to sit on this one. My brother and his wife are sitting there." I point to Alexander and Charlie, and then to the only chair that doesn't have any of her belongings on it. The woman continues to look at me mistrustfully. "I've come to watch my godchild," I add.

"Oh," she replies, somewhat apologetically.

I sit down. "Sorry, Marcus was late for the meeting, so I couldn't get here any earlier."

"Don't worry, they haven't even started," Charlie says.

"So, is Marvin nervous?"

"Yes, they're performing a dance the teacher taught them, and she used to do jazz dance or something. Anyway, she's set the bar pretty high. Marvin has been struggling with it." Charlie smiles. She doesn't look like the average mother walking around here. Since her clothing line has become an international success, Alexander has mainly been the one taking care of Marvin, which seems to work fine for him.

The show is supposed to begin in a couple of minutes. Children rush to and fro, talking away; parents and grandparents are everywhere, looking for seats; a man with a curly mustache is filming the audience with a video camera, which I find a bit odd.

"So, are you optimistic about his chances?" Charlie asks.

"Dad's? I'm trying to be. I think I failed him, though."

Alexander leans forward to hear me better. "What do you mean?"

"We did mention it to each other. Charlie, when was that? At that dinner for my thirty-fifth, we noticed that Dad had lost a lot of weight."

Charlie nods. "He said he wanted to lose the belly and that he was much more active now that he'd retired. And he was eating fewer sweets. It all sounded reasonable. He went for lots of walks with that bird guide he bought, which he'd wanted for ages. And he cleared out the garage and the attic and that old shed at the other end of the garden. He was constantly doing stuff."

"Yes, but I should have asked more questions. I should have known you have to with Dad. The doctors said we caught it quite late."

"Do you know what Mom is saying now?" Alexander's expression is serious. "That he was doing all those odd jobs so slowly because he couldn't go any faster, and that he didn't really go out walking, he just drove somewhere and went to sleep on a bench." My brother recounts this dryly, factually. "He was also eating more than he used to, trying to compensate for the weight loss."

"Why is Marie only telling us now?"

"I was talking to her about it the day before yesterday, and she told me she'd known for some time that something was wrong."

"Why didn't she ever say anything to us, then?"

"Dad didn't want her to, apparently. I always thought it was weird that he gave his dental practice to that young guy. He's only sixty-one, after all, and he's done nothing but work his entire life."

"That was exactly why it made sense to me. He made it sound convincing, anyway."

"Yes, he was always good at making things sound convincing. That was his specialty, wasn't it?" Alexander seems somewhere between irritated and pitying as he says this. "Mom said he simply couldn't keep up the pace."

"When did he stop working?"

"A good year ago?" Charlie glances at my brother. Alexander nods. "Typical of your dad, really, that he kept going, despite those warning signs. He's always been scared of illness and doctors, like a lot of people in the medical profession, in fact." Charlie points at the stage. "Look, Marvin is standing in the wings. Can you see him?"

We wave, but he's already gone. I think about Dad, about how quiet he was at that party. And the way he hinted about it being bedtime at ten thirty and the way I lovingly laughed it off, assuming that he was just teasing me.

"He did look exhausted at that dinner for my birthday."

"What did you say?" Alexander asks, his gaze fixed on the stage as though he still has a chance of spotting Marvin, I suspect.

"Nothing. Never mind." The family of the woman with the besieged chairs turns up. The man who sits next to me smells of gym locker rooms. I turn a little more toward Charlie. "I don't get why Marie didn't encourage him to go to the doctor sooner."

"Marie encourage Vincent?" Charlie adds a little laugh.

"Mom doesn't have any influence over him, Mona. You know that."

"I don't understand how I missed it, I'm usually so—"

Then music blares from the speakers, a Christina Aguilera song, I think. Around twenty children walk onto the stage, one at a time. Then suddenly they all jump into the same pose. Marvin is in the front row, his face a picture of concentration. They adopt a different pose and then move from one foot to the other as they do something rhythmic with their arms. You can hardly call it Art with a capital *A*, yet I feel myself getting goose bumps. I wave at Marvin while his act is still going on, a silly, poorly timed gesture, pride expressed clumsily.

I wonder whether Dad ever attended one of our school shows. I'm not sure, but I don't think so. I can't remember him ever having done that.

3

The gastroenterologist, a new doctor, is speaking. He talks in a muted way, as though words are less cutting when spoken more quietly. He has adopted his most neutral expression. It wouldn't surprise me if he'd practiced it in front of the mirror in his student days. Not a trace of a frown, corners of his mouth turned neither up nor down, eyes neutral—it's an art in itself. Not that I expect doctors to writhe around on the floor in misery at each depressing diagnosis, but something that could be taken for sympathy, that would be nice. As his colleague speaks, Cleavage looks down, sniffs, coughs, clicks his ballpoint pen in and out four times, runs his hand through his thin hair, and straightens his shoulders as though he's suffering from back pain.

Marie perceives these men differently than I do. She's the daughter of a cardiologist, she knows her way in this world—that's what she wants to project. She uses slightly less common medical terms that aren't necessarily useful in the context: *carcinoma* for tumor, *sedative* for tranquilizer, *rubella* for measles. She names this childhood illness as part of the list of complaints she's had to bear, to show that she's experienced in suffering pain and afflictions. She comes up with questions that aren't aimed to solicit replies but to show off what she knows. She goes out of her way to compliment the doctors on their skills and knowledge, which, if you ask me, they haven't demonstrated yet. Alexander attempts to use each of Marie's pauses for breath to try to find out what exactly is going on.

And I look on from a chair I've pulled up. I don't like it that Dad isn't here himself—Marie didn't want him to be. It amazes me that the doctors agreed to it, but there are many things here that amaze me. I don't feel like listening, a few words tell us enough: the operation will be palliative. That the tumor in his bowels is probably quite substantial. There's a genuine chance that it's stuck to other organs. They won't be able to tell until they open him up. In the worst-case scenario, he'll need a stoma, temporarily at least. Each sentence rules out certainties. Right at the very end, the gastroenterologist adds that, if all goes well, he'll still have some time. They don't want to put a number on it, of course, but somewhere between two and five years is imaginable if all goes well.

Suddenly, Cleavage wakes up from his little coma. "If all goes well," he repeats for the third time.

If you know you've got five years to live at the most, are you dying? Can you say goodbye to someone for five years?

The doctors shake our hands, wish us the obligatory good luck, and send us back out into the hallway. And we stand there, the three of us, outside of time for a moment. No one speaks, no one looks at anybody, no one takes the initiative. You need space for a realization to sink in.

When Cleavage comes out of the consultation room, we're all still there. Marie looks like she's been caught out. "Come on," she says, hurrying toward the cafeteria, as she tells us all the things you can get there, like we wouldn't know.

"This is a sorry excuse for pie." Marie sighs as she eats her apricot pie.

She rarely eats sweets in public, but the large slice of apricot pie—
The portions are comfort-sized in the hospital, I couldn't help but think when I saw the way they cumbersomely filled the plates—is disappearing

fast. Alexander sips his coffee and looks at me as though it's my turn to speak. I avert my gaze.

The cafeteria is located in the hospital's new wing. They tried to make it look cheerful: a wall painted dusky pink next to a pale-green one, everything else in fresh whites, laminate tables and dark-gray chairs with aluminum legs, shiny tiled floors and wacky light fixtures in the same creamy white as the ceiling.

Marie and Alexander are in agreement and they want me to agree with them too. That's how we do things in this family, we agree because we love each other. And that love must be constantly reaffirmed by, for example, uniting in support of a single, clear-cut vision of things. Often Marie's vision, because we don't want her to be unhappy. Her happiness has always been very important, probably because her unhappiness is so toxic. A woman who has done so much for you, when you're not even her own child. I look at her, I can see that she's suffering, the face hovering above the pie is not open to misinterpretation. But this request of theirs is difficult for me.

"Dad is an intelligent adult, doesn't he have the right to know what's wrong with him?"

Marie's eyes grow cold.

Alexander takes off his watch and lays it beside him on the table, like he wants to measure how long it will take me to change my mind. "Mona, you know that Dad can't handle it. He was so afraid of having cancer that he ignored the pain all that time. The idea that there's no cure would destroy him. It would be a form of egotism for us to burden him with it. What's more, it's better for him medically to remain optimistic, isn't it? It would increase the chances of him getting a few more good years. That's how you should look at it."

That's how I should look at it. Alexander means it kindly, I get that. Marie is scraping the last bits of pie from her plate with her fork, not looking at me. I want to make a plea for all that is authentic and honest, for people to be taken seriously even if they are afraid, for looking hard reality in the face even when that's not easy. But experienced as I am at weaseling, I just say, "I think Charlie would agree with me."

"Charlie's not family," Marie says. Alexander looks at her. "Well, not really. You know what I mean."

I finally surrender. As we get up, Alexander grabs hold of me. He never does that. And then Marie turns it into a group hug. I feel her bony body against mine; she smells of hair that hasn't been washed for a long time and coconut lip balm.

"I don't know what I'd do without my children. I love you. You know that, don't you?"

"Of course we do, Mommy," Alexander says.

"We have to be there for each other at times like these. We'll help each other through it."

Marie goes in to Dad; I wait outside the building with Alexander. He smokes a cigarette nervously and looks at me like he wants me to ask him something.

"Are you all right, bro?"

"I'm so glad I never became a doctor." He throws his burning stub onto the asphalt and lets it smolder there. I stamp it out and smile at him, but he doesn't notice. My brother's face hardens. So cold, now of all times. I should probe further, there's something behind it, guaranteed.

"Isn't it high time we got in touch with Anne-Sophie?" Asking a new question is easier than providing an answer sometimes.

"We should suggest that to Mom and Dad, shouldn't we? Let's wait until after the operation, then we'll know exactly what we're dealing with, right?"

4

"Oh, that was it. You asked if I'd go to see your dad with you tomorrow, but it's not going to work, because I've just reached a crucial chapter and I can't stop now." Louis says this casually as he breaks a sugar lump in two and puts half in his coffee.

"How sweet of you."

"I don't need your sarcasm."

"My last bit of sarcasm dates from before the Punic Wars. I'm just fed up with having to nag you about this kind of thing."

"What kind of thing?"

"Um, well, your egocentrism, your lack of empathy, your way of dealing with people: how they're hurled into the deep freeze whenever you're busy with something and not allowed out again until it's convenient for you. Take your pick."

"I'll just pretend I didn't hear that."

"Whatever you want."

"You don't understand. Only people who write can understand."

"Fine. I already said I didn't feel like nagging." I turn back to my book.

"Listen, honey pop, you know I sympathize with what you're going through, but you've known me long enough now to know how important it is for me not to stop when I've reached a crucial section."

"And last week it was important you took part in that library event, and two days ago you absolutely had to attend that launch as though literature's fate would be sealed without you."

"You knew I was a writer when you got involved with me."

"And last weekend, Arlette needed you desperately, and last Thursday you were coming down with something there was no trace of the next day, I have to say."

"I filled a whole hankie with snot. What if your dad had caught something on top of it all?"

"Even if you didn't have a real excuse, you'd invent something so you didn't have to come."

"As if your dad's so eager to see me."

"I absolutely don't expect you to come with me every time, but now and again, I'd really appreciate it."

"You know all this reminds me of those terrible things I went through: my brother dying, my godmother passing away three years ago. I find it really hard to cope with."

"And where was I when your godmother was on her deathbed?"

"Yes, you came with me a lot and I'm grateful for that. You're stronger than me."

"That's easy enough to say. It wasn't easy for me, but I did it for you."

"As if I haven't done an unbelievable amount for you already."

"Name three things. They don't even have to be recent."

"Just two weeks ago: I took you to that Michelin-starred restaurant you'd wanted to go to for ages."

"That was a late birthday present, which was a tiny bit fancy because you didn't give me anything at all the year before. Plus, you wanted an excuse to go anyway."

"OK, fine. But when you were worried about keeping your father's long-term prognosis from him, I discussed it with you at length."

"You didn't discuss it with me. You launched into a monologue about the way you saw it, mainly making me feel like I shouldn't stick up for myself. It's been bothering me ever since."

"Come on, that was a good conversation."

"You thought so. But let's take that as one example. Now two more."

". . ."

"That's what I mean."

"You're pressuring me so much I can't think. But you know how much I love you."

"Nothing is easier than saying that, eh?"

"No one will ever love you more than I do, and you know it. You're playing a perverse game, tripping me up on my words."

"I asked a simple question and you don't have an answer."

"Mrs. Manipulator at work."

"Like manipulation's not your greatest talent."

"Here we go again. I'm good with words, yes. If I'm not mistaken, that's one of the things you fell for about me."

"That's true."

"It's sweet of you to say so. Really, you're a good girl, with a good heart, I know that."

"You're the one who slipped up, you know."

"You're stopping me from doing my work, making a scene just because I have to write, and *I'm* the one who slipped up? Well, everything's a matter of perception."

"I said right away that I didn't want to get into a discussion, and I always—and I mean always—go along with your wishes when it comes down to it."

"Exactly—when it comes down to it. But not without nagging my ears off for hours first."

"I bite my tongue all the time, Louis. It's just—I often feel let down, and now, with this whole horrible business—"

"If life with me is so shitty, then you should look for someone else. A nice boring man with a dull job who sits down next to you on the sofa every evening to have a nice chat about the trivialities of the day and the concerns of your heart."

"Don't be ridiculous. But you're the other extreme. And now, now that my father's ill, I'm finding it harder than usual. Is that allowed? I'm only human, you know."

"Mona's only human—I've never heard that before, that little line."

"Maybe I have reason to say it now and again."

"If I make you so unhappy, I'll leave you. Then you'll be free and everything will be better."

"Ach."

"No, not ach. I will say this now: I'm sick and tired of it, this crap about me being an egotist. Well, wake up—we live in individualistic times, everyone's looking out for number one. You too; you want to claim me for yourself, while I don't have any space for that in my head. This is not what I expect from a relationship. I expect support and understanding and—"

"And I'm not giving you that?"

"Sometimes, yes, but not all the time. You have no idea what it does to me, constantly having to hear that I'm failing in my duties. I don't know if I can keep dealing with it. I sometimes think seriously about—"

My stomach clenches. "Sorry, I didn't want to hurt you. I just feel—I . . ." I fall silent.

"Yes? What?" He pronounces the words as though he's carving them into my skin.

"I miss you. I love you. I don't want to be angry with you. It makes me unhappy too."

"You silly goose. Don't be unhappy. I'm here. You don't have to miss me."

I sit down next to him and he hugs me. At that instant, all thoughts stop. I'm just happy the harmony has returned, that these arms are around my body. People being angry with me, I really can't handle that.

5

This one is a little older, her hair black with a blueish tinge; she probably dyes it herself with one of those shampoos from the supermarket. She has green eyes, big teeth, a jolly double chin, and remarkably thin lips. She's wearing orthopedic sandals, definitely one of the top three footwear choices of the women who work here. When she comes in, she draws her mouth into a broad smile and says good afternoon so cheerily it's like she's on Prozac and hasn't gotten the dosage right yet.

"We're going to have a bite to eat, eh?" she cackles. She dashes around the room, presses the knobs on my father's bed to turn it into a kind of armchair in which he sits bolt upright. She pushes pillows behind his back and his neck. "There we go, everything's just fine." She ties a bib onto him, pulls the side table with wheels over to the bed, and puts the tray on it. "So, my boy, the pill in this cup is for after the meal. Don't forget it, all right? Eat well now. Bon appétit!" And she blasts out of the room in the same way she came in.

Dad is left looking at the plate of food in bewilderment. An intelligent, youthful man in his sixties being treated like an unruly toddler. I can hardly bear it.

"Shall I?"

He nods. I take off the bib, make the bed less upright, and take out one of the pillows from behind his neck. The plate contains a pile of floury potatoes, an unidentifiable slab of gray meat, and some broccoli. There's a fruit yogurt cup on its own little plate that serves no other function; a dessert here belongs on a plate even if it's in a plastic cup. They don't want any chaos to spoil their orderliness. Dad makes no attempt to pick up his knife and fork.

"Want me to go and see if I can find you something more appetizing?"

"Don't go to any trouble. I'm not hungry anyway."

I don't want to be the girl who forces the patient like the nurses do, nor the school teacher who admonishes him to eat something to be strong for the operation. The hell he's in is palpable to me now.

"They'll be on my case if I don't eat. Would you take a few bites to make it look like I did?"

In the last phase of this life, we have to clean our plates again. I wrestle down some broccoli and a couple of potato chunks. I cut the meat and hide it under the rest so that it looks like some has been eaten.

"There we go. Want your bed back down again?"

"Yes, please."

It's only when he's lying down again that Dad seems to relax a bit. A few people rush past in the hallway, heavy shoes pounding and sneakers squeaking as though a life is in jeopardy not far away. Probably just my imagination, I reassure myself. My imagination is always worse than any kind of reality; do I get that from my father? How many worries does he have? Does he believe the story Marie and Alexander sold him? We both look outside even though there's not much to see from here. The silence hangs heavily between us like mist between ancient mountains.

And then all of a sudden, out of the blue, he says, "Mona, will you hold my hand?"

Dad lays it ready, that hand, on the white sheet, palm upward. It must have happened before, my hand in his, but it's been so long I find it hard to picture, too infant-sized to be a lasting memory. Aside from Marie, who is prone to getting all gushy at dramatic moments, we don't do hugs or other variations of the affection theme in our family, as though it's a luxury we simply can't allow ourselves. And now this hand. I look at it. Of course I have to take it, but something is stopping me. What kind of a daughter am I? I breathe in and take the hand, his right one, in my left. I sit there feeling like a monkey wearing a wig, but I persevere. I look at the door; it probably won't be long before Marie arrives. She has written herself into the visiting schedule in abundance. She gets restless, she says, when she doesn't see him. It must be hard, of course, two people who've lived together for twenty-five years, day in, day out, and then you suddenly find yourself alone in a big house. If Marie gets the chance, she even hangs around when we're visiting. Today she had to be at home for the new bed that was being delivered. They'd ordered it months ago and already paid for it; it would last at least twenty years, Marie had said when she picked it out. I look at my hand in his hand and hope she doesn't come in now. If she sees this—I push away the thought.

"I'm going to live to be eighty-six," he almost squeaks. His voice is so thin suddenly. "That seems like a good age to me."

Everything inside me is breaking. I say nothing because crying never seemed more inappropriate than now in this bell jar of aging, ailing, and ministering.

Dad turns his head toward me, he wants an answer, apparently.

"That's a good old age."

He smiles. "All these tests. The operation in two days. I'm not exactly looking forward to it."

"I get that."

"I'd like to ask whether—"

Then the door swings open, the black-haired nurse makes a beeline for the bed, and I let go of his hand.

"Oh, but what did I say? That pill. You seem to have forgotten it. You were supposed to take it with your meal, I told you that." She pushes another button and the bed zooms up again. She gives him a glass of water and the pill. "Down the hatch." My father places the dull white pill on his tongue and swallows it with a small gulp. "And we haven't eaten much, have we? You have to learn to be a big boy, otherwise you'll never get stronger." "A big boy." She really said that. It's the kind of thing you say to a kid who just pooped in his potty rather than in his pants, or learned a poem by heart, a little boy who's eaten all of his brussels sprouts. "Maybe lie on your side now for a change?" She's learned not to wait for an answer, so with skilled movements, my father is laid on his side, a row of pillows behind his back. "That's better now, my boy, isn't it?" She's already heading for the door. It closes behind her.

"Is it comfortable, lying like that?"

"No."

"Why didn't you say so?"

"You need to pick your battles if you want to win at the game of life." He laughs. I try to carefully roll him back into his previous position. Then Marie comes in. I'd recognize her footsteps anywhere. Maybe because when I was a child I learned to be such a good listener and observer. I wrestle with pillows and limbs; a nurse's dexterity is to be envied. Dad lets me tug at him without complaining.

"Hello, everyone."

I hear her depositing her bags and pulling a chair up to the bed.

"I was just helping move him onto his back." I kiss her right cheek.

"Aren't the nurses better at that?" She stands close to Dad. "Well, how are things here? A little better than this morning?"

Dad nods.

She pulls her magazines out of her bag. "Which nurse did he have this afternoon? The friendly one, that blonde?"

"No, the dark-haired one." I begin to gather my belongings.

"You're leaving already?"

"I've got a meeting with Marcus and the production designer about a new project."

"I thought I might have a nice drink in the cafeteria with my daughter, but well, if you're busy, you're busy."

I know I'm disappointing her now. I pick up my coat, kiss my father's cheek, inform him that Alexander is coming tomorrow and that I'll see him after the operation. There's something questioning in his eyes that confuses me. I walk into the hallway and out of the hospital.

I don't breathe properly again until I'm in my car. Sadness is infectious. Then I start the engine, put in a CD, and "Asleep" by the Smiths begins to play. I open the window and my hair blows all over the place. I sing along, very quietly, even though the music's turned all the way up.

That evening, there's a phone call from the hospital. It's Dad, he wants to ask me something important. I'm to look in his old dental office, at the bottom of the drawer with the hanging files—I have to take out about ten of them—at the bottom, there's a file. Can I take it away? If something goes wrong during the operation, he doesn't want Marie to find it. I have to promise him. He repeats the bit about the promise even though I'd agreed immediately.

6

"I think you're just being negative now." Marcus stretches and produces an extended yawn, as though he just got out of bed. It's already afternoon. He puts on his sunglasses even though we're indoors.

I wouldn't have minded missing out on this whole project. Since Marcus became artistic director of this large theater, I'd prefer to work with the young performers who develop productions for the smaller auditorium, but I don't dare ask him if he could work with the other dramaturge from time to time. And of course he's still a top director, so I realize it's an honor to be involved each time.

Marcus has commissioned a play from a German who Louis says has written two exceptionally mediocre novels and one reasonable play. Leniency isn't one of Louis's main character traits. It was to be a piece for six actors. Marcus wants to launch four young talents and have a friend of his, Elise, play the lead role. She's a real diva but also one of the most remarkable actresses of her generation. The other lead role is for Nathan, an actor with a big personality and some good roles on his résumé.

I received the script six weeks ago and wasn't enthusiastic. Hans, the writer, revised it slightly after we gave him our feedback, and Marcus thought the new version good enough, so I had to translate it. I did what he asked but it's still a translation of an inferior play. I'm seriously unhappy about it and I've just explained that to him in depth, but he doesn't have patience for my grievances.

"What do you suggest, then?" Marcus doesn't really look at me.

"Pick a different play while it's still possible."

"Mona's feeling funny, is she?" Marcus gets up, stations himself behind me, lays his hands on my shoulders, and begins to massage my neck. If I ignore the fact that he's the person doing it, it feels wonderful; my whole body is stiff. "I think you're having a tough time because of your dad, so you're being pessimistic about everything. Rehearsals start in barely two weeks, so we'll stick with this text. And your ideas about possible revisions aren't that bad, so make them."

"That'll make it quite different from what Hans wrote."

"Well, he had his chance. You have my blessing." He stops kneading and lets go. "I'm counting on you." Then he leaves the room.

That's nice, I think, *dumping all the responsibility on me.* Rewriting a play is the most thankless task there is. If it's bad, it'll be my fault; if it's good, then Hans will get the credit. I catch myself sighing; I hate when people do that.

I gather the ninety pages of text and my book of notes. I open the window, I need oxygen—and a grand gesture, that would help. Throwing the play out the window and watching the pages be carried away on the wind, or sweeping everything from my desk with my arm, or theatrically breaking my keyboard so that it's impossible for me to work. That's what they do in movies and on TV: angry people throw things. There, the things don't belong to the people whose lives they're messing up, and they don't have to clean up the mess afterward. In real life you rarely see someone do a thing like that, if at all. I wonder why it happens so much in fantasyland.

I think: *Stop procrastinating, girl, get on with it, time is of the essence.* Just as I've sat down to start, Marcus comes back into the room.

"I forgot to ask how your dad's operation went." He gets a chair and sits back down. Sweet of him.

"They removed quite a lot of his bowel and there was some adhesion to the bladder wall, that's what they call it. But all in all, it went well. He has to recuperate now and when he's better, they'll give him some form of light chemo."

"And that will buy him time?"

"Yes. But they won't say anything concrete about what will actually happen. The vaguer they can be, the better, eh?"

"We had a fantastic doctor for my dad."

"Ours said it was impossible to make any predictions but that we should remain optimistic and not get ahead of ourselves. Literally, the same things he said before the operation, but then he'd promised we'd know more after the op, i.e., now. But we don't."

"Uncertainty is a nasty thing," Marcus says with a sigh. "Well, gal, chin up and keep the faith. I've got my fingers crossed for you." There's something warm in his gaze when he says this. "And when you've finished the revision, you'll bring it straight to me, OK?"

I nod and he leaves. *I must do this well,* I think. *I must.*

7

It's lying in front of me on the table: a binder, boring black like a civil servant would have, with bands around the corners that have long since lost their elasticity. Here and there a crease in the cardboard, and no label or anything. Louis couldn't understand why I didn't open it right away when I got home. I wasn't even sure whether my father had intended for me to remove it from his house. Maybe he wanted me to do that only if he didn't survive the operation. I considered telling Alexander, but given his relationship with Dad, that just seemed like pouring oil on the fire.

He hadn't forbidden me from looking in the binder. Admittedly, I hadn't asked, and since then, I haven't seen him without Marie being there too.

I get a beer from the refrigerator.

The mere fact that Dad has something in his possession that has to remain secret is surprising to me. I always saw him as a man who sought peace in routines, in the escape of a full waiting room and paperwork that had to be kept up to date. People who "never have time" never need to stop, never have to think about things that perhaps aren't right. But now this same man turns out to have contraband goods. I pour the beer into a glass, take a big sip, return to the table, and open the binder. There are letters in it, handwritten on unlined paper. Not my father's illegible scrawl but elegant handwriting with lots of long loops, probably my mother's. They begin with "Darling." I turn the first one over, it's signed "your J." Mom's name was Agnes.

A photo slips out and falls onto the table. A woman in her forties, reclining nonchalantly on a beige sofa; she sinks into the cushions, one knee raised, as though the photo was taken just as she was sitting down. She's smiling effusively, her eyes squeezed into slits. She's wearing black glasses with a heavy frame; her hair is playfully short; black pants, blue-gray sweater: simple and tasteful. A spontaneous, pleasant, warm woman, that's what she looks like.

I begin to read in total concentration. There are twelve lovely, original love letters from this intelligent, sweet lady, at least that's my impression. And the image of my father she projects, he's like a different man: a romantic with stormy emotions and a great sensitivity, and openhearted too. She responds to things he must have told her about, things that imply real conversations between the two of them. There are no dates anywhere, but she refers to a line by Tommy Cooper who had recently dropped dead during one of his shows, just like that, at the age of sixty-three. She wrote that she was a fan of Tommy Cooper, that life was short so we should dare to live it well as long as it lasted. I look up which year that was: 1984, on April 15. I was seventeen and Anne-Sophie five. I try to remember that time, but I can't. I don't have many clear memories of the past. Nowhere in the letters is it clear what did or didn't happen between them, or how long they knew each other, and nowhere is there any sign of an impending ending; the letters simply stop.

I look at the photo of this J. I try to imagine what my father looked like at the time. His hair was a bit longer, I believe. I try to imagine them together. I don't know what to think and yet I think all kinds of things. I take another beer from the refrigerator. I wish I still smoked.

The phone rings. It's Louis, he wants to take me to a party tonight. I'm not sure I feel like it, but it's a nice gesture all the same.

Louis never writes letters, even though writing's his job, and he thinks love letters are ridiculous anyway. People shouldn't use certain words too much because they lose their meaning. He thinks couples who say sweet things to each other all the time are pathetic in their melodramatic thirst for validation—that's what he calls it.

I need to write to Anne-Sophie, I think. If I was her, I'd be offended that we hadn't already.

8

Marie's sitting on a chair at an angle to Dad's bed. She's knitting something gray, black, and red. Some people find the clicking of knitting needles relaxing, but it makes me feel nervous, like clocks that tick loudly or faucets that drip. And once you've noticed, it becomes impossible not to hear it.

"What's it going to be?"

"A sweater for Daddy, a nice warm one."

I go over to his bed and give him a kiss. He smells of disinfectant and something sour.

"How are you, Dad?"

"A little less tired than yesterday, eh, Daddy? That's good, isn't it? Because yesterday, well, we had quite the day. He woke up and suddenly said to me: 'I have to take Mona to school.' I said, 'What are you talking about?' I said, 'Mona's thirty-five, she's had a job for years.' At which point he dozed off again. Funny, isn't it, Daddy, you coming out with all these foolish things."

Dad says nothing. He believes that resigning yourself is an art.

"I asked the doctor whether that's normal but he assured me that the moments of confusion were a result of the narcotics. They can take a while to wear off."

"Are you in pain?" I ask him.

"The pain's not too bad today, is it, Daddy? It's all right today, but yesterday and the day before it was a different story. First he was hooked up to all kinds of devices, eh, that squeaked and pumped, it looked horrible. Even though I'm quite at home in the medical world, you know I was going to the hospital with my own father before I'd even learned to read or write, but it's still a shock when it's your own husband. I even thought for a moment: *Am I going to faint? Am I going to vomit?* But well, I hadn't eaten anything, of course, so I couldn't. I'd rather not eat, but I force myself because I have to stay standing. If I collapse now, that would be a calamity, wouldn't it, Daddy?"

Dad reaches for his drink, in a red sippy cup, like a little kid would have.

"And the pain he was in, eh, Daddy? Pain! At a certain point he was lying there whining like an animal. So I complained to the nurses. 'The doctors decide how much pain medication he's allowed,' they said. 'Then call the doctors, for god's sake,' I cried, which made them stare. Yes, but well, no one should have to feel pain these days, that's what people say, isn't it? But you did, didn't you, Daddy? In the end, they gave him something extra due to my intervention." Marie beams as she says this.

Dad stares out the window and says nothing. I notice a large clear bag on the floor under his bed, there's dark-brown piss in it. Is that color normal? I don't want to look and move my chair back a little.

"Good thing I'm here, eh, Daddy? Take this morning. A physical therapist came along to do a few exercises with him. That person has hardly said three words when Daddy interrupts him, saying he's not yet ready for it. Well, then I stepped in. I said, 'Yes, but well, we're not going to get anywhere like that, are we? The road to recovery is long, but this will make it even longer.' Yes, that's what I said. 'A person sometimes needs a push in life.' I did that myself when I had that operation on my foot, do you remember? That was no laughing matter, but I went to the physical therapist and I bore the pain. All right, I have a high pain threshold, but that's not the point. The point is, if I hadn't done the exercises, I wouldn't have gotten back to being my old self as quickly. The hospital therapist, he agreed with me. He said, 'Sir, let's just give it a try, maybe you'll surprise yourself.' He was a friendly man, wasn't he, Daddy?"

My father makes the smallest nod possible.

"Finally, he cooperated. With a lot of groaning and puffing and panting, but I'm sure he was glad in the end that he'd done it, weren't you, Daddy? I was proud of you." Marie looks at him with a sweet smile on her face. "The faster you recover, the sooner you can come home, that's the way to think about it."

"And are you coping, yourself?" I ask as she pauses for breath.

"Well, I have to, don't I? They're long days and all the stress, it's bound to affect you. But well, I'm doing it for Daddy. I'd do anything for Daddy, isn't that right, Daddy? Yesterday he even said, 'I'm glad you're here. What would I do without you?' He can't cope with being on his own in any case, he's never been able to. And now with all this to-do, he needs a woman at his side more than ever. It's normal. So I'm here for him, always, at least as long as visiting hours permit, because I don't want to get dirty looks from the nurses, of course." Marie throws her ball of yarn a little farther away to lengthen the skein. "That nurse, the blonde, she said to me, 'It can't be easy for you, ma'am, spending so many hours here each day.' I replied: 'I can't help it. It's in my nature, always thinking of others before myself.' She also said she could see that I was doing it all on my own. 'Well,' I told her, 'the children are always busy. That's normal too, they've got jobs, our son's got a baby.' And—"

"You know I wish I could come more often but you always say you get nervous when you can't sit with him, and Dad finds too many visitors hectic."

"Yes, it's all fine for me the way it is. I'm only repeating what the nurse said, that's all."

There's a momentary silence. Only the click-clack of knitting needles and the sound of a quiet conversation in the hall. After the storm, there's something magical about silence. I smile at Dad and he smiles weakly back.

"Have a chat with your father, eh. You're here now and you've hardly said a thing."

I look at her, wanting to respond, then there's a knock on the door. Alexander comes in.

"Oh, it's busy in here," he says.

"You were on the roster for tomorrow."

"Oops, my mistake, sorry. Bye, everyone." Then my brother looks at me, reads my expression, I suspect, and asks Marie, "Hey, Mom, would you like to have a coffee with me downstairs? It will give you a break."

"Gosh. Daddy, do you mind if—"

"Of course, Mommy, you deserve a break," my father reassures her.

She puts down her knitting and picks up her handbag and the two of them leave the room. My father exhales loudly, in relief perhaps, or from the pain, that's also possible.

"I try to sleep as much as possible, or I pretend." He coughs, it's a wet cough and it looks as though it hurts.

"That's not good, having to fake it in your own hospital bed."

Dad stares outside as though he needs a moment to consider this. Then he turns back to me. "Mom has shed a lot of tears since I've been in here. But those tears, you know, they're for herself." He scratches his cheek, which makes a scraping sound because he hasn't been shaved today. "Oh well. When everything's back to normal and she can return to her hobbies, it'll be more bearable."

At that instant, a nurse waltzes in. "I've come to take care of you, young man. How are things here?"

"When my favorite daughter's here, things are always good," my father says.

I feel happy and embarrassed at the same time.

Understandably, none of this matters at all to the nurse. "Are you going to stay?"

"Um, no, I'll wait in the hall."

I look around. I wish I had a better idea of what to do. Charlie told me a few days ago I should stop humoring everyone, that this would help him, not just me, to broach certain matters. What should I talk to him about, then, exactly, I asked. Charlie smiled and said I already knew the answer to that.

9

I didn't think Louis would be home, so I just walk into his study. There's an immediate commotion. I see him slam his laptop shut, his pants are down around his ankles, his bare knees stick out awkwardly on either side of the chair. He's sitting with his back to me and he doesn't dare turn around now is my guess.

"Oh, um—" I don't continue because I can't think of anything to say. I close the door again behind me. I don't think he'd come yet, I would have noticed the smell of sperm in such a small space. I go into the kitchen. Is he finishing the job now?

I start making dinner. As I rummage around in the vegetable drawer, I wonder whether he still visits the site with women fucking each other with fluorescent strap-on dildos. I stumbled on it once in the search history on my computer. Apparently he uses both mine and his own computer to satisfy his pornographic needs when he's in his writing cave. Later, I discovered that this particular site seems to be his favorite—it came up a remarkable number of times. To be honest, I was surprised something like that would be so exciting. The women first have to fight each other and the one who wins is allowed to fuck the other one roughly with a brightly colored fake penis, larger than any I've ever seen in real life. The winner always acts mean, the girl who has lost groans with pain, her face contorted. I've never asked him why this excites him so much.

When was the last time we made love? About three weeks ago? We were watching a movie together and when the man fucked the woman against the kitchen counter, horny and hurried, I cuddled up to Louis, at which point he reached for my breasts and kissed my neck. He used his tongue, he knows that turns me on. It was a simple lay with the movie on pause. Afterward, he fetched both of us a whiskey. His leg rested against mine while we watched the rest of the movie in the bedroom. Louis was asleep the moment the credits started to roll. I was still wide awake. I got up again, lay down on the living room carpet on my side. The wool prickled my cheek, I could see my hand and my arm, I could hear cars out on the street, music coming from the apartment beneath us, just the bass, an ambulance or fire truck somewhere in the far distance, and all I could think was: *What if I just lie here forever?*

I cut the eggplant into thick slices, sprinkle them with salt. Then I peel the tomatoes and in the meantime, I try to think of things I like. I like a lot of things Louis considers ridiculous. I like brightly patterned shirts on men, doughnut holes from the funfair, cats when they are kittens. I like falling stars and making a wish and believing it will come true. Books with happy endings. Words invented by me or by somebody else. White- and milk-chocolate-flavored Mister Whippy. Paintings by Van Gogh (according to Louis, he'd never have achieved the fame he enjoys today if he hadn't cut off his ear) and by Richter (pathetic pseudophotography and gloomy ambient abstracts, says Louis). Passport photos of children in women's wallets. Pastel-colored boas, very short skirts, and plunging necklines on women who can get away with it. Playing a particular song on repeat during an endless journey. Corny sunsets in colors that look like a child's painting. Escalators, Christmas lights, cuckoo clocks, felt-tip pens, snowballs, disco balls, bubble wrap and being able to pop each bubble one by one, plastic flowers, ladybugs, four-leaf clovers, five-leaf clovers, wishbones, and greeting cards that play music when you open them. Cookbooks, men's hats, women's suits, pinball machines, the poems of e e cummings (empty form experiments, Louis thinks). Notebooks and then having too many of them with too little written in them. Believing that coincidence isn't a coincidence. People who are kind to you, just because, without your having done something for them first. People who dare to show their vulnerabilities without being afraid of being seen as pathetic. People who try harder to save the world than I do. People who spontaneously burst into song when there's no reason for it. Goodwill, naivete, assertiveness. Optimism. Poorly lit spaces, busy streets, the way stillness is captured in the arts. Rainbows. Old trees, fog and mist, sea views, big shells and then listening to the sea in them, baby clothes, sour candy. Romance, even when it verges on the gooey. Big words and big feelings.

Louis comes into the kitchen and kisses my right temple. "Oh, eggplant, delicious, my lady of the pan."

"Pasta alla Norma," I say.

"When will it be ready?"

"No more than half an hour, I expect."

"Great. I'll just pop out for some cigarettes. Want me to bring you anything?" He never usually asks.

"No, thanks."

When we're sitting at the table, he wants to know whether Anne-Sophie has replied yet. He pours me a large glass of red wine, says he picked a good one, then shows me the label.

"No, not yet."

After talking to Alexander, we decided I should email her. Neither Dad nor Marie has even mentioned her name since Dad went into the hospital, but I didn't want to wait any longer. For more than four years, Anne-Sophie has been traveling around South America. She's even spent time in Africa. Her whole life fits in a backpack. I have no idea when she'll read my message, often she doesn't check her email for weeks. And she's never had a cell phone. I miss her.

"I wonder if she misses me."

"Maybe. But she rarely gets in touch, does she? Is there any more pasta? This sauce is yet again delectable in its simplicity."

I get up and put the pans on the table.

"How are rehearsals going?"

"A read-through without much enthusiasm this afternoon. I think the actors think as little of the piece as I do, only they don't dare to say it."

"They're not very courageous, your actors."

"I'm not either, so . . ."

"Oh, my poor sweet coward. Do you want some more too?" He holds a spoonful of sauce above my plate. I wave my hand, no thanks. "And on the home front?"

"Dad's getting better every day, I think. He's walking the full length of the corridor and spending at least an hour upright in a chair three times a day. But Marie looks terrible, dark circles under her eyes, lost a lot of weight."

"Really? And she already was so skinny. Poor woman."

I nod.

"Hmm, yeah, Marie," Louis says.

He turns his fork in his spaghetti, creates a massive bite, and then puts it all in his mouth at once, smacking his lips. Before his mouth is empty, he begins out of the blue to describe a dream he had. It's about a woman with fleshy legs that rub together when she walks. She came up to him and he didn't know what to do. I wait for the point, but it doesn't come. Marie is in almost all my dreams, sometimes she has a bit part, other times, she determines the whole sequence. I wake up from a lot of my dreams feeling suffocated.

"I saw Charlie very briefly this morning."

"Hmm," Louis says, seeming to focus all his attention on his plate.

"She said she hates the term *dysfunctional families* because that's the type of family she sees as exceptionally functional. The kind that isn't focused on people flourishing individually and feeling good, but on a system that has to be kept in place, a system in which everyone plays a role, even if it's at the expense of everyone in it."

"Yeah," Louis says with his mouth full.

"Interesting to think about, isn't it?"

"Golly. Well, to my mind, Charlie's read too many self-help books. What herbs did you put in this sauce?" He points his fork at a green bit.

"Basil, like I always do."

"Really exceptional, honeybun. And I was ravenously hungry." He sucks up the last strings of spaghetti, making a squishing sound.

I think about the many meanings of the word *hungry*. I consider going to take a sniff of his study, but decide not to.

"I'm going to finish the whole pan if that's OK?" Louis scrapes his spoon across the bottom of it.

I think about Dad. What does he dream about? Dying and giving up? Marie and her knitting? I start to feel cold. "Want to watch a movie together?"

"No, I want to finish that essay." Louis wipes his mouth, gets up from the table, puts his plate on the counter, not in the dishwasher, and refills his wineglass again.

I go over to him, press myself to his body, hold him tightly, and just for a moment I never let go.

10

There's a long line at security. A kid with a whole lot of hair isn't allowed by her mother to sit on the floor and begins to whine fretfully. A man with helpless ankles beneath too-short pants stares at the ceiling as though something interesting is about to happen there.

"Airports have been loony since 9/11," Marcus says.

He puts his perennial pair of sunglasses in his hair, runs two fingers under his nose for the nth time, and straightens his right shoulder. The question is how *much* coke he's snorted. It isn't even afternoon yet, and I thought just now that I smelled alcohol but was hoping I was wrong.

He'd been doing well for just over three years. He checked into a reputable clinic and, after that, seemed rid of his worst demons. But bit by bit, the habit crept back in. He seldom uses when he's working, he says, so he doesn't think it's a problem.

"I've got the feeling we've hardly moved three steps in twenty minutes. We'll miss our flight at this rate." He puts his sunglasses back on his nose. I'm mildly tempted to smack the glasses from his face when he begins to complain like this, but I tell him we've got plenty of time, everything will be fine. Marcus insisted on going to Berlin and back in one weekend to talk to Hans because, along the way, he'd begun to have more and more doubts about the material too.

It's almost our turn. Marcus constantly shifts his weight from one leg to the other and talks at top speed about a book he's reading. He gives away the entire ending, even though he'd started by impressing on me that I had to read the novel urgently. We arrive at the conveyor belt, I take a plastic tray, put my phone in it, my laptop, my shoes, and my coat. I pick up my suitcase and lay it on the belt, ready to be checked too. Everything's carry-on; it's a short trip. Marcus puts his bag on the belt and dumps his keys and phone into my tray, then he walks toward the detector, where one of the security men points at his shoes. Marcus points back at the man's shoes, laughs, and keeps walking.

The man barks, "Your shoes need to go on the conveyor belt, sir."

"These sneakers never beep, you'll see." He tries to walk on, but the man holds him back.

"Sir, I must insist that you follow the rules." He adopts a stern expression, like a father who doesn't know how to react or a teacher who isn't very happy.

Marcus goes up to him and stands too close. "Do you enjoying humiliating me? Is that it? First make us wait forever and then you behave like a motherfucker?"

The man doesn't bat an eyelid; he's been trained for this. A female colleague discreetly comes closer. Before she's said anything, I go over to Marcus.

"Marcus, please, just do what they say or we'll miss our flight."

I carefully lay my palm on his shoulder, he looks at me without looking at me, shakes off my hand, but does go to the plastic tray, takes off his shoes, and puts them in it. People behind me stare, some of them visibly annoyed. Marcus goes through the metal detector as though he's walking onstage to accept his applause, his arms spread theatrically. He looks at the security man, who ignores the provocation. I presume Marcus is disappointed in some way. He probably just watched one of those documentaries about recalcitrant rock stars who claim that artists must resist all forms of authority.

As I'm putting my shoes back on, the woman on the other end of the conveyor belt asks, "Whose luggage is this?" She points at Marcus's bag. Murphy's Law and me.

I feel like just walking on, but I put away the rest of my stuff, take my luggage, and go over to the lady. She's a large woman, almost as big as Marcus. She has a slight squint, not a bad one but just enough to confuse you. She's holding Marcus's toiletry bag and taking out all kinds of bottles: shampoo, shower gel, aftershave, deodorant, night cream. Night cream, you can only be so tough, apparently. I try to imagine Marcus late at night in front of the mirror, having just snorted a line of coke, now dabbing at his skin with delicate fingertips.

"Sir, don't you know that liquids and gels have to be packed in a transparent, resealable plastic bag?"

"I didn't have a bag."

"Well, you can get them here." There's something implacable about her, she's probably been like that all her life. "Besides, these bottles are all much too big." I look at Marcus. I see the veins in his neck tighten, they rise up out of the skin, blue and threatening. "You understand I'll have to take them from you, sir."

"Christ, what shocking treatment people get here. Those are my things and I don't want to arrive in Berlin stinking to high heaven." He looks at her defiantly. I consider doing something, but I don't know what.

"Complaining won't get you anywhere, sir. We're just doing our job." She takes two small containers from his bag, vitamins, I think, and a strip of pills. "And do you have certificates from your doctor to say you need these supplements and this medication?" She opens the containers, looks inside, and sniffs at them.

"Pardon?" Marcus roars.

"I've never heard of that either, that you'd need something like that," I say, adopting my friendliest expression.

"You can find it all on our website, ma'am. You should try that sometime: reading up on important matters beforehand. It would save us a lot of time and hassle." She turns around and bends down to get a trash can.

And then it happens. Marcus gives the woman a shove; she falls and cracks her head on the table; he grabs some of his belongings and runs off. This is the kind of craziness that only an intoxicated Marcus is capable of. With two security guys running after him, Marcus bumps into a woman with a stroller, falls over, and scrambles to his feet again. Now the men have caught up with him. They attempt to stop him, but he strikes out, his fist clenched, and smacks one of the men in the face. The man falls to the ground and grabs at his nose with both hands. A third security guard turns up, a real burly-looking fellow. After some pushing and shoving, they manage to get Marcus under control and two of them cart him off. I stand there watching, frozen to the spot, amazed by the absurdity of the situation. The woman is back on her feet again by now, she seems slightly more cross-eyed than before, but that could just be my imagination.

"I'm so sorry," I say prissily. "He's a little on edge."

The woman doesn't reply, doesn't even glance at me, and I don't blame her. A colleague puts our baggage to one side. The flow of passengers is moving smoothly again.

I say to the security man standing nearby, "We're supposed to board in a minute."

"Well, your husband should have thought about that earlier."

I don't want them to think we're married, but I don't have the energy for an argument. "Where did they take him?"

The man simply points.

"Sorry," I say again, and then think about how sick I am of having to apologize for him. I put his things in my purse, pick up the bags, one in each hand, and head off in the direction the finger pointed. I've already had enough of this day.

More than two hours later, Marcus emerges from the small room: a small boy, walking dejectedly, lost his mommy on a busy shopping street. He looks around, one hand over his eyes. It's because the sunglasses are gone, I think, that the gaze strikes me like this, so suddenly. He comes over, barely dares to look at me, and leaves his nose alone. Adrenaline sobers you up, and time in this case.

"The flight—"

"I know."

"I've informed Hans that we're delayed. What do you think, should we try to get another flight or—"

He interrupts me again, very quietly. "I'll have a long talk with him over the phone tomorrow."

I give Marcus his things back and roll the bag right next to his legs. He doesn't even look up.

"They called the police, that's why it took so long. I broke my sunglasses when I fell, goddamn it."

"What now?"

Marcus shrugs. He takes his bag and goes outside, I follow him. When he reaches the automatic doors, he stops and lights a cigarette. He sucks on it and stares ahead. Regret always comes later with him. Then he looks at me from under his bangs, sheepishly almost. "Headache," he says. "They come on suddenly, like storms." He just stares. "You must be so angry with me."

"Less angry than you probably are at yourself. Maybe it would do you good to go back to—"

"It's not normal, I think, you being so nice."

"Probably not, no." After I've said this with a forced smile, I wonder why, actually.

"Can I please take you to lunch at a fancy restaurant, my treat, to make it up to you? Then I'll drop you off at home."

"Oh, Marcus. I think I'd rather—"

He throws his cigarette in the gutter and suddenly hugs me. This big, tough man clamps his strong arms around my body. Strangely fragile, it feels, and intimate. It takes him a long time to let go. "You're my best friend, do you know that?"

I smile a little, almost sarcastically. "Indispensable. To the theater too."

I let Marcus take me to lunch at a restaurant he apparently remembers that I like. We order the four-course menu and drink wine. We talk about the play but also about life, and his problems, and my father. He says I should say what I still have to say, before it's too late, he really regretted not doing that. Without his sunglasses on, everything seems to go much more smoothly. Marcus doesn't even drink too much, he is human, a warm man. As he eats his dessert—he has a sweet tooth—I look at the famous director sitting opposite me, this big kid, and I wonder what binds me to him. Maybe I unconsciously know the answer.

11

Cleavage told Marie yesterday that he'd hoped the gentleman would heal more rapidly after his operation but that, even so, things were progressing in the right direction, step by step. From a man who makes everything sound like a hopeless drama, this almost feels like optimism.

It's a gloomy day, clouds threaten outside, but I'm fine here. I have finally managed to spend a few hours with Dad on my own. He's telling me about the quiz show he watched last night: if he'd been one of the contestants, he'd have had a good chance of winning. That must mean he's getting better, he thinks. He gives me an encouraging look, as though I'm the person who needs to get better. And then I say it, just like that, having wanted to subtly steer the conversation in that direction, test the waters. I say it, I lay it down, carefully but unavoidably, between us: the hidden story, the letters, J. Dad doesn't seem angry. There's a touch of dismay in his eyes, though.

"You haven't mentioned it to anyone, I hope?"

"No, Louis is the only one who knows about it."

"Promise me you'll keep it between us."

This is tricky because of my brother and sister, but I don't want to be difficult.

"I promise."

"Are you angry with me?"

I wouldn't know how to be, I realize. "No, just curious."

Then he begins to tell me. First hesitantly, but then more eagerly. As though he'd been waiting centuries to be able to.

Her name was Joanna. He'd met her at a party that Marie hadn't attended because of a headache. He noticed Joanna in the far corner of the room, she was drinking a cocktail through a straw, he still remembered that, and he wanted to keep on looking at her, he tells me. Not only because he found her attractive, not only because she had an infectious laugh, but because there was something about her, in her, something he wanted to be close to, that's how it had felt.

He'd gone to talk to her because he couldn't not, and they started chatting. They skipped the dinner and took a walk in the late-evening light, and during those few hours, he'd been more honest about himself than he ever had to anyone before. Because it was easy with her, because she was open too, toward him.

He talks about her like everything in his life was supposed to lead to that one point. A softness has come over him since he said her name, a softness that I've always suspected more than actually seen.

Four days later, they met up again, and then—he wavered for a moment—they made love. He seemed to want to explain how exactly it had gone, but when he suddenly seemed to realize he was talking to his daughter, he stopped. He'd thought that it might blow over if they did that, perhaps it was about the conquest, that's what he'd told himself, but it hadn't worked that way. She was the loveliest, strangest person he'd ever met, he says, so different from the others. He'd never believed that one person belonged to another person before, but she'd made him, the sober-minded man, reconsider. It was something he'd wanted all his life.

There is vastness in his eyes, and rain and whispers and wind blowing, as though he's elsewhere, which he is, I believe. "Joanna wanted me," he says, she wanted him. She'd said so after a good five months. Five months in which they'd seen each other when they could, in which she'd written him letters, in which they'd found each other and comforted and helped each other, in which they'd told each other their whole life stories, and then all over again, in which they did things for the first time: skinny-dipping in the pond at the back of the Goovaerts' family estate (they were never there in the summer anyway), licking a single ice-cream cone together, chocolate—both their favorite—with teasing enjoyment, and then really greedily as though they were momentarily adolescents again, and then licking each other, with chocolate on their faces, where anyone could see them, and then taking a taxi into the city just to be able to kiss in the back seat, like in the movies, and setting off in the car and driving until it was nice enough outside to be able to sit on the grass and stare up at the sky and then even more at each other. Like life had begun there and only there, for both of them, that's how it sounds to me.

And that she'd suddenly said, just as she was putting her glasses on, he still remembered that, that she thought nothing was right in the world if they couldn't be together and that difficult wasn't the same as impossible. He'd replied that it felt the same way to him and then he'd added a *but*. And she'd cried and held him and delivered a wondrous speech, and he had never been so completely moved, he had never wanted something so much, never. But.

Dad stops talking and stares at I don't know what. I look back and wish I could do something.

"*But* is the worst word," I say.

Then he looks at me, with a touch of gratitude, I think, perhaps only because I'm listening, perhaps because he can tell that I feel it too.

"Why did you let that chance slip away?"

"How could I choose to be with her instead? After everything. And Marie, she'd have—" He deliberately doesn't finish his sentence.

The biggest truths can be found in half sentences, I can't help thinking. I pull up my knees and wrap my arms around my legs.

"A person can't have everything, that's how it is. And maybe it was too good to be true." He fiddles with a needle in his forearm. "It doesn't matter. I did what I had to do. I pulled the plug."

"And when you look back now?"

He only stares into the distance. Sometimes people don't have to say anything to answer a question that wasn't a question.

I drive home. Rain gushes down the windshield, the windshield wipers swish fanatically back and forth; each time I turn off the heat, the windows steam up. I imagine children who would be upset by a story like that. I simply wonder what my life would be like if that woman had taken Marie's place. I accelerate, turn up the radio; R.E.M.'s "At My Most Beautiful" comes out of the speakers, as though everything works out as long as it's tackled on a large enough scale, that's what it sounds like. I drive too fast on wet roads, sometimes I do that.

12

Louis calls to me from the bathroom, yelling like something's on fire and I'm the fire department. I find him over the toilet bowl, red-faced and busy with a plunger. He states the obvious, his voice filled with despair: "It's blocked again." Then he looks at me.

"I'll call a plumber."

"I've been there before, they won't be able to come for five days. Can't you try?"

I take the plunger from him, notice that he used the toilet before realizing there was a problem. I try not to look and push the red rubber monster in and out of the hole, my face averted, and then again, and then again, and just as much happens as when he did it. I even get the impression that the cloudy water has risen somewhat. I quickly close the lid and give him his weapon back.

"Plumber, then. I'll say it's urgent. We've still got the bathroom in the hall."

"Goddamn it, a person can't even take a shit in this place. It's going to start to stink and I still need to take a shower. Christ." Louis heads toward the bedroom, grumbling.

A few minutes later, he comes into the kitchen holding his suit jacket. "Look," he says, pointing at a greenish stain on his lapel. "What's this?"

"How should I know? It's your jacket."

"Not only can I not shower, now I don't have anything to wear either. I'm not going to that party. Fate is conspiring against me."

"Wear the black jacket."

"It's gotten too small."

"Then we should buy a new suit sometime."

"Yes, but that won't help me now." He walks off again.

I consider for a moment trying to get rid of the stain, but say nothing and do nothing. I didn't feel like going to that party anyway. The plumber's answering machine says that I can leave a message after the beep. I think about Dad and Joanna's story, I can't help it.

13

"Look, I don't like to speak ill of people, especially not now. And I do want to understand, because he is sick and afraid and what do I know, but the way he's criticizing the hell out of me, I can't cope with it anymore." Marie holds a hand to her mouth.

"Shall we play chess in the dining room?" Louis asks Marvin.

"If you're a good loser," my godchild says, with his most waggish expression. My father taught him. I can't remember Dad ever playing chess with any of us, but things are different with his grandson. "I've already beaten Grandpa four times and he's a chess master, so . . ."

They get up and disappear into the dining room. I don't know what it is with Louis and Marvin but, all of a sudden, they've found each other. Marvin let Louis read him a fairy tale he'd written for school and Louis was truly amazed at his linguistic dexterity and originality. Since then, Louis has liked to spend time with him whenever the family's together, certainly when he wants to avoid a conversation he finds boring or irksome. All the same, it's nice to see. He never wants to have any kids himself, he claims. "But what if it was another little Marvin?" I once asked. "Yes, that would be all right, for a few hours a week," he'd replied, "and then we could tie him up outside again."

Marie gasps for breath, she hadn't finished yet. "Gives me a complete dressing-down, just like that, you know, out of the blue, while I try to do everything for him."

Alexander tops up her glass and lifts the bottle to check whether anyone else wants more wine. "Terrible. What did he say?"

"All kinds of things. It's too painful to repeat them."

"Maybe he just had a bad day, that can make you say things you don't mean," I suggest.

"Or perhaps he was being his real self for once," Charlie murmurs. I knock my knee against hers under the table.

"Oh no, he's done it several times now. And he lashes out at the nurses too, or snaps at them. You should see the looks they give him. They're only trying to do their jobs."

"Shall I try to talk to him?" Alexander asks overconfidently.

"God, no. He'd only get angrier if he knew I told you. Daddy likes to play the hero in front of his children." She sits completely hunched over. "Of course, I'm hoping he'll be well enough soon to be able to come home. But at the same time, how's it going to work, all of that? A bed in the living room, some extra pajamas, and a tray on legs so that he can eat lying down if necessary. That's the least of it. But his rages, his stubbornness, his panic when the slightest thing goes wrong, his—" Then she stops talking, raises her eyebrows, and hold her hands up in surrender.

Alexander squeezes her upper arm encouragingly. "I understand that it frightens you. But let's take things one day at a time and deal with problems as they arise, Mom. There's no point getting so upset about it."

"That's true," Charlie adds, "and perhaps it won't be as bad as you think."

Two fat tears run down Marie's face, drawing blueish trails of eyeliner. She takes a deep breath as if to pull herself together.

"Maybe." Then the crying stops. Trying not to cry looks even sadder than letting the tears flow. "I'd thought, you know, that at moments of crisis, people grow closer, but that's not true, is it? He never touches me. I'm not even allowed to get close to him, he says he can't breathe. And he doesn't talk either, I have to drag each word out of him, a few sentences about how he feels, what he's lying there thinking about. And my feelings, well—"

"Dad's not an easy person, we know that," Alexander says.

I think about how Dad used to rant and rave at her. It was like he could only handle her scornful silence, her meandering whims and moods, if he could explode from time to time. And then there'd be a lot of sorrys afterward and a large bunch of flowers. I remember the sticky tension of that silence, waiting ages for the calm to return. It must have been awful for Marie, all those days, all those nights. "Have things been any better in recent years?"

"It couldn't get much worse, could it, eh, Mona?" There's defeat in Marie's gaze. "Of course, you always took your father's side, whatever he did."

"All those bad things were really bad, Mom. It just sounds a bit strange now because he's been gentler to me than ever before."

"Oh, so you're saying I'm lying?"

"No. I think sometimes there isn't just one truth but versions of the facts that mainly say something about the person sharing them, and that people only hear what they're able to hear, or want to hear, and sometimes that's the same thing. But that says just as much about me, doesn't it?"

"And then you talk me under the table, that's how you always win. Oh well, your mother will just have to manage on her own." She folds her hands and twiddles her thumbs.

"Yes, that's the reason we're all here, to prove that you have no one you can count on." Charlie gets up and goes to the bathroom.

"I didn't mean anything by it. I'm just—I don't feel very well, I'm so worried. What if Dad dies? I sometimes think I won't be able to manage. He looks so dreadful sometimes, so absent and almost green in the face, and he's been eating like a bird for so long, and he—" She breathes rapidly and wheezes a bit as she talks.

Alexander lets a silence fall for a moment, then says, "They said that if all goes well, he may have five years. Five years is a long time. You can't let yourself immediately think the worst, it won't help anyone."

I don't know whether this is the most constructive way of comforting someone, but I can't think of anything better either.

"If he dies, what do I have left? Anne-Sophie has run off. You've got your own lives." She looks at us. "I do understand that, you know. You're busy with all kinds of things. And Marvin has gotten too clever for his grandma. I mean, I already know: I'm going to be all on my own." She rubs her forehead and stops for a moment. "I think I'll just go with him when the time comes. I won't need to live anymore, and then you can all get on with your own lives without the burden of your mother."

Alexander jumps to his feet and leans over, his face right in hers, and he says, "I'd really appreciate it if you never said a thing like that again. Never, *never* ever again." He speaks in a muted way, slow but hissing with white rage. "I wasn't even ten when you—it's—you can't . . . You're allowed to be sad, you're allowed to complain about Dad, you're allowed to whine and cry as much as you like, but dumping this on us now, now after everything, it's more than I can take."

I blanch.

Marie starts to cry again, really sobbing now. "Nobody understands me, nobody."

"No, we understand you too well. Maybe that's the problem."

"Why are you turning on me now, son?" She looks up at the ceiling and fights for breath.

285

"Why don't you understand?" Then Alexander starts to cry. I don't believe I've ever seen him shed a tear in his adult life.

"I've done everything for you, everything." She monotonously plants the words between each sob. "And I'm constantly misunderstood. How is it possible?" She holds her head in her hands, distraught.

Charlie comes back in, shrugs, and raises her arms and hands as if to say: *What's going on here?*

"We're all under pressure because of Dad." I make it sound reassuring.

Charlie kneads Alexander's shoulders.

Marvin stands in the doorway. "Are you having a fight?"

"No, no, my little Marv," Marie says with a red face.

"Sometimes grown-ups need to have a fight and then they can make up again, the way you do with your friends at school." Charlie goes over to Marvin and leads him back into the dining room.

"Whatever we do, it's never good enough," Alexander says. He sits down again. The flag is at half-mast. He's as unsteady now as he was firm a moment ago. "That's how it feels to me, anyway."

"But it is," Marie says. "I'm very happy with everything you do for me, and for Dad. I do say that all the time. I don't get it."

"The queen of mixed messages, that's what you are."

Charlie comes back into the room.

"Of what?" She looks at me from under her brows, a child that doesn't understand why they're not allowed to poke their fingers in the socket. "I don't know what I've done to deserve this," she sobs, more quietly now.

"Well, I don't either," Alexander bites back.

"In such difficult times, other families support each other." Marie stands up and walks over to the cupboard containing the napkins. Her blouse is crooked, and I can see a glimpse of her belly—a triangle of white flesh, creamy, it folds over her skirt slightly. I don't know why, but the sight makes an impression on me: such a well-groomed woman letting everything go for a moment.

"Let's agree that we don't always understand each other but that everyone means well." *Someone's got to try something,* I think.

Charlie asks, "Shall I top up the wine, or does anyone want coffee instead?"

"Yes, coffee, yes," Marie says. She sits down again, her gaze on the big wedding photo of her and Dad hanging on the wall, she in bright yellow, her face radiant, Dad in a subtle dark suit, as though everything is still possible.

"The coffee's brewing. I'll have another glass of wine, anyone else?" Charlie announces.

"No, thank you," Marie says, rubbing a napkin over her whole face.

"What about you, sweetheart? Alcohol's good for forgetting." Charlie smiles cautiously as she says it and lays her hand on the back of Alexander's neck.

Some forgetting is difficult, I think as I fill up my glass again.

14

Marvin comes over with three thick photo albums. He has to make a family tree for school and he wants photos of us when we were little, and one of now. He lays the fat books on the table, pulls up a chair close to mine, and kneels on it.

"Come on, let's choose together," he says. He leafs and leafs and asks how old I am in one shot.

"Four or five perhaps," I say.

I'm wearing a short white skirt with red flowers and a sweater with sleeves like wings. My mother has picked me up, probably just for the photo, because, in my memory, she stopped doing that once I started nursery school. My left arm rests on her shoulder. We're in the garden and, in the distance and blurred, I see a swing in front of green bushes. I'm looking straight into the lens; in my eyes there are dreams and a sad knowingness.

"And that's your real mom?" He points at her.

"Yes." She was a beautiful woman, it has to be said. "Your daddy looks like her, don't you think?"

"No," Marvin says seriously. "Daddy looks like himself."

"Oh yes, of course."

"I'm glad my mommy isn't dead."

"Me too."

"Is Grandpa going to die?" He poses the question in exactly the same tone as the previous one.

"I hope not."

"Me too. Grandpa can be funny sometimes." He continues to leaf. "Do you still miss your mom?"

Only when I hesitate does he look at me. How much honesty can a boy of ten take?

"Sometimes I miss having a mom," I say, which isn't a lie.

"Yes, but you do have a mom, right? Granny?"

"Yes, that's true."

He points at a photo showing people, popsicles, sun, and a garden. Adults shelter in the shade, children sit in a circle, I stand in the middle of the picture, looking down, my silent mouth drawn into a thin line. "What was this party?"

"I think it must have been my birthday, twelve, I'm guessing."

"I wish I was twelve." Marvin turns a few pages and stops at a portrait of the family together on the sofa. Dad, Marie, Alexander between them, he looks down to the right as though there's something more interesting happening there. "That's Daddy there, with the dirty face?" Marvin asks with a laugh.

I nod. Marie is holding Anne-Sophie with her right arm, still a baby with large eyes and a straight back, she looks into the lens, Marie and Dad look at her with something of a smile and deep longing. I'm sitting on the arm of the sofa next to Dad, looking at Alexander. The circles under my eyes are so dark you'd think I was a thirty-five-year-old woman with a mild drinking problem.

"Dad says Anne-Sophie might fly back at some point," Marvin says.

"Yes, she probably will."

"Dad says I knew her when I was little, but I don't really remember."

"That's normal, you were very young."

"It's strange that you can forget relatives."

He picks up a second album and goes through it much more quickly.

"Can't you find anything you like?"

"I want a picture of you looking happy," he says in a matter-of-fact tone.

I pick up the third album and begin to leaf through it.

15

We stroll around the pond in the park near the hospital. At times like this, the world becomes smaller in every way. A toddler is feeding the ducks; every sixty seconds she shouts, "Ducky, come and eat!" Her little voice squeaks. Her mother tears chunks from a baguette before giving them to her daughter, who throws the bread as far as she can. *This woman is good at vicarious pleasure,* I think.

Marie asks if we can stop for a while, she wants to smoke a cigarette, and women shouldn't walk and smoke at the same time, it's inelegant. *Now I have to ask,* I tell myself. Most people would consider it a very normal request, but there are different laws in our family, that's the way it is.

"I wondered—I wondered whether I could visit Dad on my own from now on." I let a silence follow. "And if possible for a bit longer than just an hour."

"Oh, so you're keeping secrets from your mother now."

"Of course not. It's just, I've realized it's what I need."

"Oh, right." She tries to light her cigarette, which is difficult in the wind. I cup my hands to help her.

"It's just—he's my father."

"Yes." She smiles. "And my husband."

"Yes." I'm happy the toddler is so actively engaged; we can look at her instead of each other. "I'd just like to have a real conversation with him and that's easier when it's just the two of us."

Marie rubs the tip of her shoe along her calf. "That's possible, yes, that he does want to have a proper conversation with you."

There's not much I can say to this, so I give it a wide berth. "I don't need more than the three times a week you've allocated in the schedule."

"I start to worry when I'm not with him. What am I supposed to do then?" She inhales deeply and holds in the smoke for a long time.

"You live nearby. You could pop home, have lunch with a friend, or do some shopping in town, something relaxing, and then come back with renewed energy."

Marie looks distressed. "You know I find that difficult."

I nod.

Marie's cigarette sparks. "Fine, of course you can speak to your father. I hope it does you some good."

The little girl shakes the bread bag empty, and her mother has to hold on to her or else she'd plunge into the pond, she's that enthusiastic. "Bye-bye, ducks!"

"Thanks, Mom. That's sweet of you."

Marie throws the butt on the ground and uses her heel to twist it into the grass, then she looks at me. "What do I always do wrong?" She stares ahead. She sounds calm, not accusing. "I'd really like to know."

I stare into the distance. I see a large building on the edge of the road that has been partially demolished. The arm of a crane dangles uselessly. There's something touching about destruction when it's incomplete.

"Shall we go back?" As though she's uncertain what the answer will be.

"Yes," I say.

16

"Well, pal, you'd have been better off asking me to write that play."
Louis makes it sound like a joke.

"Oh, so your girlfriend shares all our state secrets with you, is that
it?" Marcus wraps his arm around Louis's neck as though he's trying to
strangle him. With that muscular arm around him, Louis looks even
more like a little boy.

"Mona does everything I ask."

They both laugh.

"Wait until I'm finished with the text. Have a bit of faith in a director's genius, eh?" Marcus grins and puts his sunglasses back on his nose.
"Get yourselves a good seat." Then he moves on, the engaging host,
doing his rounds.

"Someone needs to tell him his new look is ridiculous—sunglasses,
I mean, really," Louis whispers, too loud.

"Admit it, you'd like to be him."

"Him? Don't be ridiculous."

"Without the coke habit and the sartorial excesses, perhaps, but
the rest."

Louis looks around, as though he's not listening, which might be
the case.

"And who's that?"

"Which one?"

"The good-looking man, tall with dark hair, there in the corner."

"Oh, Nathan, he's in the play, very good actor. Why?"

"He's glanced over at you three times already."

"Don't be silly."

"No, really." Louis pinches my cheek teasingly. "Stick with your master, all right?"

I hear the announcement: "It's starting in three minutes, folks. Three minutes, everyone take a seat."

The national broadcasting channel has made a documentary about Marcus, a sixty-minute portrait with clips of his work and interviews with artistic buddies and other friends. Now his assistant is having it shown on a big screen for the whole gang. Around thirty people have been invited, actors, the production crews, and associates. When Louis goes to greet Elise, I watch Nathan, who's standing with Frank, the youngest of us. Nathan talks with his hands, I like that in people. When Frank begins to answer, Nathan suddenly looks over at me. When he sees that I'm also looking at him, he smiles quickly, then he turns his head away at once.

Everyone sits down. Louis has taken a seat two rows away from me, next to Elise. The documentary begins with shots of Marcus in action during rehearsals in the theater, the voice gushing about him as one of the pioneers of Low Countries theater. Marcus has his sunglasses on top of his head so he can see properly.

At the twenty-minute mark, it turns out that Marcus's mother is also in the documentary. She's a leggy, tall woman with a skinny neck and a disproportionately large mouth full of teeth. She looks as though her thoughts are elsewhere the whole time, and she talks in a brisk and measured manner, like she'd worked out her responses in advance. I remember Marcus's drunken stories about his mother; he only ever talked about her when he was drunk. I'm on the edge of my seat.

"It was already apparent at an early age: Marcus was a gifted child—creative, dreamy, elusive—not a typical child, but his parents weren't typical either, of course." She chuckles at this, there's something forced about it. "Not an easy child either, he knew very well what he wanted, he tried to bend things to his will from a very young age, and from time to time he'd have tantrums so extreme it would sometimes worry me." I glance sideways at Marcus. He sits there watching as though nothing else exists, in the kind of total concentration he can have during a rehearsal. "What I'm the most proud of?" The woman fans back her endless hair and reflects: "That he exploited his talent and turned his weaknesses into his strength." Her expression is thoughtful. When the interviewer out of frame asks which weaknesses she was thinking of, she replies, "No comment," like it's a political talk show and they're trying to corner her. The interviewer allows the pause to go on a bit, and she adds, "Marcus is an artist *pur sang*, I've always encouraged him in that." I look at the woman, who doesn't seem the least bit like a mother talking about her child. While the audience had been watching with merry, distracted interest, passing the occasional comment, it is now deathly quiet. The mother shares a few anecdotes from his early childhood, names one of her favorite shows of his and explains why she liked it. Then the interviewer asks how she'd describe their relationship. With a moment's hesitation, she replies: "It's awful that I can't give him all my motherly love, which is so much, so powerful, so unescapable. He is my only son, but he has abandoned me. In the emotional sense, at least." Then she holds a hand more or less in front of her eyes, as though she wants to hide tears from the camera. They switch to a clip from a rehearsal in which Marcus is giving a tongue-lashing to a technician who has done something wrong. The cruel power of editing.

Marcus, the man of grand gestures and the endless show, certainly in this kind of company, certainly at the moment in which he is also expected to be the star, sits bolt upright in his chair. I wonder why he gave the filmmakers permission to interview his mother. Some kinds of hope never fade, maybe. Everyone remains silent until there's a clip of Marcus's *Hamlet* production from a couple of years ago, a widely praised production. Then Elise makes a comment. It's not a very funny remark, but everyone laughs all the same. Marcus doesn't join in.

17

He huffs and puffs as though he's just climbed a mountain, but he's only pulling up the pants I'd gotten to his knees while he was still lying down. I help him into his suit jacket. He looks helplessly at the pair of shoes I've laid out.

"Come on, up on the bed," I say before putting a pair of socks on him, and then the shoes, a minor victory over my aversion, anything for a good cause. I roll the wheelchair up to the bed and put the note of apology to the nurses on the pillow.

We're almost through the door when he says, a touch of alarm in his voice, "My aftershave." I look for the bottle in the small hospital bathroom, give it to him, and he sprays twice. "Enough?"

I move in closer and sniff. "Perfect."

I push him into the hallway, past the nurses' office—they're much too busy to notice us.

In the parking lot we have to go over a rough patch, and I bump a protruding stone. He bounces in the wheelchair. I apologize, but he simply tells me to hurry.

We arrive at the car. When I open the door on his side, he stands up and looks helplessly at the seat as though he doesn't know how he's going to get into it. He turns his backside toward the car, his face toward me, and slowly lowers himself down. He almost hits his head on the roof, but I cry "Watch out" just in time. When he's finally sitting, he keeps staring at his legs as they refuse to obey. I lift them up and move them inside. Then to get the wheelchair folded, heave the thing into the trunk. I'm bright red by the time I get in.

When I close my door, Dad suddenly bursts out laughing. He holds his belly and tries to stop by taking deep breaths, but each time, he bursts into giggles again. How long has it been since I saw him laugh?

"You've actually kidnapped me, you realize that, don't you? A help-less, sick man kidnapped by his dynamic daughter, in the service of an old flame." Then he squeaks with laughter, like a little girl. Perhaps it's nerves too, but nevertheless it's infectious and so we pull onto the road, both of us shrieking with laughter.

Very unusually, Marie has gone out with her cousin for the day. Gilda had insisted on taking her to shop in Holland for the day, which worked well for us.

At first he was terrified when I told him I'd gotten in touch with Joanna and that she wanted to see him again. What if Marie found out? What if he and Joanna couldn't find anything to say to each other? What if he found it too hard? And now he looked so awful. But the more we talked about it, the less he resisted. *A heart never forgets,* I thought.

We drive past the flattest stretches of land, the sun is high in the sky. There's almost no wind. Dad has picked a radio station that plays non-stop classical music. Handel gently spills into the car. For a while, he complains about his nurse, the one with the curls and the noticeably large chin who always speaks in diminutives. He says he feels sorry to whoever's married to her. But the closer we get to our destination, the quieter he becomes. I park in front of the café where Joanna arranged to meet him.

"What if I don't recognize her?" Dad clenches my forearm as I pull on the handbrake. "What if I don't know what to say? What if I bore her?"

I give my dad my everything-will-be-fine smile. I put an old cell phone of mine in his breast pocket and say he can call me when he's ready to leave by just pressing this one button. I say I've brought a good book and some work so he doesn't have to hurry. I announce I'm going to get the wheelchair out of the trunk, but he wants to walk, he says. Passion fires the foolhardy. He looks in the mirror in the sunshade. I've never seen him do this in my whole life. I help him out of the car and guide him on my arm to the entrance. The café has a heavy glass door with cast-iron ornaments. I hold it open so that he can go inside at his own pace. I see Joanna looking and waving.

She still looks very much like in the photo, her hair slightly grayer, her skin looser, it's true, but she still radiates a lust for life. She sees my father walking over and closes both her eyes, a lovely, small, tender sign of recognition. She gets up and keeps a close eye on him, springy grass and crocuses in her gaze, fiery-red cheeks. They embrace, prolonging the gesture. It's a shame I can't see my father's face.

The shadows fall low across the road. The sky is unhappy. People walk past, some of them slowly, others in a rush. A little girl screams because she's happy or angry, or both. A dog sniffs at the wheel of my car, I hope his owner isn't going to let him piss on it. Dad is sitting next to me. His right hand is clenched around the door handle and he stares tensely through the windshield, as though there's something behind it that demands his attention. Starting the car seems rude, but just sitting there feels nosy. I try not to stare at him. Then I hear him gasping for breath. *He's going to say something,* I think. I turn my head, but nothing. When I asked him just now how it had gone, he simply said, "Good, very good," like a child when asked how school was.

Just as I go to insert the key in the ignition, ready to leave, it breaks like a summer storm: a fit of sobbing like I've never seen him have before. Everything in his face tenses and a long, low scream issues from somewhere deep within. He raises his arms and buries his face in his hands and stays like that, sobbing soundlessly now, his whole body jerking. I lay my hand awkwardly on his shoulder. We're not used to sharing emotions, the two of us. I simply wait, though I don't know what for. Being able to cry is already something, perhaps.

The sobs become infrequent, he asks me to start driving, starts to worry about the time, he definitely wants to be back in his room when Marie calls after her day out. We drive along without talking. I turn up the radio: Bach at his most fragile, the math a thing of the past, a variation on the most serene silence.

"The fact that you've done this for me—might this mean I wasn't a total bastard of a father?" It comes out as half question, half statement.

"Why do you think you were a bastard of a father?"

He shrugs.

"Of course not, Dad. I love you."

"I just wonder—I wasn't—" Dad stares at the road as though the words he's looking for might be there. He pulls the seat belt away from his chest.

I almost do what I always do, but then I take a deep breath and say, "Not a courageous father, perhaps."

He doesn't flinch. "Maybe not, no." Then he stops talking and stares ahead. "You were so strong."

"I was ten."

While we talk, Bach's strings make the sun shine soberly, make despair dance, and turn roads into festive dead ends.

"I couldn't cry, after the accident," I say, trying to overtake the car in front of me, which is dangerous on a road like this one. *Don't hesitate now,* I think, *go on.* There's a car coming the other way, I hope it slows down, I have to accelerate hard now and just in time to duck back to the right. Dad doesn't comment. I want to try to explain. "Mom was so—"

Dad interrupts me. "I couldn't, after the accident, I couldn't look at either of you. I couldn't—" His voice breaks, a fit of coughing that won't come. "I looked for a new mother for you as quickly as possible. Everything back the way it belonged—that seemed like the best thing to me."

"'The best thing,'" I repeat his words, keeping my eyes on the road.

Dad spins his wedding ring round and round with his index and middle finger. "I had to keep going."

"I know. But I wanted—"

"Me too, Mona, me too."

"I was scared my whole childhood, scared that—"

My father puts his hand on my arm to stop me. "I don't know how. I was—"

"The father, you were the father."

The weather has completely closed in now, the sky just as gray as the road, mist over the fields, the rows of trees barely visible. My stomach is full of concrete. Not a courageous father. The responsible adult who looked the other way. I've said it. I wish we could say a lot more. I hope he doesn't start hating me now. It's good we're in the car, I don't dare look at him, not really.

And then, all of a sudden, he says in a thin voice, "Mona, what an unbelievably good idea it was, having you."

18

Louis only really likes nature in paintings, he hates walking and there's no sport more boring than swimming, he says, but he's told me to put on comfortable shoes and bring along my swimsuit or be prepared to reveal my naked body to the world. He felt I needed a break, so he's taking me somewhere. He doesn't give me any details, it has to be a surprise. Louis can be really sweet sometimes.

When we arrive, he asks whether I know where we are and I shake my head.

"This is the Goovaerts' family estate. I had to give a reading nearby recently and the organizer told me the house is only used as a vacation home these days. There's rarely anyone here. We can go for a swim, like your dad and Joanna did twenty years ago." He lifts a cooler from the trunk. "Bought it myself," he says proudly.

I try to imagine Louis in the kind of shop where they sell things like that. Disconcerted by all the ugliness but still going over to a salesperson who takes him to the right aisle, and then hesitating, trying to pick out the least hideous cooler, the blue or the green, and then full speed to the checkout, dying of shame that someone might see him there. Louis opens the rear passenger door and takes two large bags from the back seat. He gives me the one containing the towels.

I'm impressed he's gone to all this trouble just for me. I kiss his neck. "What if someone turns up?"

"I'll talk my way out of it. You know me." He takes me to a section of fence that is loose and lifts it so that I can crawl under.

The house has a beautiful, old-fashioned grandeur to it and the estate looks vast. We walk through tall grass, there are bushes in the distance, old trees in shades of green and gray, white-blue skies. Birds chirp, insects buzz around our heads, and in the distance a horse whinnies.

"Better than your average nature documentary, isn't it?" I say.

"Mosquitoes don't bite you in documentaries," he replies as he shakes his head furiously; his hands are full.

Once we reach the pond, Louis sets everything down in the grass and begins to get undressed. He turns out to be wearing red-and-blue swimming trunks under his clothes, the large, baggy sort, no idea where he got them. And then he stands there in those trunks with his skinny legs and his milk-white belly. When he sees me looking, he adopts a dumb bodybuilder's pose. "And all this virile splendor is for you." He laughs and takes some sunscreen from one of the bags before smothering himself from head to toe and then passing the bottle to me. SPF 50, a person should only take risks if they might lead to something interesting, Louis says. Then he gets out a mosquito repellant roller and rolls it everywhere he can reach. Now he smells of the drugstore and a chemical factory combined. I take off my clothes and throw them in a heap. "Sexy lady." Since he's standing there in those enormous trunks, I get out my swimsuit and put it on—it's a musty, faded thing that's God knows how old. "Sexy bathing suit," he says. I smile at him. "You've got the sunniest lips," he says. Then he kisses my nose and says, "Into the water with you, woman. Whatever your father and his Joanna could do, we can do too." I don't tell him that the point of their swim was that they were skinny-dipping.

When we're sitting on the towels and almost dry, he opens the cooler. It contains a bottle of champagne, a carton of strawberries, and three types of French cheese. He takes a couple of half baguettes, a knife, napkins, and two glasses from the bag, polishes the glasses with the dish towel they'd been wrapped in, and hands them to me. He gently pops the cork rather than letting it shoot out—Louis knows his way in the world—pours, and says, "To everyone beautiful and sweet and here right now: so, you," then he grins and kisses me between my breasts.

We sit there and don't talk for a while, unsure what to talk about. Then Louis starts on about his love of Samuel Beckett and his hatred of James Joyce; he never tires of that. We talk about whether or not people can change. He doesn't believe they can, or only to a limited extent. "The bad things are going to get worse, I think, we're going to abandon each other." About Dad he says that it's criminal to force people into conversations they don't want to have. I wonder whether quiet people aren't just waiting to be asked the right question. Suddenly he gets out a notebook and reads a Robert Frost poem aloud and gets emotional about it. I thought it might be about death or saying goodbye or fathers or something, but it isn't.

The sun slowly sets and we watch it. I don't believe we've ever consciously done this before. I don't know whether we stop talking so we can focus on it better or because there's nothing else to say.

These days schools teach children to understand their feelings. For a while, Marvin hung an angry, or happy, or sad face on the corkboard each morning, as a kind of homework. I look at Louis and wonder why there are different words for loneliness, sadness, and fear because they often all feel the same. Perhaps the problem is me.

19

"Quiet down now, everybody: service announcement." Everyone looks at Marcus, who is standing theatrically on the table, his bare feet horribly close to me. "I'm not telling you anything you didn't know when I say that this play has been a struggle." *Finally,* I think. Marcus has put the problem into words, which is a start. All that walking away over the past weeks, all that fake enthusiasm from a man who purportedly knew what he was doing as a director, and his unwavering belief in a glorious end result, had brought us not one step closer to a successful production. "And now I think I know why." Here and there people look at each other, curious about what's coming. "The adaptation, that's the problem." Marcus doesn't look at me. "And how did I come to realize this? Because no one less than Elise"—*his Elise,* I can't help thinking—"came up with her own version. She's quietly been working on it, apparently, and didn't come to me until she'd finished." *Elise? Adapting? She's never done anything like that before.* I see the others looking at me, their expressions somewhere between pity and malicious glee. "And I read it and had my socks blown off." I roll my eyes at the cliché.

On Marcus's command, the director's assistant hands out packets to everyone. They immediately start to leaf through them, a din that seems to point to enthusiasm, or at least to curiosity, which I can understand.

"Let's start the rehearsal today with a read-through around the table and I hope you'll soon share my great excitement." Marcus jumps down without affording me a glance.

Elise looks elatedly at Nathan, who looks at me. I stare at the packet. I hate Elise, I love Elise, I want to be her.

I wish I could run away, hide myself somewhere in a dark cave and never come out again, or move to a country where no one has to know what a sad sack I am. I wonder why Marcus didn't even let me know beforehand. *Because that would have demonstrated some empathy,* I think. Then I'm angry with myself for trying to pin the blame on somebody else.

"Quiet everyone, Nathan's got the first line."

20

Dad's got peritonitis, Marie told me when she called. I was annoyed that she hadn't wanted to tell me at first what the problem was. At the same time, there are things that, once you know them, you wish you didn't. At the place where my father's intestines were sewn back together, there was a leak. In the beginning it was "spontaneously encapsulated," so the doctors didn't suspect anything, but all the same, poop slowly trickled into his belly, and of course, it got infected. This explains why he found it so hard to eat and why his fever came back. When a CAT scan revealed the problem, they operated as quickly as possible and gave him a colostomy bag, "to give his stomach a bit of a rest," said Doctor Amsons, the man whose name I thought I would be able to forget.

I felt shivery when I heard that. I wanted to swallow and couldn't. Panic does strange things to your body. The doctor's line "if everything goes well" was suddenly ominous again, a fearful mantra in my head.

I tried to imagine a world without my father, I don't even know how to, let alone how I'd live in a such a world. *Not right now*, I can't help thinking, not after I've just discovered a man I'd always wanted to know. I shake my head to get rid of the images. A person can try.

Under no circumstances does my father want to talk about the colostomy bag. The fact that he and I are having different kinds of conversations now doesn't suddenly make everything open for discussion. I do understand this. In the list of all the possible human humiliations, a bag of shit attached to the outside of your body scores fairly high. Marie concluded her story about the operation with the comment that she would be the person who'd have to clean the bag once Dad was out of the hospital. I wondered whether I'd be able to face doing it.

I'm visiting him now for the second time since the new operation, and Louis has come with me. He's startled when he sees the way my dad is lying there. The sheets are low, it's hot in here, his pajamas are crooked, making the bag visible through a white mesh net they've wrapped around his body. It's like a car crash on the highway—I don't want to look but I can't help it. I see Louis's gaze follow the exact same route. Then the thing begins to bubble in an alarming manner, like meat stewing in a pan. I don't even like stewed meat. *I hope it can't leak*, I think, and start to feel a little nauseated. I consider pulling the sheets up over it but I'm afraid I'll wake Dad. Louis says nothing, he just stands there. I feel awkward in a different way than he does, I notice. A person should be able to handle a thing like that with their own father, but a father-in-law, it's different. I go over to Dad and hover, staring at him. Then he opens his eyes, clears his throat, looks at me in confusion, pulls the covers up to his armpits, and says hoarsely that he's happy to see me. Then he notices Louis. "Oh, are you here too?"

"Of course," Louis says. It's the second time he's been to visit.

"That's kind of you."

"And how are you feeling now?" Louis takes a chair and sits down behind me.

"Not too bad." People minimizing their suffering always seems sadder than complaining openly. It's what I thought when Dad finally told me about his reunion with Joanna.

It had been really special the way they'd found each other again. They couldn't stop talking and asking questions as though they'd forgotten how to answer. They sat there in that café just staring into each other's eyes, remembering the moment they first saw each other in great detail, and the last time, how lost they'd felt afterward.

As Dad talked about it, I tried to imagine them, there at that table. Did they sit knee to knee? Did they kiss? Did they feel like doing a lot more than that? Did they wish they could run away there and then together, to somewhere no one would ever find them, or were they too levelheaded for that? She'd said something like she still thought of him when she opened the fridge, or took a hot bath, or looked up at the sky and saw swallows flying past, on their way to somewhere else. He'd only smiled at this and told me he regretted it afterward. He'd glossed over the word *regret*. Regret might be the most bothersome of all feelings, I find myself thinking, there's no possible defense against it. I'd like to think it's never too late, but is that true? He went on to say that, since he'd been in the hospital, the hour he spent in that café was the first time he'd really felt like living. His expression was cheerful. It was a cheerfulness intended to wipe away the wistfulness. Wouldn't everyone have been happier if he had dared to be with Joanna, he asks me. Even Marie, he said, if you could hear the things she says sometimes . . . He didn't finish his sentence. He certainly didn't want an answer.

How had they left it this time, I'd wanted to know. Neither of them had said anything concrete about what was going to happen next. Perhaps they found silence better than a conversation that would lead to impossibilities. Perhaps they should know what the prognosis was? Would that change anything? Would you or wouldn't you choose to be with your great love if you knew it was only for a short time?

Louis suddenly stops asking my father questions and begins to shuffle around in his chair. He needs to use the bathroom, he says, and gets up to go to the one in the room.

"Not here," I say, more harshly than I'd intended. "Down the hall-way, on the left."

"Sure. I'll be right back."

Dad seems to breathe more easily once the door closes, but it could be my imagination.

"Do you want to watch something with me?" he asks as he turns on the television. He picks a nature documentary. After a while, a voice says that the male fertilizes the female and then disappears, raising offspring is not for the males of the species; the voice punctuates this with a rogu-ish chuckle. Dad looks at me and then laughs out loud, very briefly. *He'll recover,* I think.

When Louis comes back in, he looks at me somewhat pointedly. I interpret his look to me: *Is this what I came here for? To stare at a TV with the two of you and watch wild animals eating each other?* Maybe I'm projecting. I get up and give Louis a kiss on his temple. At least he came and I didn't have to ask. Didn't have to ask *again*, I mean.

21

Anne-Sophie wrote back, finally. She hadn't had the chance to check her email until she made a trip to the nearest big city, João Pessoa. She wrote that the neon light in the internet café flickered every few minutes, which was distracting; that she didn't know what to write at this point. She was going to travel to the capital and take an international flight back, but she couldn't predict how long it would take.

Anne-Sophie never really wanted to talk to me about her decision. And we've always been pretty close, I hope I'm not mistaken about that. We're all so good at telling ourselves things, as though that's the only way to be.

She just did it. Without telling anyone in the family, she cleaned out her student apartment, terminated the lease, and gave away her few belongings to friends—or loaned them, she said, but it's been four years now. She left with all the money she had saved and everything she could fit in a large backpack. She sent us an email from Santiago to say she didn't know when she'd be back, that we didn't need to worry about her, she needed some time, she needed to live awhile, that's how she formulated it.

I felt sorry for Marie. Her only real child, the girl who had to make up for all the areas in which Alexander and I had fallen short—and there were many—had let her down. That's how Marie described it.

"That child, she's broken my heart." She repeated this dozens of times in those early months. "A mother is only as happy as her least happy child." Marie came up with an explanation, like she always did. Anne-Sophie hadn't sounded like herself for a while. Someone had put strange ideas in her head, probably that friend who was studying psychology—he couldn't be trusted, Marie sensed these things immediately. When Anne-Sophie had once come home with her hair cut short and dyed black, Marie had been absolutely certain: there was something really wrong now and she wanted to look like a boy. Marie infused the word *boy* with all the pity she had. No, this wasn't her child turning her back on the people who'd given her everything, everything.

I write letters to my sister—some emails are still letters—and I've asked her several times now what drove her to take such a drastic step. I heard she'd had a huge fight with Marie. Dad hadn't been able to follow it, he said, because it had taken place outside. Anne-Sophie had screamed lots of things he couldn't make out and Marie had come into the house as pale as a corpse and refused to tell him anything, which wasn't normal with her. Dad hadn't insisted, he considered any blows he experienced as just part of life, so there was no reason to try to intervene or insist she tell him about it. Anne-Sophie had come to say goodbye, with bloodshot eyes, Dad said, before returning to school. She couldn't visit for a few weeks because she had to study, she'd told him on the phone, and then all of a sudden, that email from Santiago.

All Anne-Sophie wrote to me was that she wanted to stay away from people who tried to control her, who didn't respect her, who were responsible for everything that was wrong. The only way she could live her life was far away from "her." The abstract "people" suddenly turned into "her." And, in one email, she asked a question that has always stuck in my mind. Did I remember a certain game that Mom used to play with us when we were younger? But she didn't explain why. I asked her to be more specific but she never replied.

Dad rarely or never talked about Anne-Sophie, as though he'd gotten used to people simply disappearing and never coming back. He always acted like that, a pill for the pain: eyes shut, mouth zipped, and look away.

I can hardly believe I'll see her again after all these years. I suggested going to visit a couple of times, there in her foreign country, but it was never a good time for her. Perhaps I remind her too much of herself, perhaps in the flesh she wouldn't be able to hide what she so dearly wants to keep hidden, perhaps she just doesn't miss me as much as I miss her.

22

Nathan returns to our table with two Westmalle beers and a large bowl of peanuts. He asked during rehearsal whether I had time for a drink afterward. I wanted to ask some others to join us, but he said he'd rather it was just the two of us. I grab a handful of nuts from the dish and stuff them into my mouth one after the other at top speed. *Why do I eat peanuts in bars?* I think. *They're unhygienic.* I take another handful. The glass bowl is almost empty now. Only then do I stop to think that Nathan might have wanted some too.

"Do you want one?" I ask awkwardly. I reach over and present him with a handful.

"I was about to ask," he says, pincering almost all the nuts in a single movement and then chewing on them for an awfully long time. He smiles teasingly and then gets up for a new supply. As he's waiting at the bar, he keeps his eyes on me. There's something ostentatiously manly about Nathan and yet he still gets dimples in his cheeks when he smiles. I always like contrasts in a face, I can't help but think.

"I wanted to talk to you about the show."

Tactful, just the two of us, without Marcus. I look at him and wait for him to start.

"I don't know what you think of the new version, but it doesn't solve anything for me. On the contrary. It's the play itself that isn't good enough."

"Are you saying that to make me feel better? Righting the cosmic balance after my embarrassing public humiliation?"

"Absolutely not." He touches my arm briefly. "I have a problem with it myself and it's making me very unhappy."

"Have you talked to Marcus about it?"

"Yes, and then he tells me I have to *go deeper*." Nathan crosses his eyes for three seconds to underline his despair.

I want to say that I see right through Marcus's directorial bombast, that I feel completely miserable after his stab in the back. I *could* chivalrously protest that Elise's version is better, although I'm not convinced either, but I consider my words carefully. "Well, it's not an easy project, I think—"

"I don't think Marcus can see clearly himself anymore, and he just doesn't want to hear that, certainly not now that it's his own girlfriend who has come up with the so-called salvation." He politely offers me the bowl of nuts but, after my initial grabbling, I don't dare take any more. "And the projects he gives us, come on, they don't amount to anything, do they? And he's never shown that much vision. I had such high hopes when I started working with him, but . . ."

I can't attack Marcus now, I think. "That second monologue of yours, it's beautiful, the way you do it."

"Yes, but that's the only piece of text that stirs my imagination. Apart from that . . ." Nathan eats the last few nuts. "We're clearly hungry, we should go get something to eat."

Is this an invitation? I act as though I haven't understood. "The four young actors seem relatively enthusiastic."

"No, actually, they just don't dare say anything to the great Marcus, even though they're just as depressed as I am." He wipes his hands on his jeans. "Can't you help me?" I simply smile. "You should write your own play, you know." Nathan's expression is serious.

"Don't be an idiot."

"I'm not. You could."

"Do you need something from me, Nathan?"

"You can try to seem unapproachable, it won't make any impression on me."

"Because you're just as unapproachable, is that it?"

His smile is broad. "One–zero." He takes a sip of his beer. "I think Marcus is snorting more than usual too." I feel like telling him about our adventure at the airport, but I still hold my tongue. "Whenever I run into him at the pub in the evenings, he can't stop touching his nose."

"It used to be much worse."

"Why do you keep working for a person like that? When I see the way he treats you sometimes—"

At that very moment, the door swings open and Marcus and Elise come in. They never just enter a place, they always make an entrance, the way Roman emperors did in bygone times, I imagine. And we'd deliberately avoided going to the regular bar.

"We're not safe anywhere," Nathan whispers. "Hey, maestro," he calls over to Marcus, "Elise."

I hope they won't come and sit at our table, but they do.

"Do you guys want anything?" Elise asks, her wallet in her hand. Marcus takes a chair and puts it next to Nathan's.

"No, thank you," I reply. "I was already about to leave ten minutes ago."

Nathan gives me a questioning look, but then waves his hand to turn down the offer too.

"Don't go trotting off, little lady. Just because you didn't prove yourself as a dramaturge this time doesn't mean you have to run away."

Marcus puts his hat down on the table and gives me a provocative look, although maybe I'm projecting.

"Give me a pint of Duvel, then," Nathan calls over to Elise. She is waiting at the bar to order. She studies her hands—perfectly manicured, the nails painted cherry red, as always. She is beautiful and elusive and completely perfect, this woman. It's no surprise that Marcus is so crazy about her. And then I hear Nathan suddenly say, "Listen, I'm going to be honest with you, Marcus. I don't think the new adaptation is any better, and I'm seriously concerned about the play."

I look at the two men in astonishment. I pick up a placemat and fold it in two, and then again and again and again.

"Oh, that's interesting," Marcus says with a sardonic glint in his eyes. "And what about you, Mona? What do you think?"

"It's not really my place to have an opinion, I think."

Elise arrives at our table with a whiskey, a pint, and a glass of white wine. Her wallet is clenched between her teeth, her usual elegance momentarily forgotten. She puts down the drinks and arranges herself. "You really don't want anything?" I shake my head and she sits down.

"Mona was just about to share her views on your adaptation," Marcus cries.

"No, I—"

Nathan interrupts me. "With all due respect, Elise, I think it's wonderful that you've attempted to make the play workable in your own way. But to me, it's no better than it was before. The real problem is that Hans's text is a shambles."

"'A shambles.'" Marcus repeats the words, slowly and emphatically, as though he has to ponder them long and deep. "And what do you suggest, then, three weeks before the premiere?"

"I'd risk choosing a different play. The timing's tight, but it's not impossible. I'm sure Mona could find a better script in no time." He doesn't know I suggested this before we started rehearsing.

Marcus pushes his hair back behind his ears, and then again; he always does that when he's irritated. "Are you in love with Mona? Is that what this is about?"

"Come on, Marcus," Nathan says.

"Just find a new play? With this crappy cast? And then bash a production out of it in just three weeks? With four rookies in the cast? And you think that would have more chance of meeting with success?"

"To be honest, I do."

"Mona?"

"I'd be happy to make some suggestions."

"Looks like you've got Nathan wrapped around your little finger." Marcus rubs Elise's back.

"I simply asked her to have a drink with me," Nathan says. "I wanted to discuss the play with somebody."

"Oh, and what did she tell you? I'm curious about that. It wouldn't be the first time that Mona's loyalty has been shaky." He makes this sound heavy with meaning and I genuinely have no idea what he's talking about. I look at him questioningly, but say nothing.

"Marcus, come on. I just want us to make something good, that's all." Nathan frowns.

"Duly noted," Marcus says, throwing back his whiskey in one gulp. "Weren't you two just about to leave?"

23

His small head is sunk deep into the plumped-up pillows, his mouth is half-open, his lips are creased and dry, he hardly moves. Dad is sleeping more and more. I hope this isn't a bad sign. Cleavage said yesterday that the gentleman was severely weakened after the operation, which couldn't be considered abnormal, and that we had to wait and see how things developed further.

I pick up a newspaper and begin to read. I try not to think about the play or the theater or Marcus or anything related to those things. I've never felt like my back was to the wall as much as it is now. I read an exposé about child abuse in the weekend supplement. I suddenly realize: I'm able to sit here next to him. I can bear the bag of urine, the strange noises he makes, the helplessness of him lying there listlessly.

Then my phone rings. Nathan. I don't pick up and quickly turn the ringer off, but Dad wakes up anyway. I apologize.

"Don't worry, don't worry," he mutters. He yawns a few times, smacks his lips, tries to open his eyes fully, and maneuvers himself a little straighter. He slowly comes to life. "I can sleep when I'm dead." He looks at the clock next to the TV: almost four. Then he stares out the window as though he's trying to get a handle on the world outside, on the time that keeps slipping away from him.

"Do you want some water?"

He shakes his head.

"Can I get you anything else or do anything for you?"

He still says nothing, looking deep in thought. I turn a page of the newspaper. I don't want him to feel like he has to perform for me.

"You should have kids." He suddenly comes out with this, decisively.

"What makes you think of that now?"

"I just thought I should say it."

"And why should I have kids?"

"It would do you good."

"I'd mess up a kid, I think." It sounds light, nonchalant. "Anyway, Louis doesn't want any, so, but I don't mind."

"You're thirty-five, there's still time."

"Louis is fourteen years older than me."

"I didn't say you should have children with Louis, did I?"

"Dad." I add a touch of indignation, almost teasingly.

He ignores it. "You won't mess up your kids." His gaze seeks out mine. I feel cold for a moment and don't immediately understand why. He buzzes his bed a little more upright. After all this time, he's figured out the control panel. He's not the most dexterous; I must've inherited that from him. I don't know whether it's because he keeps on looking at me like that, but something in me summons up the courage.

"I've been wanting to ask you something. About Mom."

Dad waits in silence.

"What was wrong with her? I mean, I've never dared to talk about it, but . . . that coldness of hers. She was so—"

"Damaged." Dad finishes my sentence, the word has been waiting there for centuries. Dad looks at the door with a regretful gaze, as though he's worried someone will come in. "Your mother was a woman who'd been through a lot." He lays down the sentence and then stops talking.

"Yes?"

"Oh, child, it was all so long ago, all of it."

"She was my mother, I'd like to understand."

"Her father, he was"—he hesitates—"a tyrant, there's no other word for it. They were terrified of him, her and her sisters, your grandmother." He turns his gaze to me and I give him a very brief nod of encouragement. "When he got home from work, for example, he demanded total silence, and all those women had to tiptoe around to make sure he didn't . . . Sometimes I had to visit the house, that's the way things were in those days, you couldn't just go out on the town with your girlfriend, it all started off at a snail's pace. First you'd have coffee with the parents in attendance. Then you'd go for a walk together. Later you might go to dances organized by the Christian Youth Club, but home at twelve at the latest. That was . . ." He rubs his cheeks. "I remember one time your mother served her father a bowl of soup. We weren't eating with him, I don't know why, but we did sit down at the table. Whether your mother had cooked it or not, I can no longer say. But he tasted it, laid his spoon down on the table, and, looking at Agnes, threw the bowl of soup onto the floor. It splashed up onto the wallpaper, onto Agnes's skirt. 'Inedible!' he roared. And without a word, your mother cleaned it all up. The rest of them acted like nothing had happened, you wouldn't believe it. And I can tell you another twenty-five stories." He lets a thoughtful silence follow. "And then Agnes got pregnant. We'd known each other for about a year or so. Those things, none if it was allowed, of course, but we were young and we managed to escape now and again. We thought we'd been careful, but well. Now, as you can imagine, back then, a pregnancy out of wedlock could ruin a family's reputation for good. It was a disaster, to be honest. Her father arranged for her to be sent to France to stay in a kind of convent to have the baby and then give it up. Give *you* up." He looks at me for a while and then away again. "When her mother heard about it, she plucked up the courage to warn her daughter. Agnes packed her bags immediately and came to me. I still lived with my parents at the time, and they weren't amused either. The only thing we could do was get married as quickly as possible, before

anyone could see she was expecting. Your grandfather helped me set up
my dental practice. I was lucky. He never let me forget it for the rest of
his life, of course, but hey. That's what happened."

"You didn't really want to marry her, then?"

"There was no other choice. In those days, that was how it went."

"Was she different when you fell in love with her?"

"In love." He emphasizes the words. His face tells a whole story,
but his mouth doesn't join in. "I didn't really get to know her until after
we were married."

"Was she the same way with you? So—"

"Hmm, Agnes was—I don't know—"

He sounds like he's about to get shut down, I think, though I'm not
sure. "That hardness in her, with me she was so often—"

Dad doesn't let me find the right words. "I didn't know how to arm
myself against that either." He falls silent.

It feels like I have no skin. A tree losing its leaves after a gust of
wind. So, I was what tied my father's fate to that woman. I let the
thought blow through my mind.

"I'm tired. Really, terribly tired." Without waiting for a reaction,
Dad zooms his bed back down again. "Can I sleep a bit?" He closes his
eyes. "A little nap."

"Yes," is all I say. I decide to go get myself a coffee, maybe with
something cloyingly sweet to go with it.

As I walk down the dismal hallway toward the cafeteria, I spot Uncle
Artie coming my way. It's been a long time since I last saw him. He's
visited a few times, though my father usually manages to get rid of him
in less than thirty minutes. *Strange the way everyone keeps their distance,*
I think, *even his own brother.*

"I thought I'd give it a go," Uncle Artie says, shrugging apologetically.

"Just keep insisting, that's the way to do it with him."

Uncle Artie gives me a kiss. "I'm happy to see you again, pretty lady." Uncle Artie was always the kindest.

"You're looking pretty sharp yourself." I laugh. "Are your men making you happy?"

"Just one man these days, sweetheart." With a big smile, he takes a photo out of his wallet and shows me a guy in brightly colored swim trunks. "Handsome, isn't he?"

"Fantastic," I reply.

"Is it all right if I drop in on your father now?"

"He's taking a nap."

"Then shall we have a drink together first? Do you have time?"

I nod and we head for the cafeteria.

"How are you? You look a little troubled."

"Dad and I just had an intense conversation about my mom. He told me they had to get married because of me, and that he actually hadn't wanted to."

Uncle Artie whistles through his teeth. "You didn't know that before?"

"No, you know Dad. We were never allowed to talk about her."

We walk over to the self-service counter, each take a tray, and push it toward the sweets section. I choose a bowl of chocolate mousse and cream, and Uncle Artie copies. He insists on paying. Once we're seated, he says, "I still can't believe you never knew."

"I'm sure there are a lot of things I still don't know about." I sum up what Dad told me.

Uncle Artie gives me a questioning look, then rests his spoon next to his bowl. "It was an unhappy marriage, your parents'. They didn't talk to each other. Vincent hid in his office and, if he didn't have to work, he'd ask us to hang around, us or the neighbors—anything to liven things up a bit. I was there a lot in those days, maybe you remember that. I was a bit younger, so it was nice not to have to spend every weekend at my parents'. And when there were people at your house, it was so much fun, there was eating and drinking and we played cards and talked until late at night, and you two little kids would hang around with us." He sips his coffee.

"I remember my mother wasn't happy about you coming around all the time, or am I mistaken?"

"Eh. Agnes let it happen. She complained about it sometimes, but not when we were there. I think both of them were happy to have the distraction. They'd run out of things to say to each other before you were even born. First they lost hope that they'd ever connect, I think. After that there was the fear of never connecting again." He eats another spoonful, leaving a brown stripe above his lips.

"She was a very unhappy woman—depressed, I realize now. Only, back then that word didn't exist. I don't think she ever forgave your father for getting her pregnant. Well, she was there when it happened, of course." He laughs like a child who has told a dirty joke. "But I imagine *he* was the one to take the initiative. Vincent, he was—" Then he looks at me, smiles apologetically, and doesn't finish his sentence. "People said Agnes's father, a terrible man, the whole village knew it, anyway they said he messed with his own daughters. Excuse the expression. I don't know whether it's true, but that's what they said. And I know that your parents' marriage wasn't exactly, um, passionate. That doesn't have to mean anything, but still."

"Dad once told me his sex life with my mother was better than with Marie."

"That's odd. He complained about it a lot to me, at the time." He scrapes his spoon across the bottom of his bowl. "Strange fellow, your dad, always has been." I try to picture my mother, but I don't really manage and it bothers me. "But the way she treated you, Mona, that was—it often pained my heart." He touches my shoulder and then squeezes it.

Mice run through my thoughts. I remain sitting on my chair, my head spinning, as though it's the only thing I can still do.

24

Alexander found the message on his answering machine in the morning. Marie had called late the night before, saying, "It's a big emergency, can you come to the house tomorrow morning? I'm going to *try* to get some sleep now, *try*." He'd called her back immediately, but she hadn't picked up.

My brother said he thought something was really wrong with Dad, the water on his lungs was already a sign of total exhaustion, and what about his heart? I asked what made him think that, simply because I didn't want to draw the conclusion myself. Alexander repeated, irritated, "'A big emergency.'"

"As though there were degrees." I sighed back.

He and Charlie were going to take Marvin to school and then pick me up on the way.

I go outside immediately after the phone call, even though I'll have to wait at least twenty minutes. I try to call Louis from the portico of the apartment building. He'd gone up to his writing den quite early. The phone rings six times, then the answering machine. I leave a message. The sun is shining, but the clammy morning chases a chill through everything. *I should have put on a jacket or a sweater,* I think, but don't go back in.

"Come on, Alexander, hurry." I say it out loud. I'd like to talk to him about all the things I've learned, and yet I know already that I won't. I can't cope with the horrible things he might say about Dad. When I told Louis that same evening, he'd been very intrigued. He was disappointed I hadn't asked for more details.

They pick me up, we drive and talk about all kinds of nonsense, and then we ring the bell. In our hurry, we've both forgotten our key. No reply. We ring again, the ding-dong echoes into the neighbor's garden. "Maybe she's at the hospital?" I say.

"She said we had to go to the house," Alexander replies.

"Maybe she died in her sleep, just to do us a favor," Charlie says, and I have to laugh, partly from the tension.

Alexander hisses at us, "Come on," and points at the door as though he's afraid Marie has her ear glued to the other side of it.

A minute later, Marie does appear. "No key?" She lets us in. "I was in the kitchen," she adds then, as though to explain the long wait. "What would you like to drink?"

"Tell us what's the matter first." I sound brusquer than I'd like.

Alexander sits down at the kitchen table, in Dad's seat, which bothers me.

"Yesterday, it must have been about eight, I suppose, quarter past, maybe, I took the inner ring road to the hospital, and suddenly, along that stretch with the row of trees, you know, the beeches they once wanted to chop down, until they set up a committee to stop it, all the cars in front of me slammed on their brakes. Me too, of course, but I bumped into the car in front of me. I was only going around fifteen miles an hour, so at first I thought, *Oh, it can't be that bad.* I get out and the other driver gets out and we stand there in the middle of the road. Terribly dangerous, actually, because Yvette's daughter, you know, she got run over and she still has trouble with her leg, and how long ago was that?" She pauses to take a sip of her coffee. "But anyway, so we were standing there. There wasn't much damage to his car, he was driving one of those giant Jeep things, a bit like Francis's, but in black, almost indestructible, those things. I don't like them, such big vehicles, but actually you should have cars like that because at least they're safe. But the state of mine: the whole hood crumpled, the bumper dented, the right headlight broken, and God knows what inside, of course. I stood there just quaking. The man acted friendly, he asked whether I was all right. 'No,' I said. 'I hit the steering wheel really hard and now my car looks like the driver should be dead.' To which he says, 'Fortunately, you're not.' As though that solved everything. People today, there's no politeness anymore."

In the meantime, she has pulled back her hair and pointed, her finger like an arrow, to a cut on her forehead.

"See that? And my neck hurts, oh it hurts, and around here too, guaranteed it's whiplash, can't be anything else, and whiplash, well, that'll be months of misery, won't it? Bettina had that once, the woman didn't sleep for months afterward. So now I'm stuck here, without a car, and just when I have to get to the hospital every day and all. And Dad really wants me to—"

Charlie interrupts her. "So everything's OK with Vincent?"

"Given the circumstances, you can hardly call that OK, Charlie, but I'm terribly concerned. Now, nothing new has happened, no, just the pulmonary edema. But I ask myself, how am I going to get to the hospital every day? And what about my neck?"

"Yes, it's all dreadful for you," Alexander soothes.

"You could take a cab, it'll cost about ten euros a ride," Charlie says, "or get a rental car until the damage has been repaired. They usually have those available at the larger auto shops."

"The towing service dropped me at home first and then they took my car to the shop, apparently they always do it that way. And then I called them this morning, about nine, it could have been ten past, and they said it would take about a week, depending on how fast they got the new parts in. I said: 'What do you mean, about a week? I can't cope without a car, because my husband's in the hospital and it's not looking good at all.' And then I said, 'So, I need a car.' 'Yes, ma'am, but we can't help you with that,' he said. He said—"

"And that's why all of us had to drop everything and rush over here?" Charlie says, turning away from Marie.

"I didn't ask you all to come, did I? I called Alexander because I didn't know what else to do."

"We thought Dad was dying," I say, keeping my voice level.

"Whatever made you think that? If Dad was dying, I'd have said that Dad was dying, wouldn't I?"

"That's true," Alexander says.

Charlie looks at me and rolls her eyes.

"So, a rental car." She grimaces like she's imagining a vacation in a run-down hotel. "Well, I have to do something. Dad can't be without me, not for five minutes. When I leave in the evening, he can't stop begging me to stay a little longer." She rotates her neck, her face suggesting someone is breaking her leg. "I think I'll have my neck checked out in the hospital. Can you take me? You're here now anyway, you'll want to see Dad, so perhaps someone can come with me if they want to take an X-ray, if that's not too much to ask. If you're too busy, I'll understand, you know, then I'll look after myself. But you can't be careful enough with a neck, Dad would agree. Oh, he's going to get such a shock, he doesn't even know about all this yet."

We walk to the car. When Charlie goes to sit next to Alexander, Marie says, "Oh, so your mother has to climb into the back seat? All right, no problem."

Alexander drives a four-door car, so there's actually no difference between getting into the front or back, but Alexander looks at Charlie, who says, "Why don't you sit in the front, then?" When Charlie joins me in the back, she squeezes my knee and makes a face like a silent scream. I giggle. I can't help it, relief after the panic, I suspect.

"Oh, you think it's funny, do you?" Marie says without looking back.

I recover myself. "Of course not," I say, seriously. "Absolutely not."

"There's a strange stain on this seat, Alexander."

"No idea what that is."

"Well, and Daddy. That pulmonary edema is really not good news, sometimes it's an indication of heart failure." She looks in the sunshade's mirror and studies her forehead. "I think it's ketchup or something."

"What?"

"The stain, ketchup. Have you been eating fries?"

"Huh?"

"Eating fries, in your car. I can still smell it a bit, I think, and that stain really could be ketchup."

"I can't smell anything." Charlie lays her hand on Alexander's shoulder.

"If I was you, I'd try to wash it off. They've got a good product for that, I'll write down the name of it for you if you want. Otherwise, you could hang up one of those air fresheners. A car is part of the way you present yourself, dear."

As he parks, Alexander says, "I'll take Mom to get her neck checked out."

"I want to see Daddy first," Marie says as she wriggles out of the car.

"No," Alexander says, "you're going to think of yourself first. Come." He takes her by the arm and, with some grumbling, she lets herself be coaxed along.

Charlie and I walk to the elevator.

"Hallelujah," says Charlie. "I don't know where you two find the patience."

"Years of practice." I grin because I always do when I say something like that.

An hour and a half later, Marie comes into Dad's room. She is wearing a cervical collar, a very wide one, and moves her upper body as though there's a plank in her skirt that reaches right up to the top of her spine.

"Are you all right?" I ask.

"Hmm, I have no choice, do I?" she says. "Whiplash, just as I feared." Her blue eyeliner is slightly smudged, adding a grayish ring around her eyes, which already looked so sorrowful.

"Good thing you got it checked out."

"Yes," she says.

"We're really going to have to get going now, though."

Marie goes over to my father, bends over him, kisses his cheek, and keeps her face just a hair's breadth from his. "I'll tell you the whole story in a minute."

"Yes, why don't you make yourself comfortable on a chair." This is a charming attempt by Dad to get her face at a bearable distance, I guess.

She hovers where she is. "Well, any better than yesterday?"

My father tries to sink away deeper into his pile of pillows. "Yes, yes, absolutely. Already a little better." He sounds like he'll say whatever she wants to hear after hours of torture.

"Oh, I'm glad about that." Marie sits down.

"We really have to go. Sorry. Take care of yourself, Dad, and you too, Mom. See you tomorrow."

"Thank you," she says.

As I kiss my father again, he squeezes my hand and looks at me. His expression is somewhere between desperation and resignation. I wonder whether I've made things worse by getting him in contact with Joanna again. Charlie asks Marie where Alexander is.

"He went outside for a smoke. I think he assumed you might stay a bit longer."

Charlie only smiles.

As we go to the elevator, I picture them sitting there, the two of them, her talking about nothing, him saying nothing. *It's important to choose your partner wisely,* I think, *if only for the last part.* I'm going to call Joanna, maybe she'd like to see him again.

25

I stopped going to Louis's readings a long time ago, but if we want to see each other for more than fifteen minutes this week, accompanying Louis to this one is the only option.

In the car I tried to talk about the problems at the theater, it's getting harder and harder for me to know what to do during rehearsals, but Louis apologized and asked whether we could keep that subject for the way home, he wanted to prepare himself.

The organizer is a young woman, orangey-red lips, high cheekbones, red hair pulled tightly into a ponytail. She takes us on her high heels to the building's greenroom, a route past hallways highly reminiscent of bunkers. Louis says he's glad her beauty can help us forget the ugliness of these trenches, then he laughs at his own joke, to make clear that it is, probably, a joke. She turns her head and gives him a sideways smile. Once we've arrived in a room they've clearly tried to make cozy—you can see that from the color palette—she indicates the snacks that have been laid out, "All from the region," she says, smiling with those lips of hers. Louis thanks her twice.

Louis is good at evenings like this one. He reads some excerpts from his work and embroiders stories around them, smart and sensible but engaging too. Afterward, there are questions and a woman raises her hand like she's in school. "How autobiographical is your work?" she wants to know. "Not in the slightest," Louis replies. "My life is much too boring for that." Cue laughter.

When it's over, Louis wants to have a drink with the people, "because it's polite," he says. An hour and a half later, we're still there. I talk to the woman who asked the first question; she works in a store where they sell everything you need for equestrian sports. With more than average enthusiasm, she holds forth about different kinds of fodder and their advantages and disadvantages, about riding hats, of which there are more than ten different types these days. In the meantime, Louis wanders from group to group, bathing in their praise, he really needs it. The room empties out and, in the end, the one person who has made no attempt to leave is him.

When we finally get to the car, he asks me to drive because he's had two beers after all, and he's a bit tired. "Nice that you came along," he says, "evenings like this are always nice, aren't they?" Within five minutes, he's snoring. I turn up the radio. Who knows, it might wake him up.

26

"That'll be her," I say when we hear someone tapping on the door. Dad wanted me to put the bed as upright as possible, he refused the oxygen in his nose, the sheets had to be neatly pulled up to under his armpits, hair washed, chin shaven, aftershave on. He was even more nervous than the time before.

First he'd refused when I said that Joanna wanted to see him. What about Marie? He couldn't leave the hospital now. But since Marie had to lie down for at least an hour every day after lunch for her whiplash, the coast was clear, and I would keep a lookout in the hallway. We talked things through a while and then he came around. Some longings are stronger than any fear.

When Joanna pokes her head inside, he beams. He suddenly looks healthier than over the previous days, but perhaps I'm only imagining it. I immediately go to the door to leave them alone. She gives me a kiss. She smells of roses and autumn mist.

I've brought along a book, but I'm too restless on their behalf to be able to read. I look around aimlessly. There are three elderly women waiting in chairs. They're all wearing glasses and similar skirts and blouses, like a kind of uniform for the aged. One of them has a coughing fit, holding her hand in front of her mouth. The other two stare at her like they want to intervene but are bolted to their chairs. The mouth of the one on the far left gapes a little, alarmed by the coughing, or maybe she simply forgot to close it. *I don't want to get old,* I can't help thinking, *at least not like that.* I wander over to the window and then back and wonder how things are going in there.

Barely forty minutes have passed when I hear footsteps I recognize right away. I try to get a good look, someone is approaching, a skinny woman in a muted red dress. Marie has one like that. Let it not be true, not now, not her, but oh yes, I can see it's Marie. What is she doing here now? I can't warn Dad and Joanna, it's too late for that. Think of an excuse, but what? Marie draws ever closer. It's like she's constantly clamped to my feet, pulling me down with all her weight.

"Mona, what are you doing out here?"

My mouth talks but my head doesn't join in, it's on too high a state of alert. "The nurse is busy with him—want to go get a coffee together or something?"

"No, thank you, I've already had some coffee and too much gives me diarrhea if I don't watch out." She goes toward the door, her head too upright in the neck brace. "I'm going—"

"You're not allowed in, the nurse—" I say, realizing it isn't good enough. I have to get her away from here.

"Oh, I always stick around when they're nursing him. I've had enough medical—" And then she opens the door. I waltz into the room with her. For a few seconds, there's silence. Everyone looks at each other. Dad's eyes fill with panic.

"That's Joanna," I say, "a friend of my mother's, of Agnes's. I bumped into her here and when I told her about Dad, she said she wanted to come by and say hello."

Marie looks her up and down and then again, her lips in a thin strip. "Pleased to meet you," she says, without proffering a hand.

"You too. Yes, I was actually about to leave. I just wanted to—after all this time." She smiles, slings her handbag over her shoulder, and stands up.

"Don't let me drive you away," Marie says in the highest pitch I've ever heard her reach.

"No, no. I'll leave you to it." She turns to Dad, gives him a chaste kiss on the cheek, and says, "Take care of yourself. Get well soon." There are tiny chicks in that voice, and puppies, the softness. Then she nods to Marie and comes over to me. I'm standing near the door.

"I'll just accompany her out," I say, and as that slips out, I wonder whether I *can* leave Dad alone with Marie now, but to do anything else now would be more suspicious, so I let Joanna pass and then close the door behind us.

"Want to get a snack downstairs, or would you rather not? Whatever you want to do." I see her pondering. "And I'm sorry. Since the accident, Marie hasn't been here at all around this time, and then she had to pick—"

"It doesn't matter." She rests a hand on my shoulder. "And yes, let's pop down to that dreadful cafeteria."

Joanna is having a glass of beer; they only have a couple of kinds here, but she chose the darkest, a stout, which immediately endeared her to me. She isn't a sherry-sipping old woman, she's still very much part of the world. I just have a coffee, who knows what this day still has in store. We sit at a small table in the corner, next to the pale-green wall, at the window.

"To Vincent," she says, clinking her glass against my cup. She takes a few big sips, and then lets out a sigh. "I'm glad you called me."

"Does it upset you that—"

"It's terrible," she says. "You can't imagine how . . . He and I were so . . ." Then she falls silent. She stares at the sky outside, where birds are flying and clouds are slowly sailing by. She drinks a little more of her pint, it's already half-empty. "Do you mind me saying that? It might be—"

"No, on the contrary," I hurry to say.

"Will you take good care of him? You can do that."

I nod.

"Someone needs to take good care of him," she says, as though she's speaking to herself, so quietly. Then she smiles at me.

There's so much I want to ask this woman, but everything feels so odd. I continue to stare at her bashfully. "I think my father regrets it now, that he didn't—"

"Regrets." She rubs her finger and thumb along her bottom lip, the way Dad does sometimes when he's thinking. "We get up every day, do what's expected of us, and then go to sleep again, and we call that life. We sabotage our lives without realizing it because we unwittingly just do the things we saw people around us do, and we assume that's how things should be done. And in the meantime, we arrange things in a way that doesn't give us time to stop and think about our deepest feelings. We forget what we're worth and don't dare believe that we genuinely deserve something good. We find it easier to come to terms with our suffering, easier to console ourselves after the pain than to opt for what really would make us happy." She runs her hand through her hair. "Look at me ambushing you with all of this. The wisdom of an old crone, you're thinking." She smiles generously.

"Not at all." *Go on, don't stop talking.*

"You know, it's, I've been thinking so much since . . ." She stares into the distance, rubs a few fingers over the palm of her hand. "We always just carry on and then we're old, and we feel it in our joints that things aren't actually right, that something else would have been possible if only we'd dared. But then we think it's too late. And soon we're secretly dreaming of dying, or of a heaven where everything turns out right. It's such a pity, all of it, such a terrible shame." She turns her glass in her hands, then empties it. "How old are you now?"

"Thirty-five."

"Can I tell you something? You have to live well and dream harder. You have to learn to look at yourself, to ask yourself why you do what you do." She takes both my hands in hers and smiles as though my life could still work out OK. We look at each other. "By the way, just a practical thought, I wanted to ask whether there's a time of day I might call Vincent."

"After about eight, eight thirty, he's usually alone in his room."

"Ask him first whether he'd like me to call, will you?"

"I'll do that and let you know."

Joanna gets to her feet and so I do too. I don't want her to leave yet; I don't know why I don't want that. She hugs me, maybe because she wasn't able to hug Dad. When she lets go, she looks like she wants to say something but then turns on her heel and walks away. I watch her go for as long as I can.

When I go back into Dad's room, Marie is telling him something about the neighbor's daughter. Dad is dozing off because he's tired and about to fall asleep, or because he doesn't want to suggest any kind of exaggerated awareness of things. It's hard to guess. When I go in, he shoots a peevish glance in my direction, then closes his eyes again.

After a while, Marie asks, "So you just happened to run into that woman?"

"Yes, I recognized her when I was buying a newspaper downstairs. Some people don't change at all, even though it's been years."

"Hmm," Marie says. "And why wasn't I supposed to see her?"

"Well, everything that's got to do with my real mom, I mean Agnes, it's always been a bit of a sensitive subject, right?"

"You always act like it is, but I never say anything about it."

"Well, in any case, it was stupid of me. I'm sorry."

"Lying is always wrong and the truth will out." Marie looks at my father, who is keeping his eyes shut. My mother always used to say that too. "And Daddy didn't mind seeing her."

"Um, sure?"

"While he always tries to get rid of the rest of us as fast as he can." She talks as though he's not present; Dad continues to act like he isn't.

"I might have forced him into it a bit. I thought it would be nice for him, after all this time, a different face. I didn't really think."

Marie picks up her knitting.

"Sorry," I say again, just to be sure. "And she was here for less than fifteen minutes."

"Right." Marie sticks the knitting needles under her armpits. The back of the sweater she is making for Dad is almost done.

27

When they bring him back, Dad's face is ashen. He lies there not moving, groggy, an animal who has been transported in a dark box all day
and is now adjusting to daylight again.

"Was it a little bit bearable?"

"No," he says, sighing deeply, which he seldom does. My father
doesn't believe in sighing, just like he doesn't believe in hope—or faith,
I think. I should ask him sometime.

"The needle was this big, and they sucked out all the fluid with
it. There was a lot, the doctor said." He swallows, loudly. "I hope you
never have to go through that." He grimaces in a way that worries me.

"But you feel better now?"

"Breathing's easier, yes."

"Get a bit more sleep, maybe."

"The waiting's the worst. They leave you lying in a hallway where
anyone might walk past, and the sheet was too thin, I was cold, and I
was worried the bag would get too full." These days he refers directly to
his colostomy bag, calling it simply "the bag." "I'm not wearing a watch,
how long was I there?"

"You've been gone almost two hours."

"Why do they do that to a person?" His voice breaks. He takes a sip of water. "I think I will take a nap. Will you tell Marie it turned out better than expected?"

"Why? It didn't."

"And you think Marie knowing that would be helpful to me in any way?" He lets out a wheezy laugh, somewhere between disbelief and astonishment, then closes his eyes and turns his sallow face a little. "Thank you, dearest daughter." Then he opens them again briefly. "By the way, she called me last night. Thank you for passing on the message." He smiles broadly.

Within a few minutes, his snores are whistling away. I wish I could take him away from here to a place where lives are long and wide and the sun glitters on seas and nights remain blessedly warm.

As I drive away, I think about Dad and about Dad and Joanna, about the days as they are, what lies behind and ahead of us and everything that slips away. I turn up the music and croon along with Andy Williams, "Moon River."

28

This isn't shouting, it's barking. In a few days we'll move to the theater to put the production together. There's been no progress, as far as I'm concerned, but no one's asking me. I've never felt so painfully redundant. Nathan has just performed his long monologue; he did it just as he has done over the past days. Then Marcus hadn't commented, now he goes ballistic. The others look on in shock, even Elise bites her cuticles, a habit she's trying to quit. When he's finished with his tirade, Marcus sits down on a chair, cross-legged as usual, sunglasses on top of his head, and says nothing for a while.

No one dares to speak, until Nathan himself starts up. "Maybe it would be a good idea if I—"

Marcus interrupts him, icily calm all of sudden. "Quit, left this production. Yes, that's an idea, yes. I've been thinking about it for a few days now, perhaps Frank can take over your role. I'll have to talk with the PR and planning people, whether we can delay the premiere for a week or maybe two even, but it can't go on like this." He holds a hand in front of his face, an elbow on the table as though he's the victim.

Nathan looks like he doesn't know whether to laugh or shout, amazement's two ports of refuge. Elise knew nothing about this, based on the way she's staring at Marcus. The young actors stare at their shoes and their cups of coffee and their scripts, anywhere as long as it's not at Nathan or Marcus. Even Frank looks uncomfortable.

I observe the tableau. All these people, dedicating their lives to art, Marcus in the lead, and the result: Nasty situations like this one? Toying maliciously with a man who hasn't done anything wrong?

I straighten my shoulders and say, just as calmly as Marcus, "You can't do this."

He emerges from behind his hand and turns his goading eyes on me.

"Blaming something on an actor when it has nothing to do with him, and forcing another young man to learn his role in three weeks. It's going too far." It rolls out of my mouth and I sit there staring at it, as though I'm not actually present myself, not really.

Marcus gives me a penetrating look. "It might be to your credit that you're defending your admirer, but the fact you can't see that Nathan is lowering the standard doesn't say much for your skills as a dramaturge."

"Maybe it's time you admitted you no longer know what to do." I keep my eyes fixed on him.

Marcus paces up and down, pushes his hair behind his ear at least five times. "What do you want, Mona? For me to kick you out as well? Is that it? For me to finally admit what you really are: a girl who sits there quietly being intellectually correct, while all the rest of us are doing the real artistic work? What do you know about making theater, at the end of the day?" Marcus has always known exactly where to strike to hurt somebody; despite everything, he's an excellent observer. "You've got no part in this production anymore anyway. And let's return to this conversation, once all the rave reviews have been published."

No one speaks. Nathan lays a hand on my shoulder. I gather my things; Nathan begins to do the same. I leave; he follows. It isn't until we're outside that what I've done and what the possible consequences might be really sink in. Nathan suggests we go drink whiskey or something. I'm not sure that's the best plan now. I withdraw and call Louis. He says we'll go out and eat together, he wants to hear the whole story. Then I calm down a bit.

29

Anne-Sophie wanted to go straight to the hospital from the airport. She didn't say why it had taken her so long to come. I didn't want to bring it up myself, didn't want to subject her to a barrage of questions; it must shake you up a bit, returning to your home country after all that time away.

We stand outside the door to his room, her face as blank as white paper, arms crossed. She taps the nose of her sneakers on the floor, each in turn, like a runner warming up for a race. She looks good: deeply tanned, hair fairly long, blond again, no longer dyed, tied up loosely, muscled arms, weathered hands. She's not wearing any makeup like she used to. She looks a lot older than when she left, more adult. She's one of those girls who is intriguing because she's so hard to read.

I hugged her, there in the arrivals hall. Perhaps because everyone does that there, perhaps because it was so odd, her suddenly standing there, in the flesh, perhaps because I wanted to show her how much I'd missed her. She was the first to let go.

In the car she was relatively quiet. When Anne-Sophie was little, her mouth never stopped moving. She was always asking questions and telling me things, and when she wasn't, she'd have a song ready to sing. Sometimes I thought she was trying to keep one step ahead to prevent anyone else from saying something awful, or having a fight, or doggedly refusing to talk. She became quieter in her adolescent years. Perhaps the trend simply continued, or the years of relative solitude have truly changed her. She was continually meeting people, she wrote in her sporadic emails—but does that cure loneliness, I always wondered, that fleeting coming together of people in transit? Perhaps her Dutch has grown rusty, she probably hasn't spoken it for four years.

"Are you coming in with me?" She smiles almost shyly.

"If you want me to."

She nods, then presses the door handle and goes into Dad's room.

He knew she was coming. When I told him, his first question was, "What did Marie say?" and his second, "So she does want to see me?" And when I only said yes, he continued, very calmly: "Because she thinks I'm dying?" In all this time, that word hasn't been spoken yet. I just sat there, but it was like I fell and kept on falling, like everything underneath me fell away, crumbled, unraveled. I told him never to say stuff like that. His reply was, "Just when I thought I could say practically anything to you." Then he gave me a teasing tap on the nose.

Dad is sitting there ready; there's something ceremonious about it. Anne-Sophie goes over and gives him a kiss. If she's shocked by the way he looks, she hides it well.

Dad smiles and says, "There you are," and his eyes become even smaller than they already are.

"Yes." She takes a chair and moves it closer.

"You've gotten even prettier."

Anne-Sophie smiles.

"Four years is a long time."

"Yes."

"Are you happy?" he asks.

"Happier than I used to be."

Dad takes Anne-Sophie's hand in his own, she squeezes it, then he lays it back down on the sheet. "But tell me, how are you doing now?"

It's strange for me to be here too, so I say, "I'll just head downstairs."

"No, Mona, grab a chair and stay. I haven't seen you for so long."

There isn't a question but a request. Big sisters always remain big sisters, and this makes me happy, I realize.

They talk a lot, mainly about all the things she's seen and done. Everything that might potentially be problematic is politely side-stepped. Dad does ask a lot of questions, and I see that Anne-Sophie is pleasantly surprised.

A good half an hour later, she hasn't been here any longer than that, the door opens without anyone knocking. It's Marie. She's put on her new skirt, the brown one that almost reaches her ankles, bought with her cousin Gilda. Her white blouse is neatly tucked in, and the broach her mother gave her two Christmases ago is pinned just above her right breast. It even looks like she's been to the hairdresser's. She walks behind me to Dad, kisses his cheek, mumbles something by way of a greeting, and then sits down in the armchair at the head of his bed. Dad looks at me, glassily, as though he no longer dares to look at Anne-Sophie. No one says anything; the air is deadweight.

"Hello, daughter."

"Yes." As though that word is her lifeboat.

"You're back."

"For a little while, yes."

"How long are you staying?"

"I don't know."

"If you'd like to stay at home, I can—"

"No, I'm staying at Peter's. He's got a spare room and it's not so far from here."

"Oh right, that's good, yes."

After each reply, there's a new silence, more painful than the previous one. Marie rests a hand on my father's shoulder, something I've never seen her do before.

Then Dad says, "Anne-Sophie's had a really interesting time over there, haven't you, Anne-Sophie?"

"I'm sure." Marie coughs, a fake cough from a throat that doesn't need clearing. "And were you planning to give your mother a dressing-down along the way?" Something in her voice trembles. She must have resolved not to say this, not like that, and certainly not at once, but now there's no escape from herself. She bites her lip as though she wishes she could take back the words. With the cervical collar, she effuses a new kind of helplessness.

"I've come for Dad, not to argue."

"Fine, so I can breathe again, can I?" An awkward giggle follows.

"It's always all about you, isn't it?" Anne-Sophie keeps stroking her hand with two fingers, she looks at Dad and then at me, a face that refuses to betray anything.

Marie scoots her chair even closer to Dad, fiddles with her broach, moves Dad's drip to one side. A large group of people, chattering noisily, walks past in the hallway. "What on earth happened? For you to become like this?"

Anne-Sophie looks at her, and says curtly, "You. You happened to me."

Marie's bottom lip begins to quiver. She gets up, looks as though she'll say something for a moment, but then leaves the room.

Dad's face is frozen. The door closes on its latch. I look at him and go after Marie.

I find her smoking on the bench where she always sits when it's not raining. I look at the red glow between the V formed by her fingers. When the cigarette is finished, she uses the stub to light another one, her cheeks all sucked in, which makes her eyes larger. She has crossed her legs one over the other, the higher foot bounces up and down; if you didn't know better, you might think she'd gotten carried away by some up-tempo music. Once the new cigarette's lit, she feels around in her handbag for something.

"Are you all right?"

"No, not really." The smoke circles her head.

"Of course I don't really know what's going on between the two of you but—"

"Lies," she snaps at me. "I don't know where she gets these things from. But well, apparently I deserve this punishment, apparently I do everything wrong." I hear rattling in her handbag, God knows what she carries around in there. "No one cares about me, that's the truth. I should just learn to accept it, right?"

"But Mom."

"No, don't 'but Mom' me. Do you really think I'm stupid?"

"I don't get it."

"Oh. You don't get it? 'You can't go in, there's a *nurse* in with him.'" Marie imitates me. "A nurse." She looks at me. "Do you think I really didn't know who she is?"

I almost die of shock. She looks away again, at two little girls wearing matching dresses chasing each other in circles. She gets out a handkerchief, gives me her cigarette to hold as she blows her nose. I grip it between my thumb and index finger, the bit where the ash isn't burning and where her mouth hasn't been.

"Does Dad know?"

"Oh, Dad, of course. It's only ever about Daddy. No, I haven't said anything. What would be the point?" She takes a third cigarette from the pack, sees the burning cigarette in my hand, and throws the new one over her shoulder. A black dog with a square head comes sniffing over to her, trots past the bench, and presses its nose to her leg. "Hey, boy, where's your owner? Shouldn't you be on a leash?" She strokes its ears and it looks grateful. "Sweet dog, you like that, don't you, me taking care of you, you like that, don't you?" A man whistles twice, the animal reacts at once and walks off without looking back. "You should go back up and let me know when Anne-Sophie's done. Then I can sit with Daddy for a while," she says.

"I'm sorry about—"

"Yes, yes," Marie says.

30

He smells of Calvados and cigars at four in the afternoon. He's sitting on our deck, staring into the distance. A Louis not doing anything, that's a sight I rarely get to see. I give him a kiss.

"Everything OK here?"

"No." He stares listlessly at the plant with the incredibly complicated flowers, a gift from Marie.

"What's the matter?"

"Writing. I think I'm going to have to throw away the entire manuscript, it's so bad."

"Why do you think that?"

He shrugs.

"You're a major writer, it's just a dip."

"It's not," Louis says, suddenly decisive.

"Want me to read it?"

"No, I'm too embarrassed."

"But—"

Louis shakes his head. "Sometimes I think I've lost it, or it's run out, or something."

There's a silence. I look at him.

"I wish you could see yourself the way I do. I love reading your writing, always. Honestly."

"Yes, but you like me."

"Sometimes I do." I smile. "I thought you were a great writer before I met you, so. That's even one of the things that attracted me to you, I think."

"You're sweet." He makes it sound almost pitying.

"I wish I could help you."

"Me too," he says then. In his gaze: black sheep, plumes of smoke, and screaming. This isn't the Louis I know, the man who's always able to deflect all self-doubt. The way he's sitting there now, so lost, really affects me.

"I believe in you, totally and completely. Does that help?" He just smiles weakly, but I persist. "Shall we go out? Do something fun? A change of scenery might change your state of mind."

He shakes his head. "Let me sit here a while. It'll be all right. I hope."

I look at him. I fetch the bottle of Calvados and an extra glass, top his up, and then pour one for myself. I see us sitting there, both doubting our own capabilities, worrying about what to do, even though his concerns are unjustified. Heads are closed spaces, I'm afraid.

31

Then Louis puts down his knife and fork and simply asks her, "What exactly happened between you and Marie?" Anne-Sophie is all eyes and hair behind her large glass of red wine. "Do it for literature, for this poor man who has to create worlds in isolation while, in real life, things happen that he would never be able to invent." Classic Louis, this. The whole evening we've been talking about all kinds of stuff, everyone has been trying to put Anne-Sophie at ease, and then he does this. Louis, a master of elusiveness, the man who in the same situation would employ his entire arsenal of words in order not to have to answer. Anne-Sophie looks at him. "A good story and my belief in my writing career may remain intact if you do your good deed for the week. Here's your chance." Louis grins.

"If Anne-Sophie would rather not talk about it, that's her right." Charlie licks her knife.

"But you can tell us everything if you feel the need, I hope you know that," Alexander adds.

Anne-Sophie folds in her lips until it looks like she doesn't have a mouth. Her large eyes are just slightly too far apart to be really beautiful, but it makes her gaze all the more piercing.

"I think . . ." Her voice rises, then pauses.

Let it come, I think. *It will do you good.*

Then the waiter arrives to clear away our plates; he's neither fast nor dexterous. Anne-Sophie falls silent. I look around: two people sitting opposite each other in silence, a man helping a woman into her coat, the drawer of the cash register pops open, someone behind the bar has five glasses in one hand, the man in that group of six looks like he's been out of it for quite some time. And then the sauce of sounds on top of everything, in stark contrast with the silence at our table. When the waiter finally disappears with his hands full of plates, we all turn toward her.

"It's—I don't want—" Then she stands up and goes toward the bathroom, serenely, without drama, not a tear to be seen.

"Well done," I say to Louis.

"What do you mean? I only asked what everyone's wanted to know for the past four years."

"Should we go after her?"

"I'd leave her," Alexander replies.

My sister is so different from the enthusiastic, chatterbox infant I carried all around the house. I hope that it helps her, all that hiding, and I hope even more that she doesn't have to put on her suit of armor in that far-off country.

Ten minutes later she sits back down. She looks at her plate and says very collectedly, "I can't talk about it, or I don't want to, I can't really tell which. Maybe I will later, at some point."

"Of course," Charlie says.

"Please tell me about your lives. I've got so much catching up to do."

What a shame, I see Louis thinking—for all the wrong reasons, I'm sure.

32

"Ouch," Louis says at the weak applause, "and for an opening night."
He adopts his calamitous face.

The actors wave and gesture to Marcus to come forward, as though
he might need an invitation. He walks over, hugs them, and takes a deep
bow, hand on his heart, as though wild applause has broken out. It's a
bit painful to watch, but people begin to clap a little louder. Two girls
come up with flowers; he kisses the one who hands him a bouquet, full
on the lips. They're all able to come back onstage just one more time,
then the applause dies out. The polite minimum on an opening night
like this is three.

We shuffle toward the foyer. We press forward in the throng moving slowly toward the free drinks. The concentrated smell of all that life
imposes itself. *Thirsty,* I think. I look around for the first time in ages at
this beautiful theater of old, the place I love so much, and now I'm lost
here. I considered not coming, like Nathan, but I'm still the company's
dramaturge, and there are other productions I am working on, so.

Louis cranes his neck to see how much farther we have to shuffle
along. "You were completely right, it was a hopeless play. And there was
that strange bit about twenty minutes in."

"They must have cut a large chunk out there after I left."

"That's why it's impossible to know what the hell's going on. Proof of how important the dramaturge is, right?" Louis smiles at me. "Red or white?" He points at the glasses standing ready.

"Red. The white here's undrinkable."

Louis takes two glasses from the high table and installs himself at a spot by the bar that just about everyone will have to walk past.

"Can't we stand more to the side?"

"Why?"

"Louis."

"It was stupid of you to make such a fuss about a dead horse, I still think that, but that's no reason to hide away as if you embezzled production money to buy expensive shoes or something, huh? You had a difference of artistic opinion with the director, you two can solve that, you're adults." Life is simple for Louis.

"Just do it for me," I say, but now Fred, a film director Louis knows well, has come up to us. Louis turns to him immediately and says something that makes Fred laugh. His night has begun now. That's the way it always goes with us: him on one side of the room, me on the other. At some point, we decided that was normal.

The cast will arrive in a minute too, after a toast backstage. It's the first time I'm not with them. Out of all of them, Frank's the only one who has told me it was a shame I wasn't there anymore. Frank's a sweet kid. Nathan hasn't heard from anyone, he told me on the phone. He sounded weak when he said that.

I see a lot of people I know; I try to figure out whether they're looking at me differently, maybe the story of my incompetence and Marcus's grandiose speech about the emptiness of my dramaturgical existence has already made the rounds, but no one looks at me. As the thoughts wheel around my head, I feel a sudden tap on my shoulder. Marcus, in a smart suit, sunglasses in his breast pocket, giving me a challenging look.

"Well? What did you think?"

I want to walk away, blow away, fade away. I shrug and smile apologetically.

"I've heard some great responses from people with brains and good taste. Wait until the general public sees this, they're going to go crazy."

"I'm glad you're so confident, Marcus." I try not to make it sound cynical.

"Say, Mona. I want to talk to you. Can you be in Tamar's office around midday tomorrow?"

Tamar is the HR manager, you don't have informal chats in her presence.

"Are you firing me?"

Marcus loses his countenance for a moment, or perhaps I just hope that. "I wanted to deal with it the right way, take the time, but fine, if you're asking to know now, if right now is necessary for you. Do you know what your problem is, Mona? You're not an original thinker, you don't have a big personality. You're like a chameleon and chameleons can never be artists. And it's simple, I realized it over the past few days. I want to work with artists, even those in a questionable role like that of dramaturge."

It's like a pickup truck is dumping a few tons of sand on top of me. "And you've only just discovered this? After all these years?"

"You're a sweet girl, Mona, but we're not a charity, are we? I want people around me who inspire me, drive me on, make me wild, challenge me. You get that, right?"

I stand there staring at him without moving. I'm a cloud of dust in the distance, a blind bend, a rut in the road.

"So, just let it sink in. Tamar will be expecting you tomorrow." He stands there as though waiting for meaningful last words. All I can think is: I'd rather he'd launched into one of his unreasonable tirades, made a scene, fired me right away in rehearsal. He plucks a glass from a tray and takes a few sips. I don't want to cry, not with this man, here, at this launch party where everyone is looking their best. "How is your father, by the way?"

"Ah, you know," is all I say.

"I'm not thrilled that the decision had to be made now. I know the timing isn't great for you, but hey."

I lower my eyes. I think: *I want someone to come and help me at last, or I want to find the words that would knock him so low he'd need anti-depressants again.* I gulp, look at him, continue to remain silent, then I turn around and wring my way through the people. I want to leave and now I am leaving. I storm down the stairs and, once I'm outside, I accelerate my pace. Birds fall from the sky, mirrors burst behind house walls, a scooter narrowly misses me. And soon, soon night will fall.

33

The pulmonary edema is back. Already. Dad looks more and more like an outstretched snow-covered landscape, the way he's lying there, sinking away palely into the white sheets and pillows, as though he's slowly erasing himself from the world. He talks less and less because talking takes effort, breathing is an effort. Life tires him out. Marie has hung up cards on the wall behind his head, brightly colored cards featuring bears and balloons and flowers, as though they might make him better. I'm sure he doesn't mind the fact that only visitors can see them.

I sit on the concrete window seat, my back to the pane. The sun is hot through the glass, and the heat does me good, but part of me thinks the weather should play along so that I can at least look back on these times against a suitable backdrop of falling leaves and gusty showers of rain and a crisp kind of cold.

My father is very ill. And now I don't have my work anymore, work that was more than a job, and soon everyone in the theater world will know it. In our circles, gossip like this travels faster than a homing pigeon. What will they think of me? What will they tell each other? I remember one time, I was about seven or even eight and I'd wet my bed. Waking up after a scary nightmare to the sickly smell. I gathered up the sheets, went downstairs in the middle of the night, put them in the washing machine, and pressed the wrong buttons. When my mother discovered this the next day, she asked me, in the presence of my little brother and my dad, why in God's name I'd been washing my sheets in the middle of the night when I clearly didn't know what I was doing. I could have broken the washing machine. I saw even Alexander, as small as he was, understand what had happened, even though it wasn't actually said. The same crushing feeling of humiliation, it comes over me each time now when I think about being fired. I made Louis swear not to say anything to my family, for now at least. He thought it was a bit ridiculous, but he did promise.

Dad is sleeping, his mouth slightly open, a patch of drool on his pillow. I'm glad people don't sit around watching *me* sleep. The newspapers lie next to me, I barely dare look at the culture section, but curiosity gets the best of me. The headline reads: **Great Master Completely Misses the Mark**, and the last line of the critical review says, "After an hour and fifty minutes of poorly worded and miserably constructed babble about nothing, it's a delight to finally be able to go home." I also find "the boundaries of boredom skillfully extended" and "hopeless blundering on a pompous set." I try to picture Marcus reading these reviews. Might he think about me for a moment? Would he dare admit to himself that he got things wrong this time? *I wish I could have a good cry,* I think, but there's just weight in the middle of my chest.

Dad suddenly opens his eyes. He rubs them, sees me sitting there, and stares in confusion, as though he has to check twice who it is. Then he waves, just with his hand, he leaves his arm lying next to his body. I move closer. He has an oxygen tube up his nose, a drip-feed and an infusion with various medications, and every so often he has to wear an oxygen mask for twenty minutes, which he detests.

"Has Anne-Sophie come today?"

He nods.

"Does it help you, seeing her?"

He nods again.

"Is Marie reasonably OK?"

He makes a cautious gesture. I suppose.

"Alexander said he'd pop in with Marvin later. He's missing his grandpa."

Then Dad smiles with just one corner of his mouth, as though raising the other would require too much effort. "What time are they coming to get me for the treatment?" His voice sounds rusty.

"Soon, the nurse said."

We say nothing together. The silence is different than it used to be: richer, more proof of nothing being necessary than fear of saying the wrong thing.

"And you, are you happy?" His gaze is penetrating. After Anne-Sophie, it's apparently my turn, or did he notice something? Did someone get wind of it and tell him about me getting fired?

"With you here in the hospital, how could I be—"

"Apart from that. You, your life, in general?"

He hasn't heard anything, that's already something. I reflect on his question. "I don't know," I say, not knowing if this is true.

Dad looks at me; the whites of his eyes are pinkish. "I've always said you should learn to be happy with what you've got, but maybe that's not entirely true." He closes his eyes, as though he's exhausted all his strength pushing out these complete sentences.

Then the door opens. Cleavage comes in, along with Marie. He nods at my father. "Well, how are things?"

Dad doesn't go to the trouble of answering his superfluous question, he just smiles weakly. "What time are they going to come get me for that edema treatment?"

"Hard to say, but it won't be much longer."

"I'm really dreading it."

"Yeah, you'll just have to grit your teeth for a while, no other option."

"Easy for you to say," Dad replies in a rare moment of cautious assertiveness.

Cleavage takes hold of my father's foot, sheets and all, moves it back and forth—a strange, pointless gesture—and then says, "Well, sir, you waited too long to come to us, didn't you? The human body can only take what it can take, and we can only do what we do. The second operation has placed a lot of stress on his heart, it seems." He lays two fingers on his chin—to underline his authority, I suspect.

I take a step forward. "Perhaps you haven't noticed, but *sir* is present in the room. Sir is not a toddler, nor senile, and the last time they did this, they left him lying in some hallway for two hours, as though it wasn't horrible enough, and that's just one of the reasons sir is dreading it, which seems totally understandable to me."

Cleavage avoids my gaze. "Right, any questions? I've got dozens of patients waiting."

"Yes, of course," Marie says hurriedly. "I'll just accompany you a moment." She tries to catch my eye, but I look away.

When the door has closed, I say, "Want to bet she's apologizing on my behalf?" I give my father a giggly look, but he remains serious.

"Yes, sorry, I found that man trying right from the first time I saw him. I couldn't keep it in."

I don't regret it either, I think, but I don't say this.

"Tell me what's really happening. With me, I mean."

Any satisfaction about my minor flash of civil disobedience drains away at once. What's he asking now? I can't, I won't reply.

"Medically," he adds, as though there could be any doubt about it.

I continue to hold my tongue, searching for words that are meaningless enough.

"Come on, Mona. Marie will be back in a moment." He grips my arm. "I won't be running any marathons, will I?"

He's not really asking, he knows, I think. Who else could know it better than the man who has been living in this body, the vehicle that is coming ever closer to breaking down? He swallows and then coughs, awkwardly slowly.

"I've never fought this hard before," he whispers, making it sound as though he's done it only for us.

"Just one more go at that horrible treatment and, if it works, that will probably be all."

"Probably."

"*Probably* is a better word than many others."

He closes his eyes again.

"Yes, have a rest," I say as though he needs permission.

Outside, demolition work has begun, they're building a new wing: sick people are a booming business. Trucks reverse, beeping, chunks of rubble are pushed this way and that, workmen shout at each other above the clamor. The sun continues to shine mockingly in the sky.

34

"You mustn't give up hope." He adds six apples, a bunch of grapes, and a box of strawberries to the shopping cart, even though we hardly eat any fruit. Louis rarely goes to the supermarket, if at all. Today he grabbed my keys when I said I was going to leave. "These things are unpredictable sometimes. Your dad could sputter his way through this and then steadily improve."

"You haven't visited my dad in weeks, though. You should see the way he just lies there."

Silence.

"This one or this one?" He holds up a box of pasta in each hand, different shapes, but the brand is the same. I point to the left one; he casually dumps it on top of the grapes.

"You mustn't give up or else he will too." Louis stares at the legs of the girl who passes us in the candy aisle. I take some white chocolate from the shelf.

"Oh no, not white."

I put it back reflexively.

"By being strong, that's how you can help him, make him believe that anything's still possible."

"Wouldn't being honest with him help more?"

"But what's honest? You don't know any more than the doctors do, and they keep saying to wait and see, right?" I don't reply. He hurries along the aisles. "You'd be amazed by how strong those tough old dogs can be sometimes." *My dad's not an old dog,* I think. "Hopefully things will return to normal soon and then you'll have time to look for a new job. Then you'll feel better. Since I started the novella, I've regained my faith in myself. That's the way it is, we're that kind of people, what we do determines who we are." We walk past the fish. "Oh, do you want to cook your cod tonight? With lemon and thyme sauce and fennel? I really like that." *I don't,* I think. I don't want to eat colorless food and I'm not hungry and I feel even less like cooking. I pick up two pieces of packaged cod, look at them, and then ram the cart against his shins. He grabs his leg and hops around on one foot. "Fuck, that hurt."

"Good," I say, throwing the fish at his head.

Louis ducks. "What?" He looks somewhere between confused and indignant.

"Make your own fucking cod. And don't lecture me on when to look for a job or how to speak to my dad. That urge of yours to compensate for your endless absence with pedantic little speeches, I can't cope with it anymore."

He puts his foot back down again, stands staring in amazement for a moment, and then moves closer to me and says, "But, sweetie, are you angry? It's all been too much, hasn't it? I understand. I'm not angry with you." He hugs me, smiles encouragingly, takes the cart from me, and rolls it on. "Come on, they're closing soon and we still don't have everything yet."

I bend down to pick up the cod. A woman stops nearby, she has a little boy in the seat of the cart. As his mother studies the meats, he sits there with his wiggly legs, looking around. Suddenly he notices me, standing there next to the dead fish. He looks at me inquiringly, takes his thumb from him mouth, and smiles. I smile back and wave at him, even though I'm thinking: *Don't do it, don't be so endearingly sweet.* There are some things I really can't handle.

35

The nurse simply wakes him up. Not because he needs to be awake, but because it's quicker for her this way. "And I'll be back shortly for the oxygen mask, my friend. That'll do you some good." She checks the drip, turns around, and clacks out of the room in her mules.

"'Some good,'" my father repeats, and if he had the energy, he would have smiled pityingly. "As if anything could still do me any good."

I kiss him by way of a greeting. He smells different from normal. There's something hurried in the way he immediately starts talking when he sees me.

"Will you call Joanna for me? You've got her number, don't you?" His voice sounds like it has to come crawling from somewhere deep under the ground.

"Yes. Now you mean?"

He nods. I type in the number, pass him the phone, and gesture that I'll wait outside. What might they say to each other? I resist the temptation to try to eavesdrop. When there's silence again, I go back into the room.

"Was that nice?"

He nods again. My father has become so small, so defenseless lying there. He lays his hand on my arm.

"Mona, I need to tell you a few things." I shake my head. I don't want to hear them, I suspect. But he doesn't seem to have time for hesitancy today. "There's something else you have to get rid of at the house. I suddenly remembered it." He closes his eyes momentarily, then opens them again, with effort. "In the wardrobe, in the sock drawer, somewhere in a gray pair, painkillers. Acetaminophen, ibuprofen, aspirin. Marie mustn't find them. Will you take them away?" It clearly makes him nervous.

"Of course," I reply. I can hardly believe that he's worrying about this now. How long has he been slowly giving up hope? "If that's ever necessary, I'll—" I feel his hand again.

"You won't forget?" He opens his eyes wide.

"No, of course I won't."

He clears his throat, blinks, for a moment there's a fathomless silence, then, "I'm never going to get better, am I?"

I say nothing. I feel my tears running down my cheeks, almost imperceptibly, as though the liquid just belongs to my face.

"I'm glad you're still able to cry for your old dad." He takes my hand in his. "But listen to me, I want this to progress now. Morphine, or whatever they use."

"Dad, you mean—"

"Yes." He's never been more emphatic about something not explicitly voiced. "They often do that: passive—" He doesn't formulate the next word. "Would you organize that for me?"

There we are, closer than we've ever been, and further away too. I take hold of his other hand too. I'm a girl holding hands with her father; I never want to let them go again.

"But there's still so much. We can still . . . You can still . . . Maybe you could . . ." I'm sobbing too hard to finish my sentences.

"Mona, I can't anymore." He emphasizes each word. He looks at me. *Don't look at me like that,* I think. He continues to look at me like that.

"It's too soon," I say.

"Yes," he replies factually, "but also not."

"But I can't." I lay my head against his. I can feel his clammy sweat, the stubble of his beard, his baking-hot cheeks.

"Will you ask the others to come too?"

I nod and I keep on nodding, just nodding away, as though I'm broken and this is the only movement I can still make.

36

"Well?"

Marie closes the door to Dad's room behind her, comes over to us, and rubs the shoulder of her coat a few times with the flat of her hand, and then, with the other hand, the other shoulder. "What do you mean?" She looks at her shoulder, not at Alexander and me.

"Shall we start the process, then?" Since Marie doesn't respond, Alexander adds, "That friendly nurse, the blond one with the tattoo on her wrist, she told us that a duty doctor is coming to relieve Doctor Cleavage for the weekend. A young woman, apparently, and the nurse said she might be open to Dad's request."

"What do you mean?" Marie repeats.

"Dad's request for passive euthanasia."

"What? Did he say that? To who? To the nurse? Why is she sticking her nose in? I'll give her—"

"No, Mom. He said it to Mona. Didn't he just tell you himself?"

"No. I don't believe it." She turns around and goes back into Dad's room, clearly irritated. We try to keep up with her. She bursts through the door, shouting, "What's this I hear? You want to abandon me and you don't think it's necessary to tell me to my face? Me, the person who has been at your side for weeks on end? Your *wife.*" She makes that last word sound like a cannon shot. Dad lies there breathing squeakily, trying to breathe, even though the oxygen is turned up to the max. She goes over to his bed, holds her face about two inches away from his, and repeats, at almost the same volume, "Why, why you didn't say anything to me?" Dad can't get a single word out. And she stands there as though a physical protest might change anything.

I move a little closer. "He can't go on, he said so."

"Well, I can't go on either," Marie roars. Then she storms out of the room. The heavy door slowly swings shut. Alexander glances at me and then goes after her.

"Afterward, just go along with whatever Marie wants," Dad squeaks to me. "You two have each other anyway." He slides his tongue along his lips. "Did you manage it?"

"We found someone who will probably be able to help. We're going to talk to her now, all right?"

"Yes, hurry," he says, closing his eyes.

37

Louis has to be in Amsterdam today of all days. I did let him know, but he said the earliest he could get away was this evening after his reading. He'd been planning to stay the night there, but given the circumstances he'd do his best to drive home and of course I could call him any time I needed to.

I find Alexander sitting in the cafeteria with Marie, they're at the table in the far corner nursing empty glasses. I join them. I'm suddenly reminded of times long past, how often the three of us had sat together like this when Dad was still at work and Anne-Sophie had gone to bed or something, and the way we'd talk because we didn't trust silence. Now there's a very lengthy silence.

"Don't you want a drink?" Marie asks, probably just to say something.

I shake my head.

"Mom has agreed to it."

I smile at her. "Will you come with us? The nurse told us where we might find the doctor."

"Don't ask me to do that," she whispers, staring at the table.

"Then, well, um, we'll see each other upstairs, with Dad, then?" Alexander gets up, I follow.

She nods without looking at us.

Alexander points. "That must be her—young, short dark hair, not very tall, red shoes."

We go up to her and ask whether we can ask her something. There's something unbelievably soft in her face, and a lot of vigor in her movements. The three of us stop at the end of the hallway, just near the elevator. We explain the course of Dad's illness and tell her what he's asked us. Alexander and I interrupt each other as we tell our story, as though we're trying to get to the end of it as fast as possible, as though we can't wait for her response, which we fear and also long for—sometimes those things go hand in hand. The doctor nods the whole time we're talking, as though she wants to reassure us that she does actually understand. She lets a silence fall when we're done, and then says, without the slightest hesitation, "I understand your situation. I experienced more or less the same with my grandfather." She purses her lips briefly. "I'll drop by and examine your father and see whether we can agree that his suffering is too great—unbearable—so that a much higher dose of pain medication would be appropriate. That's what we can do." She looks the way mothers look at their children when they're about to take an exam in their weakest subject. "What do you both think? Is that all right?"

Alexander and I both nod.

"And then . . ."

"And then your father will drift off very quickly, within a few minutes, and then he'll slip away."

"How long will it be before he dies?" I need to call it what it is because no one else has spoken the unspeakable yet.

"It's hard to predict, somewhere between very quickly and around seven days. Three to four is about average." She's the first doctor who hasn't given the impression that she's needed elsewhere urgently. The silence lasts awhile.

"OK, so when can we expect you?" Alexander asks.

"Dad is really anxious to know," I add.

"I've got a couple of my own patients to see, but I'll come to you after that. In about half an hour or so. Room 316, right?"

"That's right."

"Thank you," I say to the woman who is going to kill my father. It's odd that it's been so easy. I look at Alexander, he looks at me. I check my phone, maybe there'll be a message from Louis.

38

Charlie is taking Marvin to her mom's, but she'll be here soon. Marie is sitting bolt upright in the armchair next to Dad, plucking hairs from the coat she has laid across her knees. Anne-Sophie is leaning against the wall; she's wearing an oversized, thick sweater. Alexander and I are standing next to Dad's bed, explaining. He listens tensely, breathing heavily, he stretches his skinny neck. "How much longer?" He makes it sound like he'd rather the answer was two minutes instead of twenty.

"She's doing her rounds, so she couldn't say exactly, but it won't be more than an hour," Alexander says in his softest voice. We smile until our faces hurt.

"Are you afraid?" I ask.

"Only healthy people are afraid of death," he replies.

Alexander takes a chair next to Marie. I wonder whether he's talked some more with Dad over the past weeks, really talked. Or not. I wonder why we don't know that about each other. I take a stool and sit at the foot of the bed.

I look at my family. Anne-Sophie is biting her nails. She stares at a point on the wall where there's nothing to see. She crosses her legs one way and then the other. I ask her discreetly how she is; she tells me that everything's fine. Everything's always fine with her, which is what worries me the most. Alexander sits there typing a message into his phone;

it takes a while, he's clumsy with those things. Marie tries to stroke my dad's cheek, and Dad smiles but stops her hand and carefully lays it on the mattress next to him. Is it awful for him that Joanna isn't here now?

We can't practice this, this waiting together for death. It's a shame, because I've rarely seen so much united awkwardness, so much combined impotence, so many people who can't just be themselves together, not even at this kind of hour of truth. When I die, I hope there'll be a lot of people and they'll drink and kiss and hug and tell stories and laugh at the dumb jokes they make out of awkwardness, and cry about the absence they'll feel, about this unfair leave-taking, or from drunkenness on my behalf. Anything would be better than this, in this cool room filled with congealed silence, this tense not knowing.

The kind nurse comes in and tries to put on Dad's oxygen mask.

"No," he says with a weak flip of the hand.

"Rather not? As you wish." She smiles heartily. It's the first time one of the nursing staff has so clearly taken what he wants into account. Clemency when push comes to shove, that's what this is. "The doctor will be here soon." She touches his arm briefly.

Dad stares at the clock next to the TV and we sit there in a semicircle, just sitting, without words. From time to time someone looks at someone else, from time to time someone changes their position. When Charlie comes in, I see that our silence startles her. She gives Dad a kiss. "Can I do anything for you?" she asks in a very normal manner.

"Be here," Dad says. "Oh yes." He points at the cupboard next to his bed. "That box." Charlie opens the door and takes out the wooden case.

"This?" She slides it open. It contains chess pieces, very old ones.

"My grandfather made them, by hand." His voice sputters. "For Marvin."

Charlie looks at the box, then at us, as if she needs permission to accept it for her son, then at Dad.

"He'll be thrilled to have it." She swallows. "Do you mind him not being here? I wondered whether—"

Dad makes a dismissive gesture. "No place for children." He tries a small smile.

Charlie sits down close to Alexander. He takes the box on his lap and looks inside, his expression somewhere between shocked and moved, I guess. Then the room falls quiet again. I look at my father, he closes his eyes and then opens them again momentarily.

"Maybe you'd like us to talk about something?" Marie suddenly inquires. Dad smiles weakly at her. In just a few hours, he seems to have grown weaker, as though he's let go of everything, as though he wants to pass the test the doctor is going to put him through to see whether he's allowed to leave. "Perhaps everyone can tell us something nice they remember about Daddy." Marie's voice rises to unnatural heights. Then Anne-Sophie springs to her feet and leaves the room. Should I go after her? I check to see whether anyone else is going to. Everyone stays in their seats, so I do too.

39

"I've asked the nurse to take care of it," says the young doctor in the hallway. "Why don't you all go in? She'll be there in a few minutes and after that he'll fall asleep very quickly. Are you going to sit up with him tonight?"

Everyone looks at me automatically. True, I'm a notorious night owl, and no, I don't have any children to look after, and no, I'm not the estranged sister who has just returned to the country, and no, I'm not the fragile wife with whiplash who needs her sleep more than ever.

"All right, I'll do it," I say. I wonder whether I immediately agreed to the unvoiced request because I want to be with him or because the chance he'll die that soon is statistically small.

We all go in again and stand around his bed. He looks at us, one by one, there's more sweetness in his face than I've ever seen there before.

"I did fight hard," he says then. Again that same line, as though it might bring him absolution, as though a person is allowed to just decide they've had enough, as though he didn't already give up years ago.

"Very hard," a couple of us say in chorus.

"You can go now, Dad," I say, because I have a vague sense he needs to hear it spoken clearly.

"Yes," he says, sounding almost cheerful.

Marie looks at me and then at Alexander, her expression bleakly anxious. Anne-Sophie is standing right at the foot of the bed and doesn't seem to be looking at anything at all. She looks like she hasn't slept for a week. Alexander hangs his head between his broad shoulders, to be closer to Dad, or out of general despondency, it's hard to say. Charlie leans against the edge of the mattress, her face a picture of charity. She looks from Dad to Alexander in turn.

The nurse comes into the room. "Now?" Dad nods. She hangs an extra bag on the infusion stand, turns up the dripper, gives us an encouraging look, says we can always press the buzzer if we need anything, and then slips out discreetly.

Dad looks at us all one more time, slowly and emphatically, with a combination of a strange kind of peacefulness and great attention. There's nothing more to say, or everything, it's almost the same thing. I look at Dad, my father, breathing, my father who was always there, who didn't know how to live, who couldn't cope with the arrival of fall, the fact that things pass, the fact that some things don't pass. I see him close his eyes with a cautious smile. His left index finger jerks furiously as though someone else is controlling that one muscle, his chest rises and falls, his smile becomes a thin strip, then everything seems to fall still. It took barely two minutes and now he's asleep. The longest and shortest two minutes ever.

40

I'm against it. I'm against death as a concept, but no one's asking my opinion. I'm sitting here at Dad's bedside, all alone. Outside, the night is dark and starless; inside, I'm keeping the lights down, Dad didn't like too much brightness. A strip of light shines through a gap around the door to the small bathroom, the only warm light I could find in all the white fluorescent of this room, as though illness and death were things that had to remain clearly visible. Outside, the sputtering sound of car tires on wet roads, and somewhere behind the poplars, a dog barks incessantly as though it's been locked up or out. Inside, there is only Dad, he's never sounded this loud before. The friendly nurse had warned about the death rattle that could come. She looked at us sympathetically and called it "pulmonary secretions," as though the name might make it less unpleasant. A long time ago, when death was something I'd only read about in books, something for other people, I'd wanted to know what that would sound like. I find that perverse now. It's a sound that's like nothing else: somewhere between shaking an empty spray can with tiny bullets in it and wet heavy breathing. The nurse said it wouldn't bother him at all. Comfort can sometimes be found in the strangest places. I try to see safety in it: as long as the machine is making a racket, it's still working, that idea. I've always been good at making a virtue of necessity, I've been wondering recently whether that's actually a quality or not.

I look at his left hand, his blue-tinged nails. There are reddish-purple blotches on his arms that remind me of rotten fruit; I don't want to look at them. The shorter of breath Dad becomes, the closer he is to death, the nurse explained, so I count to get an idea. One as he starts to breathe in, and then continuing until he has fully exhaled: one, two, three, four.

"It won't be before tonight." I say it out loud and am startled by the sound of my voice. I look at him and then away again, as though too much reality will break me up in bits.

I feel a little sorry I volunteered; it's not the only thing I regret, but it's one of them. I've heard horrible stories about the way people die. I don't know how to do this, I don't know whether I can.

I study his face, narrower than it has ever been, the skin between two shades of gray, cheekbones pronounced, lips dark and cracked, silver-and-white hair messy and combed back, cheeks and neck neatly shaven, as though he had to look nice for his death. Dad sleeps and his chest rises and falls. He's still alive, that much is sure. I think of the expression: *to slip away peacefully*. Is this the kind of scenario they mean? I'd never choose those words for it. How are *kicking the bucket* and *slipping away peacefully* related?

I want to moisten his cracked lips. They've given me a kind of giant cotton ball on a stick to use for this. Moistening the lips apparently brings relief, and a bone-dry mouth is typical of the dying. Charlie had read somewhere that champagne was even better than water because the sugar makes the effect last longer, so Alexander got some. I dip the tip in the glass of champagne and rub it along his lips. They spontaneously begin to suck, so I push it deeper into his mouth. Suddenly he tugs the whole thing into his mouth like it's a lollipop. I'm scared, worried he'll choke because of something I did wrong. At the same time, it's the most ridiculous sight, a father on his deathbed with a stick coming out of his mouth. I laugh out loud, from the stress maybe, and carefully tug at the stick. He doesn't let go. I'll have to call the nurse in a minute, and what will she think? It's nice, though, that he's able to enjoy something at a time like this, or is it just like a mindless reflex? I carry on tugging and finally he lets go.

If I live to be his age, I'm already more than halfway there, I suddenly realize. I pour myself some champagne in a water glass. "What shall I toast to, Dad?" He seems to rattle even louder when I say that, as though he wants to answer. He'll never answer anyone again, I think, and then the tears come. "I'll drink to you, to the man you turned out to be."

I look at the clock that he'd lain staring at so often, counting his own hours when there was nothing better to do. Only fifty minutes have passed since the nurse left again. Tomorrow night, Alexander will keep watch, he'd promised quietly. In the early evening, I tried to reach Louis, but he didn't pick up. Ten minutes later, he sent me a text message: I'm tied up at the moment, will call you ASAP, stay strong.

"What am I going to do about Louis, Dad?" Does a dying person find the drone of a human voice pleasant or annoying? Would he sense that there was another person with him if that other person sat motionless in a chair? I get up, briefly touch his cheek. "You're not alone. I'm here with you." I say this in a quiet, hoarse voice, then sit down again.

Charlie had brought a few magazines and newspapers for me, but I can't even look at the pictures. I can't do anything other than be here, experiencing every minute, hyperconscious. I wish I knew what exactly was happening. I wish I knew which dreams were taking place behind his eyelids; I wish I could be certain he wasn't feeling any pain, that nothing was irritating him: an itch or a pillow that was too hot, or the chemical smell of the hospital sheets. One, two, three, four, he's still breathing in the same rhythm, that's good. The door opens. This nurse is wearing clogs, white, like the ones I had when I was a child. Her nails are painted orange and her hair is an unnatural yellow. She takes a few steps toward us. The hall light spills into the room.

"Well?"

"He's still alive," I say.

She looks as though I've said something shocking, then merely nods, turns around, and closes the door. What else is there to say to a nurse wearing clogs? Except: Will you stay, please, so that I don't have to be alone, so that I don't have to be so restless and scared, will you promise me that he won't die now but tomorrow, during the day with the blinds down, when there are a few of us gathered around his bed? And would you also guarantee that this won't have to take too much longer, for his sake, and perhaps also for my own? To her, my father is simply another dying man. She works on a ward where more people might die than get better, that's why they invented the word *geriatrics*, a word that sounds like an illness you never recover from, which old age is, of course. And Dad, he's not even old.

My phone beeps, a family member probably. I look and it's a message from Nathan: I heard your father wasn't doing so well? Thinking of you. Should I answer? Then Dad begins to cough. I jump to my feet, but it stops immediately. He lies there, motionless as stagnant water, arms beside his body, eyes closed, less and less of a person, a father who is evaporating.

I picture Dad, his nose pressed against the steamed-up window, like a child. Looking out of his office window into the garden, where Alexander and I are building a snowman. He holds up his thumb, I can still remember that, and he's smiling, I think. I wave to him, then he steps away from the window and I can't see him anymore. So thin is the boundary between being there and not being there.

Once, when I was little, Dad told me about an animal that made the same sound as a dentist's drill, but I've forgotten the name of it. He also told me that crickets chirp by rubbing their wings together and that seahorses don't whinny and that frogs in England don't say "quack" like here in Belgium, but "ribbit." I didn't know whether to believe him, I didn't know how he knew such things. I've forgotten the name of the creature that sounds like a dentist's drill and I can no longer ask him.

I think back to the time I asked Dad to put my hair in a ponytail, like Ellen's. Mommy had always done that, but then she died. At first I didn't dare ask him but in the third week, there was a morning when his face seemed slightly less stormy, so I asked then. He took a long time with a brush and barrettes and a hair tie, and he pulled my hair, which hurt, but I didn't mind, I believe. "There you go," he said when he'd finished; he smiled proudly. I took my coat from the hall and looked in the mirror. The ponytail was ridiculously high on my head and too far to the left. I thanked my father and left for school, but once I'd turned the corner, I pulled out the tie and the barrettes and decided never to ask him again. Remaining silent is also a way of taking care of a person sometimes. As I think this, I wonder whether it's actually true or not.

I hear Dad shouting, that too, shouting at Marie, shouting at Mom. I can't help thinking that powerlessness can sound very loud. Maybe I'm being too charitable, looking at it like that.

I picture Mom. "I've never missed her." I say it out loud as though I want someone to hear me, for Dad to hear me. I never ended up telling him this in so many words. I think about Joanna. I wonder whether she was the last person he thought about, just now, or not.

I wonder whether people really do things for their children, or whether they only tell themselves that. He didn't marry my mother for my sake, but to save them and their families from a scandal, and because, in those days, abortion was not only emotionally charged but also difficult to acquire. Did he get involved with Marie because Alexander and I needed taking care of or because he himself was afraid of being alone? Because he didn't dare believe that waiting might bring him greater happiness?

At ten past four, the nurse comes in, fiddles with his drip, smiles, and leaves again. I mustn't fall asleep, he mustn't be alone. I walk around the bed and touch his hand, just briefly. It feels cold. I pull the sheets up a little higher and sit down again.

Perhaps getting fired is the best thing that could happen to me, I suddenly think, then I wonder whether I'm just telling myself this to be able to process it better. "Dad, Marcus fired me, just last week. Let go, dismissed, given the heave-ho, handed my walking papers. I'm really upset; it's totally awful, to be honest." I say it out loud, then burst out into a liberating fit of giggles that I only half understand myself. Confessing and the relief of getting it off your chest perhaps. I stretch, crack my neck by moving my head from left to right, then I get up and pace up and down the room. God, I need to pee. I don't want to pee in his toilet, so close by, the sound of a stream hitting the toilet bowl while a person lies there fighting death, it feels sacrilegious. The restrooms out in the hall, then? But what if something happens? I can hold it. I find a position to try to ease the urge. "Yes, that's it."

I intertwine my hands and crack my knuckles, which I was never allowed to do when I was little. I'd get rheumatism, Dad said. I take a sip of champagne, wonder whether I should moisten his lips again, and as my gaze goes from the bottle of champagne to his lips, it suddenly stops. The death rattle stops. I shoot to my feet, rush to the edge of his bed, grab his arm, my whole body is tense. Is this it? This stupid sudden stop? Or is he still breathing, only not in stereo. "Dad?" I can hear my own panic. I look and wait. *I should check his pulse,* I think, but I don't dare. I don't know what to do. "I'm here," I say. "I'm with you, let go, Dad." And then: a rattle, an exhalation of breath, a short one, and then it's quiet again, ridiculously quiet. Is he dead now? Or not yet? Tears run down my face, a lot of them. *A nurse,* I think, she has to come now, someone who knows what to do. I press the buzzer above his bed. I feel his chest, no heartbeat, I think, but I'm not sure. I stand there waiting. I count, all the way to thirty. I think he's gone. I suspect he is, but I don't know anything. Where's the nurse? Do I have to go and look for her? Then he'll be alone and I don't want that under any circumstances.

Who knows, perhaps he's still in the middle of dying, perhaps this is just a strange false alarm, the average was three to four days, wasn't it? I press the buzzer again, minutes pass, minutes that crawl past, torturous minutes. I'm still holding his arm, but I don't dare to look at him.

Then the door opens. "Is it time?" She flips the switch and light smashes into the room. These people don't think.

"Off, turn that light off!" I sound hysterical, but I don't care. I stare at her, at the nurse and the lines around her mouth, the furrow in her brow that I can see clearly now in the sea of white light. "Please, light off." Only then does she take a step back toward the switch and turn it off again.

She comes closer, feels his wrist, and then, without looking at me, says, "The gentleman has indeed passed away."

My whole body jerks as though, in all the hours I've been sitting here, I hadn't seen it coming, as though everything in me wants to fight against this acute loss. My cheeks are wet, my body lost, my head spins.

"Do you have a suit here so that we can dress him?"

I don't have a clue. I don't want to think about this now. I say nothing.

"Would you like us to close his mouth, arrange him nicely?"

Stay away from him, I think. *I want to get out of here,* I think. I leave the room. I have to call the others. I melt, blow away, settle, and wash away. I have to call the others. I go to the bathroom, run cold water over my wrists, rub my face with my wet hands, and run my fingers through my hair. I look in the mirror and see my face. It looks eighty years old.

41

Alexander is walking up front with his characteristic springy step. Marie is trotting along about three or four feet behind him. He's carrying a gray suit wrapped in plastic over his left arm. She's holding a fabric bag in her left hand that must be the shoes and socks; it swings back and forth, hitting her legs. I see them approaching but don't get up from my chair in the hall. *I'm just going to stay sitting here,* I think. Inside my head, the night is dark, the fog thick, the ground damp. I'm alone, no one to guide my way.

"Well?" my brother asks. He balls his left hand into a fist, relaxes it, and repeats.

I shrug.

"I don't want to see him anymore, not like this, dead. I'll stay with you." He sits down on the chair next to me, elbows resting on his knees, hands supporting his forehead.

"What?" says Marie. "You're not going to say goodbye to your father?"

"I did that already when he was still alive. I'll wait for you here, if you don't mind. Or . . ." He gets up and sits back down again immediately. "I'll wait here, yes."

"Ah." No one can instill that word with as much meaning as Marie. "Are we expecting Anne-Sophie too?"

"Yes, but she has to come from farther away."

Marie disappears.

Alexander arches his neck and breathes in deeply. We don't look at each other. "Was it scary?"

"It was disconcerting in its apparent nothingness. Death is staggering in its triviality, the most shocking thing I've ever seen."

He lays his hand on my arm, lets go instantly, and I start to cry again. "Have you called Louis yet?"

"Yes, he didn't pick up. He must be asleep. I could hear from the way it rang that he was still abroad, so it doesn't really matter anyway."

"You deserve better, sis." He bangs his fist gently on the arm of his chair twice, to add a show of might to his position.

Then Marie comes back out of the room. Her voice hoarse, she says, "His mouth is still open." She waits for a response, but neither of us speaks. "I can't look at it. It's so unpleasant." Her breath catches, and she swallows loudly. "Why is that?"

"Um. I don't know."

"They normally close it, don't they? That's the standard procedure, right? Precisely to spare the bereaved from such a sight. At least, that's what I thought."

I just stare. I don't know to say.

"Where are the nurses?"

"I just saw one go into the kitchen." Alexander points.

Marie rushes along the hallway as though there's haste after death. She returns a few minutes later. "Apparently, you told the nurse his mouth had to stay open." She gives me a furious look. "What is the meaning of this? Haven't you seen how dreadful—" She's unable to finish her sentence.

My self-composure is in danger of shattering. I can feel it, I purse my lips. "The nurse asked some questions, but I didn't know what to say. I left the room. I said nothing as far as I remember."

"I hope it's not too late now." Her voice trembles. "What time exactly did he die?"

"I don't know."

"Did you wait a long time before calling us?"

"No. I don't think so, no."

"Do you know what happens if you wait too long?" She raises her eyebrows. "Do you know what they do? Then they have to glue the mouth shut with a special kind of adhesive. Oh yes, having to do a thing like that to a person after their death. And I find that a strange thought, no, a horrific thought, that he'd have to be buried with his mouth glued shut."

To be honest, I don't want to hear the words *buried* and *death*, not now, let alone stories about glue and mouths. Alexander breathes in like he's going to speak but she vanishes again.

My brother looks at me; he suddenly feels close in all his restlessness.

"Why do we talk so little, Alexander? I mean really talk."

He rubs his hands over his face, then turns to me. "Don't we talk much?"

I shake my head. He squeezes my neck, and I wonder whether he knows that Dad used to do that sometimes to me, a long time ago. I squeeze his hand by way of a reply. He breathes heavily and opens a button of his shirt.

"What's the matter?"

"I—" He shoots up from his chair. "Air," he says. He hurries off. I try to keep up with him. He stops at the first window he comes to, pulls on the handle repeatedly, but it doesn't open. He wheezes even harder.

"Are you all right? Should I call a nurse?"

He shakes his head and goes to the elevator. "Outside," he says. I press the button three times. It arrives fast, it's still very quiet here.

Alexander gets in, paces around the tiny space, and undoes another button. Downstairs, the doors open again, he rushes out, through an emergency exit, the only one that's open at night. I run after my brother.

I see him stop in the parking lot and sink to the ground. A dark shape in the wary light of a single streetlamp, a shuddering heap of Homo sapiens. When I reach him, he's sitting there crying violently and struggling for breath. I kneel next to him. I can barely look: my giant of a brother, always the brave big guy, the way his body shakes. I don't know what to do now. I rest a hand on his shoulder and stay with him. Sometimes it's better not to try to make things better. He wasn't ready, he was even less ready than me. He keeps trying to get his breathing under control.

Then a car pulls in nearby, a door slams, footsteps on the asphalt, heavy heels, not clogs or sandals or sneakers, more the way cowboy boots might sound. I glance up, someone's coming, it must be Anne-Sophie. Then Alexander sees his little sister approaching and he quickly scrambles to his feet. He breathes in and out deeply and calms down, slowly but surely. He feels around in his pockets for a handkerchief he doesn't find. I give him my packet of tissues, he smiles, jerks violently one more time, then wipes his nose and dries his face.

"All right here?" Anne-Sophie asks. Her face is red and puffy from tears, or maybe exhaustion. She looks infinitely alone. I wonder whether that's something that will ever change.

"Yes, yes," Alexander says as though he urgently has to act like the big brother again. He coughs and puts away the tissue. "We should go back up again. Mom will be wondering where we are."

We stand waiting for the elevator, the three of us in a row. Alexander is breathing normally again. I look at Anne-Sophie, who looks at the floor. When we reach Dad's ward, Marie comes up to us. "Oh, there you are! I was wondering, *Now where have they got to?* And the nurse didn't know either." She stands close to us. She smells of stale sheets and an excess of floral perfume.

"Alexander needed some air," I say.

Marie nods as though this is entirely normal, then she turns to Anne-Sophie. "Go and say goodbye, but I'll warn you because I wish I'd known: he looks dreadful."

Anne-Sophie looks embarrassed. Suddenly, Marie takes a big step toward her and hugs her, unabashedly. Anne-Sophie stiffens. It lasts about thirty seconds and then she breaks free with strong, fierce movements.

"Don't do that," she roars, a shout that sounds twice as loud in this kind of silence.

A nurse pokes her head around a door and disappears again when she sees that things have calmed back down. Anne-Sophie goes to one of the chairs and sits down, trembling. She pulls her shoulders back, which looks strange. Alexander gives me a questioning look, then goes over to her. I sit down beside her. Anne-Sophie holds one hand in front of her mouth.

Marie stands there, demonstratively at a loss. "The nurses are putting his gray suit on him now. The striped one, you know, from Gilda's party. I hope everyone can live with that?" Nods of agreement. "Do you want to go first, Anne-Sophie, or can I go in again, so I can see him dressed?"

"Go." Anne-Sophie sounds weary. Marie disappears again.

"We all deserve better." I say it, thinking back to Dad's final words: *Just go along with whatever Marie wants.*

Anne-Sophie sighs, stretches out her legs, and sinks down against the wall as though she wants to release all the tension for a moment. The hallway is silent, I've never heard it so quiet here before. I look at my brother and my sister, three children with the same dad and yet all so different.

"What happened back there?" Alexander asks after a while. He leans forward so that he can see Anne-Sophie's face.

"She's not allowed to—" Anne-Sophie shakes her head, she doesn't finish her sentence. Then there's another pause. "It didn't have to last much longer for Dad, I'm happy about that," she says finally, as though that's an answer.

"You're happy?" Marie is holding the bag again, folded up and empty now.

"No. She—"

"Everything's arranged," she interrupts, folding the bag smaller and smaller. "And his mouth was all right in the end, thank God." She continues to look at us like we ought to be saying something we keep refusing to say, maybe because she doesn't know what to say herself. "Are you going to have a look or not, then, Anne-Sophie?" My sister nods, but doesn't get up. "If so, we'll wait here for you, because getting into the car alone after a thing like that, that's not nice." Marie emphasizes the words.

"No, don't wait," my sister says. "Really. Don't."

"Ah, yes," Marie replies. The rainy-day weariness of those two words.

Anne-Sophie takes a deep breath, gets up, and goes into the room with a weariness that doesn't match her years.

"Which of you is coming with me?" Marie comes and stands very close and looks alternately at Alexander and me. "I can't be alone now."

I feel us faltering and saying nothing. We let it go on, both of us, as if we'd agreed on it beforehand.

"Not me," I say, calmly and decisively.

"Oh no? Why not? Why can't you?" Marie widens her eyes.

"I could, but I stayed here all night and I want to be alone. I don't want to go with you, not now."

Marie doesn't reply instantly. She looks angry and surprised at the same time, injured by the daughter who pulls out at such a crucial moment. It's the anger I've unsuccessfully been trying to avoid all my life. The feared anger that was more important than my own anger. I look at her without even the slightest bit of apology, without the slightest compulsion to explain further. For too long, I lived like the crows that fly up into the air, forgetting themselves. Enough.

After a few seconds of speechlessness, she begins to talk again anyway. I don't feel like listening. "I'm desperate for a restroom," I say. I turn around and walk down the hallway. I look out the window, night is still happening outside. Streetlamps shine their yellowish light over the roads, the houses, the people sleeping, at the same time in the far-off distance, a glimmer of morning light. Dikes have burst, avalanches have been caused, tidal waves have risen up. My father is gone, gone forever, and nothing has changed, dawn is breaking, there will be another night. Nothing has changed and everything is different.

When I return, Alexander and Marie are getting ready to leave. I'm not going to ask what they agreed on, and I'm not going to invent some kind of excuse even though I know Marie is expecting one, or at least hoping for one.

"We'll be going, then."

"Fine," I say. I smile and give them both a kiss.

Marie continues to look at me. I sit down again. Then they're gone and I don't watch them go. I put my bag on my lap and look for my phone. Maybe Louis got in touch after all. Ah, two messages. One is from Anne-Sophie, just confirming she was on her way, and the other is from Nathan letting me know that, as an insomniac, he's a good person to call for a nighttime conversation if I could use one. I type: I know where to find you. Who knows? Maybe. I hesitate, type Ha! after it, then delete those two letters and press send because I've run out of energy to think. Then Anne-Sophie comes out of the room. She walks like she's been carrying a heavy weight for days.

"What about you?" I ask.

"I'm going to take the first flight I can get. I have to go back."

"Even before the funeral, you mean?"

She nods. "As soon as possible. I can't be here. It's too much. And Dad's gone now, so."

I look at this young woman, wishing I knew her. "I hope you'll feel better there than you do here."

She nods again.

"I hate seeing you like this. If you ever . . . you'll know where to find me, right?"

She nods again. "What about you?" she asks.

"Me? I'm going to write a play, I think." She looks at me uncomprehendingly. "Or open a theater myself, or something even more daring." I make a dismissive gesture, then I smile at her.

She comes to sit next to me. I look down the ugly hallway I never want to see again. And then, suddenly, Anne-Sophie lays her head on my shoulder. I smell her hair, something with honey or other sugary things. She breathes quietly, barely moving. I am reminded of the time when she climbed onto my lap, crying. She must have been about three or four, four maybe. She'd hurt herself by falling hard onto the kitchen floor. I said to her, "I'll give you a kiss and that will make it better." I kissed both of her knees. She looked at those two knees in embarrassment at first and then at me, and then she said, indignantly, in that high voice of hers, "No, it's not better. Your kisses don't work," and carried on crying. I remember that feeling of powerlessness like it was yesterday. I lay my hand on her head. *I wish I could help,* I think, though I don't say it.

42

I'm woken by the sound of a key fumbling in the lock of the front door. I realize I must have dozed off in the armchair; it's ten to one in the afternoon. I hear the door close, the quiet swish of a zipper, the sound of a handle being pushed back down into a suitcase, footsteps coming my way, familiar sounds. He comes in, stretches as he always does after a long journey, and then sees me.

"Oh, you're here. I thought you might be with your family. You look dreadful, my sweet creature. What have you been through? Come here so I can kiss you."

I look at him and stay where I am.

He sits down next to me and takes me in his arms. *He smells like himself,* I think. Smells tell you everything. Empty and listless, my shoulders touch his, my arms his arms, my breasts his chest, my left leg his right.

He rocks me back and forth. I think he imagines this is how you comfort someone. "It's so terrible for you, so terrible."

"Really?"

He lets go, looks at me, there's affection in his incomprehension. "Of course. Losing a father, that's—yes, it must be terrible."

"If it's so terrible, why weren't you here?"

"Who would have thought your father would go so quickly? And you know how soundly I sleep, I must have slept through your calls. I had to stay overnight there, I was really too tired to drive. You understand, don't you?" He looks at me and gives me a slightly waggish smile. "But I'm here for you now, all for you." He pulls me to him again, almost flattening me.

I kiss his right temple and break free. "That would be the first time, then."

Louis frowns. "Are you really going to pick a fight now? Now?"

"No, not a fight. But I don't want to have to understand, for once. I think I've been understanding about too much, for much too long."

"But, honeybun, what's got into—"

"Do you think we're really together?"

He hesitates. "What kind of a question is that? Together enough, right? We have a reasonable time together, the two of us. And we've managed to get this far. And we don't argue very much. We respect each other's freedom, each other's particularities, anyhow. And there's always some problem, whoever you're with, isn't there? But why on earth do you want to talk about this now?"

"I don't think I want this anymore."

Louis twirls his hair around one finger, he always does that when he's nervous.

"The way you treat me, well, and the way I react. I'm not claiming it's all your fault. I let it happen. Because I'm so used to it. When I see the way Marie—"

"Are you going to start comparing me with her now? Gee, thanks."

"That's not what I mean."

"We should sit down and have a good talk about this. We—" Then Louis falls silent.

I can feel myself shaking. The way he's sitting there now, his voice full of doubt and an expression as cold as a polar wind—*Coldness is what protects him,* I think then, I've seen it so often—I want to hold him in my arms again, but that would be for all the wrong reasons.

I breathe in and gather myself together. "Yes, we should talk. But I think we both deserve better, both of us. I once decided that you were my life preserver and if I let go of you, I'd drown. Now I think I want love."

He looks at me as though I'm speaking Chinese. I squeeze his arm and, without saying anything, I stand up. I look for my shoes, put them on, take a coat from the rack, and put on my backpack.

"What's this? Where are you going?"

"Out."

"What do you mean? Don't be so stupid. Sit down and let's talk about it."

I go to the door.

"What we've been doing for eleven years, that's not love, then?" He almost shouts it as he struggles his way into the hall with me. I open the door. "Wait, then." He grabs his coat. I go down the stairs, into the hall, out the front door. He rushes after me.

"Just let me go," I say.

"No," he replies, "not until you explain it to me." He grabs my shoulder, holding me back.

We stand in the middle of the footpath. I look at him. "I've started to realize that live and let live, make your decision and stick to it, and try not to be unkind to each other, is not real love, no." I button up my coat. He looks somewhere between lost and furious, but I keep going. "I want to be with someone because it feels like I can't not be, because no one understands each other better than we do, because we feel compelled to get involved in each other's business, because we really want to help each other to become the best versions of ourselves. Those kinds of things."

"And which stupid magazine have you read that definition of love in?" His eyes are piercing.

Then I begin to cry. Two people walk past, staring unashamedly at us. Louis hates public scenes. Normally he'd have gone back inside already.

"I saw Dad with Joanna. And I've thought a lot about what she said to me." I gulp once, and then again.

"Yes, so what?" He squeezes my shoulder too hard. *It's not deliberate,* I think.

"I want to do what he never could. I don't want . . . It seems to me . . . We're the answer to each other's weaknesses, I can see that now."

"What do you even mean?"

"Do I really have to explain it here and now?"

"No, you should come back inside, with me."

I stay where I am. "If I was insecure about my appearance, I'd be with you because you told me that my butt didn't look fat, get it? I want to learn to be OK with my butt regardless, from here on out."

"What's all this about your butt? Christ!" Louis rolls his eyes.

"I mean: we can't do that together, love each other for the right reasons. I've repeated what I learned, I chose somebody who gave me what I knew. I have to fight for love and attention with you. You pull me toward you and then push me away again. You make me feel like you could disappear from my life at any moment and I'd only have myself to blame for it. You make me think it's never enough, that I'm never enough, that you are more important than me. And that says something about me, I realize that all too well. It's exactly what used to happen at home when I was a child. I've made myself so—"

Louis makes a dismissive gesture. "I'll just assume that this is your grief talking, or something like that, and that you'll return to your senses later today, or tomorrow."

And now you're doing it again, I think. I smile at him, turn around, and begin to walk. Tears run down my face as though the supply of them is endless, and I—the girl who'd eternally put on a brave face—I don't go to the slightest trouble to hold them back. *If you're always strong, you lose yourself,* I think. Louis runs after me half-heartedly, I can sense.

"Don't overreact, Mona! Come back."

I don't want to go back, I want to move on.

"For fuck's sake, Mona!"

I look back. He's stopped in his tracks, there on the worn cobblestones. "I don't want to hurt you. Quite the opposite." I say it too quietly, he won't be able to hear. But I walk on, turn the corner. On the other side of the street, the sun is shining, and I cross over. The wind is blowing hard, but it feels warm, or warm enough. I want to love, I think, because I'm capable of it, and live, I want to live fully and eagerly, because I have to live anyway, so I'd better do it well. I want to continue walking into the wind, past houses, trees, water, clouds, walking and walking until I reach the far horizon, there where all beginnings begin. I see a father, he lifts up his young son and puts him on his shoulders. The little guy holds on to his ears like they're reins. I want to stop hoping and do what it takes to make it happen. I put my hands in my pockets and quicken my pace. I want to finally be who I am, not the person I always thought others wanted me to be. I see birds in the distance. They're flying in a big flock to wherever they need to be. I think: *I don't want to forget, because that's the only weapon we have against that bastard death.* I look at my feet and the way they are doing what I want and I think: *I never want to leave myself behind again.* I want to walk until I've lost track of the streets, and the sky. I walk and I see before me everything that was, and then I dream of everything to come, it's so much. I see three people on a quiet bench, perhaps they're smiling, perhaps they aren't, it's hard to tell. I see a man with a beard, a little boy with a backpack, two girls looking longingly at something or someone, a cat darting away into the bushes. I feel my telephone in my coat pocket. I think: *I want to understand what love is, remember that it's everything, or almost everything.* I want to save what still can be saved—myself, for example. I want to know what I am worth, choose what is right and good, believe that it is possible. I think: *That's what I want. I want to dare, at last. Yes.*

ABOUT THE AUTHOR

Griet Op de Beeck, born in 1973, lives in Belgium and has taken the literary world by storm since the publication of her highly successful debut novel, *Many Heavens Above the Seventh*. Her work has been translated into several languages, including German and French. Her second novel, *Mona in Three Acts*, was embraced by readers in the Netherlands and Belgium and is her first novel to be translated into English. For more information, visit the author at www.grietopdebeeck.be.

ABOUT THE TRANSLATOR

Photo © 2017 Elma Coetzee

Michele Hutchison was born in the United Kingdom and has lived in Amsterdam since 2004. She was educated at UEA and Cambridge and Lyon Universities. She translates literary fiction and nonfiction, poetry, graphic novels, and children's books. Recent translations include *La Superba* by Ilja Leonard Pfeijffer, *Roxy* by Esther Gerritsen, and *An American Princess: The Many Lives of Allene Tew* by Annejet van der Zijl. She is also coauthor, with Rina Mae Acosta, of *The Happiest Kids in the World: How Dutch Parents Help Their Kids (and Themselves) by Doing Less.*